THE DRAGON AND THE DJINN

THE DRAGON AND THE DJINN

GORDON R. DICKSON

ACE FANTASY

THE DRAGON AND THE DJINN

An Ace book
Published by The Berkley Publishing Group
200 Madison Avenue, New York, NY 10016

ISBN 0-441-00297-8

Printed in the United States of America

To Craig Dickson—
and those who love him

CHAPTER 1

For six days and nights the wind blew steadily out of the northwest; so that the servants huddled in their quarters, wrapped in everything warm they owned, and thought they heard voices of dark prophesies in the wind. It blew until it blew steep drifts of snow against the great doors in the curtain wall of the castle; so that men had to be lowered by rope from the battlements to shovel it away to get the doors open.

Finally it ceased; and there was a day of perfect quietness, terrible coldness and blue sky. Then the wind began again, worse than before, this time from the southeast; and on the second day it blew Sir Brian Neville-Smythe in through the now-open doors of Malencontri.

The blacksmith and one of the men-at-arms from the gate led Brian, still on his horse, across the courtyard to the entrance to the Great Hall and helped him (stiffly) down from his horse, helped beat the ice off his outer garments, where it clung thickly to those parts of his over-robe that covered armor underneath; and the man-at-arms took the horse off to the warm stables. The blacksmith, since he clearly outranked an ordinary man-at-arms, went in with Sir Brian to announce him.

But the blacksmith never got the chance. Because once they were within the Hall they saw Lady Angela Eckert, wife to Sir James Eckert, Lord of Malencontri and all its lands, taking her mid-day meal there and she, in the same moment, recognized the visitor.

"Brian!" she called from the far end of the long hall. "Where did you come from?"

"Outside," said Brian, who was a literal-minded person.

He advanced on the high table, set on a platform raised above the hall floor and looking down the two long tables at right angles before it, and stretching away toward Brian, to accommodate diners of lesser rank—but empty at the moment. Angie was lunching alone, but in all proper state.

"I can see that," said Angie, lowering her voice as he came closer. "But where did you start from?"

"From Castle Smythe. My home," replied Brian, with a touch of impatience; for where else would he be coming from at this, the end of January after a heavy winter storm?

The impatience was only momentary, however, for he was already eyeing the food and drink before Angie on the high table. To Brian, what Angie—who, like her husband, Jim, had been an involuntary importee from the twentieth century to this fourteenth-century world, some three years before—thought of as lunch time, was dinner time. It was the main meal of his day; and he had had nothing since breakfast, shortly after dawn on this icy morning.

"Well, come sit down, and have something to eat and drink," said Angie. "You must be frozen to the bone."

"Hah!" said Brian, his eyes lighting up at the invitation—expected though it was.

The table servants were already readying a place for him at one end of the table, so he and Angie could half face each other; for she sat behind the length of the table, itself, close to that end. Even as he sat down, another servant ran in from the serving room with a steaming pitcher, from which he poured hot wine into a mazer—a large, square metal goblet placed before Brian.

"Mulled wine, by God!" said Brian happily.

He took several hearty swallows from the mazer, to check on what his nose had already told him. Putting the mazer back down, he beamed at Angie with affectionate goodwill. Another of the table servants put a meat pie in front of him and spooned a large serving from it on to his trencher, the large, thick slice of coarse bread which served as his plate. He nodded approvingly, neatly picked out the largest piece of meat and wiped his fingers afterwards neatly on his napkin by the trencher.

"I thought to find you dining in your solar when you were alone, Angela," he said, as soon as his mouth was empty.

"I have done that," said Angie. "But it's more convenient here."

Her eyes met Brian's and a look of complete understanding passed between them, twentieth century and fourteenth century for once in complete agreement.

Servants. Angie would by far have preferred to eat in the solar—which was the bed-sitting chamber at the top of Malencontri's tower and the private chamber of the Lord and Lady of the castle.

The solar was a warm, comfortable place, with its windows tightly glazed against the weather with actual glass, and the floor heated under foot by a reconstruction by her husband of the type of hypocaust that the earlier Roman conquerors of Britain had used to heat their homes, but which the Middle Ages had forgotten. It was simply a space between two stone floors where air could circulate that had been warmed by continuous fires burning in fireplaces outside the room.

There also was an actual large fireplace in the solar itself—ornamental as well as useful in weather like this.

The Great Hall, of course, had fireplaces of its own. Three, in fact, huge ones. One behind the high table where Angie sat right now, and two others; one each halfway down the long walls of the hall. At the moment all three were burning brightly with fires in them, because Angie was there; but the hall was still cold for all that.

Still, against their real preferences, Jim and Angie had taken to eating at least their mid-day meals here. No servant had come to them on bended knee and pleaded with them to eat in state in the Hall; though there had been veiled references made to the convenience of the serving room—so close to the high table—so that food could be brought in hot. But no one had officially protested.

But there were still invisible limits to what a Lord and Lady could do—even if the Lord was a famous knight and magician. Those who served the gentry would obey any order. Men-at-arms would go forth and die for their feudal superiors. But neither servants nor men-at-arms, nor tenants, nor serfs, nor anyone else on the estate, would go against custom. When custom spoke, everybody obeyed; right up to the throne of the King himself.

And at Malencontri, a general attitude, unspoken but very clearly felt, had finally had its way with Angie and Jim. A Lord and Lady of a castle like this were supposed to eat their mid-day meal in proper fashion, in the proper place. That was what the hall was there for. The table servants who had to bring food from the outside kitchen to the serving room might freeze in the process. That was beside the point. There was a way things should be done; and that was the way it should be done here.

"Where's James?" Brian asked after a few moments, having managed to take on at least enough meat pie and wine to begin satisfying his clamoring stomach.

"He'll be along shortly," said Angie. "Right now he's up there."

She pointed her finger vertically.

"Ah, yes," said Brian, meaning he understood. This gesture of Angie's, which might have either baffled a stranger or seemed to imply Angie's husband had left this earthly scene, was something completely reasonable and understood between these two.

"He thought he should take a look at our people on the lands outside the castle," said Angie, "and make sure all of them came through the storm all right."

Brian nodded, his mouth full. He swallowed.

"Then, with your pardon, my Lady, I shall wait until he comes back," Brian said, "and tell you both at the same time what I came to say. I would like the two of you to hear it together. It is great news, indeed. You will grant me mercy if I do not speak of it now?"

"Certainly," said Angie. In spite of the courtly question at the end of Brian's little speech, Angie knew that Brian had no intention of speaking until her husband got back; and that was a red flag to her. If Brian wanted to talk to the two of them together, he wanted or needed something from Jim; and in that case experience had taught Angie to be ready to resist. Forewarned was forearmed.

"He should be back soon," she said.

CHAPTER 2

At the moment Jim was on wing over the southeast corner of the lands he owned as Sir James Eckert, Baron of Malencontri. This part was mainly meadow and open farmland; and he was searching the white landscape below for those relatively few of his tenants and farmers who lived in isolated spots farther out from the castle, to see if any of them needed assistance after the storm.

He was feeling a keen delight in being airborne. It was strange, he thought now, how he forgot about the sheer joy of it when he was not translated into dragon form; and how strongly the feeling came back to him once he was aloft. It was a far more gratifying feeling than flying a small plane, which Jim had taken a few lessons at doing, back in his original twentieth-century world, or even like soaring in a man-made glider, which he had done as a passenger, twice. In this case it was his living, feeling self alone that was riding the air currents; and there was a triumphant sensation of both freedom and power.

In his large dragon body, with its much higher mass-to-surface ratio than that of his human one, he was not bothered by the cold. Heat would have been something else again. He had almost melted down trying to walk through the summer heat in the middle part of France as a dragon, a couple of years ago; and the rush of cold air about him now was only pleasant.

He was alive right out to the tips of his enormous wings, which reached out an awesome distance on each side of him, in order to make it possible for that body of his to plane through the air. He was soaring, not flying, as most of even the large birds preferred to do, because of the enormous expenditure of energy required to keep him aloft by flapping his wings alone; but once at sufficient altitude, he could ride the air currents and the updrafts with careful adjustments of his wings; the way a sailing ship might adjust both fore-and-aft and square sails to cause the wind to propel it across the surface of the water.

This adjustment was purely instinctive on the part of his body. Nonetheless, he appreciated it as much as if it had been a skill. It made him feel like a king in this airy realm.

However, he had now covered almost all of his estate and it was time to be heading back to the castle. He would be late for lunch. He started the long swing to his right that would send him homeward; but just then he spotted the widow Tebbits's little sapling-and-clay igloo.

"Igloo" was not really a proper name for it; but he could think of no other architectural name that fitted it. It had been built out of saplings and thin branches woven together and plastered airtight with clay. It either had no proper roof, or the roof had settled into the walls over the years, giving it roughly the shape of an igloo. In any case, in the middle of the roof was a hole that was right above the sand-filled firebox in which the widow lit the fire for her cooking and heating.

That hole was not showing any escaping smoke now. What was more, it was covered from the inside.

Jim circled down and landed with a thump before the door, which the new direction of the wind had cleared of snow. The sound of his coming to earth evidently alerted whoever was inside; for someone fought with the door for a few seconds, then it popped open. The widow herself stepped out, bundled up in clothing, blankets and assorted rags until she looked more like a teddy bear than a human being, and recognized him immediately.

She gave the small obligatory scream that the Malencontri people had decided was the proper way to acknowledge their Lord in his dragon form, and then tried to curtsy. It was a mistake with all the padding she had on, and she almost tumbled over. Jim stopped himself just in time from reaching out to catch her. She would never have forgiven herself if her Lord had had to do something like that. Happily, the frame of the door kept her from going all the way down and she recovered her footing.

"M'lord!" she said.

Out of her swaddling of coverings, her round, soft, aged face peered at him with two sharp dark eyes.

"How are you, Tebbits?" asked Jim. The widow had a first name, but nobody on the estate seemed to remember what it was. "I noticed there was no smoke coming up from your roof."

"Oh, no, m'lord," said the widow. "Thank you, m'lord. It's good of you to speak to me, m'lord. I'm ever so grateful to you, m'lord. There's no smoke because the fire's out."

"Is something wrong with the firebox?" asked Jim, remembering to use delicacy in approaching the subject.

"No, m'lord. Thank you, m'lord."

"Why is the fire out, then?"

"It burned up the last ember and just went out, like fires do—with your grace and pardon for saying so, m'lord."

Jim sighed inwardly. He felt rather like a man in the dark with a ring-full of keys, trying to find the right one that would unlock the door in front of him. All of the tenants had a horror of openly complaining. They had ways of making their wants known to him—roundabout ways—and the pretense was always that they were perfectly in control of things and needed no help whatsoever . . . but if he happened to notice, just at this moment they could use . . .

"You wouldn't have gotten a little low on firewood, during the snowstorm?" asked Jim.

"Why, I believe I did," said the widow Tebbits. "I'm so dreadfully forgetful these days, m'lord."

"Not at all," said Jim heartily. How she had survived, in spite of all that padding inside, an unheated shelter for the last few days, particularly at her age, was beyond imagination. "You know, I think I saw a fallen branch off in that patch of woods over there. It might be useful to you. I believe I'll just go and get it for you."

"Oh, pray don't put yourself to the trouble, m'lord," said Tebbits.

"Tebbits," said Jim, in an autocratic, warning voice, "I *choose* to go get you that bough!"

"Oh, pray forgive me, m'lord. Very sorry, m'lord. Crave pardon!"

"Be right back," said Jim.

He turned around and with a thunder of wings leaped into the air, winged the short distance to the nearby stand of trees he had been thinking of and flew far enough over them so that when he came down he would be out of sight of the widow Tebbits. There were no fallen branches handy, nor had he any intention of going to the trouble of searching for them under the snow. He picked a fifteen-foot limb from an oak and simply tore it loose from the frozen trunk. On second thought, he found another limb of about the same thickness and length and tore it off. Holding the limbs by their ends so that they dragged beneath him between his feet and did not interfere with his wings, he sprang into the air once more, flapped back dragging them, and landed at the widow Tebbits's.

"Here!" he said gruffly—and then noticed that she was eyeing the thickness of the branches where they had been attached to the tree somewhat wistfully. "Oh, come to think of it," he said, "have you an ax where you can get at it conveniently?"

"Alas, m'lord," said Tebbits. "I'm afraid I lost it, like."

She had almost undoubtedly never had one, thought Jim. Iron was expensive. He must do something about getting her at least some sort of tool for cutting up thicker pieces of wood.

"Ah, yes, I see," said Jim. "Well, in that case—"

He picked up one of the two frozen tree limbs he had brought her and began breaking off—quite easily with the strength of his dragon forearms—the heavy ends of its main stem, as well as any extended limbs that would keep it from fitting neatly into her fire box. He reduced the branches to burnable lengths and, picking these up, put only as many as she could carry into the arms of Tebbits, who clutched them awkwardly, but obviously gratefully, in spite of the thickness of the cloth insulation in which she was wrapped.

"I'll have Dick Forester send someone down here with some of the castle wood sometime later today," Jim wound up. "Have you flint and steel? Can you get the fire started?"

"Oh yes, thank you, m'lord," said Tebbits. "You're always so kind to a useless old person."

"Not at all. Be old myself one day, no doubt!" he said bluffly. "Heaven bless you, Tebbits."

"May Heaven bless you, m'lord," said Tebbits.

Jim sprang into the air with a thunder of wings, feeling rather smug at having been able for once to bless one of these people of his before they could bless him. Once back to altitude he resumed his flight to the castle.

But, in the process, something new caught his eye. Something not on his land at all. On the small estate of Sir Hubert Whitby adjoining his, Sir Hubert was waving his arms, shouting something incomprehensible at this distance, and directing several of his own tenants or servants over some problem or other—Jim's telescopic dragon-sight informed him.

Sir Hubert was not the best of neighbors. In fact, he was probably not far from being the worst of neighbors, Jim thought. But then he checked himself. Sir Hubert was not really bad, dangerous, evil, dishonest or rapacious—or any of the many things that neighbors could be in this fourteenth-century England. But he was a never-satisfied annoyance; always angry about something, always insistent and complaining about it at great length.

For a moment Jim was tempted simply to complete his turn and forget that he had seen anything at all. But then his conscience, plus the strong social feeling of obligation to neighbors that existed in this time, turned him back and he soared in the direction of Sir Hubert and his problem.

As he got closer, soaring this time on a convenient slant of the wind, he saw what the problem was. One of Sir Hubert's cows had evidently fallen into a snow-filled ditch, or small ravine, and Sir Hubert, with the four men he had with him, were trying to get her out.

But the cow could not help them—or else she did not understand what she was supposed to do to help—and her weight was such that the four of them could not lift her or drag her from it. Sir Hubert was making so much noise that none of them realized Jim was even close to them until he landed in their midst with the same sort of thump with which he had landed outside of the widow Tebbits's home. They all whirled about and for a moment they merely stared at him.

"A dragon!" roared Sir Hubert, whipping his sword out of its sheath. His face was pale, but the sword was quite steady. In spite of all his other faults, Sir Hubert was not a coward. No one was likely to live to adulthood back in this time if they were, of course, no matter what level of society they belonged to.

Clearly they had not recognized him, the way Jim's own tenants and people did. The four men with Sir Hubert were actually not armed, aside from their ordinary all-purpose belt knives. But they all snatched these out and hefted whatever else they had in their hand that might be a weapon—in this case a couple of long poles which two of them held; and in the case of one man, rather ridiculously, a rope he was holding.

It was foolish of them, of course. Even fully armed and armored, on foot the five of them would probably never have escaped alive if they had seriously tried to battle a dragon of Jim's size. While they might do some serious damage to Jim before being killed, Jim would certainly be the last to die.

"Don't be an ass, Sir Hubert," said Jim, finding the British phrase rolled quite happily off his tongue. What a handy sort of phrase it was for situations like this, he told himself. "I'm James Eckert, your neighbor—only in my dragon body. I came over to see if I could help."

Sir Hubert's face stayed pale and his sword stayed pointed, but its point dropped a few inches.

"Hah!" he said doubtfully.

"I happened to be flying by, taking a look at how my own lands had come through the snowstorm," said Jim, "and I saw you having some trouble over here. So I came."

Sir Hubert's sword dropped down, but he still did not sheath it.

"Well, if it's you, why didn't you come like a man?"

"There's a lot more strength in this dragon body of mine, when it comes to helping with something like this," said Jim. "Stop and think for a moment, Hubert!"

"Well, damn it! How the bloody hell was I supposed to know?" the knight said. "You could have been any dragon, ravening for our blood!"

"I don't raven," said Jim. "You've eaten dinner at Malencontri often enough to know that, Hubert."

"Well . . ." Sir Hubert sheathed his sword. "How can you help us?"

"I'm not sure yet," said Jim. "Let me take a look at the situation. What kind of hole is she stuck in?"

"Little dimple in the ground, that's all," grumbled Sir Hubert. "If she had any sense in her head she could walk out of there. Damn cows, anyhow!"

"Steep sides or sloping sides?"

"Sloping," said Sir Hubert. "If she'd help a little, we could have got her out of there."

"If they're sloping, maybe I can get down in beside her. Then if I lift and the rest of you tug, maybe she can scramble out," said Jim.

"She'll kick you," said Sir Hubert with relish.

"Maybe," said Jim. "Let's see."

He approached the hole, and the cow, who had been upwind of him until now, suddenly smelling and seeing a dragon in her immediate vicinity, bellered in terror. Jim tested the slope of the ground under the snow and after a moment slid down beside the cow's flank. She cried out for help again; for now Jim's body was pinning her against the opposite side of what Sir Hubert had described as a dimple and she could not manage a good kick through the hip-deep snow.

Whether she actually succeeded in kicking him or not, Jim never knew. But he managed to get down beside her, low enough so that he could get leverage for the shoulder of one folded wing beneath her belly. Once he had her firmly pressed between his shoulder and the opposite side of the depression, she stopped bellering, gave one sad moo of utter despair and fell silent.

Jim took a deep breath and lifted, like a man lifting a weight balanced on one shoulder. The cow was no lightweight; but on the other hand, the muscles Jim was bringing into play were awesome compared to any human's. The cow rose upward and sprawled out on her side on the far edge of the dimple; Sir Hubert's men immediately laid hands on her, skidded her across the snow away from the depression and began to coax her to her feet.

Jim climbed out of the depression himself.

"Well, you did it easily enough," said Sir Hubert grumblingly, almost as if he was accusing Jim of doing him an injury.

"You're entirely welcome," said Jim, knowing that Sir Hubert's words were as close as the knight could come to saying thanks. He leaped into the air and began to climb once more for the long soar home.

With the wind in the southeast, he had to climb for altitude and make a long sweep over Sir Hubert's land to get himself turned about and headed back to Malencontri. He was in the process of this when he suddenly realized he was high enough and looking in the right direction to see the woods in which Carolinus had his cottage; and his conscience niggled at him.

He had been meaning to talk to Carolinus—his Master in magic—ever since he and Angie with young Robert Falon and their personal attendants had gotten back from the Christmas party of the Earl of Somerset almost a month ago. But one thing and another had kept him from getting together with the older magician.

This was an ideal time to call in briefly for a quick chat on a couple of points that dated back to the Twelve Days of Christmas at the Earl's, and had been bothering Jim since. For one thing, he had the sneaking feeling that he owed Carolinus an apology—having gotten somewhat annoyed with the other man during those twelve days.

But, back at the castle, it was already past lunch time. Angie would be waiting for him in the Great Hall. And there might be something to do with Robert that would call for him to be there . . .

Robert had become a concern that seemed to crop up in all sorts of otherwise ordinary situations. In fact, Jim was not at all sure that he was the right man to bring up an orphan boy of noble birth in the fourteenth century, where all such were raised to be warriors. He was no real warrior himself. The youngster could well be hampered by Jim's different, twentieth-century outlook on life—

Jim pushed that thought from his mind. Robert was still far too young to eat lunch with them in the Great Hall. Still—Jim's conscience pulled him both ways. But then he reminded himself that Angie would not wait very long before going ahead and eating by herself; so actually no harm would have been done. He, himself, could eat anything that was available after he got back to Malencontri, whenever that might be.

He altered the angle of his wings and headed toward the tops of the trees that still obscured the little clearing in which Carolinus's cottage stood.

The clearing, when he got to it, was pretty much as he had expected it. It was completely surrounded by very tall oaks and yews, and roughly oval in shape. It was also roughly the size of a football field. Snow hung on the trees around the clearing and coated the ground up to within about ten yards of the cottage, leaving a perfect circle in which it was still summer.

Within that circle, the cottage stood, snow-free. The grass was green, flowers bloomed, and a fountain tinkled its jet of water in the middle of a small pool from which occasionally small golden fish—or were they very small golden mermaids?—leaped like miniature dolphins into the air. Jim's eye had never been quick enough to make sure.

Beside the pool was a neatly raked gravel path leading up to the door
of a small, oddly narrow peaked-roof house that ought to have looked out
of place here; but what with the pool, the grass and the occasional flash
of a golden jumping figure from the pool, it looked as if it could not have
been any place else.

Jim landed with a thump at the end of the gravel path; but no one
immediately tried to look out from the house to see who had arrived. He
turned himself back into a human, complete with warm clothes (he had
had a little trouble with the clothes part in the early days of learning how
to use magic, but had it under control now), walked up to the door of the
house and tapped gently at it.

There was no answer. He pushed gently on it and it swung open. He
stepped in.

"Eh? What? Oh, it's you, Jim," said Carolinus, looking up.

He was seated in his large, wing-back chair, with a thick and heavy
volume of some book or other, open on the table at his elbow; and the
small green, sylphlike and fragile, female figure of a naiad perched on one
of his knees, as lightly as a butterfly on a twig. Carolinus looked at her.

"You'd better run along now, my dear," he said gently to the naiad.
"We can finish our talk later."

The naiad drifted off his knee to stand before him with downcast eyes.
She murmured something incomprehensible.

"Certainly!" said Carolinus.

She turned and went toward the door. Jim stood aside to let her pass
and she approached him with downcast eyes, glancing up for just a moment and murmuring something else equally incomprehensible.

"Not at all," said Jim. He had not understood her, as Carolinus obviously had a moment before; but the words he had chosen ought to be
fairly safe as an answer. She went on out the door and it closed behind
her.

"Well, well, my boy," said Carolinus cheerfully. "It's good to see you,
and particularly to see you in your human body, rather than the dragon
one. This is a small house, you know."

It was indeed a small house; and what was more, crammed to the rafters
with books and everything else imaginable, ordinary and occult. In fact,
it looked more like a warehouse than a home. But since Carolinus was
accustomed to merely ordering whatever he wanted from whatever was
piled around to appear in front of him, this made no difference to the older
magician.

"Well, yes," said Jim. "I've been meaning to drop by ever since we
got back from the Earl's, and I happened to be close so I simply came

on. I'm not interrupting anything, or catching you at a busy moment, am
I?''

"Not at all, not at all," said Carolinus. "Lalline and I can chat at
anytime. You and I see each other all too seldom."

The last words were a perfect invitation for Jim to point out that he had
made a lot of efforts to see Carolinus. It was Carolinus who had been
hard to find. However, he did not.

"But never mind that, now that you're here," went on Carolinus jo-
vially. "You're looking rested and in good spirits. Ready for your next
adventure?"

CHAPTER 3

"Adventure!" said Jim, with a sudden cold feeling in his stomach. "Certainly not. I'm looking forward to having nothing to do with adventures for a long time. Angie and I are going to try to live as ordinary people for the next few years."

An evil suspicion crept into his mind.

"You haven't got something up your sleeve for me, have you?" he demanded.

"I? James!" said Carolinus. "I certainly wouldn't impose another set of duties on you so quickly after the last affair at the Earl's. No, no. I don't have the slightest thing in mind for you. If you get involved in anything, it will be because you do it yourself."

"I'm sorry," said Jim. "It was just that those twelve days rather took things out of me. Do you mind if I sit down?"

"Sit down? Of course," said Carolinus. "Of course—that is, if you can find a chair. There are some around here, someplace."

He peered about the interior of the cottage shortsightedly.

"I know there are some other chairs. Try under those volumes in the corner there."

"Sorry for overreacting," said Jim, seated finally after a small but necessary delay. "But Angie feels that I spend far too little time with her; and I can't say I blame her."

"Of course not," said Carolinus. "Is the chair comfortable?"

"Well . . ." said Jim. "To tell you the truth, no."

"It should be!" said Carolinus in a terrifying voice.

The chair instantly was. It was possibly the most comfortable chair Jim had ever sat in, in spite of the fact that it had four single legs, a stiff upright back, no arms and no padding.

"To tell you the truth, Carolinus," he said, "I came here because, after thinking it over, I may have been a little too suspicious and a little too short-tempered with you during those twelve days. But I was used to having you around to check with in emergencies; and I could never get in touch with you.''

"Dear me!" said Carolinus.

"Oh, it's all right," Jim went on. "I understand now you were deliberately leaving me on my own, as the best way of doing things. But I'm glad to be back to where I can find you when I want you and check with you if I need to.''

"Find me, and check with me by all means, Jim," said Carolinus. "Bear in mind, though, there is no going back. You have now tried your wings as an independent magickian; and you will have to fly by yourself from here on.''

"I will?" asked Jim. A couple of years before, Carolinus's words would not have had a particularly ominous sound. Now that he realized the possibilities of magic better—as well as its limitations—he found they worried him.

"What are the limits, then, to what you can do for me?''

"You can ask me questions," said Carolinus. "And within certain limits I will answer them. Absolutely complete answers to anything simply do not exist. You will discover this yourself, Jim, once you are an established magickian of at least A level and dealing with those of a lesser level; or even with an apprentice of your own.''

"I can believe you," said Jim, who had about as much intention of ever taking on an apprentice in magic as he had of setting himself on fire.

"Remember always," said Carolinus, "there's never any point in offering information to someone until they're ready to receive it. But, if you wait until they ask, then the two things that need to happen are happening. One, they'll be ready to listen to what you have to tell them. Secondly, now they give a value to what you say; whereas until they had a need, they might have been inclined to question or even argue with your instruction or advice, out of sheer ignorance.''

"Had I been doing that?" said Jim.

"As a matter of fact," said Carolinus, "you haven't. But then, you don't fit the usual pattern of apprentices. Your problem lies in a different area, one in which I'm helpless to be of any use to you; and that is, your thinking is entirely conditioned by this—what shall I say—mechanistic . . .''

"You mean I've been conditioned by the technology of the twentieth-century world I came from," said Jim.

"Yes," said Carolinus. "That's it exactly.''

"I don't know what to do about that," said Jim.

"Well, it has to be your problem; but it's also, paradoxically, the basis of your unusual ability to find solutions, outside the normal bounds of what a learning magickian might, in dealing with a problem. For me to try to correct your habits and preconceptions in this area would probably throttle the very abilities that are your greatest asset. Therefore, you must sink or swim on your own, Jim; even more so than the ordinary apprentice."

"That's fine if I get into something on my own," said Jim. "But if you, yourself, give me something to do and I need help, then I can call on you, and you'll answer and give me the information I ask for?"

"Not necessarily *all* the information you ask for," said Carolinus. "I have a great deal more information than you imagine, Jim. Most of it you couldn't use, even if you could understand it. But I'll always give you as much information as I think you can use."

"But if I solve problems in ways you can't and don't, yourself, because I come from somewhere else, you can't know what information I can't use, or understand."

"That may be, possibly. It may be a remote possibility. But," said Carolinus, "one of us has to choose what information you are to receive. And since it is my information; and I'm one of only three AAA+ class magickians in this world, where you are only a C-class magickian, my apprentice and a relative newcomer—I shall be the one who chooses."

"In other words," said Jim, "I've got no choice. Well, I suppose I can't force you to give me any more information than you want to."

"You've always been very quick to see the point, Jim," said Carolinus. "That's one of the things I remarked immediately about you when we first met."

"But you'll do the best you can to help me within what you see as possible limits, right?" asked Jim.

"Yes," said Carolinus. "Remember, Jim, I have a great consideration for you—wouldn't have taken you on as my apprentice otherwise—and I rejoice when you succeed and am concerned when you are in difficulty. In short, I hope you feel you can trust in my goodwill."

"Actually, I never doubted that," said Jim. What he had feared, of course, was Carolinus jumping to the wrong conclusions because the older magician was thinking purely in terms of his own fourteenth-century experience. Or at least, that was the way Jim had felt most of the time. For a little while during the Christmas party at the Earl's he had wondered whether Carolinus wasn't necessarily using him for his own convenience, and had been for some time. But that proved to be wrong. "No, I trust you, Carolinus, of course. So does Angie."

"I appreciate that, my boy," said Carolinus. "Nor have I forgotten how you saved my life when those two local healing women were about to heal me to death with their potions and rough treatment."

Jim remembered. That had indeed been a time when Carolinus had been helpless; and Jim and Angie with some of their men-at-arms, plus the fortunate appearance of John Chandos, Giles and Chandos's squire, had appeared in the nick of time to rescue the elderly magician and get him to Malencontri where he could be nursed back to health. Jim's guilty feeling for doubting Carolinus at the Earl's, grew to an even greater self-accusation.

"I'll trust you, Carolinus," he said. "You can count on me."

"And you can count on me, my boy," said Carolinus. "Opportunely, since we have just established our mutual trust, there is something that I have been meaning to speak very seriously to you about, since you are moving—let us say—into a new area of the use of magick. You know, of course, that you have this unlimited drawing account on magickal energy because of your unusual status, and that this has caused some upset on the part of other magickians and their apprentices, who feel you're being especially favored."

"I know," said Jim grimly.

"Their upset doesn't concern me," said Carolinus. "They'll get used to the fact that your difference supports it. But you also remember that you used this drawing account quite freely at the Earl's Christmas party. You managed to get a number of things done with it. But still you were rather prodigal with its use."

"You think so?" said Jim.

"I'm very sure so," said Carolinus. "As I say, I'm not worried about the other magickians complaining about this. What does concern me is that you are not observing something that, as a magickian operating essentially on your own, you must never overlook."

"Oh?" said Jim. He had never heard a note this serious in Carolinus's voice before. He found himself suddenly alert. He and Angie had been in some danger because of other magicians' complaints about his handling of magic before this.

"I would like you to remember something always," said Carolinus in the same voice. "No matter how little energy you may draw to do a certain amount of magick, no matter how large your resources may be, it is always wise, at all times, to hoard those resources. In other words, do not use your magick if there is at all any other convenient way of getting done what you want to get done. I know, you've seen me hopping around hither and yon—and even taking you with me sometimes—magickally. But I am a much older man than you and, well, there are other reasons you'll understand when you've learned a little more. The rule remains: do not use magick unless you have to."

He looked severely at Jim, who looked suitably impressed in return.

"The simple reason is," Carolinus went on, "that you may have a sudden, unexpected demand on the most magickal energy you can command at that particular time and under those circumstances. You have no way of predicting either what that demand will be, nor what your circumstances will be; so be safe. Keep as much in reserve as possible. This is very, very important, James!"

Jim felt a slight coldness on the back of his neck. Carolinus was being so serious that he was suddenly and very deeply wary.

"There isn't something—some danger—you know about that I don't know about, for which I might need magic?" he asked.

"No!" said Carolinus emphatically. "None whatsoever! I give this to you as a general rule. But I emphasize that this rule is of the greatest possible importance, always; particularly when you are adventuring into magickal situations on your own."

"Well, I'll certainly remember it," said Jim soberly.

"Good!" said Carolinus. "Remember your encounter with the Dark Powers at the Loathly Tower; and how I told you I had to make a long journey to get the magick enclosed in that staff I held. Large magick is not easy. No magick is the answer to all situations. You must first rely on yourself, your own will and your own wits."

He broke off rather abruptly and coughed.

"Now," he said briskly in his normal tone, "was there something else you wanted to talk to me about?"

"Not at the moment," said Jim, feeling surprisingly relieved that they were back to ordinary, friendly words after the almost ominous tone of the advice Carolinus had been giving him. "We're all fine at the castle. We'll be in touch with you shortly as soon as the weather gets a little better."

"I'm glad to hear it," said Carolinus. "I assume you'll be flying back there now, rather than transporting yourself magickally?"

"I'd planned to anyway," said Jim. "I like flying. But, come to think of it, isn't turning myself into dragon shape or out of it a use of magic?"

"As a matter of fact, in your unusual, individual case, it isn't," said Carolinus. "You're different, insofar as that goes—rather like a Natural— you came into this world as a dragon; and as long as you're a dragon when you go out of it, all the energy involved cancels out."

"Good," said Jim. "I'll step outside then, to turn back into a dragon."

"Do," said Carolinus. "I'd much appreciate it."

Jim did.

Back at the castle, some twenty minutes later, Jim landed on the flat, battlemented top of Malencontri's tower, under the flagpole, from which the banner bearing his coat of arms flapped in the somewhat active breeze.

He was greeted by the ritual short shout of alarm which was the male equivalent of the widow Tebbits's polite scream. He nodded an acknowledgment at the man-at-arms on sentry duty, changed to his human form, walked down the stairs, opened a door and stepped into the solar.

Angie was there, seated at a table with papers spread out before her, doing what no right-minded lady in the fourteenth century would want to be caught doing—keeping the accounts of the castle household.

Actually, John Steward should have been doing this. But Angie had discovered that John, entirely in accord with hallowed custom, had been skimming off for himself a certain amount of the funds necessary for the castle's maintenance. Shocked by this, she had checked with Geronde, who had looked into the accounts, and come to the conclusion that John was not being greedy at all in what he took. In fact, he was being rather sparing in making use of his skimming possibilities. She had strongly counseled that Angie leave the matter alone.

But Angie was determined that things should be done in a more reasonable twentieth-century manner. She had taken over the accounts herself, giving John Steward instead a twice-yearly fee, which was in fact a little more than he had been taking. Then, she herself kept the records and kept them rather more tightly than John had ever done.

"Jim!" she said, looking up from the table. "Where have you been?"

"Oh, I stopped at the widow Tebbits's—she needed some firewood," said Jim. "Then I saw Sir Hubert was having some trouble with a cow stuck in a hole; and I was so close to Carolinus's then, I thought I'd drop by and see if I couldn't mend our relationship. I was having some hard thoughts about him toward the latter part of our visit at the Earl's, you remember."

"And it's taken you until now?" said Angie. "The afternoon's almost gone!"

"Yes," said Jim, "I must have talked to Carolinus a little longer than I thought. But let me tell you—he started out by asking me if I was ready for my next adventure. I told him, 'Certainly not! Angie and I are going to live as ordinary people for the next few years.' "

"You told him that?" said Angie.

"Absolutely!" said Jim. "That's what I said to him, flat out."

"Then nothing is going to take you away for a long while yet," said Angie.

"Absolutely!" said Jim. "You can count on it."

"Good. I will," said Angie. "Brian is downstairs."

"Brian?" said Jim. "What brings him over?"

"He wanted to tell the two of us at the same time, so he's been waiting for you to get back," said Angie. She got up from the table. "Let's go down to the hall now. He's been perfectly happy sitting down there, talking to your squire.''

Jim's squire was Theoluf, a former man-at-arms who had been elevated to squire rank for Jim, when there was no one else available. He had at least a dozen, possibly more, years of experience in the same sort of martial activities that Brian lived for. Brian could hardly have sat down and chatted with him if he had been still a man-at-arms, even the Chief man-at-arms—which he had been. But now that Theoluf was a squire, he was advanced enough in rank to be someone to chat with; although Jim was ready to bet that while Brian was still sitting at the table, Theoluf was standing.

Jim, of course, could not break himself of the twentieth-century habit of inviting everybody to sit down. Angie had adapted to the business of having inferiors stand when they talked to her; and she as well as Brian and Geronde de Chaney, Brian's betrothed, had tried to break Jim of the bad habit of inviting them to sit.

Jim was better at it now, but he still slipped occasionally. His own servants, having gotten instructions from Angie, passed down through John Steward, were in the habit of simply ignoring the offer when Jim suggested they take a seat.

They had been relieved to be ordered to do that. The truth was they felt uncomfortable sitting in Jim's presence—it was as someone might feel five hundred years later, not knowing if they were using the right fork at an ultra-formal dinner.

When Angie and Jim came into the Great Hall through the serving room, next to the high table, Theoluf was standing, just as Jim had expected, before the dais on which the high table stood. Brian was sitting, in his usual upright horseman's posture, but with one elbow on the table and a forefinger emphasizing a point he was making to Theoluf at the moment.

''. . . But one thing you must always train them to do,'' Brian was saying emphatically. ''A man down does not mean a man slain!''

''And so I do tell them, Sir Brian,'' said Theoluf earnestly. ''But getting them to remember it and believe it until after they've had a close 'scape from a man they thought was dead, is something else again. When I was at Warwick Castle I had one lad, searching for money in what he thought was a corpse, gutted by it; though it had been on its feet and fighting like the devil himself, a moment before—''

Theoluf broke off and bowed, as Jim and Angie appeared by the high table. His hat was already in his hand, since he was talking to Sir Brian, so he could not take that off. But the bow was becoming a rather smooth and practiced gesture for the ex–man-at-arms, Jim noticed. It was a far

cry from the awkward way Theoluf had jerked his upper body when he
had first been promoted to squire.

"Theoluf," said Angie, as she and Jim took seats behind the high table,
flanking the end of it at which Brian was seated, "run see about some
food for your Lord. What would you like, Jim?"

"Oh, cheese, bread, some cold meat—and some small beer," said Jim.
He was actually almost coming to like the small beer. Wine would taste
infinitely better; but he was trying hard to resist the fourteenth-century
habit of drinking it on any and all occasions that gave the slightest excuse
for it.

"Yes, m'lady," said Theoluf. He bowed apologetically to Sir Brian,
and ran off through the serving room in search of table servants.

"Brian!" said Jim. "It's really good to see you. I didn't expect to have
you come in this weather, though. You look fine. And Geronde's fine?"

Brian and his betrothed, Geronde de Chaney, traded homing pigeons so
Castle Malvern and Castle Smythe could stay in touch when the weather
was bad like this, or in any emergency. Castle Malvern boasted a priest
in residence. Brian had no such luxury, but he did have a former monk
among his retainers, who could read and write a limited form of Latin.
So messages went back and forth in that language.

"Never finer," said Brian. "Wondrous things have occurred—but before I get into that, I must tell you before I forget, it was a great sorrow
to Sir Giles not to be able to see you after the tourney."

"I'm sorry, myself," said Jim. "He came all that way to the Earl's
from up near the Scottish border, and we really never had a chance to
talk. I thought he might come home with us here for a short stay; but
when I looked for him later that day I couldn't find him. I'd heard he'd
left already. I hope it was nothing I did or said."

"Not at all," said Sir Brian. "You remember that since he could not
ride in the tourney himself, he acted squire for the other Northumbrian
knight there, Sir Reginald Burgh; whom, if you remember, was the third
to ride against Mnrogar?"

"Yes, I was told that," said Jim. "That's why I didn't go looking for
Giles until after it was all over. But do you know why he left so soon?"

"It seems Sir Reginald had planned to leave early," said Brian. "He
had some matter up along the border that would require his being back
as soon as possible. But because he had taken some small hurt in his spear
running with Mnrogar—oh, nothing serious, a few ribs cracked, or a
shoulder displaced for a moment—he was in no fit shape to fight, in case
he and his men ran into the same sort of outlaws that Giles encountered
on his way down. Giles, therefore, being a fellow Northumbrian, felt it

his duty to ride with Sir Reginald; and he had barely time to pass this word to me before he was off to do so.''

"Maybe he can come down again," said Jim.

"Possibly next year—" began Brian; and they were suddenly surrounded by servants, putting down a fresh tablecloth and a napkin, plus trencher, beer, cheese and meat as ordered. They were gone again in a moment, but the thread of conversation had been interrupted.

"Well, we'll hope so," said Jim, privately wondering whether it would be much of a journey for him, in his dragon body, to fly up to see Giles for just a few days at the Castle de Mer of his family. "But you were saying that wondrous things had been happening?''

"So I did; and so they have," said Sir Brian. "You will hardly credit two such chances falling together so happily at the same time. You will recall what none of us expected, the capful of gold pieces that King Edward sent down with the Prince as his gift to the winner of the tourney? None of us, of course, were hoping for such a kingly guerdon.''

That would certainly be true, thought Jim. The King of England did not usually favor the winners of any but royal tourneys with gifts.

"But, as you know," Sir Brian went on, "it ended in my keeping. I had been counting on only the horses and armor of my opponents; and indeed both horse and armor that I gained from my opponents were of noble worth—particularly Sir Harimore's. However, he wished to ransom these back, the horse being as dear to him as Blanchard of Tours is to me; and the armor being such a cunning fit that he was fearful he would not find as good again. I could not deny him, of course, though I did allow him to force payment on me, which was not the best of chivalric manners. But then, you know how it is with me and Castle Smythe.''

Jim and Angie knew. Castle Smythe was perennially teetering on the edge of becoming a ruin; and while Brian won a tourney from time to time, most of the money had to go to supporting those in the castle who were retainers of Brian's and would not leave him, but stayed on merely for a roof over their heads and the poorest of food. But even these simple needs ate up most of his winnings, so that there was usually little left for much-needed repairs of his small castle—even though it was little more than a tower keep, with outbuildings and a curtain wall enclosing all.

"Well, I had done so well this last Christmas," Brian went on, "that I was in high hopes of at least mending the roof of my Great Hall; and still having enough to feed us all until the first spring crops come in and some of my herd of cattle''—(there were only six of them, Jim knew)— "would give birth. But then, on top of all else, came this marvelous rain of gold pieces. I counted them when I got home; and could not believe my eyes.''

He paused to let Jim and Angie both murmur polite agreement with his astonishment at that moment.

"There was enough there to mend all of Castle Smythe," Brian went on, "and keep us well for more than a year—and in a year I would have won other tourneys. For the first time, I would begin to get ahead of my necessary spendings. From that point, who knows what richness of lands and buildings I might not produce? I could clear the scrub wood from my southwest corner and put it to pasture; but, in any case, the King's gift was a gift from God. In fact I was tempted to go to Windom Priory to ask counsel of the good priests there as to how to thank Him. But it came to me that they might well say that I should give all or most of it to them for churchly uses; and I am sinner enough not to want to lose that much of it. Oh, I will make them a handsome present; but I shall decide myself how large shall be the gift."

"Well, you were the one who earned it," said Angie.

"No," said Brian, shaking his head, "fortune favored me—no more. But, though little I knew it then, this wealth was already destined for better use."

He sat back in his chair, beaming at them.

"A much better use!" he said. "For, within a few days of my return, a message came by pigeon from Geronde, summoning me over to see her. I had been intending to go in a day or so anyway; but I went right away. When she saw me, she flung her arms around me; for the best of news had come. An aged knight, returning from the Holy Land, had brought word and passed it on to a King's Justice, on regular circuit through Devon to hold his court; and he had passed it on to another gentle knight, of name Sir Matthew Holmes; who, on his way back to Gloucestershire, kindly came by Malvern Castle and told her. Her father has been seen living in the city of Palmyra, in the Holy Land—but, beyond the fact that he was recognized there, we have no word of how he is living, only that he is in good health for his age, which by now must be close to fifty."

"Then you don't know whether he's planning to come home or not?" said Angie.

"No. And it was exactly that, that showed both Geronde and I the miracle involved in my gaining the King's gift," answered Brian. "With the amount of moneys I now have in hand, I can travel swiftly to this Palmyra, find him and bring him back. Bring him back, I will, by force if necessary; because he must consent to Geronde's marriage to me."

He broke off and turned to Jim.

"Will you come with me, James?" he said. "It will be something to see the Holy Lands, of course. But, more important, I can be certain sure of bringing him back if I have you with me!"

Jim had been expecting it for the last few seconds; but the request still hit him like a fist between the eyes. He was conscious of Angie watching him.

"Brian—" he began and hesitated. "Well, you see, much as I'd like to go, I couldn't get away now if I wanted. Sir John Chandos kindly offered to see if he could not speed up matters at the King's court— whatever legal matters there are involved in our getting the wardship of young Robert Falon. But until that is actually given to us by the King, I have to be here, in readiness to go up to London myself, if necessary. You understand?"

"But, James," said Brian, "with the help of good Sir John, it should not take too long. Now, I was planning to leave as soon as possible, so as to make the trip, find Geronde's father and get back before the terrible heat of the summer season down there strikes. But I could wait for some weeks, say—"

"No," said Jim, feeling Angie's eyes stony upon him. "It's too much of a chance. You should probably follow this up as quickly as possible. I'd like to go more than I can tell you, Brian. But I think in this case, you'd better go alone."

The light that they had seen in Brian's face from the moment he had come in, the light and the excitement, had completely gone out of it. Now his back stiffened.

"Of course," he said, "you are absolutely right, as usual, James. It would be too much of a gamble; and I can indeed understand why you would want to wait here to be on hand to make sure of the Falon wardship. We will say no more of it."

"If there's any other way in which I can help you, Brian," said Jim earnestly. "I don't know what it would be; but since I have some magic at my disposal, maybe we could set up something, or think of something— some way in which I could be useful to you while I'm still here."

"No, no. Not necessary at all," said Brian. "As I say, we will speak no more of it. In any case, I should have asked you how you and your people came through the storm. I and mine were safe within our walls, with all we needed to survive; but you have serfs and tenants in out-lying buildings; and if I mistake not even some cattle in the open. Did you lose much of importance because of the snow and the wind and the fierce drop in temperature?"

"No, surprisingly not," said Jim. "I've just come back from flying around the estate in my dragon body; and I found almost nothing in the way of problems. I did help a few people, including the widow Tebbits, who had run out of firewood. But actually, it did us no harm at all."

"I'm glad to hear it," said Brian, rising from the table. "But, now that

I think on it, there is still light enough for me to get back to Castle Smythe this eve before total darkness; and while there's wind, there is no snow. Indeed, the weather is not as bad as I've endured many times before. I think I will leave, then. You will understand there are things that I must make ready, a great deal of planning and arrangement so that Castle Smythe will go forward properly while I am gone; because I will probably not be able to take anyone with me, even John Chester.''

John Chester was Brian's squire, and the last person Brian would ordinarily leave behind. A coolness had come into the atmosphere, however; and it was very clear that any protest by Jim or Angie, that Brian should stay after all, would have no success and possibly just make the situation that much more awkward. Jim and Angie stood up also.

"Well, good luck," said Jim.

"Yes, Brian," said Angie. "Be careful—for Geronde's sake as well as your own. And for ours.''

"A prudent knight takes no unnecessary risks," said Brian. "The same may be said of a prudent traveler—and I shall be both. Farewell, then. If there is any news that I can send back from this Palmyra place, Geronde will have it; and she will let you know.''

The light was going from the day, and the warmth of being together had already departed from their little gathering in the Great Hall. They accompanied Sir Brian to the far end of the hall, where servants helped him back into his armor and outdoor traveling cloak. His horse was brought around; and they stood for a moment in the doorway, watching him out of sight across the courtyard and beyond the gates, until he could be seen no longer.

CHAPTER 4

For nearly five weeks neither Jim nor Angie mentioned Brian or Geronde to each other. This was unusual, since normally they talked everything over. But in this case, Jim had a new feeling of guilt, this time about their last meeting with Brian; and he suspected that Angie had, too—so the subject was bound to be a little touchy.

It stayed there, like a sort of half-forgotten headache that would surface from time to time when there was nothing else to think about. But still, with time, it was surfacing less often, when unexpectedly there was a blast of a silvery horn from outside the castle walls—not the braying of a cow's horn, or even one fitted with a nipple to act as a hunting horn—but the sound that only a true musical instrument could make; and a man-at-arms came running to them from the guard on the gate, meeting them just as they stepped outside the Great Hall, on their way to see what was happening themselves.

"M'lord! M'lady!" gasped the man-at-arms, a relative youngster with the bright blue eyes common in the countryside and a shock of slightly reddish hair. "Yves Mortain sends to say that it is Sir John Chandos who approaches, with a dozen mounted men-at-arms."

"Well," said Jim. "Welcome him! Welcome him! Run back and tell them on the gate he's to be brought in with all courtesy!"

The message bearer spun around and dashed off ahead of them again.

"You'd think they'd all realize by this time," grumbled Jim, "Sir John's welcome here anytime."

"That's not the point," said Angie beside him. "They're doing what they're supposed to. And, anyway, how do they know but what Sir John's turned out to be an enemy, since he was last here at Malencontri? Things like that happen in this time, you know."

"I suppose," said Jim, still dissatisfied. "What I wouldn't give for just some kind of speaking tube that would reach from the Great Hall to the front gate."

He wiggled his shoulders uncomfortably, for although the day was bright, and the castle walls around the courtyard cut off most of the breeze from him, he and Angie had come out dressed as they were for the relative warmth inside the castle. It was a bright day and a relatively still one as far as moving air went—but it was still February.

"Yves Mortain is simply doing his job," said Angie.

"Yes, you're right," said Jim. Yves Mortain had been named Chief man-at-arms when Theoluf had been elevated to the position of Jim's squire. Yves was entirely competent; and, to tell the truth, Jim was secretly aware that Yves knew a lot more than he did about how a castle should be defended and a watch on the gate should be kept.

But already through the doors of the gate, opening now to the bridge above the moat, the sound of the hooves of the first two horses of their visitors were audible, and Sir John rode through the gate into the courtyard, looking elegant and barely middle-aged as usual, on a large black stallion which whisked its tail as it approached, as proudly and cheerfully as if it was just starting the day's trip, not ending it. It halted in front of them.

"Sir John!" said Jim happily. "It's good to see you!"

Sir John took off his steel cap with a flourish.

"Sir James, Lady Angela!" he said. "I bring special news for you, and I wanted to be the first to get it to you. So I have come down from London. Shall we go inside?"

"Absolutely!" said Jim. He looked around for his squire.

But Theoluf had already appeared, with a man-at-arms to lead the train of Sir John's armed retainers off to the stables for their horses, and to shelter for themselves, as well as, undoubtedly, to food and drink. Theoluf himself came forward to hold the head of the stallion, as Sir John swung down from the saddle.

"By your leave, Sir John," said Theoluf, "I will have him in the third stall from the front door to the stables and the best care taken of him. May I ask his name?"

"He is Tonnere de Beaudry," said Sir John.

"This way, if you please, Tonnere de Beaudry," said Theoluf, addressing the war horse with the courtesy its worth deserved, and leading it off.

Sir John turned back to Jim and Angie, and all three together began the walk toward the entrance of the Great Hall. Thoroughly chilled by this time, Jim would just as soon have moved a little faster; but manners dictated that their stroll to the front door be leisurely.

"I can only stay the night," said Sir John. "I have matters to deal with in the west. But my way led by Malvern Castle, where I had hoped to possibly encounter Sir Brian without turning aside—for Smythe Castle was out of my way. I wished to bring him his Majesty's personal congratulations on winning the Earl of Somerset's Christmas tourney. His Majesty was held in thrall by the description of that tourney by Richard de Bisby, Bishop of Bath and Wells. But Sir Brian was gone, unfortunately, to the Holy Land. Lady Geronde de Chaney, however, gave me shelter for the night. While I'm here, though, I must say how I, myself, was impressed by the way the Earl's troll, under your handling, of course, handled those five good knights of ours. He is indeed an unusual troll, both in size and, I assume, in attitude."

"Yes, you could say that about him," said Jim. "I didn't see you in the stands, though. I looked for you by the Earl—"

He broke off, feeling an impulse to bite his tongue, though the words were already out. By his status, if not his official rank, Sir John should have been seated very close to the Earl, but he had not been.

"Oh that," said Sir John lightly. "I was sitting with an old friend, a fellow campaigner, on one of the lower tier of benches there. But I missed nothing—"

He turned to Angie.

"—And I was most impressed by the diversion you arranged for us on the last night of Christmas, m'lady."

"Well, thank you," said Angie. "But I enjoyed putting it on, as much probably as anybody watching it."

They passed through the door into the relative warmth of the hall, still chatting. Sir John, Jim noticed, did not seem in any hurry to get to what he had come to see them about. Bad news, perhaps. The most probable thing was that there had been some hitch in the wardship proceedings for Robert Falon, and Sir John was planning to break this to them gently— possibly over dinner.

But Jim was wrong. After they had been sitting and making light conversation for a while at the high table over wine and oreoles—which were something like small, holeless donuts in fantastic shapes, with a certain amount of fruit preserves in them—Sir John's squire approached the table and stood waiting patiently until he should be noticed. Sir John eventually did.

"Ah," he said. "You found it. In good shape I see. Pass it up to me, here."

The squire handed him what looked like a square of folded parchment, its edges sewn together so that it would not open up into its normal, larger shape.

"You may go," said Sir John to the squire, and turned to Jim and Angie, the package in his hand. "I suppose I should wait until some high point of our meeting to give you this," he said. "But I know you are anxious to learn what is in it. Therefore . . ."

He passed the package to Jim, sitting next to him; and Jim overcame his own overwhelming desire to hand it on to Angie, to whom it mattered most—if it was what he thought it was. But the manners of the period were that it should pass from Sir John to him, since he would be the responsible recipient.

Jim took out his belt knife, cut the stitching that held the parchment closed; and, sure enough, it opened up into a single sheet with a heavy seal, pressed on to a strip of smaller parchment fed through two slits at the bottom of the letter; so that it hung down from the page almost the way a pendant would hang down on a human neck.

He looked at the writing on the parchment sheet.

It was in fairly readable medieval "Latin"—done by a clerkly hand with the style particular to the time and originator, with various ornate flourishes, including the fairly common so-called "clubbed ascenders"— the vertical strokes of certain letters being pushed upward and thickened, so it looked like those words were carrying spears.

He read the written words with some little difficulty, but with reasonable ease—

Edwardus Dei gracia Rex Anglie et Francie et dominus Hibernie omnibus ad quos presentes litere pervenerint saluten . . .

Even as he watched the Latin suddenly blurred before his eyes and turned into English. It was that same overall magic that he had long since decided had been doing a constant job of translating not merely different languages, such as French, but innumerable different dialects, and the speech of wolves, Sea Devils and the like, to a sort of common, modern English, understandable to both his and Angie's ear.

In English it began: *"Edward by the grace of God King of England and France and Lord of Ireland to all to whom these present matters are concerned, greeting."*

In the matter of Robert Falon, son of Ralph Falon, Baron of Chene, now deceased, concerning the wardship of said Robert Falon until he shall be of age . . .

Jim's eyes slid rapidly down the page. It was what he and Angie had been hoping. The wardship had been assigned to him; and at the very bottom was the royal seal that he had noticed the minute the letter was opened. Without a word, he passed it to Angie. Angie's eyes filled with tears.

"We must celebrate," said Jim. He turned to Sir John. "I don't know how to thank you, Sir John. We weren't expecting an answer on this for months; in fact, I had understood it might even be years before something like this was decided on."

"It can sometimes well be," said Sir John. "However, those close about the King decided that it would be best if his Majesty saw to the safe-keeping of young Robert Falon with dispatch, his royal command passing over ordinary procedure. You have the good Bishop of Bath and Wells, Richard de Bisby, to thank in part. He made a visit to court and his arguments for you to be appointed had a powerful effect on his Majesty, who may God bless."

"Amen," said Jim and Angie dutifully.

Jim cleared his throat, embarrassed; for Sir John had uttered the last words with a perfectly straight face. Jim could imagine the Bishop's powerful voice and determined attitude having its effect on a king who only wanted to be left free of state responsibilities.

"You won't mind a little celebration, considering you've got to ride again tomorrow?" he asked Sir John.

"Certes, in this instance, absolutely not," said Sir John.

So they celebrated, medieval style, with the best of wine and the best of food; and by whatever occult means it was done, the word spread through the castle to all the servants. The result was all of them also went around beaming; quite as if the wardship had been given not merely to Jim but to all of those at Malencontri, collectively.

Their general happiness, and Jim and Angie's as well, lasted until the next morning, when they waved Sir John Chandos and his troop of men-at-arms off on his further journeys.

But then it began to fade as they walked slowly together back into the castle and climbed the stairs to their solar. They had both fallen silent, and it lasted even in the solar for a little while, until Angie, looking not at him but out one of the solar's windows, spoke.

"Well," she said in a low voice, "you're free to go now."

"Go?" said Jim, with complete understanding and acute discomfort.

"You know what I mean," said Angie. She turned around to face him. "To that place—Palmyra—that Brian's going to. I mean, that he's probably gone to already by this time. You're free to follow him, now."

"No, I'm not," said Jim reflexively.

Angie looked away from him again. It was almost as if she had not heard what he had said.

"You know," she went on in the same low voice, "I started thinking, some time back, how I'd feel if I was Geronde and you were going to try to find my father; and how I'd feel about you not having Brian with you."

"It's not the same situation," said Jim. "With Robert Falon belonging to us now, we're a family. Besides"—he tried to prod a smile from her—

"I'm wounded, deeply wounded, by the thought you don't trust me out alone without Brian to protect me."

"It's not funny," said Angie, looking squarely at him. "I worry a lot less when Brian's with you and you're off on one of these things—a lot more than I would if he wasn't there."

"Anyway," said Jim, "we've already told Brian I wouldn't go. He's undoubtedly left some weeks ago; and there's nothing to be done about it now."

"Isn't there?" said Angie.

"Well," said Jim, feeling uncomfortable, "barring the possibility that I could catch up with him. But you still don't really want me to go, do you?"

"Of course I don't," said Angie. "But maybe I'm wrong. Maybe you should go."

"That's something no one can tell for sure."

"Maybe we can," said Angie. "Anyway, I think we ought to go and have a talk with Geronde."

Jim stared at her.

"You've already decided to let me go, haven't you?" he asked.

"Yes," said Angie, almost angrily. "But I want both of us to talk to Geronde first."

"Maybe that's a good idea," said Jim. "To be truthful, Angie, it's been gnawing at me a little that I didn't say yes, in the first place, when Brian asked me to go. But by all means, let's find out Geronde's point of view on it. Maybe—well, let's go talk to her anyway."

He stood up.

"You don't mean now?" said Angie.

"It's still early in the day," Jim said.

"It's a three-hour ride over there in this weather," Angie said, "and if we have any kind of a talk with her, it'll be too late to ride back. That means we've got to stay the night. That means we've got to take our bedding along with us. I love Geronde, but I wouldn't sleep in one of the beds in her castle without my own bedding unless someone forced me to it at the point of a knife. Can't you just take us over there by magic?"

"Carolinus warned me against using too much of my magic, even though I've got an open drawing account," said Jim. "I've been meaning to tell you about that. It was the day Brian came—and that drove Carolinus clear out of my head. He warned me to always be as careful to use as little magic as possible—so I'd have enough for any emergency."

"Well, then," said Angie, "isn't there some way you can turn into a dragon and just carry me over by air?"

"No," said Jim slowly. "A dragon really hasn't got that much lifting power. An adult human is more than one can fly off with. Remember back in the twentieth century how there were old folk tales of eagles flying off with babies? Well, the truth of the matter is there was no truth to them. A baby weighing much more than ten pounds would be too much for any eagle to carry. For the same reason, an adult human being would be too much for me to carry. I might be able to get you off the ground and sort of flop along with you for a short distance, but then I'd run out of strength; and we'd both come back to earth.''

He hesitated.

"I don't suppose you'd like me to go alone— No," he answered himself as he saw her mouth open.

"You're right. No," said Angie. "You don't think you should use the magic just this once?"

"That's the trouble. I've been doing too much of 'just this once' up until now. Wait a minute!"

"What?" Angie stared at him.

"It's simple," said Jim. "I'll just make you into a dragon, too. That'd take almost no magical energy at all, by comparison."

"Me? Into a dragon? You could do that?" The startled look on Angie's face changed to one of pleasure. "Yes. Why not? I've never been a dragon. Why didn't we think of that before?"

"I suppose because we didn't have to," said Jim. "But you'd better put some outside clothes on for the weather, just in case we have to turn back into humans while we're still outside." He was already moving toward his own clothes rack to get a travel cloak.

Properly dressed, they mounted to the open top of the tower, and Jim nodded at the man-at-arms currently on duty.

"You can go downstairs for a few minutes and warm up, Thomas," he said.

Gratefully, the guard disappeared down the stairs.

"When are you going to change me into a dragon?" Angie asked.

"Right now," said Jim. "Come along with me."

He led the way over to the platform on which rested the great cauldron—empty now, of course—that could be filled with oil to be heated, lit and poured down on anyone trying to storm the gates to the castle keep. He stepped up on the platform and gave Angie a hand up. Here, they were level with the top of the battlements, looking out from a flat surface into thin air and down onto the open space surrounding the castle and the trees beyond.

"Move over from me a little bit to give yourself room," Jim said. "Just a few feet there. There. That's good enough. Now here we go."

Jim visualized both himself and Angie as dragons, their clothes having vanished, but ready to come back on them immediately they were turned back into humans. It was a far cry from his early days of using magic to change himself into a dragon, in which case he invariably ruined whatever clothes he was wearing, or else had to strip them all off first.

"You make a good-looking dragon," he said to Angie.

"Do I?" said Angie. "Or are you just saying that?"

"No," said Jim. "You *are* a good-looking female dragon. If I was a full-time male dragon—"

"Well, I'll believe you for the moment," said Angie. "Now what?"

"Now," said Jim, "all you do is jump off the edge of the platform, into the air, spread your wings and start flying. I'll be right with you and you just do what I do, flap your wings when I flap mine and stretch them out and soar when I soar."

Angie looked at the edge of the platform and the empty air beyond.

"Jim," she said, after a moment, "I've changed my mind. I don't think I want to be a dragon today, after all."

"Don't be silly," said Jim.

"I'm scared," said Angie.

"Remember what you said to me when I was in a dragon body? I'd turned up in the Cliffside dragons' caves and I was alone with you. You suggested I might fly to Carolinus's for help. I wasn't too eager, either, to jump out of that cave into thin air. But you said I could try it. You said, *'It'll probably just come to you. I'd think it would, instinctively, once you were in the air.'* Remember?"

"Did I say that?" said Angie. "Well, I was wrong."

"No," said Jim. "You were right. It'll come to you instinctively, once you're in the air. That body you have now has its own instincts and reflexes, you know."

"I don't care if it does," said Angie.

"Besides," said Jim, "I'll be right there to catch you in mid-air with magic even if something could go wrong."

"I don't care," said Angie. "I'm scared. I've changed my mind about being a dragon. Change me back—Jim, *stop that!*"

Her last words ended in a scream. Jim was using his greater weight (he was a much larger dragon) to simply push Angie off the edge of the stone platform into the air. She tried desperately to hold on with her claws, but the claws only scraped the stone and slid. As she herself slithered toward emptiness.

"It's what mother birds do with their nestlings when they're ready to fly," said Jim. "And father birds," he added, as Angie reached the edge, teetered there for a second and dropped off it.

She dropped out of sight, but almost immediately there was the thunder of wings and Angie shot up past him, climbing frantically for altitude, like a fighter plane reaching for its best operating height.

It was exactly what Jim himself had done, the first time he had taken off into the air from the Cliffside cave he had been talking about. The first thought in his mind had been to keep from falling; and that human message, translated to his dragon body, had immediately made use of every ounce of the powerful climbing ability that a dragon's wings could produce.

Hastily, he leaped off and followed her, climbing after her.

This sort of intense activity was possible for a dragon, but it exhausted them in a hurry; and, he saw, after a bit, that Angie was ceasing to pump so hard and was beginning to slow down. Finally she stopped, and her wings instinctively reached out and stiffened in soaring position on an updraft. Jim swam up through the air to soar beside her.

"Where am I?" Angie asked him wildly.

"Oh, I'd say about two thousand feet above the ground," said Jim.

"Two thousand—" She looked down. There was a long silence. "I am!" she said.

"Of course," said Jim. "But that's more than enough for the straight flying we'll be doing to Malvern Castle. Now follow me. I'm used to finding thermal updrafts—that's what you're riding on now—and using them. From here on we soar to Malvern. You can think of it as coasting."

"All right," said Angie, but in a voice that signaled she still really did not trust what she was doing.

Nonetheless they went on, moving from thermal to thermal, circling upward on the warmer air of its updraft, planing down in the direction of their destination, finding another thermal and riding it up to where they could start planing onward again. It was some time before Angie spoke once more. Jim had not been saying anything to her, leaving her to get used to her new way of traveling. But finally she did speak.

"This isn't the right direction to Malvern Castle," she said.

"We have to go roundabout, because of the way the wind's blowing," said Jim. "Not far roundabout. But it's just as if our wings were like a ship's sails and we have to trim them to the wind to a certain extent. We're coming in toward Malvern Castle on a curve."

There was another long period of silence while they shifted from thermal to thermal, mounted the updraft from dark patches of trees below them, which had picked up heat from the sun and were warming the air above them to cause updrafts; and after a while Angie spoke again.

"I'll never forgive you, Jim," she said, but almost in a conversational tone. "I'll never, never forgive. That was a terrible thing to push me off the side of a building where I could have fallen to my death!"

"But I knew you wouldn't," said Jim. "Just like I didn't, the first time I tried it. You couldn't have if you'd wanted to. Your body reacted without your even thinking, just the way the body of a young bird does when its mother pushes it out of the nest."

"I'll still never forgive you," said Angie. "But—oh, Jim, this is a marvelous way to get about. I love it! Why didn't you turn me into a dragon before this?"

"Because I knew you wouldn't want to jump off the top of the tower," said Jim.

It was not strictly true, of course. Actually, it had never occurred to him to think of turning Angie into a dragon before. He hurried to take advantage of the change in her mood, though.

"But you do like it?"

"I love it!" said Angie. "And you know something? I don't feel cold at all; and it must be icy out here with the wind blowing on us."

"Dragons don't feel cold," said Jim. "They do feel heat—you'll find out about that for yourself. Also, you're moving with the wind most of the time, so it's not really blowing against you."

"Just think," said Angie, "now you and I can go places together this way!"

Jim had not thought of that, either. He was still considering the ramifications and possibilities of such traveling when Malvern Castle appeared in its clearing and he led Angie on a long gliding descent toward the top of its tower.

The Malvern tower top, like their own at Malencontri, had a single sentry on it. Besides his sword he had a short stabbing spear in his hand. He stood transfixed as they came closer and closer to the tower top.

When they came down with a double thump about fifteen feet from him, he gave what could better be described as an honest shriek, rather than the ritual male shout of alarm Jim was used to from his own people— and bolted down the hole in the tower top, where the stone steps led to the floor below.

They heard his footfalls clattering away; a door slammed, then opened again; and Geronde's voice floated up to them from what was obviously the floor just below.

"What the hell?" it snapped.

CHAPTER 5

Jim and Angie heard the patter of lighter feet coming back up the stairs in a hurry, and Geronde popped up onto the roof, with the sentry's stabbing spear in one hand and his naked sword in the other. She glared at Jim and Angie.

"All right, you dragons!" she said. "You're at the wrong castle. You want Malencontri. It's twelve miles west that way—" She pointed with the sword.

"It's just us, Geronde," said Jim. He was working his magic; and in the same instant he said this, he and Angie turned back into their human shapes, in their human clothes. Geronde stared at them, and the weapons in her hands drooped.

"You two?" she said after a long moment. "And you're a dragon as well, Angela?"

"Jim just made me one for the first time," said Angie, with perhaps a touch of smugness in her voice. "It's enjoyable. But Geronde, what in heaven's name did you think you could do against two dragons with that spear and a sword?"

"Make them sorry they ever tried to bother me—if they did!" said Geronde. "Jim turned you into a dragon and you decided to come here?"

"The other way around," said Angie. "We were going to come here, and we decided to fly instead of riding over. It was quicker."

"Oh? Well, it was kind of you to think of visiting—" she began, but the sound of two pairs of feet scuffling up the steps interrupted her, and up through the opening of the stairwell, now, came a tall, black haired, long-nosed man who was Bernard, the Chief man-at-arms at Malvern, hauling along the sentry by his collar. He stopped and held his captive still, as Geronde turned to face him.

"Shall I hang him, m'lady?" he asked. "He left his post—as well as running from the enemy in cowardly fashion."

"I suppose," said Geronde through her teeth, "though useful men-at-arms are not that easy to pick up . . . On the other hand, he's no use to us if he hasn't got the guts to fight—''

The ex-sentry, who had been half-fainting in Bernard's grasp, on hearing this all but collapsed; so that Bernard had to hold him upright by main strength. Jim hurried to get a word in.

"If I could crave a favor, Geronde," he said, "might I beg this lad's life for him? He had just a moment to see the two of us coming; and I think he ran off the top of the tower, pushed more by a feeling that it was his duty above all to warn and protect you; and that was what made him seem to abandon his post so wantonly."

"He hasn't got the wit," said Geronde, looking angrily at the half-collapsing sentry, held tightly in Bernard's grasp.

"Why, yes," said Angie quickly, "if I also may pray the same favor from you, Geronde, I'm almost sure I heard him shout something—I think, something like *'must save m'lady'*—before he ran down the stairs."

"Hah!" said Geronde. "A likely—Well, all right, Bernard, take him away. Send a man up here. As for this one, let him go without food for three days. It'll give him time to think about following his orders first!"

Bernard hauled away the suddenly joyous sentry, and Geronde turned back to Angie and Jim.

"Will you step below to the solar?" she said. "You must forgive its appearance, Angela. We will go to the Great Hall in due course; but it comes to me that you may want to talk privily for a little while first. In truth, I have been thinking of going over to Malencontri to speak so to you two."

She led the way downstairs.

Her private bed-sitting room, the solar at Malvern, was nothing to be ashamed of by medieval standards. It was just that, by contrast with Jim and Angie's own at Malencontri, its lacks showed up. But there was a good-sized fireplace with a good-sized fire in it; and, after Geronde had seen the advantage of the glass-filled window apertures at Malencontri, she had had her own windows glazed also, since she had the money for it.

Still, the room had a rather barren look to it compared to Jim and Angie's solar—although it occurred to Jim that possibly some of the feeling of barrenness about it came from the fact that the chairs were unpadded and the floor unheated, as he and Angie were used to having it at their own home.

But the fire was bright; and there was an unusually large bed, with its four tall bedposts holding up a canopy as well, thick bed-curtains hanging from them. Those curtains were the first defense against the coldness of nighttime for medieval sleepers of quality.

To further balance the difference between the two castles, Geronde's servants were very well trained indeed. There was a scratching at the door, shortly after they had sat down; and when Geronde bade whoever it was enter, a servant came in, carrying cakes, wine and water from the serving room and asking if his lady would care for them.

Since it turned out she would—it could hardly have been otherwise with guests there—these were put on the table.

"Now, leave us alone unless there's a fire in the castle," said Geronde sharply.

"Yes, m'lady," said the servant. He bowed his way back out.

"As I say, I was of a mind to come and visit you in any case," said Geronde as soon as the wine and water was mixed and they had all both drunk and nibbled at what was before them. "But perhaps I should let you tell me first why you wanted to come here."

"No, no," said Angie hastily. "You talk first, Geronde."

"Well . . ." said Geronde, slowly looking down at the table. "It is not my place really to speak for Sir Brian. He is a knight and a gentleman and can speak for himself. No doubt he told you there need no more be said on a certain subject; and yet it is that subject I would wish to discuss with you."

"Discuss away, Geronde," said Jim.

"You have a somewhat strange way of expressing yourself sometimes, James," said Geronde. "Nonetheless, I think I take your meaning. I will indeed discuss away, since that was what I was going to do if I came to see you. Now, both of you learned almost from the beginning of our acquaintance that Brian and I were betrothed."

"Yes, indeed," said Jim. "Almost the first thing he did was show me your favor."

Geronde's eyes misted slightly.

"He would do that," said Geronde. "Yes, that is the way he is. But perhaps when you first met, it was as two knights who might decide to debate something or other. Was that so?"

"He did suggest," said Jim, "that the two of us might have a go at it on behalf of our individual ladies. I had just told him that I was in love with Angie and he said that was a coincidence, because he was in love with you."

"He said that!" said Geronde. "But you did not fight?"

"No," said Jim. "It was rather awkward at the moment, because I was in a dragon body and couldn't get out of it; and then later on when I was back in my human form we had been Companions. So, for the two of us to fight would hardly have been right. But I knew almost from that first moment of the closeness between the two of you, as something that had endured for some time."

"Yes. Longer than you might think," said Geronde. "Indeed, longer than we can remember ourselves, he and I."

"You knew Brian most of your life, then, Geronde?" asked Angie.

"In truth, we knew each other all our lives," said Geronde. "Though we were not kin, he was motherless almost from birth and we were close neighbors, of course. His father and mine were good friends. In fact they were two of a kind, those fathers. The result was we grew up together, Brian and I. I was almost never at Castle Smythe, but he was here much of the time."

Angie looked at her curiously.

"Strange, is it not?" said Geronde. "It was almost as if we were to have no choice but to end up as we have. Brian's father was very much involved with his cousins, the Nevilles of Rabe; and I believe intended, or at least expected, to mend his fortunes by doing things for them. At any rate, he was always going on trips, mostly to the continent for them— the Nevilles have connections all over, there; particularly in France and Italy. When he went, Brian was left here at Malvern."

"Brian must have been closer to your father than his own, then," said Angie.

"No," said Geronde, "because my father was gone often, too. But here at Malvern, there was a well-trained staff; and, after my mother died, when I was seven, women to look after us both when we were very young. All things in order. Whereas Castle Smythe was—well, you see how Castle Smythe is nowadays. There was really no other place for Brian to be put. Sir Edmar Claive and his cousins, who then occupied Malencontri, were not the sort of men any young boy could be left with; and there were no other suitable households close. So, Brian was left with us; and, as I say, he and I grew up together."

"How young were you when all this started?" Angie asked.

"The first time, Brian was seven and I was five," said Geronde, "although we might have been brought together as babes too young to remember it also. But the earliest I remember is, as I say, when I was five; and after that we were together at least for a time almost each year; so much in each other's company, like brother and sister, that you'd think it would be the last thing in the world for the two of us to fall in love."

"You did, though," said Angie.

Jim looked out one of the windows at the cloud-flecked sky and a hawk, almost certainly wild, circling high above the trees beyond the clearing. There had been an interested, prompting note to Angie's voice that he always dreaded. The heat of the fire and the wine, half a cupful of which

he had been foolish enough to drink straight, was making him not so much
drowsy as dull-witted; and he was a little afraid that this would turn into
one of those *"Oh, was your great-uncle living in such-and-such a place,
then? I wonder if he knew some of my relatives who lived there?"* He
struggled to keep his eyes open.

Geronde was nodding in answer to Angie's question.

"We did not know it at first," she said. "We only knew as children
that we missed each other when we were apart and were never happier
than when we were together. Oh, we had some terrific fights in those days;
but nonetheless, as I say, one day it turned out we were in love; and later,
when I got older, I told my father that it was Brian I intended to marry—
that was during one of the few times when my father was home and I
could talk to him."

"He was around that little?" said Angie.

"He was always off on some errand or other that would bring him back
loaded with gold, but he never came back so," said Geronde. "As I say,
he and Brian's father were alike in chasing moonbeams of wealth. In any
case, when I told him how I felt about Brian, he stamped and roared that
I would never be allowed to marry Brian. That I should marry a duke—
a prince! It was yet another of his grand dreams—aside from the fact that
I would rather have Brian than any prince in the world."

She turned abruptly to Jim. Jim woke up and did his best to look alert
and interested.

"This was why I was thinking of coming over to talk to you both,
James. Brian told me you were awaiting the King's gift of the wardship
of Robert Falon; and might need to present yourself in person before his
Majesty—and so could not leave England now. I understand that perfectly;
as Brian did."

"Well . . ." said Jim uncomfortably. There had been no doubt that
Brian had been deeply dismayed by Jim's refusal to help him in his search
for Geronde's father in the Holy Land, now that they had found out where
Geronde's father was. For Jim to stay home under these conditions, even
at the cost of a friendship, was the only sensible thing to do, by medieval
standards. Land and wealth were everything; and the gaining of them took
precedence over everything else.

Therefore, Brian's good judgment would agree with the common sense
of what Jim was doing; but nonetheless they were literally blood brothers,
in that they had both shed blood at the same time in more than one affray;
and the ideal of the chivalric knight, toward which Brian himself lived
and reached in everything he did, would have scorned the Falon wealth
and property in favor of aiding a comrade. Geronde could not have helped
but feel somewhat as Brian did.

"Well . . ." said Jim again, hesitantly.

"James, do not think I mean to make any opposition to your decision," said Geronde earnestly. "In life, we all must make hard choices. I know well how your heart must have beaten higher, like Brian's, at the thought of a venture into the Holy Lands; let alone your natural desire to aid a fellow Companion-at-arms. Already, you will probably have decisions to make and matters to concern you, as far as the administration of Robert Falon's estates are concerned. But I thought I might come and plead with you to consider a certain decision, in spite of all that."

"The fact is, Geronde—" Jim was beginning. But Geronde interrupted him again.

"No," she said. "Hear me out, I pray you, James."

"Of course," said Jim, more uncomfortable than ever.

"I would like to tell you something that I would not otherwise tell anyone, except perhaps you two," said Geronde. "I can say this because Brian and I are so alike."

She looked at Angie.

"I never had a close woman friend until you, Angela," she said. "I could never stand them. Chattering, spineless creatures, most of them— except for some older ones; and they so stuck in their ways and determined to be right all the time that I would have fought with them continually. But you were different, Angela."

"Well, Geronde . . ." said Angie, as obviously embarrassed, Jim noticed with a certain amount of perverse satisfaction, as he had been himself, a moment before.

"It is a matter of being able to agree with each other on things," said Geronde. She turned her attention back to Jim again. "It is exactly that way with Brian where you are concerned, James. He never had any close friends of his own spirit and rank. He must always be in contest with them—better than any at anything, if it killed him; and indeed, he has been better than most. As a result, he has found few men he could respect; and of those, he had full respect only for superiors such as Sir John Chandos, who is so much older and so proven in war and peace that there could be no measuring by Brian of himself with such a knight. All others of worth he might otherwise have respected, he must be fighting with. You saw it yourself with Sir Harimore at the Earl's. Brian will kill Sir Harimore one day, unless Harry kills him. But meanwhile he gives Harry full credit for his fighting skills, only. Oh, he can *like* your bowman Dafydd ap Hywel, because Dafydd is of common birth. Therefore there cannot possibly be any competition between him and Brian; and Brian will cheerfully acknowledge that Dafydd is not only a better bowman than others, but a better bowman than he."

She turned again to Angie.

"But have you not also heard the like, from Danielle, Angela?" she said. "How Dafydd, in his own rank, like Brian cannot abide an equal? So that when she and he started to live with her father, Giles o' the Wold, and all his other outlaws—how Dafydd must be forever measuring himself against each of the band, before he would be at peace with himself— taking them on in contest two at a time, if necessary."

"Yes," said Angie. She looked across at Jim.

"Nobody ever told me," said Jim. "But I'm not surprised."

"Well, that is the point I'm making, James. You now have—according to what I was told by the good Sir John Chandos—the wardship of Robert Falon firmly in your hands. While Brian has gone on alone."

She hesitated.

"He would not expect you to follow him," Geronde said. "No, not even if he knew that the matter of the wardship was now settled. He would not ask it. But you mean a great deal to him, James. You are the one man whom he can accept as an equal. Also, you are the one man he would depend upon in any strait."

"Geronde," said Jim, "you know I'm not very useful with weapons. Brian could pick up a dozen knights, or even many less than knights, who'd be much more skilled in fighting, and protecting his back than I'd be."

"But that is not the point, James!" said Geronde, leaning forward. "It is true—and I crave your pardon for saying it to your face, James—that you will probably never be either a goo— a great horseman, nor a master of any weapon; nor even, possibly, a good average man of your hands with any such. But otherwise he admires you tremendously."

"Oh, you mean my magic," said Jim. "You must know that's an accident, Geronde. If chance hadn't made me a dragon, I'd never have become a magician's apprentice in order to take care of the magic that I happen to generate without meaning to. It all grew out of that—by accident."

"No!" said Geronde. "It is not that either. Though we all respect the courage and mind in you that would send you to study that strange Art. No. It is the fact that you are so like what Brian most admires—that which is to be found in Sir John Chandos—a *preux chevalier*; you are a truly chivalric knight, in that you could never do anything less than your knightly duty in all matters."

"Geronde . . ." said Jim helplessly. He could think of no easy way of handling a compliment like this. All he could do was sit there and suffer under it. He was quite certain that he was nowhere near being the kind of person Geronde was talking about and Brian evidently believed him to be; but he could also feel very clearly that it would be doing her no favor to argue against that fact just now.

"That is why I greatly venture at this moment," Geronde went on, "to beg you, James, that you consider following Brian and catching up with him, so that you can be with him on the rest of his trip. He will be no farther than the Isle of Cyprus by now—if he is indeed that far. I can give you the names of those he knows there; and you can find him easily by searching them out—for they are men well known on the island. James—by your favor, James—do not say no without thinking about it for a moment."

"Geronde—" interrupted Angie; but Geronde charged on, speaking to Jim and ignoring the interruption.

"This is why it is so important that you be with him on this search for my father," said Geronde. "He will listen to you, James, where he would listen to no other—and you know that he is apt to be drawn aside by a trifle chance at a passage of arms, or some such. He will be stronger and more sensible if you are with him. You are wiser than he. Yes—do not look at me like that—you are wiser than he! So, you will keep him safer by being with him; and he knows and I know that you would never fail him in any strait. That is why I beg you now—I beg you on bended knee—to follow and join him, James!"

"Whoops—whoa!" said Jim, catching her just in time, for Geronde had literally been about to kneel to him. This was not remarkable from a medieval point of view, but from Jim's twentieth-century viewpoint, the very idea made him go hot with embarrassment. "It's all right, Geronde. I'm going. That's what we came here to tell you!"

She stared up at him, and all the blood drained out of her face. For a moment it seemed as if she would collapse like the sentry who had come so close to being hung, if Jim had not been holding her upright.

"That's right, Geronde," said Angie urgently, moving to her and putting her arms around her. "Jim's decided to go. Haven't you, Jim!"

She stared at Jim. Jim had not quite realized the full meaning of what he had just said. He did so, now.

"Of course I am!" he told Geronde, with as much heartiness as he could manage. He let go of her elbows, because Angie was hugging her.

The blood came back to Geronde's face. She exploded upward from her chair. She kissed Jim. She kissed Angie. She whirled from one to the other, as if she was beginning to dance.

"It is dinner time!" she cried. "And we will have such a dinner! Ho, there! Attend me!"

The door to the solar from the hall outside burst open, showing Bernard and another man-at-arms, both with swords drawn.

"Put up your weapons, you idiots!" snapped Geronde. "Run to the cook and the serving room. We will have two guests for dinner, Lord and Lady Eckert. It will be the finest and best of everything we have. We will be down in five minutes. You hear, five minutes, and I shall expect to see a table laid, set and with the first of the meal upon it. Run!"

"Run!" roared Bernard to the other man-at-arms, who disappeared from sight immediately. "Your pardon, m'lady—your pardon, m'lord and lady . . ."

Bernard backed hastily out, closing the door behind him.

"Now, let us pray you to forgive us, Geronde," said Angie. "We should have told you this right away, without letting you go through all you had to tell us before we told you."

"What difference makes it?" sang Geronde. This time, she actually did twirl. "Howsomever the news comes, it is what I have dreamed and prayed for. I shall tell five rosaries of beads tonight in thanksgiving. I regret not a word of what I said, not a moment of not hearing until just now. It is the fact that you are going, James, that makes all the difference. Oh, how we shall celebrate!"

"I'll need to know all you can tell me about how I might follow him and where I might find him," said Jim.

"You shall know all that I know!" said Geronde. "I shall tell you every word he said, at dinner. But—it will be a long, hard trip for you, James. You do go willingly?"

"Of course!" said Jim.

"Then all is well!" said Geronde. "Though the travel itself may be none too easy."

"Not at all," said Jim. "From my standpoint—a nothing. You forget I am a magician."

CHAPTER 6

"**M**agician—hah!" said Jim morosely to himself. What good was it to be a magician, if you were deliberately never using your magic? With magic you could say, "Let so-and-so, wherever he is, appear before me!" and instantly the one named was there.

"Is something the matter, m'lord?" asked Hob, the official castle hobgoblin of Malencontri (plain "Hob" as he was once more called, like all hobgoblins, now that he had been shorn of the title Jim had given him earlier—"*Hob-One de Malencontri*").

"No," said Jim.

But of course there was. Hob was now out of the pouch on Jim's back in which he normally traveled, and perched on Jim's right shoulder. Jim, himself, was sitting on a rock on a pebbly beach in Cyprus, gazing out at the Mediterranean and waiting. He had been waiting for five hours now.

He was long past the point of being impatient. He now slumped on his rock, despondent, gazing at the Mediterranean Sea, which was in a good mood at the moment, the curling surf coming neatly in to the gray-blue pebble beach in front of him.

Before Jim, the waves came up, came up, one after the other, laid down on the beach and died. Every so often—it was either the eighth or ninth wave in the Mediterranean, except in extraordinary circumstances when it seemed to skip a whole cycle and go sixteen—one came farthest up the beach; and each time this longest wave came into the island, he waited for an individual named Rrrnlf to start emerging from the water before him. But this friend of his, a sea devil, had not appeared.

This was all the more irritating, in that the only other time he had taken Rrrnlf up on his invitation to summon him, by calling out over the salt waters, Rrrnlf had arrived almost immediately. Also, he had once told Jim—or given Jim the clear impression—that he would always hear instantly and could always be with Jim in almost no time at all after that.

A typical adult male sea devil, Rrrnlf was about thirty feet tall, narrowing wedge-shaped from a great head above wide shoulders down to feet that were only three times as big as Jim's. How he could move this tremendous mass of body easily around on such tiny feet, Jim had no idea. The contrast was particularly striking when you looked from his feet to his hands. His hands seemed big enough, not only to pick up as much of a load as a bulldozer could push before it, but bulldozer and load together, in one fist.

He was a Natural. That was to say that he could do some things that could be explained only as magic; but he had no conscious control over that magic. It was rather like a dog wagging his tail when he was happy. When a sea devil was in the sea, possibly thousands of feet down, he breathed water with no trouble. When he came up on the land, he breathed air with no trouble. He had no idea how or why he could do it. He simply took it for granted he could.

Hob—though miniscule compared to any sea devils, and ordinarily the hobgoblin of the serving room, back at Malencontri—was also one of the category of what were called Naturals; but he and Rrrnlf were, as you might say, at opposite ends of the Natural yardstick.

"M'lord," said Hob's voice in Jim's ear now, timidly, "I think you are sad. Would it help if I took you for a ride on the smoke? All you'd have to do would be to start a small fire."

"No," said Jim.

Then, he realized that his tone had been a little too abrupt. The hobgoblin's feelings were easily hurt.

"No, thank you, Hob," he said, more gently. "I just don't want to go anyplace else right now."

"Yes, m'lord," said Hob.

Jim concentrated on the waves again. Rrrnlf had to be out there, underwater, somewhere. Was something keeping him from coming, or was he simply failing to answer? Had something happened to him? There were things far larger even than he in the oceans. Granfer, the ancient deep-sea squid (or Kraken), for one.

Jim had now been on Cyprus for a week without finding Brian. Brian had clearly gotten here, because a number of people had seen him and nobody remembered him either leaving the island, or talking about leaving. But he was being strangely difficult to locate.

If he had already gone on to the city of Tripoli, Jim should waste no time in following him. On the other hand, if he was still here on the island, Jim had to run him to earth so that they could go together.

Jim scowled once more at the scene before him. It had the effrontery to be a happy, picturesque scene. The Mediterranean was in one of its brightest, most blue moods, the salt-smelling wind blowing off it in Jim's face was mild and warm, and the beach itself, although it could possibly have been improved by a few thousand tons of very clean sand spread over the pebbles, was still a kindly sort of beach, with most of its pebbles nicely rounded from water action.

The only unpretty thing in the whole scene was a brownish mongrel searching among the rocks and pebbles some little ways up the beach. It was a small, starved-looking dog, clearly intended to be coated with short tan hair, but the hair was either very dirty or else it had acquired a naturally dingy appearance somewhere in the animal's lifetime; so that the only other living thing on the beach beside Jim and Hob was definitely out of key with all else visible. On the other hand, it was not bothering Jim and Jim had no real interest in it.

Jim forgot the dog and concentrated on the waves once more. He had called out loud more than enough times for Rrrnlf. Now he was trying visualization—but with no magic command to appear—concentrating on Rrrnlf wherever the sea devil should be in the undersea, with Jim's calls necessarily reverberating over and over again in the large Natural's ears.

So far this had shown no signs of working, either.

"Oh great and puissant, compassionate magician," said a high-pitched, but oddly gruff, voice at his elbow. "Of your mightiness and strength, aid me in my terrible plight; and your reward shall be greater than any could ever imagine."

Jim came out of his concentration to discover at his elbow the dog which, a moment before, had been nosing about, farther up the beach.

That it was an animal speaking to him did not startle him—although it was the first talking dog Jim had so far encountered on this magical, medieval world. All sorts of creatures spoke, here, of course—while others didn't; and there seemed no rhyme or reason to which did and which didn't.

Also, while no dog had ever addressed him until now, one of his best friends was Aargh, an English wolf, who not only spoke but issued very definite and uncompromising statements. So, also, had a Northumbrian wolf whom Jim had met up near the Scottish border. Until now, Jim had simply assumed that wolves spoke in this fourteenth-century environment and dogs didn't. Apparently the rule was not universal. But he had heard so many unlikely speakers by this time that what concerned him at the moment was the fact that his concentration had been interrupted.

"What is it?" he asked the dog sharply.

"I am in desperate need and I cast myself on your mercy, O mighty one!" said the dog, fawning upon him.

"Yes, yes," said Jim, "but what do you want?"

The dog pressed close against his right leg and lowered his voice to a murmur. Thoughts of fleas, lice and possible skin diseases flitted momentarily through Jim's mind, but his natural instinct not to be unfriendly to dogs—even ratty-looking specimens like this—which in general he liked and usually got on well with, kept him from pulling his leg away.

"I am in desperate need of your protection, O great and invincible master," the dog went on, barely above a whisper. "I am in flight from a powerful and wicked one, who most cruelly ill-used me; and when I saw you here, casting spells upon the ocean, I knew you at once. You are as much greater and stronger than him as he is than me; and so I have ventured to ask you for protection, knowing that by your Art you already knew that I was a Djinni—as is the one who so mistreated and would now pursue me—so that I need not first show you myself in my own real form."

For the first time in some hours, Jim dropped his concern with Rrrnlf and the undersea spaces. There had been one glaringly false note in what the dog had said so far, in speaking to him.

It was not surprising the dog/Djinni might recognize him as a magician. Unlikely sorts of non-humans had done that before. Others had not, of course, but there was always the chance that some of them could feel, smell or somehow tell the difference that his magic gave him. But the other had clearly been guessing when he threw in that bit just now about casting spells on the sea—since Jim had been doing nothing of the kind.

Jim was instantly wary. Experience in this particular world had taught him it was usually wisest not to disabuse a stranger's favorable misapprehension about him too quickly. By letting the mistake slide by, he might be able to find out more of what was actually going on around him—and usually he badly needed to know what was going on around him—for his own safety's sake, to say nothing of that of little Hob.

He had been aware that he was now in the territory of those middle-eastern Naturals called collectively Djinn or Jann; and, individually, Djinni or Jinni. If this dog actually was a Djinni, then probably the most prudent thing to do was to first find out what kind of magiclike powers he had, while keeping him as much in the dark as possible about the scope of Jim's own abilities.

"You say you're a Djinni," Jim said. "But before I give you any kind of protection, I'd have to know if I could trust you. I need to know more about you. To begin with, are you really the sort of Djinni you say you are?"

"O my master, I am. I am!" cried the dog in a high, thin voice, then quickly looked around behind him, as if he expected somebody to be there, listening.

"We'll see," said Jim. "You're right, of course, in taking for granted

I knew you were a Djinni without having to see you in your true shape. But what if you're really a Djinni who's been stripped of his powers by some holy person because of evil things you did, and condemned to live permanently as the dog you pretend to be? Prove to me first you can change back to your true shape."

"Does he have to?" whispered Hob fearfully in Jim's ear.

"Hush!" said Jim, over his shoulder. He looked at the dog. "Well?"

The dog changed his appearance.

"Tell me when to open my eyes," said Hob in Jim's ear.

"That's fine. You can change back. That's just fine," said Jim hastily. "It's all right now, Hob. You can look."

What he had seen, and Hob had almost caught a glimpse of, was a huge male figure with gray skin and large belly, scantily dressed in a sort of vest plus loose billowy, purple trousers. It had possessed a hideous face, with a third eye above and between two other eyes not in line, a face with a mouth that was off to one side and tilted up at the right corner. This kind of tilt should have given the face a cheerful look. Instead it gave it a look of the deepest evil imaginable.

Then the dog had become a dog again.

"All right," said Jim. "That much you can do. Do you have your other powers? For example, if I was just an ordinary person instead of the magician I am, would you have tried to bribe me to help you by promising me great treasure?"

"Forgive me, O my master," said the dog, fawning on him again, "but I would have. Of course, I know better than to bribe such as your incorruptible self."

"Prove to me you could have done such a thing," said Jim. "For example, produce a chest full of rubies, sapphires, diamonds, and other precious gems to show me you can do it."

The chest appeared, but its top was down, its contents hidden.

"Forgive me, forgive me . . ." whined the dog hurriedly; and the lid of the chest flew up, revealing its contents which were indeed colored stones of all kinds; none of them cut and faceted, of course, since the cutting of gems had not yet been developed on this world.

"Very well," said Jim loftily, waving his hand. "Take it away. Such toys do not interest me."

The chest disappeared. Jim felt a small pang of regret—but appearances were everything at this stage.

"Now," said Jim, "I'll listen to your story and then make my decision."

"Hearken, then," said the dog. "My name is Kelb. For thousands of years, I never did a false or cruel deed, or anything evil, until one day when I was taken as a slave by another very powerful and very evil Djinni named Sakhr al-Jinni. For some centuries he forced me to do terrible and cruel things, at his orders. Finally, sick of it, I tried at last to escape.''

"Good," said Jim.

"I don't believe him," whispered Hob.

"But I was caught by the giant called Sharahiya, one of the keepers of Sakhr al-Jinni's orchard, and brought back," Kelb went on. "Sakhr al-Jinni had me thrown into a lake of fire as punishment. There I suffered for six hundred and fifty-two years, three months, two weeks, three days and nine hours, forty-seven minutes, ten seconds. But at the end of that time, I was released."

Jim had been thinking furiously, trying to remember. The names "Sakhr al-Jinni" and "Sharahiya" rang a faint bell in his head, connected possibly with Richard Burton's *Thousand Nights and a Night*. No—Sakhr al-Jinni was only referred to there. Somewhere he had read more about him. There was a connection with King Solomon of the Hebrews. But Kelb was clearly waiting for some response from him before going on.

"And then what?" Jim said in the best tone of impatience he could manage or muster. "Why did Sakhr al-Jinni let you out of the lake of fire?"

"I was released not by him, but because the great King Solomon, David's son, imprisoned him, with other evil Djinn and Marids, each in a copper bottle; stopping these up with lead which Solomon sealed with his ring, and casting Sakhr al-Jinni into Lake Tiberius to lie where he would forevermore be beyond harming anyone. Once he was embottled, his powers that kept me in the lake of fire no longer held, and I was free to go.''

"Well, then," said Jim, "your troubles are over. I don't see why you're bothering me.''

"Alas!" said Kelb. "A clumsy undersea giant, picking up the bottle that held Sakhr al-Jinni to look at it curiously, loosened the seal only five days ago; and that evil one is now free in the world again—full of rage and searching for all those who were his servants before, and particularly me, who had now escaped the punishment he had given me. He is far stronger than I. I cannot withstand him. Help me, O my master!''

It was all pretty far-fetched, Jim felt. But on the other hand, this was a world of magic and unusual creatures. Anything could be true. It might be simply that Kelb was, at most, only embroidering the story of his life.

"Who was the clumsy undersea giant that let Sakhr al-Jinni loose?" he asked.

"I know not," said Kelb. "I was only told it had happened by others like me, who were escaping at last from Sakhr al-Jinni's wrath.''

The chances of it being Rrrnlf who allowed Sakhr al-Jinni to escape from his bottle were not very large, Jim told himself. The ocean back in Jim's twentieth-century world covered something like a hundred and forty-two million square miles of the earth's surface. It was unlikely that the amount of ocean here on this world was much different. That provided enough room for a high number of sea giants, even if they weren't to be considered common.

Also, even if Rrrnlf had been the cause of Sakhr al-Jinni's release, jumping from that possibility to the further possibility that Sakhr al-Jinni had somehow managed to destroy or disable him was a second long guess. But Jim had spent enough time now trying to summon Rrrnlf, and this Kelb might turn out to be able to do a great many of the things that he was hoping that Rrrnlf could help him with.

"Have you some place where you can hide safely, until I summon you?" Jim said to Kelb.

"I have, my master," said Kelb.

"Well, go and hide there," said Jim. "I'll call you back as soon as I've made up my mind about a few things. Mind you, I'm not saying I'll extend my protection to you. I don't extend it to just everybody, you know."

"I am sure of that, master," said Kelb humbly.

"Off with you, then," said Jim. "I'll call you back when I'm ready." Jim stood up from the rock on which he'd been sitting.

"We've spent enough time here," he said. "Hob, we'll head back to Paphos and Sir William Brutnor's place."

He started back along the beach, around the headlands that separated where he'd been sitting from the town of Paphos itself—a place half village, half town, mainly filled by local Greeks; but with a fair sprinkling of the descendants of crusaders, from one crusade or another, who had never gotten any farther than Cyprus. These latter had prospered and built themselves almost European residences—not exactly castles, but very comfortable establishments; and it was Sir William Brutnor who was providing Jim with food and shelter right now in the customary fashion of British and European upper classes, when the visitor was someone they recognized as belonging to their part of society.

"Do you want me also to call you 'master,' m'lord?" asked Hob, in a small voice, as he rode Jim's shoulder.

"No, no, of course not," said Jim. "Not you, Hob."

"But you would protect me?" asked Hob. "I'm not just one of the 'everybodies'?"

"Of course not," said Jim. "You're my Hob of Malencontri."

"Of course," echoed Hob smugly. He loosened his grip around Jim's neck and sat up on Jim's shoulder, very straight.

CHAPTER 7

"So there you are, Sir James!" said Sir William Brutnor, striding into Jim's room, with the hems of his mid-eastern, silk robes flipping around his ankles. "Been looking for you!"

"Yes," said Jim. "I went for a stroll on the beach and ended up going around the headland and some of the way up the coast. Beautiful day."

"Yes. Getting hot. Bit of a stroll, I'd say," said Sir William. "You missed dinner, you know? Did you have them send up food and drink for you?"

"No," said Jim. "It hadn't occurred to me, yet—"

"Well, never mind, never mind," said Sir William. He was a short, broad man, possibly a little overweight but he carried it well. He had a square middle-aged face, tanned and wrinkled by the sun, with graying eyebrows, a small gray mustache and a hasty manner. "I'm taking you off to a coffee house—actually, a coffee house in a bath house. We can get some decent wine and food there, being Christians. You needn't dress up. It's all very informal—travelers in off the road and people like that. Oh, by the way, we've located this friend of yours you're looking for. Sir Bruno."

"Sir Brian, you mean?" said Jim.

"That's the gentleman," said Sir William, "the Neville-Smythe. I remember that much of it because of the Neville part. Related to the Nevilles of Rabe, I think you said?"

"That's right," said Jim. "Where is he?"

"Where? Oh, up near Episcopi, round the coast a bit," answered Sir William. "Not at Episcopi itself. A little further on, at a small fishing village. There's a shore-castle there. Sir Mortimor Breugel has it. He has a couple of galleys and does some off-shore pirating, from time to time. Not great, but it's a living; and Sir Mortimor doesn't want a lot, you know. He'd rather sit in his own hall, dice and drink than anything else, anyway. But, come along now—"

He broke off suddenly. The brown dog that was Kelb had just appeared beside Jim.

"Master," he said to Jim, ignoring Sir William, "if I may speak to you—"

"Go away!" said Jim. "Later."

The dog disappeared.

"A Djinni!" barked Sir William. "Look here, Sir James, I'm all for hospitality to a gentleman from home, and all that. But—a Djinni! How did you come to bring home a Djinni from this walk of yours; and into my house? Have you any idea the trouble there is getting rid of them? A good priest won't do, you know, you have to get a Holy Musselman— and then half the time it doesn't work because the Holy man wasn't Holy enough; and you have to go looking again. Give me a good old-fashioned ghost or goblin to get rid of, any day!"

"Don't worry," said Jim, "I'll take him with me when I go; and since you've found Sir Brian, if you'll forgive me, I'll go to him right away, without wasting any more time. It's important I catch up with him as soon as possible."

"You can't be in that much of a hurry," said Sir William. "There's this coffee house—"

"I'm afraid I am," said Jim. His mind scrambled for an excuse to get on the road at once. He had no particular interest at the moment in coffee houses, wine or even European style food, notwithstanding—even less in bath houses. Inspiration came to him. "You've heard of Sir John Chandos, of course?"

"Chandos?" said Sir William. "Oh, yes."

"Well, need I say more?" said Jim, giving the other as mysterious and diplomatic-level a look as he could manage.

"Ah, well," said Sir William, "I suppose so. True. True. Pity, though. You'd have liked this coffee house."

"I'm sure I would," said Jim. "I can't tell you how sad I am to miss out on it. It's very good of you to think of taking me there."

"Oh, well," said Sir William. "Just a place where some gentlemen get together about this hour. They'll be sad to miss you too. I'll send someone up with directions on where Episcopi is, the way there, and where beyond it Sir Mortimor's shore-castle can be found."

He went out of the room as abruptly as he had come in.

"Kelb," said Jim to the empty air.

The dog appeared in front of him.

"All right, Kelb," said Jim, "what is it?"

"We Djinn have our ways," said Kelb smugly.

"I'm sure you do," said Jim impatiently. "Now, what did you come to tell me?"

"By means of which only we Djinn know," said Kelb, "I was aware you were searching for another such as yourself. I have found him for you. He is just above Episcopi in a tower by a small sea-village. Do you not now see how valuable I can be as a servant to you, O great one?"

"I'm not so sure about that," said Jim. "You wouldn't have happened to have been in your dog shape by the kitchen door of this establishment, begging for scraps and just happened to overhear the servants talking about the fact that I was looking for a fellow knight and that he had just been located up beyond Episcopi?"

"Are the servants indeed talking about it?" said Kelb. "Such a strange happening at the same time is almost beyond belief; but—"

"Never mind making up excuses," said Jim. "I told you I'd tell you when I had made up my mind about you, and I will. Until then, go!"

"I go, master," said Kelb, and went.

Southeast Jim went, around the coast of Cyprus to Episcopi in a relatively small, and very smelly, boat with a huge lateen sail that seemed once to have been red in color. Their small craft hugged the shore all the way up, for fear of corsairs; and the ship owner—a cheerful, black-haired, black-eyed Greek whose three sons were his crew, explained that they stayed in shallow water so that large enemy vessels that might prey on them could not come in after them. They could go right up to the beach, which the larger vessels could not do safely without damaging themselves.

"But what if you have to sail in deep water right next to the shore?" asked Jim. As he said the words he felt a slight stirring by his right shoulder blade, where Hob was comfortably curled up out of sight in a sort of padded nest in a bag that resembled a knapsack. For a moment he was afraid that Hob would stick his head out and want to join in the conversation; but the hobgoblin said nothing after all, staying quiet and hidden.

"If there is no way we can get away and save the boat, then we save ourselves," said the ship owner with a fatalistic shrug. "It is better than being impaled or crucified if they catch us."

Jim considered this; or rather, tried to consider it. He had thought he was immune to seasickness, after all the sea travel he had had on the way down from Britain. He had, in fact, traveled by a number of means. By sea; overland on horseback, by the process of buying horses in one place and selling them at his destination; and also—more secretly—flying in his dragon form, usually at night, or riding the smoke, for the little hobgoblin could ride a waft of smoke anywhere and take him along.

He had, indeed, been tempted to ride the smoke with Hob all the way to Cyprus. But he had to follow Brian's route and make sure Brian had not been captured, imprisoned, hurt or even killed by mischance—all too likely in medieval times—along the way. As it was, he could check at the towns he passed and with the people Brian had planned to guest with, to make sure Brian had made it all the way to Cyprus before Jim reached that island, himself.

Meanwhile, Hob had been a pleasant little companion; and Jim had not regretted Angie's insistence that the hobgoblin should be with him, to carry the word home to her, if anything happened to Jim.

One of the side benefits of traveling by ordinary methods, Jim had believed until now, was that he had developed an immunity to seasickness. However, this small boat rocking and bouncing in the near-shore waves had produced an effect on him after all. He could not honestly say he was sick, but he was feeling cold and uncomfortable in his stomach area; and the discomfort made it hard for him to concentrate.

"Just suppose we had to do that—put the boat in to shore and run," said Jim. "What if they came in after us or sent another small boat in after us and caught me, for example?"

In Europe, he knew that normally a person dressed as expensively as he was would be held to ransom.

The ship owner shrugged.

"Take all you had that was worth anything, and then do the same with you as they'd do with us," he answered.

"If we stayed together," said Jim, "maybe if there was just a small boatload coming to shore after us, we could fight them off."

The ship owner nodded his head vigorously. Jim's heart lifted, before he remembered what the motion meant. He was still getting used to the fact that in some of these near-eastern areas, a nod meant "no" and a shake of the head meant "yes."

Once the proper message got through, however, he felt a touch of relief. If the others would not stand and fight with him, then he could feel a little easier about taking care of himself and Hob first; and all that was necessary for the two of them was to duck out of sight someplace. Then he could turn into a dragon and fly himself and Hob out of the reach of any corsairs in a hurry.

In the event, however, they met no corsairs, and Jim did not go all the way into actual seasickness. But he was very glad to step out on the stony beach in front of the castle of Sir Mortimor; in spite of the fact that waiting for them were a half-dozen very fierce-looking, armed men with steel or leather upper body-armor and cap, over-robes. As far as their faces went, they might have been distant cousins of the boat owner, only lacking the

boatman's cheerfulness. Jim had hardly set foot ashore before the swordpoint of one of them was at his throat.

"Take that away or I'll have you whipped for it!" snapped Jim, falling
back on the proper knightly response. "Send to the castle immediately! I
am Sir James Eckert de Malencontri, the Dragon Knight, here to see Sir
Brian who is guesting in this place. Carry that message to Sir Mortimor
or Sir Brian immediately. I command it!"

He had been in this world long enough to pick up some understanding
of how a situation like this should be handled. The two key points were
to be as richly dressed as he was, and to act as if he was the infinite
superior of any of those around him.

It worked. The man who had presented the swordpoint at his throat did
not lower his weapon, but he backed away a couple of steps and snapped
an order at one of the others to run ahead to tell them in the castle what
Jim had said.

"Come, Sir Dragon, then," said the man with the naked sword. "Come
with us!"

They escorted him up the steeply sloping beach, through the jumble of
small buildings that were evidently half homes, half warehouses; with nets
draped on posts to dry, and fish also drying on racks. Just beyond the
village the going abruptly became very steep indeed; and a sort of switchback path or road led up to the castle itself, giving way at last to a flight
of steps cut through the groundcover into the rock underneath it; so that
the last bit of distance was like climbing a staircase.

The castle was really nothing but the tower, with a few precariously
attached wooden outbuildings; a simple-looking fortress. At the same time,
Jim noticed that it was not as vulnerable as it might appear at first glance.
It was built of bluish-gray stone blocks, with a stout entrance door that
was closed until the leader of Jim's escort pounded on it and shouted to
those within—after which it was opened and they were let into a short
and narrow passage with stone walls all around them leading to another
door, equally stout.

Jim looked up as they moved toward this second door and saw a ceiling
above with holes in it through which uncomfortable things like boiling oil
could be poured down on anyone who broke through the first door and
was battering at the second; then, hopefully, it would be set alight by
burning brands pushed through those same holes—so that the space between the two doors would become a death trap.

In Jim's case, however, he was led on peacefully through the second
door into a very gloomy interior. There seemed to be only a single, further
light source—and indeed this turned out to be a fact.

They went forward until he came to what was essentially an open well, ascending through the middle of the castle right up to an opening in the top floor of the tower. A patch of blue sky and a glimpse of battlements could be seen. Undoubtedly this roof opening would be closed in bad weather with one or more covers. For now, however, it was open; and the sunlight struck strongly down through it, its gleams bouncing off the stony walls to give what little light this could to the rest of the castle. In the lower areas of even the central part of this well, itself, torches burned on the walls to reinforce the lighting.

He was led to stone stairs attached to the stone wall, the steps spiraling up against the outer wall of the tower. On the third floor he found Brian, with a tall, somewhat elderly-looking, thin man with a long, mournful face and a mustache that drooped down at the ends of his thin lips. A man who looked less like a warlord than a retired scholar.

"James!" cried Brian, starting up from the table at which he and the elderly man were sitting. The elderly man rose too, but more slowly.

But as he got up, Jim rapidly changed his first impression that the slow rise was due to age. Instead, plainly, it was the result of a casualness, a sort of studied laziness. When the man at last stood at his full height, he towered not only over Brian, but Jim; and if his mustache and hair signaled age, the rest of his body signaled some twenty or more years younger. He was at least six and a half feet tall and of that peculiar rangy, hard-muscled build that would probably mean he would be both strong and fast in action.

However, Jim did not have a chance to see more than this, because Brian had darted forward from the table to embrace him and kiss first his left cheek, then his right—a common fourteenth-century greeting among friends that Jim had learned to accept with some show of grace.

"You are here, James!" cried Brian, letting him go. "More welcome than I can tell you! And just in time as well! Allow me to make you acquainted with Sir Mortimor Breugel."

Jim knew the proper manners for this type of situation. He inclined his head in a near bow to the tall man standing behind the table, who returned it.

"Honored to make your acquaintance, Sir Mortimor," said Jim.

"Honored to make yours—" said Sir Mortimor in a remarkable bass voice, and paused meaningfully.

"Crave pardon!" said Brian happily. "Sir Mortimor, this is the right worshipful Baron, Sir James Eckert, the Dragon Knight, of whom you have heard me speak."

"You and others," said Sir Mortimor warmly. "It is a special pleasure to see you, Sir James. As Sir Brian says, you come at a good hour. Pray seat yourself with us and may I offer you some wine and meat?"

Jim was still a little bit queasy from the boat ride, but what Sir Mortimor was offering was ritual hospitality, which it would be insulting to refuse; and in any case Jim was glad to find himself welcomed so warmly. He joined the other two and they all sat down around one end of the table. It, like all the other furnishings Jim had seen so far in the castle, was of the barest, most utilitarian variety. Altogether Sir Mortimor's home reminded him of Malencontri, when he and Angie had first moved in. The previous owner of that castle had camped out in it, rather than actually living there; using it as a base for any number of outside activities.

Now he touched his lips to the mazer—the large square drinking utensil brimming with wine that was placed before him—and took a bite of the gristly meat—mutton, he decided from the taste of it—that a servant or one of the men-at-arms placed in front of him.

"May I ask," he said, as soon as he had managed to chew the piece of meat apart enough so that he could swallow it, "why you two gentlemen talk about my coming in good time?"

"Why, James, it could not be better," said Brian. "The chance of a lifetime. Have you never longed to cross swords with a Sallee Rover?"

Jim's mind went into one of its scrambles to make the proper connection with the term for a moment; then he remembered that a Sallee Rover was one name for a Sallee (or Moroccan) who was of a piratical nature. In fact, Morocco was generally considered to be nothing but a nest of pirates—at least by Sir William Brutnor and his friends, the gentlemen he had met on Cyprus.

"I have, I can tell you!" Brian was going on eagerly. "But never did I think I would have the chance. But here I was, guesting up this way; and word came that some were expected at the shore below this castle at any moment. Our good Sir Mortimor has on occasion picked up some of the eastern merchant ships; and it seems the owners of the goods carried in those ships have hired a couple of the fiercest of the Sallee Rovers to come hither and put an end to him and this castle."

Jim felt a pang of instinctive sympathy for the owners of the merchant ships. Translated, what Brian had just said meant that Sir Mortimor had been robbing some vessels to the point where their owners and shippers decided the larceny had to be stopped; and they had hired some of the more notorious Moroccans to do the job for them.

But of course, he reflected, there was no such thing anyway as justice upon the Mediterranean, any more than there was anywhere else upon the oceans of the world. The strong took anything weak enough to be taken, and fled from anything stronger enough to take them.

More than that, he had already heard that it was Sir Mortimor's way of making a living. He himself, he thought, had no interest whatsoever in getting into a fight with Moroccan pirates; but it was exactly like Brian to think of this as the greatest entertainment in the world. To say nothing of the fact that it would produce—if he lived through it—a story that he could tell back in England to the envy and admiration of all.

To be honest, Jim knew Brian well enough to believe that it was the excitement of the actual life-and-death encounter that sent Brian eagerly into these battles, rather than the wish to tell about them afterwards. But the tale of this fight later on would not be something without social value.

However, mentioning any of these thoughts aloud to his present two companions would not be the most politic choice of conversation. Jim smiled and made an effort to look not only interested, but happily so.

"Indeed!" he said. "And you say these pirates are expected at any moment?"

"We have a lookout on duty night and day at the top of my tower," said Sir Mortimor in that surprising bass of his.

Jim was ready to swear that the man was not speaking above his normal conversational tone; but the words seemed to bounce off the stone walls behind Jim and echo throughout the whole castle. Sir Mortimor had the kind of voice which could be perfectly understood by someone twenty feet away, even with an intervening crowd of other people talking at the top of their own voices in between.

"So far," went on Sir Mortimor, "none of them have reported what we expect, although sails are often seen. Of course, they are most likely to come in galleys, possibly with their sails down and on oars only. But still, in this clear weather we will see them coming and have time to arm. Meanwhile, perhaps, you would care to join Sir Brian and me in a bout with the dice?"

"I must beg your forgiveness, Sir Mortimor," said Jim. "As Sir Brian may have told you, I am a magician, and under certain circumstances, my control and use of magic depends upon my abstaining from all pleasures involved with chance. Also, Sir Brian, I have news and word to you from the Lady Geronde, and from my own dear wife, the Lady Angela, which I must not forget to tell you at some other time. If you and Sir Mortimor care to dice, I shall enjoy simply sitting and watching."

"Sad, that; but I understand, of course," said Sir Mortimor, with something in his voice that seemed to Jim a little too much like the regret of a card sharp seeing a plump but innocent victim escape.

"Howbeit," he went on, "possibly better we acquaint you with what Sir Brian and I were just discussing; which is our matter of defense of this castle of mine when the marauders do land."

"I shall be happy to hear," said Jim.

"Come!" said Sir Mortimor, uncurling to his full height again and leading them away from the table, up the staircase and on to the very roof of the tower; a level circle of stone with its surrounding battlements like jagged teeth, and the opening of the light-and-air shaft in its center. There was another opening by the battlements facing seaward, which must be above the entrance passage with holes in its ceiling.

There were as well five chimneys better than six feet tall; and a huge, soot-blackened metal kettle on wheels, with a sandbox-firebed underneath, undoubtedly to heat boiling oil for pouring on attackers.

Beside the kettle stood a framework in which was vertically suspended a circular round of what looked like bronze, some four feet across. It was not until Jim saw something like a sledgehammer leaning against one side of the framework that he recognized the apparatus as a large gong.

This gong stood midway between two men—plainly guards on lookout here, both of them gazing out at the waters of the Mediterranean. Jim, looking out himself, saw the white flecks of several sails at varying distances; but since the watchmen took no interest in them, they could hardly be the galleys of the enemy coming in.

Both these men looked about as Sir Mortimor led Brian and Jim upon the roof. Sir Mortimor flicked a pointing finger downward at the steps from which he had just emerged, and the two ran to them, disappearing from sight.

"They can learn about my plans," said Sir Mortimor to Brian and Jim, softening his voice as he led them to the battlements, well away from the ventilation shaft and to where no chimneys obstructed their view to seaward, "when I'm ready to tell them. Take a look, gentlemen. You see the situation."

Jim, with Brian, looked over the battlement and down at the beachfront below. The tower, in effect the castle itself, was no more than four or five stories high; but its slenderness, and its position perched on the spire of rock with the cliff behind and overhanging it, gave an impression of dizzying altitude; so that they seemed much farther up than they actually were. Added to this, the steep steps down to the almost as steep switchback path below it, then farther on down to the beach below, increased the feeling of height; so that it felt to Jim as if he was looking out from a precipice half a mile high.

That illusion, however, was at odds with the fact that he knew he was not actually that far above the sloping beach; and so the wooden buildings upon it gave the impression of being closer than they should be. It was as if he looked at these through a telescope at the same time as he examined everything else from the illusory height of the tower.

The stony, pebbled water's edge, at which the waves lapped, was at the greatest indentation of a small bay. The cliff behind the castle curved forward on either hand, like horns, reaching out to form two headlands.

The tops of these headlands were little higher than the castle roof, itself. As far as their tops could be seen, they were almost bare, except for some vegetation and a few sheep wandering about.

Out to sea, the Mediterranean was as peaceful as it had been since Jim had arrived here in Cyprus, its blue surface stretching to the curving horizon, with the sails Jim had noticed earlier apparently passing each other and the shore on coastal business.

"I expect no less than two large galleys, each carrying a load of up to two hundred armed landsmen," said Sir Mortimor's voice in Jim's right ear. "These, together with the crew of the galleys, will bring to face us some five hundred fighting men. They will land, burn the village and kill any they catch, then attempt to come at the castle from above. But they will find that the overhang of the cliff behind it prevents them dropping anything heavy enough to do damage from there. Also, the grass is slippery up there and the slope is steep toward the edge of the cliff. They will lose a few men over the edge of the cliff merely by trying this."

"Will they have Greek fire?" Brian asked their host.

"Greek fire is a close-held secret still, in Constantinople," said Sir Mortimor. "They will not. No more will they have bombards of any kind, although they may have some gunpowder; and they may try to place that around the base of the tower and do some damage with it. But my lower walls are nowhere less than six feet thick and up to ten feet in places. Gunpowder has been tried before and done no real damage. They will burn the village below, as I say, and of course they will make a try up the steps and through the door of the main entrance."

"They will be at a sore disadvantage while they are at that," said Brian.

Sir Mortimor nodded.

"It will cost them heavily; but if they keep trying long enough, they may get through both doors. If that is the case, they will then overrun the castle and we shall die. Therefore, a decision will have to be made at the last moment—in fact I shall make it, myself, gentlemen. With all due deference to your own skill in warfare and with weapons, this is my castle and I will fight it the way I know best to do. If it seems they have survived breaking through the outer door and the boiling oil in the passage, and done enough damage to the inner door so they will shortly be through, then we must sally."

"Hah!" said Brian.

"There is a secret way out of this castle that emerges some little way down the beach," went on Sir Mortimor. "Counting those of the village able to fight to any purpose, we will have inside with us here over a hundred and forty men. With a hundred of these, we can attack those who come against us from behind, or unexpectedly in the night, when they

have withdrawn to rest, feeling that we who are penned in the castle can
nowise escape from them; and therefore they can finish matters at their
leisure. If we have the good luck to catch most of them asleep, or unex-
pecting—and, since they will be boat people, with legs not used to running
up and down steep paths to attack or escape—we may do enough damage
to convince them that we are a rescue party come from Episcopi, or
somewhere else close. A reinforcement. So that they will break and run
for their galleys.''

"Pray," said Brian to the tall knight, "to which side of the castle does
this secret way emerge?"

Sir Mortimor looked down at him with a wintry smile.

"There is no harm in telling you that much," he answered. "Though
all else about that escape route is a family secret."

He waved his hand toward the close slope to the right of the castle.

"Some little distance in that direction," he said.

Brian considered the area.

"There are some large rocks at the foot of the steep slope on the beach
no more than fifty yards from here," he said. "Give me three score of
your men, and I will pledge to go out at night, or at some other time when
they are busy, and burn or otherwise destroy their boats behind them."

"That is exactly what I do not want done, Sir Brian," said Sir Mortimor. "If the boats are not there for their escape, then they will be left
with us—whether they or we like it or not. Recall they outnumber us now,
nearly five to one. With their boats destroyed, they will fight to kill or be
killed; and in the end they may well own the castle and all of us will be
dead—"

A shriek, followed by a wild babel of voices, unexpectedly echoed up
the air shaft.

"Hell, blood and weeping!" exploded Sir Mortimor, his voice echoing
off both headlands. He took four enormous strides to the stairway entrance
and vanished down it.

CHAPTER 8

Left alone together on the roof, Jim and Brian looked at each other.
"Brian," said Jim. "Now's my chance to bring you up to date on
things. The reason I could follow you this quickly was because John Chandos showed up with the order giving me wardship of Robert Falon."

"That was fast, indeed," said Brian. "I have known such matters to
take years. I had little hope. But it is good to see you here, James—doubly
so, considering the circumstances."

"I'm not as happy about the circumstances as you are, Brian," Jim was
beginning, when he felt Hob stir in the knapsack on his back and sit up.
A second later, the hobgoblin's small gray head poked into sight at the
corner of his right eye.

"By the way, this is Hob," said Jim hastily, "from the chimney of my
serving room at Malencontri. Did you just wake up, Hob?"

"Oh, I wasn't asleep," said Hob. "We hobgoblins never sleep. We just
dream without sleeping."

"A hobgoblin!" said Brian, staring. "What do you dream about, hobgoblin?"

"Oh," said Hob, "nice warm chimneys, good people with food down
below, plenty of children we can take for rides on the—"

He broke off suddenly, staring back at Brian.

"I don't know you," he said, shrinking back behind Jim's head and
clasping him around the neck.

"This is Sir Brian Neville-Smythe, Hob," said Jim. "My best friend.
He comes to Malencontri all the time; and he likes hobgoblins."

"Likes—" Brian broke off abruptly. "Nothing against them, actually.
You're the first one I ever met, in fact."

But now Hob was looking at Brian again, this time with fascination.

"Are you really Brian—I mean, Sir Brian Neville-Smythe?" asked
Hob. "Was your hair almost white, when you were very young?"

"Of course!" snapped Brian. "As for my hair—yes, it was. Not that that is any matter for your consideration, hobgoblin!"

"Your father brought you to Malencontri with him on the way to Malvern Castle one time when you were very little," said Hob. "That was when there were some humans named Claive in Malencontri. There was a lot of eating and drinking and singing and everybody forgot about you. I took you for a ride on the smoke. Don't you remember?"

"Ride on the smoke..." Brian frowned. The frown slowly cleared. "Yes, by God! I do remember. Yes! We went out over the woods. You showed me where the hedgehogs were sleeping, and the bear's den where it was sleeping. And you showed me the magician's house—it was Carolinus's place, but I didn't know that till later. I do remember! So you're that hobgoblin?"

"Oh, yes," said Hob. "You were very little and your mother was dead and your father wasn't with you most of the time. Didn't the hobgoblin at Malvern take you for any more rides when you got there?"

"Never," said Brian.

"Well, he certainly should have," said Hob. "I would have."

"By St. Brian, my name-saint, I have never forgotten that! You were most kind to me, hobgoblin."

"Oh, no," said Hob earnestly. "I liked taking you."

"There, Hob," said Jim. "I told you Sir Brian liked hobgoblins. Here, he's an older friend of yours than he is of mine."

"It's—it's good of your knightlyness to remember," said Hob, still a little timidly, peering around Jim's head at Brian.

"Hah—well," said Brian. "I was a youngster then, of course. No idea of rank. Still, it was a moment I'll not forget. But Jim—what are you doing on a trip to the Holy Land, carrying a hobgoblin?"

"That was part of what I wanted to tell you about Geronde and Angela," Jim said. "This is the time to say it, before Sir Mortimor comes back. You see, Angie and I went over to Malvern to talk with Geronde as soon as we had the wardship in our hands; and Geronde told us as much as she knew about how I could go about finding you. I got here to Cyprus actually over a week ago; but nobody knew exactly where you were, and I was afraid that you'd already taken a ship for Tripoli, which Geronde says was to be your next stop."

"She was quite right, you know," said Brian. "I really didn't expect you to catch me, James—particularly not this soon. Otherwise I could have left word here that would have aided you in finding me. I take it that there were no important happenings either at Malvern or Malencontri since I left?"

"No," said Jim, "outside of Sir John Chandos's bringing the parchment on Robert's wardship. He had some men-at-arms with him and was headed for the Welsh border, as far as I could understand.''

"I wonder what . . .'' said Brian. "Outside of the building of the castle at Caernarvon, I have heard no news of Wales in some time. But, James, I still do not understand why you brought the hobgoblin."

Sir Mortimor's voice could be heard up the air shaft; and it seemed to be drawing closer, as if the knight was climbing the stairs back to them.

"It was Angela," said Jim hastily. "Both she and Geronde were more concerned than usual about this trip of yours. Geronde had said she'd gone as far as actually asking you not to go—at this time anyway."

"So she did," said Brian. "However, I saw no reason to put it off. Also, you must understand, James, with that much gold sitting around, there would be a danger it might be gone by the time she felt comfortable with my leaving."

"I understand," said Jim. "At any rate, Angie, in particular, wanted something from me. That was to know, and to know as quickly as possible, if anything happened to either of us. You've ridden on the smoke with Hob, so you must remember—"

"I do remember most clearly, now," interposed Brian.

"Then maybe you'll recall how, while you seem to be moving at a fairly slow speed on the smoke, actually you're covering a great deal of distance very quickly. Hob and I used his smoke for a fair amount of the time coming down here. We traveled by other ways of course, but we used the smoke too. The point is, with Hob, if anything happens to you or to me, he can get back to England in a hurry and tell Angie—who will tell Geronde; and if there is anything they can do, they'll do it—"

He broke off, for Sir Mortimor's head had just appeared above the opening for the staircase, and a moment later the tall knight was beside them.

"I tell you what it is, Sir James, Sir Brian," he said. "The fears these easterners have are enough to drive a man out of his wits. Can you imagine what all the trouble was about? A small brown dog—a small brown dog that was not to be found when we went looking for it."

"Brown dog?" echoed Jim.

"Exactly!" said Sir Mortimor. "Rare imagination! Couldn't be a dog in my castle. If one could get in, all the damned curs in the village would be nosing about here for scraps. Man or beast, it has to come in through the front doors. There's no chance for an animal to slip in. None. But here's my cook and half a dozen others, swearing they saw it—and of course, you know what they took it for? Or at least you know, Sir Brian. Sir James, you may be new enough here not to guess. They thought it

was a Djinni. Anything in animal shape can be a Djinni as far as they're
concerned. Everything's a Djinni. Ridiculous!''

"Ridiculous!'' faintly echoed the two headlands around the little bay
in front of the fishing village.

While Sir Mortimor had been talking, the two men who had been on
lookout had come back up and silently taken up their post. The good
knight lowered his voice to conversational level again.

"But shall we forget all that, gentlemen, and go back downstairs? I
could do with a cup of wine; and I imagine the two of you could too.''

They followed him away from the bright sunlight down into the shad-
owy interior of the castle and back to the same table at which Jim had
met him, sitting with Brian when Jim arrived. They took benches, and
mazers of wine were put before them. Jim noticed with interest that his
original mazer, from which very little of the wine had been drunk, had
been taken away—the wine almost certainly drunk by one or more of the
servants back down in the kitchen.

"But,'' said Brian to Sir Mortimor, once they were seated, "if the
brown dog was indeed a Djinni, then maybe he could get in here without
being seen, or without coming by the normal route through the doorways.
They use magic, don't they?''

"Oh, yes, yes,'' said Sir Mortimor. "But it was no Djinni, of course.
What would a Djinni want here—''

He was interrupted by possibly the one thing about the castle as pen-
etrating in sound as his own voice. It was a sudden outburst from the gong
being beaten on top of the tower. There was a scurry of footsteps running
down the stairs toward them, and one of the lookouts burst in, even while
the clamor continued overhead.

"My Lord! My Lord!'' he shouted. "They are here. They are almost
on us. They rode around the two headlands, one galley around each just
now. Within minutes they will be beaching their craft before the village!''

"By the Wounds!'' exploded Sir Mortimor, leaping to his feet and
oversetting his own brimming mazer of wine on the table. "Can't a Christian gentleman have a moment of peace in his own house?''

He glared at the messenger, who was standing white-faced before him,
reached absently for his own mazer, discovered it had spilled and picked
up Jim's instead, tossing it off in what seemed to be a single swallow.
Rather a good trick, Jim thought, considering the mazer must have held
close to a full pint of wine.

The gong was still going mad overhead, and Jim's ears were beginning
to ring. He saw Sir Brian's lips move, but did not hear what the other had
said. Sir Mortimor's voice, however, rose through the din without any
difficulty.

"Front doors opened for villagers!" he snapped. "Slingers and bowmen to the top of the tower. Run!"

The messenger scuttled down the stairs toward the lower levels of the tower.

"Could that gong be silenced now, Sir Mortimor?" Brian shouted through the din. "Surely everyone in the castle has heard it by this time!"

"The villagers must hear too. Come with me, gentlemen!"

He stepped to the stairs, almost knocking into eternity a bowman who was hurrying up them at the moment; and went on up, two steps at a time, leaving Jim and Brian far behind as they began to follow, Brian behind Jim simply because Jim had been closer to the stairs to start off with.

"I am naked except for my poignard," puffed Brian in Jim's ear. "It is well you have half armor and your own sword on, James!"

It was true. Jim had been wearing the sword, simply because, as a knight traveling, it was unthinkable that he should go without it. His half armor, which consisted of a chain mail shirt and a steel cap, he had worn as a natural traveler's protection. The men who had met him as he stepped out of his boat after getting here had not taken the sword from him—possibly because it was unreasonable that he could have overpowered the dozen or so of them even with it. In fact, Jim suddenly realized, he was getting so used to the weight of the sword and the armor that he himself had forgotten it when he was introduced to Sir Mortimor.

"You better go down and arm and armor yourself then, Brian," he said over his shoulder. "I'll tell Sir Mortimor—"

"No, no," said Brian. "It would not be polite. Our host should have told us if there was need for us to dress for any trouble."

"He may just have forgotten," said Jim dryly. His opinion of Sir Mortimor so far was still something of a question mark. "If it turns out that swords are needed, Brian, I'll pass you mine. You can make better use of it than I could."

Brian made some kind of noise that sounded like a protest, but both he and Jim were too out of breath trying to catch up with Sir Mortimor to talk much further. Also, just about then they emerged onto the roof.

Already there were some three or four other men who had rushed up the stairs from below at the first note of the gong. One of these was the bowman who had almost been brushed into the air shaft by Sir Mortimor. Jim had come up expecting to go immediately to the edge of the battlements and look down at the invaders; and that Brian would do the same thing. Instead, both of them had halted where they were, their attention riveted on a man who was coming down a long rope, like a spider descending on his own thread from a ceiling; only in this case the rope came down from an outcropping of rock on the overhanging cliff behind the castle, the top of which looked as if it could be reached only by birds or angels. Sir Mortimor was standing wide-legged, looking balefully at the approaching man.

"Why didn't you see them?" snarled the knight, as the man's feet touched the top of the tower.

"Crave pardon, m'lord," said the man. "They must have hugged the shore in their galleys—at least enough so that the headlands blocked my view for several miles. They may even have slipped in to shore under darkness last night and been waiting until now to come close."

"Hah!" said Sir Mortimor. "Well, in any case we have them here now."

Even while this brief conversation had been going, men had been pouring up the staircase onto the roof. Jim counted only three bowmen. But there were a number of others; thin, dark-faced men, slim-bodied and not too tall for the most part. They seemed unarmed, unless the large, bulging pouches at their belt contained some kind of weapon.

In addition, there were other men coming up who were plainly unarmed, but had their arms full of rocks, which varied from the size of a baseball to the size of a small cantaloupe. These they were piling close to the battlements on that side of the tower that faced the beach and the village below.

Brian had already gone over to those same battlements to look down at the invaders. He was standing beside Sir Mortimor, who had also turned his attention in that direction. Jim joined them. Below them the zigzag road up to the stairs leading to the castle's now-opened door was crowded with people carrying various things, ranging from an ax to sacks holding unknown contents.

The two galleys that had been mentioned were just now turning in, prow-first toward the beach. It was clearly their intention to come in as close to the land as possible. Indeed, they checked themselves and anchored not more than ten or fifteen feet from shore; and now men were jumping overboard at the prow, landing in water varying from waist deep to shoulder deep, and wading ashore. They varied remarkably in both armor and the weapons they carried; but most had a round, obviously wooden shield, and a curved sword—the latter carried naked in their hand as they reached the shore.

No sooner was one out of the waves than he charged up the beach, shouting as he went, toward the village and those still trying to escape up the road to the castle.

There was no order to the way the attackers came, but very soon a good share of them were on the land and already in among the villages. Jim had expected to see the buildings there go up in flames almost immediately; but they did not. Instead the attackers merely rushed through the structures in pursuit of those trying to escape.

"Slingers!" said Sir Mortimor.

There were still only about half a dozen bowmen on top of the tower, but possibly as many as three dozen of the other men. These lined the battlements facing the beach, reached into their pouches, and drew forth a length of doubled leather thong with a flat leather pad in the middle of it, which had been poked or molded into a pocket. Digging again into their pouches, they came up with dull slugs of some sort of metal. Each at his own rate of speed fitted a slug into the pocket of his thong arrangement, took both ends of the thong and began one-handedly whirling the whole arrangement lightly in a vertical circle, as they gazed down at the beach, the weight of the slug in the pocket stretching the thong arrangement—which was evidently and clearly a sling—to its fullest limits, so that it rotated like a solid wand in the hand of each as he twirled it.

"Never mind any that haven't reached at least to the bottom of the road," said Sir Mortimor. "Pick off those close to the villagers. Wait for my order."

The row of men stood apparently idly whirling their slings. It was not until the first of the attackers were within a few steps of overtaking an old woman who was lagging behind the rest of those frantically trying to reach safety, before he gave the word; and by that time the section of the road that had been left empty behind the villagers was now full of the Moroccan pirates.

"Now!" said Sir Mortimor and all together, as if it had been rehearsed, one end of each sling was let go, the slingers leaning forward all together as they released their missiles—and, immediately, each slinger had another slug out of his pouch, fitted it into the socket of his sling and was whirling it again, slinging now as each one was ready.

Down below, the results were remarkable. From this height, of course, the impact of the slugs was soundless and, unlike the strike of arrows, there was nothing to be seen in the way of a shaft with feathers sticking out of the person hit.

"Balearic slingers!" cried Brian with delight. "They are Balearics, are they not, Sir Mortimor?"

"For the most part," grunted Sir Mortimor, his eyes still on the situation below. "They have to be trained from boyhood, like those who use the longbow. But some of these are cheaper, raised closer to hand, and from the standpoint of a castle like mine, it is much easier to stock great amounts of the slugs they throw, than the carefully made arrows a bowman must use, and which usually cannot be recovered when a castle is being attacked and possibly besieged. Also, they have not the range of the longbow, but at short distances like this they are wonderfully effective.''

"Effective indeed!" said Brian.

And so they were.

To Jim, looking down from the tower, it was as if half of the closest pursuers had suddenly collapsed on the ground; and those still on their feet had turned and were in panicky flight back down the road. The rearmost of these also fell; but by the time they reached the bottom of the road, most of the slingers had stopped whirling their slings and were looking to Sir Mortimor for further orders.

Sir Mortimor shook his head.

He had evidently signaled for wine, and someone had brought it to him. He stood with a mazer in his hand, nearly full with the red liquid, but was not drinking from it. There was silence on the tower top.

Down below, however, the invaders were making enough noise for both sides. Looking down from the battlements, Jim could see that most of them had crowded into the little space between the houses of the village and the beginning of the zigzag road up the slope. They howled and shook their weapons, looking upward at the battlements. A few of them evidently had bows, for arrows flew from among them, none getting any higher than three-quarters of the way up the tower before hitting the stone sides and dropping back.

"Not surprising, that," said Brian, watching beside Jim. "Hard to judge the distance to your mark looking so sharply up hill as this."

Sir Mortimor sipped at his mazer.

A few more arrows lofted into the air high enough to fall harmlessly onto the tower top. Minutes went by, and gradually the noise below dwindled and dwindled until there was silence there as well. Then a strong voice shouted alone.

"English knight!" it called. "Sir Mortimor, I know you are there. I am Abd'ul Hasan, and these are all my men. You cannot hope to hold out against us. I would speak with you. Sir Mortimor. English knight. Show yourself at your battlements!"

Watching from those same battlements, Brian with Jim saw the crowd below move apart to reveal a single tall individual in a red turban and a long, flowing white robe standing almost on the beginning of the road up the slope itself. He was taller than most of those around him; but even from this height, Jim could see that he was nowhere near the height of Sir Mortimor. His brown face looked upward, waiting.

Beside Jim, Sir Mortimor leisurely stepped forward to stand towering over the serrated rock teeth of the battlements and looked downward.

"What is it?" his remarkable voice rang out and down to those below. "We will take your castle, burn it around your ears and crucify you!" cried Abd'ul Hasan. "But this, only if you force us to fight our way in. I give you a choice. Come out now, leaving all behind; and you and everyone with you shall go safely. I repeat, come out now, and you and all with you shall go free, safely. We only want what is inside your castle!"

Sir Mortimor stood, not answering, simply looking down at him. After a long silence the man below shouted up again.

"What do you say, English knight?" he said. "Answer me now. You will not get a second chance."

"I am German," Sir Mortimor's voice over-rode him.

"I care not what you call yourself," shouted Abd'ul Hasan. "Do you accept my terms? Say yes or no now. You will not get another chance."

Sir Mortimor looked down at him thoughtfully. As the seconds fled by he lifted the mazer to his lips but only sipped at it again, then took it from his mouth. Slowly and deliberately he turned his wrist to pour its contents through the empty air, to splatter on the last few steps leading up to the front door of the castle. He tossed the empty mazer after it. The cup was of metal; it fell in a straight line to the stone steps, hit and bounced, hit again, and half tumbled, half rolled, now an unrecognizable pounded lump of metal, almost to the feet of Abd'ul Hasan. Then Sir Mortimor turned and walked away from the battlements.

For a long moment there was silence below and then a swelling roar of rage came up from the attackers. On top of the tower Sir Mortimor's voice came clearly through the tumult.

"Ten men on duty here at all times," he said. "Everyone to sleep with their weapons and—Beaupré!"

"Yes, m'lord," said a narrow-bodied man with a sword at his side and European body armor above the waist, as well as a steel helmet. His hair was dark brown and plentiful; but smallpox had made a pitted ruin of his otherwise sharp-featured face.

"You will have the charge in keeping," said Sir Mortimor. "A special watch to be kept on the stairs and a guard on the door; the kettle up here to be filled with oil and a low fire under it, ready to heat it swiftly if there's need. You will tell me, asleep, awake, or whatever I am doing, if they begin to show signs of attempting to force the front door. Otherwise, it is in your hands. I expect little for a day or so; but make note of when they try us from above, and if they try gunpowder against the walls and any else of the usual things."

"Yes, m'lord," said Beaupré.

"Well, gentlemen," said Sir Mortimor to Jim and Brian, "shall we down stairs once more; and try again if we may not have a little time to ourselves?''

He did not wait for an answer; but turned and went directly to the stairs opening and down it. Jim and Brian followed.

CHAPTER 9

"**B**eaupré will be my squire if I have need of such," said Sir Mortimor, in an unusually quiet voice.

They were seated once more at the table where they had been before, with three more of the apparently endless supply of mazers filled with wine before them. Sir Mortimor had waited until the servant who brought them had left the floor.

"As it is," the tall knight went on, "he is my second in command. If he should call on you to do something, you will please me by regarding it as a request from myself. I expect nothing much to happen for a day or two. They will try all the easy things. We may hear stones poured upon the tower from above, and some attempts to break through the walls at ground level, but nothing serious. Beaupré will take care of this, all of it, and call upon you only if needed."

"Sir Mortimor," said Brian in a level voice, "I crave pardon if I misunderstand you. But it seems to me that you are suggesting that two belted knights fight if necessary under the orders of a squire."

"So I am," said Sir Mortimor, meeting him eye to eye. "You gentlemen do not know wars as they are fought in this part of the world; and Beaupré does. I assure you he will use the best of manners in speaking to you."

"That is hardly the point, Sir Mortimor," said Brian. "We are guests of yours, I believe?"

"You are," said Sir Mortimor. "What else might you be?"

"I expect nothing else," said Brian. "But I also expect that if my host would welcome my assistance in defending his house, then my host would ask it himself, rather than sending someone of lesser rank to demand it of me."

"Very well," said Sir Mortimor. "I do so ask."

"In that case," said Brian, "I will be only too ready to help as much as I can."

Jim felt the pressure of the conversation on him.

"And I too, of course, Sir Mortimor," he said.

"Then I think we are agreed, gentlemen," said Sir Mortimor. He stood up, leaving his wine untouched.

"While I have put Beaupré with the charge in keeping," he said, "it is nonetheless my castle, and my decisions rule. I will therefore be aware of all that is going on, and this will leave me little time to pay attention to my guests. Sir Brian, if you would accept Sir James into the quarters I gave you, I would appreciate it. The possessions you brought with you when you came here by water, Sir James, have already been carried to that room. If in any way you are not comfortable, simply call a servant and say what you want. If it is possible to supply you with it, my castle will supply it. Now, if you will excuse me, I will be about my own circuit of the castle to see how things are being readied."

He turned, strode to the stairs and went down out of sight.

"Brian—" began Jim. But Brian raised a forefinger and brushed it across his lips, and Jim broke off abruptly.

Brian got to his feet, picking up his mazer as he did and beckoning Jim. Jim followed his example, but left his wine behind. Brian led him to the staircase and down a single level into a small space from which three doors opened off. He took the one to the left, and led Jim into a room that was obviously intended as a guest bedroom.

In contrast to what Jim had been used to finding in castles in England, it was more spacious than most such guest rooms were; the bed was much bigger, with four posts and a canopy all the way around it; and what might have been otherwise considered an arrow slit in the wall was several times as wide as the ordinary arrow slit—making a good bid at calling itself a window. There were, however, no shutters on it. In case of bad weather not only wind, but rain, would enter.

Jim's possessions were piled in a corner; and, among them, he was happy to see, was his personal, rolled-up and vermin-free mattress. There was also a table and barrel chairs in the room. Brian carefully closed the door behind them, beckoned him over to the table, sat down himself with his mazer and motioned Jim to a chair.

"James," he said in a low voice, "unwittingly, I have led you into a trap. If your magic gives you means of escaping from here, I beg that you will use it. This attack on Sir Mortimor's castle should be no concern of yours. I am heartily sorry you have become involved even this far with it."

Jim looked across the table at Brian and saw that he was in deadly earnest.

"Of course," he said, "I could get away by magic. In fact, we both can get away by magic. What have you got yourself into here, Brian?"

It was not until the last words were out of his mouth, that he had realized that he had committed an unpardonable social error by asking such a personal question of Brian, in spite of the fact that Brian was his closest friend. He had no right to ask Brian to tell him why he was in any kind of situation. He opened his mouth to apologize, but Brian spoke before him.

"Never mind it, James," said Brian, as if he had read Jim's mind. "I understand you speak only out of concern for me. No, if you can escape, you must do so. I, myself, am not free to leave."

"Why not?" asked Jim.

"I came here as an invited guest," Brian said, "after meeting Sir Mortimor in Episcopi, where I was visiting with some other good knights—English knights—whose grandfathers settled here at the time of an earlier crusade. Sir Mortimor has not failed in his duties as a host toward me; and I cannot fail in my obligation as a guest to him, now that he has a difficulty on his hands. It is not so with you. You came only to find me, and you find me tied here while you are free to go. I beg you, James, leave while you can; and if a message must be sent back to Geronde and Angela, say that I was well the last you saw of me, and merely had a small bicker on my hands which might delay me slightly in getting on with what I came here to do."

Jim felt Hob stir again in the knapsack on his back. The little hobgoblin had ducked down out of sight before Sir Mortimor had come back up to join them, at the time when they had been talking about Brian's childhood and his early knowledge of Hob. Now the hobgoblin stuck his head out of the knapsack, and his breath tickled the back of Jim's right ear as he looked about.

"Oh!" he said happily. "Fire and smoke. A fireplace. M'lord, is it all right if I take a look up that chimney?"

"Go right ahead, Hob," said Jim—and in a moment the gray figure of Hob had launched itself from his shoulder toward the fireplace and to all appearances simply disappeared. Jim turned his attention back to Brian. The last words that Brian had said had rung oddly false in his ears.

"Brian," he said, "forgive me—and you don't have to answer me, if you don't want to—but is something wrong? Is there something you're not telling me that's badly out of kilter? Will you really be ready to go on as soon as this is over?"

"I pledge myself to do so," said Brian. "And that pledge I am not going to fail upon. I give you my word I will do my best to go back to my search for Geronde's father, the minute I am away from Sir Mortimor and this castle."

"Then why don't we both leave?" said Jim. "Your obligations as a guest—"

"Are my obligations!" said Brian with a snap. "I have never failed on my word; and, before God, I never will."

"You're talking about your word to Sir Mortimor, now, aren't you?" said Jim. "What word exactly did you give him?"

"James—" began Brian on an almost angry note, and then stopped abruptly. He looked down at the table, looked at his mazer of wine, took a drink from it and looked back up at Jim. "James, I will continue in my search. There may be a slight delay, however. You are right. There is something I have not told you; and it concerns an error and a weakness on my part. It is—the fact is I have almost no money left to travel with."

"No—?" Jim broke off. "I don't mean to—" he continued, staring at his friend. Brian's square, lean-boned face with its blue eyes and aggressively hooked nose had something defiant about it. He checked the word "pry" that had been on the tip of his tongue and rephrased what he was going to say.

"—Ask any impolite questions of you," he went on, "but how does it happen you could be out of money so quickly? It seemed to me you had more than enough for a search here that could take you months, or even a year."

"So I had," said Brian. "The fault is my own, James. We are all sinners and have our weaknesses. One of mine, as you know, is the dice. I should have sworn off all such things for the period of this search, but I did not think of it."

"But what happened, then?" asked Jim.

"I came to Cyprus, as perhaps Geronde told you," he said, "because a certain Sir Francis Neville, a cousin twice removed, was a knight of the Hospitallers; and I hoped for advice from him. I knew that he was here on Cyprus on some business between the Hospitallers and certain well-placed and powerful gentlemen on the island. Perhaps Geronde told you all this."

Jim nodded.

"But when I got here," Brian said, "Sir Francis had already left again for the headquarters of his Brotherhood, which has long been elsewhere than the hospital they founded in Jerusalem, in the name of St. John of Jerusalem, whereby, of course, comes their name of Hospitallers. Their proper title at present is the Order of the Knights of Rhodes. I had hoped to learn from him the best way to take myself to Palmyra, and also how I should conduct myself and what I should be wary of on the way there."

Brian paused. Jim, thinking he was done speaking, opened his own mouth.

"But surely," Jim said, "his being gone shouldn't have cost you most of your money—unless it was stolen from you."

"No," said Brian, "it would be a brave robber that tried to take what I had on my person. No, my cousin Sir Francis was no longer here; but he had many friends, of course, whom I discovered by mentioning his name to other gentlemen; and those friends welcomed me in a right neighborly manner. But you must understand, James, they passed me from one to the other—since one would have some knowledge of Palmyra, but not of the best route toward it, where another might know of the route, but not the city, and yet another might know more about ships plying back and forth between here and Tripoli, that being the best port to come close to it. Palmyra, you must understand, is some distance inland from Tripoli and all other port cities to the south."

"Go on," said Jim.

"The trouble was, James," said Brian, "of course, each new gentleman I met must dine and drink and entertain me—and, of course, together with all this there was a certain amount of dicing."

"Oh," said Jim. "And it added up to your losing all your money?"

"Oh no," said Brian, "not all of it, by any means. A small portion, only. I was most careful. But then, in Episcopi, I was introduced to Sir Mortimor, who was up there from his castle for business of his own, and he joined us at the dice; and I won."

"You won?" Jim stared at him.

"Yes. I won a good deal," said Brian. "I ended up with more than I had when I first came to Cyprus. And I won it all from Sir Mortimor, who seemed then to live only for dicing and drinking. I have a fair capacity for wine, you know that, James. But Sir Mortimor's is heroic!"

"I can believe it," said Jim.

"So, I did not refuse," Brian went on, "when Sir Mortimor invited me up here for a short stay. We were to enjoy the fishing, actually. He had promised me that there was almost as much pleasure in trying to boat a fish as large as a man, on a single line, as there was besting one in single combat; and you know that we do not usually have fish that large, to be taken by only an angle, in England. Indeed, he was quite right. He did take me fishing at first, and I had the experience; and it is something to remember, James!"

"I can believe that too," said Jim. "But the last I heard you still had money. In fact, more than you had started out with."

"Not more than I had started out with, James," said Brian reproachfully. "More than I had by the time I had gotten here to Cyprus."

"I stand corrected," said Jim.

"But, of course, in the evenings we would be dicing; and—I know not how it is, James—but what I had experienced in Episcopi could only have been the most unusual run of luck; for here at the castle it has been just the opposite. I have lost steadily; until now I have lost almost every coin I possess. I cannot leave without trying to get it back; and even if I could, my sense of honor would insist that I stay here to help Sir Mortimor in his hour of trial.''

"I'm not sure he regards it as that much of an hour of trial,'' said Jim. "So you won gaming against him in Episcopi? Won steadily. But back here at the castle you have lost steadily? Were you always using his dice?''

"Why, yes,'' said Brian. "I never carry dice, James, you know that, for that I might be tempted to lose what little I own. I have this abiding fear that one day I might forget myself and even wager Blanchard of Tours, when the fever is on me—and lose him.''

Jim nodded soberly. Brian had given all his patrimony, except the run-down Castle Smythe itself, in order to buy Blanchard, the great white stallion that was his war horse, and who had the intelligence and the fighting spirit that made such horses worth a prince's purse. And indeed, without Blanchard, Brian would be hard put to win the tournaments in which he essentially made his living; and in which a horse of such weight, power and speed was a vital necessity.

"But you cannot be suggesting that Sir Mortimor has been less than honest in our bouts,'' said Brian, staring at Jim. "A knight would not— oh, I know there have been cases, hedge knights and pitiful fellows not fit for a gentleman's table. But for someone like Sir Mortimor who owns this castle and property here . . . He could not survive without the help of his neighbors; and he would not dare cheat his neighbors for fear that sooner or later it would be discovered; and then all would turn against him.''

"You may be right, Brian,'' said Jim. "But I think you forget something.''

"What is that?'' Brian was very close to bristling.

"This is a part of the world where taking all you can get from anyone else is the normal way of life. In fact, you know as well as I do it's not the only part of the world where this can happen to a visitor. And I might point out that you're a visitor here, a stranger. That could make you fair game.''

"He dare not!'' said Brian.

"From what I've seen of him,'' Jim said, "Sir Mortimor is not slow when it comes to daring things.''

Brian sat, slowly adjusting to the idea of Sir Mortimor as someone who would cheat a fellow knight. Gradually his face became more and more grim until the bones of it seemed to push against the skin.

"By God!" he said. "If he has—"

He broke off; and gradually the anger seemed to leak out of him, to be replaced by despair.

"However," he said at last with a sigh, "there is nothing to be done about it. It would be all the more impolite if I were to question his honesty without proof certain—now that I am a heavy loser to him. But game with him I must, if I am to have any hope of regaining my funds. In any case, there is no way to tell whether he plays honestly, or not."

"Maybe not for you," said Jim. He had his magic. But at the moment he could not think how he could use it to check on the honesty of Sir Mortimor's dice playing. There must, however, be a way. "But if he won't object to my sitting and watching while you play . . . if he doesn't suspect that I'm watching to see if I can tell that in some way or other he's less than honest . . ."

"He would not suspect the honor of a fellow knight—" Brian broke off. "By St. Giles, James, it just may be that if you are right, he would indeed be suspicious. How to avoid that, I know not."

But Jim's mind was working now.

"What about this, Brian?" he asked. "Would you say that Sir Mortimor was the sort of knight who could be counted on to take up a challenge?" Brian stared at him.

"Of an absolute certainty!" said Brian. "Courage, he does not lack."

"Then maybe we could get him into a dice match, where his attention would be more on the match itself with you than on any reason I might have for watching. If you challenged him to it, for example, at a moment when things were at risk and two gentlemen would normally not sit down to wine and dice. You could do that?"

"I could, of course," said Brian. "But when? And James—I have only a few pieces of gold left. It may be that I would have to give the appearance of having more. It is a great deal to ask of you, but is it possible—"

"Certainly," Jim interrupted him. "I can give you enough extra money to make him interested. That's no problem."

For that matter, he thought, he could make any amount of money that might be needed, magically. Of course it would turn back into whatever he had made it out of, twenty-four hours later—and also to use such false money to cheat someone would be against the laws of Magickdom—as Carolinus would spell that word. But to use it to catch a cheat ought to be allowable.

"We'll wait until the attack against this castle heats up," he said.

CHAPTER 10

Sir Mortimor turned out to be a true prophet, however incorrect might be his play with the dice.

Jim woke in the middle of the night under the impression that the castle was falling apart, and came fully awake only in time to hear the last tremendous thunder of something or other against the wall not six feet from his left ear. The fire had died down in the room's fireplace; there were only a few embers glowing with a dull redness that left everything else in complete darkness.

"It is the pirates, only, trying to drop stones on the castle from the cliff overhead," came Brian's voice out of that darkness, as soon as the thunder had ceased. "As Sir Mortimor said, James, the cliff overhangs enough so that they can do no real damage. You heard the rocks scarcely hitting the forward side of the castle, just grazing it, so that they will only leave scars, which you may see tomorrow by looking down from the battlements."

"Oh," said Jim. He went back to sleep.

The invaders evidently agreed with Brian, for after the first fall of stones, no more came to wake them; and the following day, Brian, pointing down from the battlements, directed Jim's gaze to the whitish scars on the rounded side of the tower where the falling rocks had scraped it. It was hard to believe in scars that slight, considering the thunder Jim had remembered hearing in the middle of the night.

The next attempt at the castle came several hours later, well past mid-morning, when an unknown number of the Moroccans crept up the steps, carrying a heavy wooden shield over their heads, so that they were able to advance to the very foot of the tower and move around it to a point where they apparently leaned it against the building as a permanent protection, and went to work beneath it.

"They will be attempting to dig down either under the wall, or far enough so that they can loosen and break out a part of the wall, so that the castle itself may sag, or that they can build an entrance through which they can fight their way in,'' said Sir Mortimor. ''But they will be disappointed. This castle is bedded solidly on and in the living rock of the cliff itself, in a circular trench that was cut in that rock when the tower was commenced.''

''Still . . .'' said Brian. They were all three, Sir Mortimor, Brian and Jim, looking down over the battlements and listening to the scrape of tools against the building and the other noises of work beneath the shield. None of the castle's fighting men had been ordered to take any action against the diggers. ''If they stay with it,'' Brian went on, ''sooner or later they should be able to gnaw through whatever is there to the interior of the castle.''

He looked at the tall knight.

''Though I would venture,'' he added, ''to guess it would take more than a few days.''

''They will not,'' said Sir Mortimor. ''Such patience you speak of is not theirs. A quick battle, a quick victory is more their way. Now, if this castle were somewhere north of the Mediterranean, far inland, you might have cause to expect such a thing. But not here.''

''You have been in the wars on the continent, sir?'' asked Brian.

''Some,'' said Sir Mortimor, briefly; and, turning, he left them to go downstairs into the castle.

But again, it fell out as he had said. As the shadows of the day lengthened, the sounds of labor under the shield became less and less and finally ceased. Finally the shield crept back down the stairs, with stones from the tower-top slingers seeking to find the space between it and the ground; and at least hit the legs of those who carried it. But it made its way back down the stairs and out of range without leaving any wounded or dead behind.

The next night was ominously quiet, except for some singing and noise of voices down in the abandoned village at the foot of the castle.

''I expected them to burn those buildings right away,'' said Jim, half to himself and half to Brian, looking down at night. The only lights visible around the village were some torches being carried by individuals going from one part of the village to another and a torch or so down by the two ships.

''I believe they have waited because the buildings give them a place of shelter to sleep and eat in,'' said Brian, beside him, ''from what little I understand of such things. How I envy Sir Mortimor with his experience in wars on the continent. I wonder if he was in the low countries, or in France—or maybe he was farther east, possibly fighting against the heathens in the Far East.''

Jim turned to look at his friend's face in the meager light of the stars and a half-full moon.

"You sound almost as if you admire him, Brian," he said.

"He is a warrior," said Brian. "More so than I, who have never seen—well, have never really taken part in, outside of some small actions in France—pitched battles, sieges, or the real meat of warfare. I may be clever with the lance and possibly with other weapons as well; but I cannot say I have really fought in any true sense of the word."

Since Brian's life had consisted of almost continual fighting, according to Jim's ordinary meaning of the word, from the time of Brian's father's death when he had taken over Castle Smythe at the age of fifteen, Jim found this exaggerated respect for someone who had been in recognized war a little surprising. But he did not think his friend would appreciate his mentioning that fact; so he said nothing aloud.

That night, however, there was an alarm of a different nature. Jim woke to the sound of voices and rushing feet in the castle. The fire in their fireplace blazed up suddenly; and Jim saw Brian turning away from it after throwing extra fuel onto the still-burning embers. His friend was pulling on his hose and shoes and buckling his belt and sword around his waist. In the light from the newly leaping flames in the fireplace, the scars on his naked upper body looked black, as if they had been painted there.

"They are trying to force the door under cover of darkness," Brian said to him briefly. "Best we were up and armed, James. It is past compline."

After midnight—Jim scrambled to his feet and began to dress, with that sinking feeling he always had when his being in actual combat was in prospect. If anything, he was at his best in a melee, where his greater than average weight and size could give him a sheer muscle advantage. But it was in moments like this he was very much aware of how inexpert he was with the sword he was now buckling about his waist.

He and Brian, finally dressed and as fully armed as they could be, left their room and went down toward the source of the most noise, which was on the ground floor.

Sir Mortimor's voice could be heard riding over the tumult by the time they reached the floor just above ground level. It came echoing up the stairwell with force and command.

"No more than thirty men here!" the knight was ordering, one floor down. "Do nothing unless they actually break through the front door. Then, if they do, open this door only long enough for the slingers and bowmen to have at them for a moment, then lock and bar here again. They should not gain through this time. So. Be orderly, be on watch, be ready. The rest of you, beyond the thirty who will stay, fill your arms with straw and up the stairs with you and pile it by battlements above those attacking. The oil in the kettle should already be heating. As soon as I come, we will throw down the straw from the tower-top on those trying to get in, pour oil on top, and throw down lighted torches. Beaupré!''

"Yes, Sir Mortimor." The pockmarked face of Sir Mortimor's second in command came toward the knight from among others in the crowd before the knight.

"Leave just enough slingers here to be effective in the passage when the door is opened for a moment. All other slingers up to the roof with us. Extra bowmen also. Make sure the torches are ready!''

"The torches are already there and lit, Sir Mortimor," said Beaupré, "and most of the other slingers and bowmen also. There are enough here to take care of any attack through the passage. I will take care of all."

Sir Mortimor turned toward the stairs, saw Brian and Jim starting down them and shook his head.

"If you please, messires," he said, "come with me to the roof."

He was up the stairs and past them, crowding them against the stone wall to his left on the stairway, within seconds of having finished speaking. He vanished upward, taking the stairs two steps at a time and leaving them far behind as they turned to follow.

Jim, his legs still stiff from the previous day's stair-climbing in the castle, gazed thoughtfully at the empty steps before him. It did not seem possible that any human being could run up the five stories worth of levels inside the castle, taking two of the eight-to-ten-inch steps of the staircase at each stride; but having seen Sir Mortimor in action, he was now ready to believe that the knight would continue his pace all the way to the roof. Possibly, even now as Jim and Brian were climbing after him, Sir Mortimor was emerging into the open night at the tower's top.

They joined him eventually; and Jim saw, by the light of torches held by men standing well back from the forward facing battlements, where the lights they held could not make them marks for archers from below, a respectable stack of straw already built, ready to be thrown down.

Sir Mortimor stood, legs spread a little bit apart, watching other men bring still more armfuls up and add to the stack. The fire was alight, in fact blazing brightly, underneath the kettle of oil, which had now been rolled on the metal wheels attached to its firebox to the aperture over the passageway ceiling. The kettle itself was held pivoted on a couple of extended metal arms, so that merely by tilting it forward on those pivots it would pour its contents out of a lip in its rim, to fall through the holes overhead in the passageway far below. The heat from the firebox could be felt a dozen feet from it. Jim was astonished to see Sir Mortimor

suddenly walk toward the kettle and casually stick his forefinger deep into
the liquid it held.

"Warm enough," he said, stepping back. Jim stared at the finger, but
there was no sign that it had been in any way cooked, or otherwise marked
by heat. A little late, he realized that such a fire would have to burn for
some time to get the oil, itself, to an actual boiling point. There was a lot
of liquid there to be heated up.

"Fill buckets," said Sir Mortimor. "Line them up close above the entrance and five men stand ready to pour."

A long iron rod was produced, and two men used it to push the top of
the kettle forward so that it swung on its gimbals, tilting enough so that
the first man to hold a bucket under its lip was able to fill it without a
problem. He carried it to the front battlements.

He was succeeded immediately by another man with an empty bucket,
and the process continued until at least a dozen buckets were lined up just
below the crenelations of the battlements.

Another man ran up from below.

"Sir Mortimor," he panted, "Beaupré sends to say that he does not
think they will get through the outer door in any time soon. Their battering
ram strikes all over the surface of the door rather than repeatedly at one
place on it. He ventures to guess, with your permission, Sir Mortimor,
that they are finding their footing uncertain on the steps in the darkness."

"Good," grunted Sir Mortimor. He waved the man away. "We will
furnish them light to work by. Tell Beaupré that."

He looked back at the activity on the roof.

"That's enough straw!" he said. "Be ready to throw it over. Get it as
close as possible before the door, itself. It will spread and scatter enough
falling down. Bucket-men, and all. Throw the straw!"

He took two enormous strides forward himself, scooped up a huge armful of it in his long arms and tossed it over. All around him everyone was
doing the same, including the men who had been standing sentinel by the
battlements around the back part of the castle. Within less than two
minutes, all the straw was over.

"Oil!" snapped Sir Mortimor.

The men who had been appointed to handle the buckets seized them
and began dumping their contents over the side, crowding each other as
they did so to get as directly above the doorway as possible.

"Now," said Sir Mortimor, when the last bucket had been poured.
"Torches!"

The torches around the roof were seized and carried to the same point
from which everything else had been thrown and dropped. Jim and Brian
crowded close to the battlements a little off to one side and saw light

suddenly blossom in front of the castle doorway—not at the door itself, but at least one or two steps down. The straw had taken fire immediately and the oil was feeding its flames.

"Slingers!" Those on the roof who were slingers had already dropped their straw and filled their slings with missiles. They were whirling their slings ready to throw. Now they stepped forward to the battlements, and as yells and screams came up from below they launched the missiles downward.

An almost equal roar of excitement rose among those at the top of the tower, with a single voice shouting out above the rest.

"They run!" cried a voice.

"Let none escape!" trumpeted Sir Mortimor. "Slingers, see to it!"

Watching, Jim saw the last two flaming figures scrambling down the steps to fall and lie still. In front of the door, but not too close to it, the straw still burned brightly, with dark areas here and there among it where a body had fallen on the flames. The dropped battering ram they had been using—a squared-off piece of timber, with the bottom edge of its striking face slanted back from top to bottom to compensate for the fact that they were ramming it upward because of the slope of the steps—was outlined by fire.

"More oil on that stick of theirs," said Sir Brian. "More straw too, if necessary. It must burn."

He looked around for the man who had brought him the message from below earlier, and found him now, hovering almost at his elbow. "Tell Beaupré to send any extra slingers and archers he has up here. Tell him he may keep half a dozen of them only."

"Yes, m'lord."

The man went downstairs at a run.

A swelling hubbub could be heard from the buildings of the village where the rest of the attackers were; but none of them stepped outside the structures to where they might be in view of slingers from the tower.

"Well, gentlemen," said Sir Mortimor, looking over to Brian and Jim. "Shall we indulge ourselves with a drop of wine?"

Brian and Jim both murmured polite formulas of acceptance and followed him down the stairs to the floor below—Jim still a little dazed, in spite of his several years now of medieval experience, by the ruthless killing of the battering ram's handlers. He pushed it from his mind as Brian and he arrived at the floor below. It was probably that extremely carrying voice of Sir Mortimor's, he decided, that caused things to start being prepared as if by magic; but servants were already putting out three mazers filled with wine on the table by the time they reached their floor level behind Sir Mortimor. And just then another servant came with cheese, bread and cold meat from the kitchen level farther down. Enclosed here, it seemed to Jim strangely stuffy after being on top of the tower. It had been a cool night, up out in the open, but not unpleasantly so. It was probably the tension and the sudden change to indoors, to say nothing of the clothing and armor he had put on, that gave him the feeling.

Also, of course, each important room had its own fireplace; and there was one here. The fire had been allowed to burn down, but it was still throwing out some heat. Jim was startled, however, to see Hob's face appear suddenly upside down, just within the upper edge of it. Hob smiled happily at him and disappeared again.

Luckily, Sir Mortimor's back had been turned to the fireplace when this happened. Come to think of it, though, Jim told himself, Hob would probably not have shown himself if anyone but Jim or Brian had been looking in that direction.

Jim wondered for a moment how the hobgoblin had managed to get from the fireplace in their bedroom to this one—then the obvious answer struck him. Of course, Hob had gone up their bedroom chimney, then over and down the chimney of this fireplace. He had probably been exploring every chimney and fireplace in the castle.

"Well, Sir Mortimor," said Brian, as they sat down. "I believe you said the only way your castle could be taken was by an attempt through its main entrance. Yet we have just had such an attempt made; and you had little difficulty repelling it. Surely, you have not much to worry about from these pirates?"

Sir Mortimor put down his cup, already a quarter emptied.

"Under any ordinary conditions, no," he said. "At least, not from a force as small and as ill-armed as this one. Against a larger, more determined set of attackers, with siege engines, with gunpowder or even bombards, possibly. But what I learned from the wars I was in on the continent was to be prepared for circumstances that are not ordinary."

"And you still would not welcome," said Brian, "my sallying with a few men to burn their ships?"

"I am not about to lose one man I do not have to," said Sir Mortimor dryly. "This burning of their ships would not be the bloodless task you seem to think it, sir. Moreover, not to mince words, you are also wrong about this castle having nothing to fear."

"I but tell your own words back to you, sir," said Brian. "I repeat, you said that except they reached you through your main door they could never get in; and from what I saw tonight that they will never be able to do."

"In God's Name!" said Sir Mortimor, slapping his large palm down hard on the table top. "What you saw tonight was not what could be. Any place of strength can be taken, given either engines to break their way in, or enough willing men to keep attacking until the place is penetrated and reduced!''

He and Sir Brian were staring at each other; and Jim was sitting with all his muscles tight. When two men with the golden spurs (golden in name, at least) of knighthood started talking to each other in this bare-knuckle fashion, in spite of whatever courtesies they larded their speech with, a fight with weapons was only inches away.

"We have neither of those here," said Brian.

"Now," said Sir Mortimor, "we have not. But you burn their boats and—as I told you—you will cut off their retreat. If they cannot leave, their only other hope is to take this castle. Such as these marauders do not go out to get themselves killed but to pick up loot. But if cornered, they will fight as well as anyone else. From being men unwilling to keep fighting, they will change to men willing to fight and die—aye, die! As they are now, they have not the heart and guts to make it in my front door.''

He and Brian were eye to eye, their faces less than the table's width apart.

"But give them no choice," Sir Mortimor went on, "and they will send men and battering rams against that front door until it goes down, no matter how many are killed. The weaker among them will be pressed into service first, and then those left who have become the new weakest will be the next to go, and so forth.''

"There is a limit to how long men will continue doing that," Brian said.

"Not in all cases," said Sir Mortimor. "If there was a *jihad*, a Mus-selman Holy War, against us here, and those outside were fighters in that cause, I promise you they would simply keep coming. They would bring battering rams against that front door and those who brought them would die; and they would send more and those would die and they would send more and those would die. But in the end, they would break through into the passage and the first of those into the passage would die and those next to follow would die in the oil and flame and smoke—but the time would come when they would break through the inner door—and then we would die.''

Jim felt an almost intolerable pressure on him to say something, any-thing, to interrupt the growing tension between Brian and Sir Mortimor, who were now leaning forward over the table toward each other in the heat of their dispute.

"I know very little about this part of the world, and such things," he interrupted, in as peaceable a voice as he could manage, "but I've got to confess I don't understand why those who attack us here should be left with nothing to do but assault the castle, if their boats are destroyed. I got the impression you believe most of them are Moslems; and certainly there can't be any lack of others of their faith in Episcopi. Why can't they simply go by twos and threes up to wander into Episcopi, find their fellow believers, and be helped to some ship that will take them homeward?''

"Indeed!'' Sir Mortimor's piercing voice and angry gaze turned itself on Jim. "You do know little about matters here. In fact, sir, you know nothing! What makes you think that simply because there are others of their own faith in Episcopi, they would be safe there? There are too many of them attacking us to try to pretend to be anything but what they are. Only a few of these would need to wander into Episcopi, before word would reach the Christian knights who are my friends, telling them who these men are, and what they have been about—''

"I see,'' said Jim soothingly. "Well, of course—''

Sir Mortimor's voice drowned his out, going right on.

"Their fellow Musselmen would not wait for answer, but seize and hold these men and any others who came after them, while approaches were made to those I do business with—as to whether I would pay to have these condemned as pirates and turned over to judgment and death— and with them any other such who wandered in from then on, no matter how reasonable their story, or how innocent their appearance, would be put to the same fate. There are those in Episcopi, Christians and Musselmen both, who do business with me. Some hold my notes-of-hand for certain sums and want them redeemed—which they cannot be if I am killed and my castle looted. Also, they know I am in a position to repay any rewards they offer for such pirates being taken up and disposed of. Surely, Sir James, you are even more of an innocent than you proclaim yourself if you cannot imagine something like this happening!''

The mounting tension between Brian and Sir Mortimor had been broken; but Jim found himself personally in an uncomfortable spot. Now, instead of Sir Mortimor crowding Brian to the point where a fight between them was inevitable, Sir Mortimor was crowding him to the point where, if he wanted to go on calling himself a knight, Jim must react as Brian might have, unless he could think of something very quickly indeed.

CHAPTER 11

He had gotten out of a sticky situation once, when he had first met Brian, by talking about Social Security numbers. Possibly, thought Jim, something else in the way of twentieth-century concepts might work now. He smiled amiably at Sir Mortimor.

"I'm indebted to you, Sir Mortimor," he said heartily. "Indeed I am very glad to hear you tell me this. I've been concerned these last few days over the meteorological situation at this castle of yours, here; the dangerous possibilities that are always there whenever a large low-pressure cell approaches an even larger high-pressure one. But what you say reassures me."

Sir Mortimor's lips, which had begun to curl into something very closely resembling a sneer with James's first few words, froze, then gradually collapsed into a baffled stare. Brian was staring at him with equal blankness.

"As you know," Jim went along cheerfully, "events have fallen out so that I have ended up being involved with magic. So the concern was unavoidable. But, naturally, I didn't wish to concern you or Sir Brian with any matters meteorological or astrophysical, unless absolutely necessary."

Sir Mortimor's stare sought Brian's face. Brian frowned back at him severely.

"Sir James is a mage," said Brian frostily. "I had thought you understood that, sir, since he mentioned his work in that art prevented him from taking part in any gaming."

"I knew of his deeds, of course, but I had thought then he spoke only in regard to his changing into dragon-shape."

"It is far more than that," said Brian. "The rules of his Order are extremely strict. For one, he must sleep every night not in any bed, but on a pallet of penance he carries everywhere he goes."

It was Jim's turn to stare. He had never imagined Brian had put this interpretation on his carefully deverminized, decontaminated, traveling bedroll. Sir Mortimor's face had gone ashen. He turned to Jim.

"Sir James!" His voice was lowered. "I crave your pardon if some hasty word of mine may perhaps have sounded improper or unrespectful; but I only knew of your deeds—your deeds as a knight, that is—I had no real notion of you as also a mage . . ."

It would have been impossible for Jim to have imagined such a thing a few moments before, but the tall knight was actually stammering.

"You mustn't call me a mage," said Jim hastily. "I'm really only experienced in lower levels of magic. Only the very top levels of magicians, those like my Master, Carolinus, should be addressed as mage. As for any hasty words from you, I have heard none, Sir Mortimor. In any case, tut! We are all three knights, here together. Pray let us forget this business of my magic, except as I referred to it a moment ago—a problem now settled. I shall speak to you, sir, as a knight; and, I will be gratified if you will speak to me as merely another."

"That—that is most gentle of you, Sir James," said Sir Mortimor. "You must understand how, living here away from normal European society, and being rather a rough fellow to begin with, I have become even rougher, and I do not guard my tongue the way I should. It is so difficult these days to get your orders executed properly. I have fallen into the habit of being more outspoken to my equals than I should be, to anyone except those of lesser worth. I will be most grateful to you, Sir James, if you will correct any tendency like that in me, which you see or hear in the future, so that I may amend my ways at once and make proper apology for them."

"Tut," said Jim again, at the moment totally unable to think of what else to say.

The color flowed back into Sir Mortimor's face.

"I am most grateful to you, Sir James—well, damn your black liver and lights!" These last words were delivered to Beaupré, who had come up the stairs during the knight's final words and was standing by his elbow, silent and waiting. "What kind of trouble are you bringing me now?"

Beaupré showed no more sign of being affected by Sir Mortimor's outburst than if he had been carved out of stone.

"Your pardon, my Lord," he said in exactly the same tone of voice Jim had heard him use every time he had spoken, "but there is some activity down in the village, which may be connected with our just driving off those who had attacked the front door. The fire from the straw and the oil in front of the castle has now burned down, and all is darkness before the door. I could let one of our men out the small panel in the door; or go myself, and creep a small distance down the slope to see what I could hear and find out about what they may be doing, or beginning to do."

"Ignore it, Beaupré," said Sir Mortimor. "They will do nothing until daylight at least, when we may see them trying to find a safe way from the village to the door. But not in darkness. Not tonight."

Beaupré hesitated.

"You may go!" said Sir Mortimor. Beaupré disappeared down the stairs. Sir Mortimor turned back to Jim.

"You are, indeed, satisfied, Sir James," he said, "that I meant no ill will? Then or now?"

"It never crossed my mind," said Jim.

"I am relieved," said Sir Mortimor. "Well, gentlemen, shall we sit and talk and drink a bit and then perhaps seek our beds for what rest we may have the remainder of this night? Mayhap we may need it tomorrow. One thought does occur to me, however, Sir James. If you will excuse me from any further offense I may give through ignorance, I do not suppose you would be willing to put your magic to use in the defense of my castle? I am not without certain resources. By that I mean that I would be more than willing to consider any price you might think right for your assistance in that direction—I mean to offer no offense in suggesting payment to a fellow knight, none at all. It is merely a thought."

"In any case," said Jim, "I'd have to disappoint you. As you just guessed, Sir Mortimor, my magic is not for sale."

"Oh, of course—" Sir Mortimor broke off. "So let us drop that matter, gentlemen, and talk of other things. Between the three of us, I am enheartened by the speed and easiness with which we repelled tonight's attempt on the castle's entrance. It may well be that whatever reward was promised or given these sea rovers was not enough to encourage them to a fully serious effort against the castle. There are fish in the sea and there will have been some food left in the village; but they will soon run out of provender; and it may be that after a few other small attempts, they may simply take ship and leave. I have known it to happen before."

"I told Sir James about the fishing you told me of and then took me out on," said Brian, avoiding Jim's eye with a faint pinkening of the flesh over his lean cheekbones, "and the pleasure in bringing to boat a fish of the size you had then spoken of. I would that he could have the experience as well. If these pirates leave, certainly it would be possible to take Sir James out and find him a like fish?"

"Easily, easily," said Sir Mortimor, taking a hearty drink from his mazer. "I have never forgotten my first experience in such fishing with an angle, myself, on coming to this island—*more wine here!*" He lowered his voice, which had been pitched up on the last three words, and went on. "Until that time I had boated only small fish, the kind that come like obedient dogs when you pull on the line. I would be happy to take you out, Sir James, as soon as we are no longer under siege.''

"Thank you, Sir Mortimor," said Jim, "but we'll have to see about that when the time comes. Brian, you remember we must be about our business, and you have been some time on Cyprus, already.''

"Surely, you could spare a few more days," said Sir Mortimor. "We deserve a certain amount of rest and enjoyment once these intruders are gone in any case. Tell me, Sir James—I honor your resolve not to sell the use of your magic, but surely if a magician should so choose, I should assume there would be a good deal of wealth to be gained by it? I have thought from time to time how useful it might be if I could work some magic myself; but I never had time to sit down and learn it. I imagine it takes a couple of weeks or more to really master a spell? But, on the other hand, once you have mastered it, I imagine it is no more than snapping your fingers; and then all things obey you?''

"Not exactly," said Jim, thinking of his hard work and the small progress in magic it had won him during the last several years, even with the help of Carolinus. "It's a little more difficult than just learning a spell.''

"Say you so!" Sir Mortimor looked at him thoughtfully. "Not the sort of thing a gentleman could pick up, to an extent at least, in a few months? I must tell you, sir, that I am reckoned to be very fast with my hands. I have small tricks with which I have amused company before now, in which things seem to appear or disappear—like magic, but tricks only, of course—and my friends have often said that I might easily make myself a famous magician with a bit of effort. But you think it would require more than, say, a year or so of work—when I had the time?''

"I'm sure it would," said Jim firmly.

"Ah, well," said Sir Mortimor, but the polite belief he tried to put into his words rang false on Jim's ear.

"How many years does it take to make a knight, Sir Mortimor?" asked Jim.

"Eh?" said Sir Mortimor. "But you must already know that. A lifetime, from boyhood upward of course.''

"That is why a magician must live much longer than any knight," said Jim. "Because it takes a lifetime for him, also, to make him a full master of his craft.''

Sir Mortimor stared back at him, puzzled. Slowly, Jim saw understanding begin to dawn as the little frown line between his eyebrows erased, and something of a flush colored his face. But before he could say anything in answer, Beaupré was again at his elbow.

"Forgive me, m'lord," said Beaupré in the same unvarying voice. "But I have had the carpenter from the village listening at the escape panel in the front door; and he says that they are now pounding stakes in somewhere partway down the steps; and in addition they are building something, or some things, in the houses of the village. He swears he can hear his long-saw at work; and he begs permission to go out and listen more closely to what is going on.''

"He is the only master carpenter we have," said Sir Mortimor irritably. "Is there not someone else who could go out and listen and be more easily spared if he did not come back?"

"I can send a man with good ears, who has some knowledge of the sounds in a carpenter shop, m'lord," said Beaupré.

"Then take care of it, Beaupré," said Sir Mortimor. "Take care of it yourself; and stop bothering me about minor matters like this."

The servant whom Sir Mortimor had called for some moments before to refill their mazers was now doing so. Beaupré went downstairs and Sir Mortimor soothed his nerves with some of the newly poured wine.

"Well, gentlemen," he said, "perhaps we shall have some peace now. It is a misfortune that you cannot indulge in play with the dice, Sir James; since I hesitate to suggest to Sir Brian that we pass a little of our time now in that sport, so that we may the more quietly go to sleep when we retire. I know not what else I can suggest by way of amusement; but it would be ill-mannered of us to play while you merely sat idle."

"Not at all," said Jim. "I enjoy watching. It is the next best thing to being able to play myself. The two of you go ahead. I'll just sit here and enjoy myself."

"Well then," said Sir Mortimor, looking at Brian. "What do you say to a short bout, sir? As it falls out, I still have my dice in my purse here, along with my winnings of the last time we played. I had meant to set both away, but failed to get around to it."

"All the better," said Brian. "On my part, I happen to have a fair amount of my money with me; so that there need be no interrupting to fetch it from the room Sir James and I share."

He reached into the broad purse attached to his belt and brought out a heavy handful of moutons d'or, broad French pieces in gold, that brought a gleam to Sir Mortimor's face, although it was gone almost as quickly as it appeared. In his turn he brought up a handful of coins almost as large, but they were all in silver, with some lesser silver and brass change mixed with them.

"Shall we say ten silver to one gold?" he said to Sir Brian.

"Willingly," answered Brian.

The dicing began; and to Jim's surprise, Brian began to win immediately. In fact, he won the first four bouts before he had his first loss, and then he won three more. Both he and Sir Mortimor were becoming caught up in the game. Their eyes followed the dice with an avid eagerness, concentrating on the dancing cubes alone to the point where Jim began to feel he was next to invisible.

He also found that he was blaming himself for not having made plans for watching a dice game that might show him if Sir Mortimor cheated. He had made a mental note to find a way to use magic to test the matter; but he had not gone beyond that point.

Also, it was awkward that Brian was continuing to win, an average of something like three bouts out of five; and Sir Mortimor's silver was swiftly moving to Brian's side of the table. Letting Brian win could simply be a clever move on Sir Mortimor's part to allay suspicion, particularly since he had come to realize that Jim had considerable magical powers which might make any cheating dangerous.

Sir Mortimor could simply be cheating against himself, to let Brian win; or he could be playing honestly at the moment; and Brian was having a legitimate run of luck.

It could even be that Jim's suspicions were unfounded.

The whole business of Brian winning in Episcopi and losing here might have been the result of honest play after all, with Brian having a run of luck in Episcopi and Sir Mortimor having his here. If it had all been honest, then Brian's only hope was to get lucky again.

The dicing went on. For a little time, luck seemed to flow against Brian after all; but this did not last. After a short run in which he lost, he began to win again and continued. They were approaching a point of decisions, since the money Sir Mortimor had on the table was now down to a few pieces. He would soon either have to call an end to dice-play for the evening or go to wherever in the castle his wealth was stored, and bring back a fresh supply of coins.

"Well, well," said Sir Mortimor, pushing his last few coins together. "The dice have not been my friend this evening. Heigh-ho, but so it goes. At any rate, we have gotten away from our present problems and mayhap we will all sleep well. We should probably call it quits for the moment, Sir Brian."

"I feel distressed, sir," said Brian. "It seems less than gentlemanly of me to stop without giving you a chance to win back what you have lost just now. If you are weary, yourself, I would not keep you from your rest. But I assure you—"

"Oh," said Sir Mortimor, "I spoke only out of courtesy. Myself, I am not sleepy at all; and, in fact, I would be up and around in the castle for the rest of the night from time to time, anyway. If you wish, I will be glad to dice on. I own, I would not be loath to win back what you just took from me. Give me but a few moments to fetch more coin, so that we can play like gentlemen with the worth of our wagers openly upon the table—''

"By all means!" cried Brian, determinedly ignoring Jim's attempts to signal him that quitting now would be a good idea. "I will be happy to wait. So, I'm sure, will be Sir James."

"Then I shall be right back," said Sir Mortimor.

"Brian," said Jim, in a low voice, after the tall knight had gone, "you really should have stopped. Even this much ahead must have recouped you for at least part of your losses."

"It does, of course," said Brian. "But, James, it is unthinkable that I should not give the man the chance to have his revenge. It is as unthinkable as if I was in a tourney, and the saddle girth of he who is to ride against me broke before we had even a chance to cross lances. I were no gentleman at all, then, if I did not lift my lance point in the air, rein in my horse, and ride back to my end of the list, to wait until he could be resaddled and ready to come again with full force."

"Well, now," said Sir Mortimor, sitting down at the table with them once more. "Since you offered to wager tonight with gold, Sir Brian, I thought it only fair to match your coins with those of the same metal."

He poured from his wallet a double handful of English rose nobles, such as Brian had won at the Christmas tournament a few months before. Almost undoubtedly, thought Jim, they had been Brian's. But now the value of the money at play on both sides was considerable.

The dicing began again. At first, Brian continued to win. Then the tide turned against him for a short time before he began to win again. But his second session of winning with the rose nobles on the table was shorter than the one before, and very soon the play settled down to an exchange that seesawed back and forth, first in one man's favor, then the other, but gradually—and, Jim noticed, steadily—Brian's pile of coins began to diminish, and Sir Mortimor's to grow.

Both men were deep in the game, oblivious to anything outside it; and Jim found himself being drawn into each pass of the dice with the same sort of tension. He was growing more and more certain that somehow Sir Mortimor was controlling the fall of the dice, one way or another. But, though he stared carefully at the way Sir Mortimor threw the cubes, he could see nothing strange about either the throws, or the dice themselves, when Sir Mortimor won; nothing different in them from the times Brian won.

Still, his feeling that Sir Mortimor was controlling the game somehow continued to grow from a suspicion to a near-certainty. There was something artificial about the rhythm of the way the winning went back and forth, with Brian regaining the lead for a moment, only to lose it again, and then to lose more deeply than Sir Mortimor had lost the time before.

Jim wished he knew more about cheating and gambling in general. All he could remember were little tags of information floating around in his memory.

Two things only floated to the surface of his mind from among these tags. One was something he was almost sure he had read in a story, rather than in knowledgeable nonfiction: a reference to some gambler putting the "happy hop" on dice when he threw them. The other was something else that he was more sure he had read; something about the edges of dice being shaved, so that when set rolling they always ended with certain sides upward.

But if his memory was not playing tricks on him, and Sir Mortimor's dice were shaved, Brian would also be winning with them every time he used them.

That is, unless there actually was something like a "happy hop"—but it could only be put on shaved dice by an experienced player with them . . . some special way of throwing . . .

However, the idea of the skill involved to make such dice work for Sir Mortimor and not for Brian rang a little far-fetched to Jim's mind. His mind, hunting for an answer, stumbled over a very obvious one. Sir Mortimor could have more than one set of dice. He could be throwing one set himself and making sure that Brian threw the other.

But this sounded almost as unbelievable as the idea of the "happy hop." Jim frowned internally. If Sir Mortimor was switching the sets of dice, he had to do it before their very eyes, without the exchange being noticeable—and that was impossible.

Or was it?

Something was tickling that memory of his again, someone, perhaps some fictional detective had said it—when all reasonable answers fail, and only one unreasonable possibility is left, then the unreasonable possibility is possible—or words to that effect. The thing to do here was to simply start from the assumption that Sir Mortimor was somehow switching two pairs of dice back and forth, and try to figure out how he was doing it.

Jim had never diced in his life, even back in the twentieth century. He was one of those unusual people who get bored by gambling, with anything less than his own life as a stake. Whatever pattern of play Sir Mortimor and Brian were using with their two cubes at a time, it was a game that involved the one who was winning holding on to the dice and calling for a certain number, and then throwing the dice a certain number of times to achieve what he had called for.

If he did so within the number of throws allowed him, he won; if he did not, he lost. If he lost, then the dice changed hands and the other player had his chance to throw, name a number and try to achieve it within the same certain number of throws.

Jim concentrated on Sir Mortimor's hands. They were very long hands, longer even than they were large; and he had not been exaggerating when he said that they were unusually quick. He would shake the dice in his fist and then release them just above the table top with his hand palm down and his fingers flicking out to start them rolling. The minute the dice had flown, his fingers curled back toward his palm almost reflexively—not into a tight fist but one almost so.

He was able to throw these dice with either hand. In fact, Jim decided, the man must be ambidextrous, because he handled the dice equally well with both hands; and both hands released dice with the same palm-down, finger-flicking motion.

Brian, by contrast, shook his dice with his fist in the same position in which he would have pounded a table, little finger bottommost; and then turned his hand palm down only slightly, to let the dice out.

By contrast, there was something unusually skillful about the way Sir Mortimor released the little white cubes from his hand. It had the flowing sort of perfection about it that Brian showed in his use of weapons—a movement that seemed to have been stripped down to its absolute essentials, and become almost a single, graceful, unthinking action. Brian's handling of the dice was nowhere nearly as graceful. He threw the dice, in fact, about the way Jim assumed that he himself would have thrown them.

The one thing in particular that riveted Jim's attention was the fact that Sir Mortimor's release and recapture of the dice, out of his hand and back again, was so swift as to make the movement of his fingers almost a blur before Jim's eyes. A suspicion crept into Jim's mind. It could be that speed was intentional, to hide something. If so, here was something where even a small amount of magic could help him investigate.

He visualized his eyes as lenses of a camera capable of high-speed recording, so that it could play back Sir Mortimor's throw in slow motion.

He concentrated on Sir Mortimor's release of the dice, then mentally reran it inside his own head. In his visualization, he saw the hand move out over the table, only the back of the hand and the knuckles visible; then they opened, with the thumb dropping away from the other fingers and the other fingers beginning to uncurl outward.

Now, for the first time in this slow-motion version, he saw that they did not open up all the way, and no dice came out from them. Instead, the two dice were held by the top joints only of the four fingers that had enclosed them; and now that he saw the whole image instead of concentrating on Sir Mortimor's one active hand, he caught sight of another pair of dice that dropped from the under part of Sir Mortimor's other sleeve, hidden beneath his outstretched wrist and hand; and it was these dice that rattled and rolled on the table top a moment later, for Brian to pick up and use.

In the same instant the fingers that held the unreleased dice closed back toward his wrist; and as Jim watched, the original dice they held, thrown by the quick action of the fingertips, flicked back up into the sleeve behind them.

Brian's hand went forward to the dice. This had been Sir Mortimor's last attempt to throw the winning point. Brian picked up, shook and threw the second pair of dice.

Jim put the visualization out of his mind, and concentrated once more on what was going on at the table.

Brian rolled the dice he had picked up, got a five showing on one and a two on the other, tried to match this point of seven and failed. Sir Mortimor swiftly scooped up the dice; and Jim, watching—even without the need for magic slow motion now—noticed that Sir Mortimor gathered them in with his other hand and flicked them back into the empty sleeve they had left only seconds before. At the same time, Jim saw the original dice, hidden from Brian by the palm-down position, drop secretly into Sir Mortimor's other hand.

Sir Mortimor shook the dice with both hands like a boxer congratulating himself. Then with his right hand again, he threw and made a point of eight; which, three throws later, he matched to win his point and another of Brian's rose nobles. The second set of dice would be the ones shaved to win—the first set shaved to lose. Sir Mortimor was controlling Brian's winning or losing by choosing which dice Brian used.

Well, Jim told himself with satisfaction, that explained how Sir Mortimor was able to win at will with the dice. Finding that out had been the hard part. Now it was simply a matter of using his magic to cure the situation so that Brian had his money back—and that should be the easy part.

No it won't, said Carolinus's voice in his head.

CHAPTER 12

Jim suddenly found himself standing, completely transparent, and looking down at his own body still sitting at the table with the equally solid bodies of Brian and Sir Mortimor. Carolinus, also wraithlike and transparent, was standing facing him; while the two very solid players were continuing to dice on, oblivious to the pair of wraiths standing beside their table.

Haven't you forgotten a couple of things, Jim? said Carolinus. *To begin with, are you sure it'd be a proper use of magickal energy to change or perhaps reverse the outcome of this dicing going on between Brian and Sir Mortimor? Remember, our great Science and Art is a defensive one; and its powers are never to be used aggressively. How sure are you that in getting Brian his money back, you wouldn't be taking it improperly from Sir Mortimor—in effect, robbing him?*

Why, he got it by cheating, Jim thought back.

The right or wrong of what humans do isn't the concern of the Accounting Office and the magickal energy that has been helping the human race this far upward on its way to Civilization, replied Carolinus. *If magick is to be put solely to that purpose, then all magickians would have their hands full just righting the wrongs in their immediate vicinity; instead of working at those things that move humanity toward a better understanding of the world and themselves. Of necessity, the Art of Magick must be apart from individual matters of right or wrong—except as those concern either the magickian himself, or those under his protection.*

And Brian isn't under your protection, is that it? said Jim.

He is not, said Carolinus.

And he's not under mine, either? demanded Jim.

Is he? said Carolinus. *That's a question you have to answer for yourself, Jim. If he's under your protection, then to what extent is he under your protection—in all things? Or just in the present instance?*

You mean I have to choose now the extent to which he's under my protection? said Jim. *And I'll be forever stuck with what I said at this moment?*

Not at all, said Carolinus. *You can amend your position in that regard at any point and as many times as you want to. But you're going to have to be careful at every decision point how far you may be stepping outside the essentially defensive nature of magick.*

Jim glared at him.

And you talked about there being a couple of things, he said. *What's the other?*

It's a simple point, but a telling one, said Carolinus. *Have you considered Sir Brian's personal code of honor?*

Jim felt as if he had just been punched in the stomach. This second question was worse than the first. If he were to magically alter the situation so that Sir Mortimor lost back to Brian everything that he had taken from him, how would Brian react if he knew Jim had arranged it?

The answer was all too obvious. Brian would be deeply—maybe critically—offended. Offended and angry. In Brian's personal code, a knight did not take an unfair advantage; not even to get his money back from one who had gotten it unfairly. Brian would insist on giving back to Sir Mortimor all that Jim had magically won back for him. Then, and only then, if he had been thoroughly convinced that Sir Mortimor had been cheating, he would undoubtedly accuse the other knight in plain terms and fight him to the death.

But the money would still have been with Sir Mortimor, if and when it was Sir Mortimor who died. Brian would not have taken it back even from the dead body. But his friendship with Jim almost undoubtedly would be severed—possibly for life.

The answer—the only answer—was one Jim would have given anything not to face. It was that he could only straighten things out here at the expense of leaving Brian, as well as Sir Mortimor, in complete ignorance of how the money had come back. Unless, that was, he could think up some excuse to explain matters to Brian afterwards; hopefully, at some distance in time, after it was too late for Brian to do anything about Sir Mortimor. Perhaps by that time he could come up with some way of explaining it to Brian that would make it all right.

Damn it, Carolinus! said Jim. *This is a gray area! A situation where the directives you talk about point in two exactly opposite ways. If I help Brian, then I'll be harming him.*

Yes, said Carolinus, *unfortunately, this is the sort of problem you bump into and have to make a decision on when you get into Advanced Magick. Here's a place where I can't help you, of course. This is something of a bittersweet moment for me, Jim. It's not unlike that of a parent watching a child growing up, to the point where the child has to use his or her own judgment; and the parent must stand aside. You've reached the stage of Discretion, Jim. It's been approaching you for some time, though you may not have read the shadow it cast before it.*

I don't know what you mean by its shadow, said Jim.

Come now, answered Carolinus, *of course you do. For some time now you've been thinking that I was ignoring you more than you'd like; and not always explaining things fully to you—even thinking that I was possibly lying to you at times. It's true that in some cases I've had to tell you only part of the truth. When at last you're fully fledged as a Master Magickian—if you ever reach that day—you'll understand. In any case, none of this alters the fact that right now you have a decision to make that you must make by yourself. I can watch; but I can't help.*

Carolinus disappeared; and an instant later Jim was back in his own body, his solid body sitting at the table, watching Sir Mortimor still taking coins away from Brian in bout after bout.

Jim's mind felt torn this way and that; and then suddenly everything fell into a simple, clear choice between two alternatives. One was keeping the relationship he valued highest—aside from what he had with Angie— a relationship with Brian that had to a large extent made his existence in this fourteenth-century world not merely bearable but possible. The other was that he could risk losing that friendship, but see Brian with a chance that might never come again—to find Geronde's father at last and marry Geronde—the chance for those two to end up married, as they had wished to be for so long.

There was no comparison between the two choices. The first was an entirely personal, selfish one on Jim's part. The other was something that could better the whole lifetime of the two closest friends he and Angie had.

The hell with it! thought Jim. *That money belongs to Brian; and Brian's going to have it.*

He had expected to have to hunt and search for the ideal magic to do it; but it presented itself to him, almost as if it had been in waiting there in the back of his mind. He half closed his eyes and visualized the two sets of dice in Sir Mortimor's possession. Magically, he would cause them to trade places under certain specific conditions. Whenever Sir Mortimor turned the dice over to Brian, it would be the winning dice that Brian picked up, and whenever Brian turned over the dice to Sir Mortimor, they would become the losing dice again.

Sitting, he watched the luck at the table change. Brian won, and won, and won . . . until Jim suddenly woke up to the fact that his run of luck had been unnaturally long. Hastily he amended his magic command, so that he could cause the changing of the dice to be such that Brian would lose when Jim decided he should, and Sir Mortimor would win until Jim decided to change the dice he was throwing back to the losing pair.

To begin with, he allowed Sir Mortimor to win back quite a fair amount of what he had lost. The tall knight had begun to look very darkly indeed at the way things were going at the table. But now his face cleared up. Jim altered things back so that Brian won again and after a short bout of winning that just about matched what Sir Mortimor had won back, Jim had him lose and Sir Mortimor begin to win again.

But only briefly so. Controlling the game silently as he sat there, Jim gradually continued to shift the balance of winnings over to Brian's side. It continued until there were no coins left on Sir Mortimor's side of the table.

"By all the Saints!" said the tall knight, getting to his feet. He was not exactly scowling, but he was not far from it. "Luck seems to have deserted me, sir. If you will wait while I fetch more coins to wager with—"

"By all means," said Brian. "By all means, Sir Mortimor. But—much as I enjoy winning, it pains me to see you losing so steadily. If you would wish to take your revenge at a later time . . ."

"Hell, no!" said Sir Mortimor.

"Then, sir," said Brian, "I'll be glad to wait until you return with fresh funds."

Sir Mortimor stalked over to the staircase and disappeared down it.

"James!" said Brian in a delighted whisper, turning to him. "Did you ever see the like? Why, I have recouped more than half of all I have lost to him, already. May Heaven be with me for a while longer; and if I once come out of this with anything like the weight of purse I had to begin, I take my oath never to touch dice again until I am once more safely back in England."

"That would be a wise decision, all right, Brian," said Jim. His voice stuck in his throat a little. "I'm delighted you're winning."

"I give you leave to be so delighted!" said Sir Brian. "It is the most perfect thing!"

He sat back, waiting and silent. Jim waited with him in equal silence; and it was not long before Sir Mortimor's steps were heard on the staircase again and he emerged onto the floor to stride over and sit down in his place at the table.

This time, what he dumped on the table was a combination of rose nobles and moutons d'or. A much greater stake than he had placed on the table before.

Jim remembered hearing someplace that seasoned gamblers, as long as they knew the odds were at all even for them, believed that the trick was to keep on gambling, because sooner or later the tide of good fortune would begin to flow in their direction.

Looking at Sir Mortimor now, particularly with eyes remarkably clear since he had made his hard decision, Jim thought he saw in the man a clear case of the fever of addictive gambling, such as he had suspected from time to time in the case of Brian. However baffled Sir Mortimor might be that his tricks with the dice were not working, Sir Mortimor had clearly set that problem aside now, and was thinking of only one thing—dicing until he won.

The pressure at the table seemed to have gone up a hundredfold; and the tension between the two men was such that Jim had the feeling that if he put out his hand he would feel it stretched between them like a tightwire.

There were emotions at work here that could explode into violence all too easily. But in spite of that, Jim had made up his mind. He shifted the winning once more back into Brian's hands.

The pile of gold in front of Sir Mortimor continued to melt, with small reversals now and then; and gradually, as it dwindled, his jaw tightened, his face darkened and his tall body settled into a crouch like that of a leopard about to pounce. All resemblance to the scholarly, elderly man Jim thought he had seen at first glance was lost and he was pure warrior.

But now Beaupré was at Sir Mortimor's elbow again.

Sir Mortimor ignored him.

"M'lord," said Beaupré, at last.

"Go!" said Sir Mortimor, without looking up from the table.

"M'lord," said Beaupré, "the carpenter and one other man I sent out have come back. The Moroccans are building somewhat in front of our door that goes level back some little distance; but is supported on the hillside some ways down. They have made remarkable progress with it in the darkness; and it may be finished before first light."

"What of it?" muttered Sir Mortimor, watching the dice rattle from Brian's fist. "As soon as there's light we will burn it."

"They have covered the wood they build with goat hides. So many it is thought they must have carried some here in their ship as they came. With that protection, what they build will not burn easily."

"I told you to leave," growled Sir Mortimor.

"M'lord," said Beaupré, "something must be done."

"See to it then, Beaupré," said Sir Mortimor.

"M'lord—"

"*See to it, Beaupré!*"

There was a moment's pause.

"Yes, m'lord," said Beaupré, turning away. He went down the stairs out of sight. The game went on with hardly a word from either of the players. Only the sound of their breathing could be heard, the rattle of the dice and the scrape of the money being pushed out as a wager, or raked in as winnings. Jim found his eyelids beginning to feel heavy. It seemed they had been at this for hours now; and he gave in a little to the temptation to let Brian's winning stretches be longer ones, and Sir Mortimor's shorter.

Sir Mortimor's face grew darker still as his supply of money dwindled; darker and more dangerous-looking. As the dice went over to Brian for yet another time, he had reached a point where Jim found his tendency toward sleepiness suddenly evaporating. Sir Mortimor was watching each movement of the dice like a wild animal about to pounce, and the tension at the table had grown to the point where the very air about them seemed to quiver with it.

Jim looked from Sir Mortimor to Brian. His friend may have been innocent in some ways, but he was not lacking perception when danger was in the air. Brian's face also was showing a change. It was not in him to show the kind of dark threat that Sir Mortimor was showing; but in his own way he was displaying a matching readiness to violence. His face seemed to have sharpened, the skin drawn tighter over cheek bones and jaw; his blue eyes appeared smaller and sharper, and their gaze was unwavering on the man sitting opposite him and on the dice.

A sudden temptation seized Jim to have Brian lose and let the dice move back to Sir Mortimor before an explosion could occur, but he hated to make Brian's winning stretch so short, when indeed he had given Sir Mortimor quite a stretch of wins; and the plan should have been at this point for Brian to match that with an even greater amount of wins.

As a result, he let Brian go on winning. The gold moved from Sir Mortimor's side of the table to Brian's.

At last, Jim let the dice go over to Sir Mortimor, on a loss from Brian. The tall knight snatched them up and stared at them closely.

"Why, these dice are cracked!" he said, jerking to his feet. "It were a shame on me that I offered such dice to a guest to play with. I will be back in a moment with another pair."

He turned on his heel and in a second he had reached the staircase and disappeared down it. Brian stared at the empty opening through which the other had disappeared.

"That was not done as a gentleman should," said Brian in a quiet but steely voice, staring at the opening around the staircase where Sir Mortimor had disappeared. "I would be in my rights if I should say that in taking away the dice he took away my luck. But though he may lack manners, I do not. Nonetheless, I will remember this."

"Brian—" began Jim.

Brian turned and looked at him, with the same implacable gaze with which he had been staring after the missing Sir Mortimor. Then his face relaxed.

"Do not concern yourself, James," he said. "If necessary, I will tell our host that I do not care to play any longer; and since I have not even yet won back all I have lost to him over the last week or so—though I am close to that amount, indeed—he can hardly object—"

He broke off at the sound of feet on the staircase, and Sir Mortimor was back with them.

He dropped into his seat and spilled from his hand a clean, white pair of dice on the table.

"These are new, and I warrant them sound," he said carelessly. He gathered them into his long hand again, shook them in his usual fashion and spilled them on the table. Jim made sure that he won.

Sir Mortimor smiled. He threw again and matched his point, taking in the wager that Brian had already pushed forward. The dice were still with him, and he threw again for three more bouts, winning.

His smile came back.

"Strange that I did not notice that crack before," he said. "A gentleman should be able to be aware of such things—"

He broke off abruptly, because Jim had just arranged for him to lose again. He stared at the two dice on the table and their uppermost surfaces as if he could not believe his eyes.

Brian reached for the dice.

"Hold—" said Sir Mortimor—and Brian's hand stopped before it touched them. Brian's eyes slowly lifted from the dice until they looked directly into the eyes of Sir Mortimor, and a wild bell of alarm sounded in Jim's mind. All he could think of at the moment was that neither man was wearing a sword. But they both had their poignards at their belts, since no one walked around without at least one edged weapon.

"I smell smoke!" cried Jim hastily—it had been the first thing he could think of, since Sir Mortimor with that one word had already crossed the border of acceptable politeness; but now that the words were out of his mouth it came to him that indeed he did smell smoke. He had been smelling smoke for some little time, and paying no conscious attention to it, as obviously neither had the other two men.

A smell of smoke where there should be none, in a castle, meant fire; and fire was something universally feared by those who lived within such stone walls.

These same thick barriers that enclosed them and protected them could make it almost impossible to come close to and successfully put out a fire once it was started inside the castle structure; so that, unstopped, it crept from room to room, while smoke was building up from it, and herding those in the castle that were alive farther and farther back from the flames they needed to come to grips with.

In the end it became an unstoppable enemy. The only escape from it was to leave the castle; and to leave this castle right now meant only one end for those within it.

Both other men lifted their heads and sniffed the air, and the sudden change in their faces signaled their recognition of the danger.

"Forgive me, Sir Brian," said Sir Mortimor swiftly, seizing on the opportunity for the one excuse that could take any possible danger out of the word he had just uttered. "I had indeed just smelled the smoke myself. *Beaupré!*"

Beaupré appeared even as the word rang on the air. Clearly he had already been on his way to them.

"M'lord," he said to Sir Mortimor, "they have built their shelter right against the outer door, and in their shelter, had burning coals against the bottom of it for some time now, without our realizing. The lower part of the door is almost eaten through by fire. The carpenter believes that they have made a flat platform on which men can also swing a battering ram. They are just beginning to hammer now."

"Five more men here! Ho!" Sir Mortimor ordered the empty air.

It struck Jim, rather ridiculously, that Sir Mortimor was the equivalent of his own PA system. All he had to do was speak with a raised voice and anyone in the castle would hear and obey. He had not specified where "here" was. It was obviously up to the five men he wanted to know where Sir Mortimor was calling from.

A second thought suggested to Jim's mind that there was no real trick in that, either. He had no doubt that when he and Angie were at home in Malencontri, every servant then in the castle would know where either of them was at any moment. It was part of their business to know; and the word of any shift of either their Lord or Lady from one place to another was transferred immediately throughout all the body of those who worked in the castle, as if by telepathy.

The five men appeared, one of them carrying a bow and with a quiver of arrows slung at his belt.

"You," said Sir Mortimor, pointing at the bowman, "to the roof. Have them empty the oil that's in the kettle up there and fill it instead with water. Get men to help you and slide it forward on its rails so that it will pour out over the walls down before the door. Keep the oil that's taken out in buckets handy to be put back in, however. Go!"

The bowman ran off and up the stairway.

"You other four and Beaupré gather everyone in the castle who can fight. Join me in the large room behind the inner entrance door on the first floor. These gentlemen and I will be down as soon as possible. Beaupré, I must be fully armed, and these gentlemen will need help arming too. See to it!"

"By your leave, sir," said Brian coldly. "Sir James and I can armor each other."

"Good," said Sir Mortimor with no hesitation. "I will meet you down on the ground floor there."

He strode off to the stairs and disappeared down them, followed by Beaupré and the remaining four men. Jim and Brian went after them.

"I think that smoke is coming in through the arrow slits and windows," remarked Jim, as he and Brian were helping each other to buckle on armor and fasten sword belts.

"Most like," grunted Brian. He paused and looked Jim frankly in the face. "I own I am happy at the prospect of action. It was becoming other than pleasant, there at the table."

"You've got the money you've won back?" Jim asked.

"As much as I won tonight," said Brian. "I am still lacking somewhat of what Sir Mortimor won originally; but he is welcome to it. I would rather not dice with him again."

"But you'll fight alongside him," said Jim, as they began to leave the room.

"I have eaten his food and drunk his wine. What else can I do?" said Brian. "Also"—he added, looking over his shoulder at Jim—"if those outside get in, we all die. We fight for our own lives, you and I. That Sir Mortimor does the same thing beside us is of less import."

CHAPTER 13

However, as Brian said these words, he did not look to Jim as if he was facing a fight for his life. The expression on his face was more the happy excitement of someone going to a picnic.

It was characteristic of Brian to look like this before any action. Jim had seen it before; and curiously, in this strange place, under these strange conditions, it made him feel better. They finished helping each other put on their armor and weapons and left their room to go down to the ground floor.

Jim had not paid close attention to the ground floor when he entered the castle, since his escorts had hurried him up the stairs to Sir Mortimor and Brian. Now he saw that it was mostly taken up with a large open space, one end of which had been divided with wooden partitions some five feet high, as stalls for horses, so that these could be brought inside if necessary; though Jim found it hard to imagine what kind of horse could climb the switchback road up to the steps leading to the castle's front door—let alone up the steps itself.

Right now, however, these stalls were filled with villagers. All the rest of the space was taken up by what looked like a hundred or more armed men, packed as tightly as sardines; and all, to Jim, looking rather pale, caught between the ominous figure of their Lord, towering over them, and the ominous knowledge of the enemy outside who was burning a route into the castle.

"Sir James! Sir Brian!" roared Sir Mortimor, as he saw Brian and Jim coming down the stairway. He broke off what he had been saying, pushed his way to the stairs and took three double-step strides up to meet them before they reached the floor.

"It is good to see you two gentlemen!" said Sir Mortimor, his voice ringing off the walls. "Particularly at this moment when the enemy is becoming troublesome. There could be no two chevaliers I would rather have with me at this moment than the famous Dragon Knight, victor over ogres and evil men alike, and Sir Brian, well known as the best lance in England!''

The statement was obviously for public consumption; and it was not without effect. Jim saw some of the paleness begin to disappear from the up-staring faces below them, and less of an atmosphere of panic seemed to pervade the area.

"A word with you gentlemen privily, first," barked Sir Mortimor, pushing past them and beckoning them to follow him back up to the floor above. Once out of the sight and hearing of those beneath them, he lowered his voice to a murmur that could not possibly be heard below.

"You are a Godsend at this time, sirs," he said in that low voice. His face and manner had completely changed. It was as if the dice game had never been and money was of no importance. In fact, though Jim found it hard to believe, there was something of the same happy excitement about Sir Mortimor that Jim had just seen, and was used to seeing, in Brian.

"Here is the situation," went on Sir Mortimor. "My men are good fighters—none better—but like all such common cattle, an unfamiliar situation takes the heart out of them. They become little more than sheep. They know how much those outside outnumber us; and now this business of burning through the outer door has made them feel helpless—with no hope but to wait to be slaughtered when the enemy finally breaks in. But they will rouse themselves and do what needs to be done—and indeed there is a great deal more that can be done and no certainty that this castle will be taken after all. But first, let me ask you again, Sir James. Would you be willing, for any way at all by which I may recompense you, to use your magic to help in the defense here?"

"As I said, I'm afraid not," said Jim. "I regret having to continue to answer you that way, Sir Mortimor; but I've got duties and obligations."

"I fully understand, Sir James," said Sir Mortimor. "In fact, I had not really hoped for that help from you. The aid you give simply by fighting with us is all but magic in itself. No doubt you felt the difference down below, the minute I announced my pleasure in your presence. They already knew who you were, of course, but I think they had not fully realized what paladins you are; and knowing that has enheartened them greatly."

"We will hope to live up to your expectations, sir," said Brian.

"I had no doubt you would in any case, sir," said Sir Mortimor. "Now, as to the situation. Let me give it to you in as few words as possible. Beaupré has privily assured me that they have made a roof over the fire they have built against my door, so although we will be pouring water from the roof even now, there is little chance the fire can be dealt with that way. Also, this roof is covered with fresh animal hides, which would resist even burning oil—though it would be hardly sensible to pour oil of any heat upon already burning fuel.''

"This," Brian said, "we have heard Beaupré tell you."

"Yes," said Sir Mortimor. "The fire must be gotten rid of, however; and it is my intent to make a rush from the inside, by weight of men and bodies, unbarring the burning door and attempting to push it open. It may be the attackers have gone to some trouble to make sure that it cannot be pushed open; but if it can, that very opening will sweep the fire aside. So men can rush out and hold any attack at bay while some inside douse the fire with water; after which we retreat once more within the castle. The door is weakened, true. But if the fire were out, and no easy opportunity to light it again for an hour or so, it could be greatly strengthened from inside by our carpenter using wood that is already in the castle here in the shape of doors and furniture. This is my plan and I intend to use it; but I would welcome any advice from either of you."

He paused. Jim could think of nothing to say, but Brian spoke again.

"I have offered to lead a sally through your private escape way," he said. "May I offer to do it, once again. It seems to me that the best way of dealing with this structure outside, let alone the fire at the door, is to attack whoever is out there unexpectedly from outside, and not only free the burning matter from the door itself, but put to flame all the rest of what they have built, with fire from the inside. A relatively small force of men, moving fast, could do that, sir, and I would be honored to lead them!"

Sir Mortimor looked at him and slowly shook his head.

"We are not in that desperate a pass yet, Sir Brian," he said. "You must know as well as I do, that such ways as you speak about are the secrets of the lord of the castle only; and not to be easily shared with others. If need be, I will share it with men of honor like yourselves; but any others who go out with you must die before they come back in, to ensure that they do not pass on to others word of this way out of the castle."

Jim winced internally, but Brian seemed to take this in stride. Sir Mortimor went on.

"Once it were known," he said, lowering his voice still more, "there are many here—and not just the villagers—who would want to escape immediately, hoping to get away and hide themselves in the hills. Therefore, as I say, any you took with you must die. I do not know how you would encompass that; and even if you did, it would further reduce the force I have here to resist those who come against us."

"I see no other way," said Brian coldly. "My offer remains open, sir. You may take it up at any time in the future, if the situation here has not changed so as to make it impractical from my standpoint."

"I will keep it in mind," said Sir Mortimor, equally coldly; and for a moment they were back as they had been at the dice table. Then, to Jim's relief, the hardness of both their expressions cleared.

"It remains then," said Sir Mortimor, "to attempt what I had in mind, forcing the burning door from the inside. We will proceed with that."

"If you wish, then," said Brian, "I will be glad to lead the charge on the door."

Sir Mortimor grinned at him. A grim and martial grin.

"Right willingly would I see you do so," he said, "and give you most hearty thanks. But my fellows fight best when they are under my eye and within arm's reach. No one but I can lead the charge on the door. What I would wish of you and Sir James is that you take charge of what I shall call the afterguard, those who stay behind while the rest of us charge."

He glanced at the stairway for a moment.

"Your appearance here, and my naming you to them, has heartened them mightily," he said. "But there may still be some faint hearts among them. If you stand with them, none will dare skulk off, hoping by hiding to at least prolong their lives by a few moments or an hour."

"It is a strange train you have about here, Sir Mortimor," said Brian. "Without offense, Sir Mortimor, I seem to gather that these men of yours are lions one moment and mice the next."

Sir Mortimor shrugged.

"What would you?" he said, still in a low voice. "It is their nature in these parts. They do nearly all things for profit; and if there is no profit, then they think only of their skins. Honor is but a word, except to those who are great men among them—as Sala-ad-Din was during the First Crusade, or Baybars, who won the battle at 'Ayn Jalut."

He turned abruptly and led his way down the stairs. Within moments he had separated out those he wanted to join him in a charge on the outer door, and those who would stay with Brian and Jim.

"Keep the inner door open for us, messires!" he called to Jim and Brian over the heads of those around him, as they clustered facing the opening revealed by that same door right now. He turned to face the open passageway and lifted a long sword in one large hand high over his head. "With me, children!"

He ran forward into the passageway and they ran with him. Jim and Brian, standing near the front of those who were left behind, watched as they swiftly approached the door, which was now smoking visibly around its bottom edge.

"Use your swords!" he shouted at those about him. "Lift the bar that way. It is too hot to handle!"

The foremost men obeyed. The heavy bar was pried upward out of the iron sockets that held it firmly to the stone on either side, and tumbled to the floor.

"Now!" roared Sir Mortimor. "Open it!"

The mice had become lions. Fearlessly, more than half a dozen men threw themselves bodily at the door, which must be even hotter than the thick piece of timber that had been barring it. They fell back, only to have others throw their weight against it, and gradually the door opened with jerks, obviously pushing a considerable load of the burning material piled up against it.

A spear flew through the opening from the other side, and Sir Mortimor's long blade caught it in mid-air, cutting it in half and throwing the parts aside before it could pierce one of the packed bodies behind the knight. Bowmen and slingers at the back of Sir Mortimor's attacking group began to send their missiles in return through the opening, and no more spears came.

Meanwhile, bit by bit, the door was being forced outward, opening an ever larger gap as the fire beyond was pushed aside. Finally, there was room for a man to slip through—and one did, followed by others as swiftly as they could, while the rest shouted in wild triumph and threw themselves even more heavily against the burning door.

Suddenly the door gave all at once, its lower half breaking off, and a couple of men falling directly into the flames beyond. If they screamed, their voices were lost in the general uproar; for immediately the rest of Sir Mortimor's fighters were going out, either through the open gap or over the broken half of the door like hurdlers.

Clearly, there had been only a small party tending the fire and guarding it in the wooden passage that had been built almost up to the door. Those guardians were now suddenly in flight, with Sir Mortimor's men after them like hunting hounds who had already tasted blood.

The men with Jim and Brian stirred, talking, moving toward the passageway, now eager to be in on the fight.

"Hold!" shouted Brian.

They hesitated, then stopped; looking at him, and then quickly looking away again. Clearly they still wanted to rush to join their fellows around Sir Mortimor; but from the way their Lord had talked about these two knights, perhaps that would be imprudent. Brian now had his naked sword in his hand, holding it up over his head in plain sight; Jim drew his and held it up likewise. The two blades shone and the men stood still.

"Messires!" came the voice of Sir Mortimor. "Come forward to me—alone!"

The last word was added as, once more, the fighters around Jim and

Brian began to move toward the passageway. But they stopped at the sound of Sir Mortimor's last word. Brian and Jim went forward alone.

"You see what they have built," said Sir Mortimor, sheathing his sword, as they came up to him. "A fine platform for using a battering ram, if the fire did not work for them, and a roof over all. I wonder that they should build so quickly—but then, they are seamen; and seamen are used to making such things, quickly, on order. Though Beaupré did say that the number of hides they have covering this structure suggests they flayed more goats than they would find in my village alone. What do you think of it, gentlemen?"

Jim and Brian looked about at it. Neither had anything to say. What they saw was simply a long, roofed shed made of wood and heavy cloth, stretching out and backward from the castle door on a level with the top step of the stairway. Its farther end was open; but there was nothing to be seen there but darkness, with stars above, and—far below—some flickering lights among the still-standing structures of the village.

"I will have my men start to tear this down, before those below can get more people up here. We will use the timbers to barricade the front door from the inside," said Sir Mortimor. "Also, we will take away the goat hides, so any future advance on the castle will not be protected from fire. Sir Brian, you offered yourself earlier. Would you go up and take charge of the watch from the top of the tower right now? Sir James, I have nothing to ask you at the moment. Perhaps you will think of something yourself—or you might even wish to join Sir Brian at the top of the tower. I will be up there shortly, as soon as barricading the door is well underway."

"I will be glad to hold the tower," said Brian. "James, will you accompany me?"

"Yes," said Jim thoughtfully, as they turned away from Sir Mortimor, who had already started to turn away himself to give orders for the dismantling of the structure and the scattering of the burning embers of the fire. Jim and Brian went up the stairs, climbing them side by side, in silence. Once they reached the floor that held their own room, they both turned toward it without needing to say anything to each other.

"James," said Brian in a low voice, once they were inside with the door closed, "Sir Mortimor thinks only of holding his castle until these pirates grow tired of attempting it, and sail away. That is not the way to deal with a situation like this. He should be thinking of ways in which he can attack and defeat these who have come against him."

"If you say so, I'll believe you," said Jim. "I've got a lot more faith in you than I have in anyone else where it comes to fighting."

Brian looked embarrassed.

"That is a kind thing to say, James," he said. "I know not if I truly deserve it, considering that Sir Mortimor has had war experience; and I, in any real sense, have not. But I have had experience with castles attacked, and the attacking of castles, and I vow I am right. But it warms me that you should take my word for it so easily."

"It shouldn't," said Jim. "I wouldn't have ventured a guess that way myself; but the way you think sounds better to me than the way Sir Mortimor is obviously thinking. I'll think along the lines you've just mentioned, myself; and tell you if anything comes to me. Is that all right?"

"Nothing could be better, James," said Brian. "Now, shall we go up to the top of the tower?"

"You go ahead," said Jim. "I'm going to try to get hold of Hob, and see if he can't go out and spy over the enemy territory for us. I think if I call him through the fireplace that he's used to us being close to, he'll hear me; even if he's in another chimney. I'll join you at the tower-top as soon as I talk to him."

"Good," said Brian.

He went out.

With his going, the room suddenly seemed unusually empty. Jim looked around himself. It was a small room, not too clean, now lit—but poorly so—by the flames of what was unburnt of the fuel in the iron basket of the cresset on one wall. Beyond the wide arrow slit, or window—whichever it was—the blackness of night still showed. Yet it must be getting on toward dawn. Also, it was cold.

Jim looked at the fireplace. It, like the cresset, had burnt down to the remains of its fuel. There were some pieces of glowing wood; a few of these were putting out feeble flames, but not throwing much in the way of heat—an unthinkable situation in any inhabited room of Malencontri during cold weather. Equally, it was something he had never encountered as a guest in any other castle or ecclesiastical building where he had been a guest.

Happily, some extra wood had been left by it; although it was equally unthinkable that someone of Jim's rank should have to feed the fire in his own fireplace, except in an extreme emergency. Jim thankfully put it all on the embers; and they were hot enough so that the flames licked up freshly.

It would be some time before the cold stone walls warmed up, but the very sight of the fire was warming and he could feel some heat on his face as he leaned down toward the fireplace opening and called into it.

"Hob!" he shouted. "Hob, would you come here, please?"

The words were hardly out of his mouth before Hob's face appeared upside down peering into the room under the top edge of the fireplace opening.

"M'lord!" he said, and popped out into the room, to sit cross-legged on a waft of smoke that seemed to pour endlessly forward from the fire, but vanished completely an inch or so beyond Hob, so that Jim did not even smell smoke.

"I suppose you know what's been going on, Hob," said Jim.

"Oh yes, m'lord," said Hob cheerfully. "I know all about what's been going on here and just about everything else as well."

"I see," said Jim.

"You're looking tired now, m'lord," said Hob, concernedly examining Jim's face. "And you've still got that sad look. I wish you'd let me take you for a ride—"

"I'm sorry," said Jim. "There just isn't time for that now. Look, Hob, I was going to ask you if you could leave the castle and go down and look around the village below, where those men are who're attacking this castle. Do you suppose you could do that—ride the smoke and just sort of listen at the walls and look around and things like that?"

"Oh, I've already done that," said Hob. "There's nothing to it. I go up on smoke here and ride it down there; and then I can go anywhere I want from their fires in their buildings, coming out the smoke holes at the top. They don't really have fireplaces there, m'lord. They've got sort of a hole dug in the earth and they build the fire in that. There's no stone floors there. Just dirt."

"That's excellent," said Jim. "In that case, you can probably tell me what they've been talking about."

"Talking about, m'lord?"

"Yes, I mean generally, the men down there, particularly when they aren't doing anything toward the castle, but are just sitting around by themselves. What do they say to each other and what do they talk about?"

"Oh, all sorts of things," said Hob. "Ships and fish and things to eat and just about everything. Of course, at night like this they talk a lot about demons. It's very scary. I've been very careful when I go out at night, but I haven't seen any demons so far."

"I don't think you will," said Jim. "Anyway, you're dark and almost invisible at night, and riding on some smoke you wouldn't attract attention anyway."

"That's good," said Hob. "The kind of demons they talk the most about are called Djinni—you know, like that dog that was pretending to be one?"

"Why do you say pretending?" asked Jim.

"Well, you remember," said Hob, "when you asked him to prove he was a Djinni, he just turned into a sort of fat man."

"That fat man was a Djinni," said Jim.

Hob was suddenly on Jim's shoulder clutching him tightly around the neck.

"I didn't know," he whispered in Jim's ear. "I thought he was just a dog and lying. He's here, you know."

"Here? In the castle?" asked Jim.

"No, not in the castle—not since he tried to come in and they chased him all over the place and he couldn't find anywhere to hide," said Hob. "He was being a dog then, you know. But is he really a Djinni? Oh, dear!"

"Don't be frightened," said Jim. "He won't hurt you. He wouldn't want to hurt you for fear of offending me."

"Is that true?" Hob's grip on Jim's neck relaxed. "I feel much better, then. Anyway, as I say, he's not in the castle. He's around someplace, probably in the village or near it or something. But those men down there don't seem to know. A demon, right there amongst them. And I never knew it, either."

"He's not a demon," said Jim. "He's a Natural. Like you."

Hob bounced from Jim's shoulder back onto a waft of smoke that appeared unexpectedly about two feet in front of Jim's face.

"He's not like me!" said Hob, staring at him.

"Well, I mean, he's a Natural, as you are. Like you only in that sense," Jim said, "just like trolls, and naiads and sea devils, and all sorts of others are Naturals—as opposed to people like Angie, Brian and me."

"But demons are full of bad magic, the men down there say; and—now that I remember—the dog-Djinni not only changed himself into a fat man, he made that chest with all the colored stones in it appear. The chest you didn't want."

"He has some powers that are like magic," said Jim. "Lots of Naturals do. They'll have a special power or two, or even more, but they don't have a lot of control over them. They can only do certain things—sort of turn them on and off—like the way you ride the smoke. That would seem like magic to anyone who had never heard of hobgoblins."

"Is that magic?" said Hob. "I never thought it was anything special. You mean I could be a demon?"

"No," said Jim. "As I just pointed out, you're a Natural. Naturals aren't demons, and demons aren't Naturals. Demons belong to a different kingdom than Naturals."

"Oh, that's good," said Hob with a deep sigh. "For a terrible moment there I thought I'd have to be afraid of myself."

"Well, there's no need," said Jim. "But this is valuable information, what you tell me about these attackers being afraid of demons. Are they particularly afraid of demons just because they're here?"

"Maybe," said Hob doubtfully. "I know they know there's a great magician in the castle—that's you, m'lord. I don't know how they know, but they do; and they think maybe magicians and demons go together."

"I can assure you," said Jim, "they don't. Different kingdoms, absolutely. But now I think, for the first time, you've given me the beginnings of an idea for doing something about this situation here. Tell me one more thing, Hob. Is there some way you could move smoke from the castle's chimneys into the far end of each of the two boats touching the shore in front of the castle here? I'd like it to look as if there was a fire going on back there in both boats."

"Move smoke?" said Hob. "Oh, certainly. I'd just do the same thing I do when I move the smoke to carry me along."

"Bingo!" said Jim.

CHAPTER 14

"**B**ingo?" echoed Hob, staring at him.

"Never mind," said Jim hastily. "That's just a word that means I'm pleased."

Hob's small round face with its tiny sharp-pointed chin broke into a wide smile.

"I'm happy you're happy," he said. "I'll be glad to move the smoke for you, m'lord. When? Now?"

"You can do it in the daytime?" asked Jim.

"Oh, yes," said Hob. "I'll just bundle the smoke up small, then ride a waft of it high up, so people won't see me take it far out over the water. Then I can come down very low some distance away out to sea and ride the smoke back just above the waves. Then I'll slip into the boats when nobody's looking, bundle the smoke in with me and tell it to rise up the way I want it to. The way *you* want it to, m'lord."

"Thank you, Hob," said Jim. "Now, there's something else to be done first. Will you be where I can get you quickly if I call for you in a fireplace? I've got to go and talk to a couple of people. Then we'll come back here to talk; and you can listen."

"I'll always be right where you can get me, m'lord," said Hob.

Jim left the room and headed for the top of the stairs. He had two others to convince, and the first one was Brian. That should be relatively easy; but the second one was Sir Mortimor. The tall knight should see the advantage of what Jim had in mind, but might have some reason against it that Jim could not now imagine. But that, Jim would have to argue down when he came up against it. Brian was the easier, and the sensible thing would be to talk to Brian first.

Brian did, indeed, turn out to be the easier. He liked Jim's idea, which was in essence a sally by the full force of fighting men under Sir Mortimor's command, just at daylight, when presumably the enemy would still be either half asleep, or just beginning to wake up; and while those who had worked during the night would still be sleeping.

"I've been recommending a sally in any case, as you know—don't see how anything can be done without one," he said. "As for anything else, James, I have complete trust in your wisdom. If you think this will work, then I will ask no further assurance than that."

"Good," said Jim. "Can you leave this tower-top? I'd like you to come along with me to find Sir Mortimor, so I can suggest we talk it over in our room—yours and mine."

"I see no reason why not," said Brian. "Beaupré is just over there. I'll go have a word with him."

He stepped across to the pockmarked man, spoke quietly to him for a moment, and then came back to Jim.

"As I thought, there's no real need for me here, except in an emergency; and any emergency at the top of this tower is most unlikely. I left word with Beaupré. He will send a messenger to Sir Mortimor saying we would be honored if he would meet with us privily in the room he gave us, to talk of matters that should not be noised about. I said we would await his answer or him there."

"Good," said Jim.

They went down the stairs together and back into the room.

By this time the fire in the room's fireplace had been further refreshed with fresh fuel, and the room had a brighter, more lively look to it. There was also a jug of wine and two pewter cups now on the table. There had been time for the small cubicle to warm up slightly; and the whole place had a more comfortable air. It was even pleasant, sitting at the table with Brian and drinking some of the wine. Water had not been provided.

"Well, gentlemen," said Sir Mortimor, sitting down with them less than ten minutes later. "I understand you have something of import to discuss."

He glared at a servant following him, who hastily put another metal cup in front of his lord, and filled it from the wine jug, then ran off with the wine jug, presumably to refill it in no time at all.

"It is a plan of Sir James," said Brian. "He has been so good as to tell me of it; and within the limitations of what I know, I find it most attractive. But let him tell you, himself."

Sir Mortimor nodded; but at that moment the door opened behind him and the servant came back with not one, but two, jugs of wine, brimming. Sir Mortimor glared at him again, for his own cup had been empty for some seconds.

"Sorry, m'lord," said the servant miserably and ducked out, closing the door behind him.

"Well then, Sir James," said Sir Mortimor, taking another hearty draught of wine from his cup. "What is it you have in mind?"

"Something that'll have to be done before full sunrise," said Jim, "otherwise I wouldn't have been in such a hurry to talk to you about it."

"It's a good time to talk." Sir Mortimor sat back in his chair and took another deep swallow from his wine cup. His face was harsh with the lines of middle-age tiredness. They were all tired. "Those Moroccans have given up and gone to sleep down in the village. My men are sleeping too—all those who aren't required to be awake."

"That's the very reason I wanted to talk to you as soon as possible," said Jim. "Because if what I have to suggest to you is workable, we'll need to move quickly before the sun is up. It's all to our advantage that those attacking us are probably asleep right now."

"Well, well," said Sir Mortimor, drumming his fingers on the table top. "What is this you wanted to say?"

"I think there's just a chance we might drive them off," said Jim. "My problem's been I don't know these people and this part of the world as you do, Sir Mortimor. How would they react, say, if they saw smoke coming out from the seaward end of each of their two ships?"

"I've already told you two gentlemen," said Sir Mortimor, "I will not countenance a sally through my secret escape route in the vain hope of firing the ships—since the last thing I want to do is to deprive the villains of the means of escaping."

"Hear me out," said Jim, sharply enough so that some of the signs of fatigue about Sir Mortimor's face vanished and his eyes narrowed on Jim. "I'm not suggesting any such thing. I asked for information. I asked how they'd react if they saw smoke coming up from the seaward end of their vessels. Would you be kind enough to tell me, sir?"

"If they saw smoke," said Sir Mortimor, "of course they would sound the alarm and all rush like madmen for the ships to put out any fire there. But I repeat—I do not want those ships fired!"

"And I have said I am suggesting no such thing," said Jim. "I'm making a suggestion that could involve my helping you with elements of my magical art."

Sir Mortimor's face changed markedly.

"And I do not want any payment," said Jim. "I would be doing this in the spirit, and only in the spirit, in which a guest helps out his host under special situations. Now if you will assist me with information and listen, Sir Mortimor—"

"I'll most gladly tell and listen, Sir James," said Sir Mortimor. "Most gladly. Forgive me if I sounded overhasty."

"Well then," said Jim, "picture all of them who are sleeping now, suddenly woken up by a shouting that there is fire in their boats. They rush to the boats to find out where the fire is. While they are all clustered around there, some of them scrambling around inside the boats and finding no fire, only smoke, they are suddenly struck by all your men, fully armed and ready for battle. Most of them will have nothing but their belt knives, or perhaps not even that; having just been roused from their slumber, and not expecting to fight men, but a fire.''

Sir Mortimor's face lit up.

"We could cut them to pieces!'' he said. But then he frowned. "They would have to remain disorganized, however; and all must go perfectly so that we come upon them at just the right moment. If we could only be sure they would stay alarmed, disorganized and not knowing what to do— then, I believe we could simply slay at will. Until a few woke to the fact that there was nothing here for them but death, scrambled aboard their ships and pulled away. By that time they would be too few in numbers to come back again at us. They would leave. But there is that problem. They are fighting men. They might grasp the situation, escape our first rush, get back to their arms—and, as we know, they outnumber us almost five to one.''

"Don't you think they'd stay disorganized?'' Jim asked. "Particularly if they saw an eight-foot-tall demon fighting with your men? They already know there's a magician with you in this castle—myself.''

"How do you know that?'' said Sir Mortimor. "How do you know they know you are here and a magician?''

"Because I am a magician,'' said Jim, in the most ominous voice he could manage.

"Oh, of course—'' Sir Mortimor's features suddenly became as obliging as Jim had remembered seeing them the moment he had first set foot in the castle. "Of course. Forgive me, I do not mean to doubt your word at all, Sir James. Can you indeed produce a demon to fight with us?''

"I can,'' said Jim. "It will take me perhaps half an hour. But there may be a difficulty. How will your men feel, having a demon among them?''

Sir Mortimor's face, which had lit up, lost a good deal of its illumination.

"Now,'' he said, rubbing his chin, "that is a question. What I must do is introduce the demon to them here, in the castle before they go out. You would not be willing to change into demon form before them?''

"I did not say I would change myself into a demon,'' said Jim. "I said I would produce a demon to fight with you and your men.''

It may have been an illusion of the firelight and the cresset-light, but

Jim was almost ready to believe that Sir Mortimor's face had become slightly pale.

"A real demon?" said Sir Mortimor.

"I have said what I said," said Jim. "It does not become me to explain myself. Either you approve my plan, or not. The how and why of it involve matters not spoken of with those who are not magicians."

"No, no. Of course not," said Sir Mortimor.

He gulped from his wine cup and did not refill it.

"A half-hour, you said?" He got to his feet. "Indeed, it will be light, then, but the sun is not yet up. The best of times to strike at men who think they now can spend the morning sleeping, and have been up all night. True, our lads have been up all night too; but they will forget that once they are in the mêlée. Half an hour from now, then, messires, I will have all my fighting men on the lowest floor of the castle. If Sir Brian will come down first to hold the men, I will then come up to meet this demon and walk down with you to introduce it to them all. Seeing it with you will give them courage to let you close to them. But you will be with me, Sir James, will you not, when I bring the demon down?"

"No," said Jim.

Sir Mortimor paled once more.

"Oh," he said.

"I will be where I can control everything the demon does. You may not ask where."

"Wouldn't think of it," said Sir Mortimor hastily. "I was only concerned with allaying the fear of my men."

"As for that," put in Brian, "I will venture to guess that the greater their alarm on seeing the demon, the greater their courage once fighting the pirates begins."

"You are right in that." Sir Mortimor got to his feet. "I will leave you now, Sir James—Sir Brian. In half an hour, look for me again."

He went out.

"James," said Brian, "will you really raise an actual demon?"

"Not exactly, Brian," said Jim. "There's something I should tell you. I haven't had a chance to, up until now. I had a talk with Carolinus shortly before I left to follow you—about the Christmas party at the Earl's a few months back—you remember that—"

"How could I forget it?" said Brian.

"Well, I used my magic rather freely there, as you know," said Jim. "I was able to do this because I've got a special drawing account. However, afterwards, and before the assignment of wardship came to me for young Robert, I had this talk with Carolinus; and he explained something to me, for reasons which I'd rather not go into, even with you. Reasons why I shouldn't be so spendthrift with my magic. Just believe me—they're serious.''

"I had not guessed this, James." Brian looked concerned.

"It's nothing to worry about," Jim said. "But because of that talk, I now need to be a miser with my magic. So, I'm not going to raise any demon—a magician's not supposed to, anyhow. I am, actually, going to make myself look so much like a demon it'll have the same effect. To do that I'm going to have to be completely alone for the next twenty minutes or so. Could I ask you—I know it's asking you to do something beneath your rank, but we're strangers here, and I don't trust the servants—would you stand guard outside the door of this room and see I'm not interrupted for that time? I think if you simply tell anyone I'm doing magic here, nobody would want to come in."

"Gladly will I do this for you," said Brian. "And I promise none shall enter."

"Thanks, Brian," said Jim.

"It is but a little thing," said Brian.

He stepped out; and Jim, left to himself, gathered his attention and visualized a make-up kit appearing on the table. It was a good deal smaller use of magic than transforming his appearance. He visualized very clearly what he wanted, and what those things he wanted should be able to do for him. The tusks should seal to his present teeth and look natural. They and the green skin dye should disappear, the minute he visualized himself as no longer needing it. The horns should fit naturally to his scalp through his hair; and vanish as conveniently, when the time came . . . and so forth. Last, but most important, he should have some boots that enabled him to walk quite naturally, but extended his legs a good two feet above whatever he was standing on.

There was a moment's pause. Then the things he had ordered appeared, with a puff of displaced air, on the table where he, Brian and Sir Mortimor had been sitting a few moments before.

They were all small items, except for the boots, which looked perfectly ordinary, except that their tops appeared as if they would reach well above his knees if he tried to put them on. He decided to leave trying them on until the last.

Instead, he tried the tusks first, simply laying them against his upper teeth under his lip, at the right and left corners of his mouth so that their sharp points curved out over his lower lip, with their points almost touching his chin.

They stuck firmly. The green dye for his skin only required dabbing on the back of one hand, and it spread by itself over all the skin of his body that was exposed—and for all he knew underneath his clothes as well.

The two horns fastened themselves to his head as firmly and easily as the tusks had attached themselves. His only difficulty was with placing them so that they would be level with each other. He found himself wishing he had a mirror to look in as he worked; and then suddenly realized that with only a small extra expenditure of magic he could have one.

He visualized it. It appeared, standing on the table, eight inches high and five wide, as ordered. He stared at what he saw reflected in it. The tusks and green skin by themselves were enough to make a remarkable change in his appearance. He had not counted on the fact that the tusks pushed out his upper lip at the right and left corners, distorting the skin of the rest of his face.

It occurred to him suddenly that he might try this trick of making himself up to amuse Robert—but Angie would never permit it.

The thought of Robert was unfortunate. He had a sudden vision of Robert, about ten years old, after hearing Brian's story about this, asking him, "What did you do in the battle?"

Jim found himself suddenly depressed. Brian should be bringing up Robert—but Brian, like just about everyone else he had met so far in the fourteenth century, was too rough. He had seen Brian playfully cuffing his squire around. In spite of the years that he and Angie had been here now, he, at least, really did not fit this time. Those belonging here ignored pain and expected all others to do so.

He pushed the feeling from him. No time for that now. Getting the horns on straight helped take his mind off it. He added contact lenses, which from the outside made his eyes look as if they had diamondlike pupils surrounded by blackness.

He attached claws to his fingernails. From inside he could see through the contact lenses quite clearly, with as good a view as he had possessed without them; and to his relief, they were not uncomfortable. He had never worn contact lenses in the twentieth century—which now seemed a long time ago rather than something in the future. The last things to go on were the boots. He sat down and pulled on the left one, gingerly.

But his foot slipped easily into it and seemed to go the full length of it. Encouraged, he pulled on the right boot and stood up, banging his head on the room's ceiling. He had not banged it hard enough to do damage, but the contact was painful. The pain made him angry; and since there was no one else around to get angry with, he was angry with himself. He adorned himself with the few more items of make-up that remained.

He took another look in the mirror—and almost jumped. He was the ugliest creature he had ever laid eyes on. He had thought Kelb, in his manlike Djinni body, held this record; but if ugliness was considered as a subdivision of beauty, he was more beautiful than a dozen Djinn, rolled into one.

However, he reminded himself, this was no time for speculating. He raised his voice. "Brian, would you come in now?"

"Gladly, James," said Brian, without. The door opened; Brian stepped into the room, and checked, his right hand jumping to his left hip, to the hilt of his sword in its scabbard.

"James?" he said uncertainly. "Is that you, James?"

His other hand had now flown to his opposite hip and seized the handle of his poignard, so that he was ready to cross-draw both weapons.

"It's me, all right," said Jim hastily. "Do I look that much different, Brian?"

"By all the Saints!" said Brian, staring at him. "If you had not answered me finally with your ordinary voice, James, I would be sure that some demon had seized and eaten you while I was outside. It is you?"

"Yes, it's me, Brian," said Jim. "Sorry I startled you. But at the same time, I'm pleased. If I can do that to an old friend, I should be sure of scaring our foes."

"By our Lady!" said Brian. "They will die of fright!"

"So much the easier," said Jim. "Now, I've got to get hold of Hob, and put him to gathering the smoke to make the pirate ships look like they're on fire. Brian, could I bother you to step outside again; and if Sir Mortimor comes along, would you hold him up and knock on the door first, so I'll have some warning before he comes in?"

"Better," said Brian, "that I knock on the door, then come in myself and make sure you are ready, before you call him in. I would like to see his face when he sees you!"

"Fine," said Jim. "Let's do it that way."

With Brian out of the room he went over to the fireplace, leaned down—way down, it turned out, with the boots on—and called into the top of the fireplace opening.

"Hob? Hob, would you come here a moment? I want to talk to you."

"Yes, m'lord!" chirped a cheerful little voice. Hob popped into view, stared at him aghast and immediately popped back out of sight up the chimney.

"Hob!" called Jim again, awkwardly bending even farther to make sure his voice carried all the way up the chimney. "Come back. Never mind what I look like. It's me, Sir James, your Lord. Pay no attention to my face. This is just a false appearance."

There was no answer. He kept talking up the chimney, pleading with Hob to come down, with his belt buckle earnestly trying to dig its way through the middle part of his body to his spine. It was hard to find breath to talk with, bent awkwardly double this way. Finally, however, a small voice answered.

"You're not m'lord James," came Hob's tones tremulously. "You're a Djinni."

"I am not a Djinni," said Jim earnestly. "I'm a demon—I mean, I'm your Lord James Eckert that you know very well, just pretending to be a demon. I know I've made myself look like a demon, but it's me. Come down here, Hob! I have to talk with you! It's time for us to rush out at the men who've been trying to get into this castle; and that means I'm depending upon you to get things done too. Come on down so we can talk about it."

The top of Hob's head inched into view upside down. It took a good half-minute for all of his face to appear.

"If you're m'lord James," he said, "what was the name you gave me, before you had to take it back?"

"I named you Hob-One de Malencontri," said Jim. "And I'll still call you by that name when I want to. It's just that the rest of the world can't."

Slowly, fearfully, Hob came out into the room. Jim was very careful not to move at all.

"If it's really you, m'lord," said Hob quaveringly, "what do you want from me?"

"I want you to do what we talked about you doing," said Jim. "Sir Mortimor's going to be along in a moment; and I'll be going down with him to let the rest of his men see me, and reassure them all's well. I'm not going to tell them I'm Sir James; but I don't want them to be afraid of me, looking like this. Also, I want them to believe I'm there to help them, fighting on their side."

"You look terrible!" said Hob, coming slowly but fully into view. "Are you sure you're you?"

"Of course I'm sure," said Jim. "But all that means is we're just about ready to go; because the sun'll be up soon. I want you to get busy right away gathering smoke so that we can have it coming up from the end of the ships for perhaps a good fifteen or twenty minutes. They may not notice the smoke going up right away."

"Oh, I've already got the smoke all bundled up," said Hob, more strongly now. "There wasn't anything to that. What do you want me to do next?"

"There's a fireplace on the ground floor where all Sir Mortimor's men are gathered," said Jim. "Will you take the bundle of smoke, go down that chimney and listen from that fireplace to what we talk about down there? Then, as soon as it looks like we're just about to start the attack, I want you to go ahead to the boats and start the smoke going up. We'll probably all come outside the castle, but wait there until we see the smoke, ourselves; and until the men who have been attacking us start running down to the ships to put out the fire they'll think is on them. How long will it take you after you stop listening to reach the ships and start the smoke rising?''

"Oh, almost no time at all," said Hob. "By the time you and everyone else are outside, I'll have the smoke going up. I can't do anything about the men down in the village seeing it, though."

"That's all right," said Jim. "I don't expect you to—"

There was a scratching at the door.

"Brian?" called Jim. "By all means come in. I'll be gone when you get here, because I have things magical to do. But the demon will be waiting for you. Have you told Sir Mortimor what he may expect to see?"

"I have," said Brian. "Do you want me to step in alone, first?"

"If you please, Brian," said Jim. "If Sir Mortimor will be so kind as to wait just a moment, there are things I must say to you before I leave— things unconnected with matters here."

The door opened and Brian came through.

Jim beckoned him to come close and whispered to him.

"Brian, I'm going to use a different voice for the demon. Don't let it bother you. And you can tell Sir Mortimor that I just simply vanished after speaking a few words to you. I think that takes care of things."

"Doubtless," said Brian.

"Then let him in," said Jim.

Brian turned to the door now, and spoke to Sir Mortimor outside. The tall knight came in, saw Jim in his demon's make-up, stopped, opened his mouth, closed it again and crossed himself in the process of reaching for his sword.

"I am invincible!" boomed Jim in a voice a full octave below his normal tones and one that he tried to fill with menace. "None can stand against me; and I take commands from no one! But I will assist you in this matter. Now, you may lead me to where others like you await."

Sir Mortimor stiffened and some of the color came back to his face. Slowly, he let go of his sword.

"Then, demon," he said coldly, "come with me."

CHAPTER 15

"Where the hell," demanded Sir Mortimor of himself, but aloud, stopping them both just above the floor on which his men waited, "is Sir Brian? He was with us upstairs!"

"That great magician, Sir James," boomed Jim, for the first time making full use of the magical voice he had invented to go with his demon persona, three times as loud and a full octave deeper than his ordinary human voice, "required that Sir Brian wait outside the room. Consequently he had no chance to make his devotions before battle—as is his custom—before you arrived. He should be with us in minutes."

Sir Mortimor looked stunned—probably, Jim thought, not so much by the idea of Brian praying before fighting as by finding himself outvoiced. But he recovered quickly.

"Now, damn it, they'll have heard you down there! Why didn't he—" Chancing to look up at his companion just then, Sir Mortimor's voice underwent a sudden change to a much milder and more pleasant tone. "—didn't Sir Brian tell me he intended that when he met me outside your door? Well, we needn't wait for him. Since they did hear you, best that we go down right now. I'll lead the way."

He moved off, down the staircase, and Jim followed a few steps behind. They descended under the ceiling that had been the floor beneath their feet a moment before, and into full view of the space packed with men armed to the teeth. In spite of their weapons, at the sight of the demon these were already trying to crowd into the corner of the room farthest from the foot of the stairs.

"Rejoice, my children!" Sir Mortimor's voice rang out. "Sir James has provided us with what we need to be sure of victory. You see behind me a demon under his command, who will fight along with us; and in whose company we shall send those who attack us flying from our shores."

It hardly seemed possible; but by this time, the crowd of armed men below them had now managed to compress itself to three-quarters of the size it had been a moment before.

Sir Mortimor continued to descend the stairs, with Jim behind him. They reached the floor.

"Fear not!" shouted Sir Mortimor. "This demon, named Invincible, is completely under the control of Sir James, my good and loyal friend. Sir James's magic forbids him from coming with us himself; so he has sent this deputy to make sure we cannot fail. Now, outside with all of you—but quietly so as not to wake them below. Sir Brian will be joining us soon. We must watch for the first sign that their boats are on fire!"

With grateful and surprising speed, the population of the room emptied itself through the inner door to the passageway, then the now unbarricaded outer door, on to the steep hillside. They poured out around the steps on to the stairs and slopes before the castle. Below them, the whole land and sea was monochrome, most of its color lost in the pale light of the not-yet-risen sun. No one was moving in the village. There was no sound. No more was there any sound or movement aboard the two ships; so that the repeated talking of the waves, coming up and breaking on the pebbly shore, came clearly to the ears of all of them.

"Ah, Sir Mortimor—demon!" said the voice of Sir Brian behind Jim and the tall knight.

He joined them, fully weaponed and ready. And stood beside them.

"Anything happening yet?" he asked cheerfully. Sir Mortimor scowled at him.

"We are waiting for a sign that the ships have been fired," Sir Mortimor said. "So far there is none."

"I have little doubt we will see evidence shortly," said Brian. "A fine, clear morning, is it not?"

This was Brian's usual high spirits before any kind of a fight showing themselves, as Jim well knew. Sir Mortimor was evidently of a different nature; and not necessarily pleased by cheerfulness over the prospect of a dawn encounter after a sleepless night that might cost him everything he owned, to say nothing of his life.

"It's taking long enough—" he began; but at that moment, a gray wisp of smoke lifted from the seaward end of the ship to their right and a second later another wisp went up from the nearby end of the ship beside it.

The columns of smoke went straight up in the still air. They thickened and darkened.

"Wake up, wake up, you blind infidel idiots!" muttered Sir Mortimor between his teeth. "Haven't you at least one hell-bound sentry awake?

Isn't there at least one of you who has to step outside for some reason or other?''

The village slumbered on, deaf to his complaints. The smoke poured up even more thickly from the seaward ends of the two boats; and now voices began to cry out from the boats themselves, yells and screams of alarm. Still, there was no sign that could be seen from the hillside of anyone moving along the visible deck portion of either one.

''All praise!'' breathed Sir Mortimor; and then suddenly his voice rang out in its full force to the men around him, more than loudly enough to wake most of those in the village. ''The rowers are taking alarm! They will be slaves chained in place and fearing to be burned to death!''

Sir Mortimor's men started a cheer—and throttled it immediately as Sir Mortimor glared at them. Below, a first few figures began to stagger, still half asleep, out of the buildings below. They stared about, focused seaward, saw the boats, and began to run toward them, shouting as they ran. Other figures began to boil from the flimsy village structures.

''Wait, wait,'' ordered Sir Mortimor in a lower voice, one pitched just enough to reach his own men. ''Let them get well away from their weapons. Wait . . . wait. Now!''

''A Breugel! A Breugel—''

Shouting his war cry, he went leaping down the steps, three and four at a time.

His men streamed after him, waving their weapons. Jim and Brian followed, more cautiously until they were on less steep ground; then Brian began to put on his best speed, charging into the mass of Sir Mortimor's men ahead of him and pushing them aside.

Jim followed as quickly as he could, but matching Brian's speed of foot was impossible, let alone that of most of Sir Mortimor's fighting men; with the exception of those who were, he suspected, deliberately lagging back a little. In any case, it was only a moment or two before they were upon the stream of corsairs, headed toward the boat, and these, turning to discover an armed group descending on them and themselves unarmed except for knives, were bolting in all directions.

Sir Mortimor had reached the shore end of the two ships. He turned and shouted to his men.

''Turn! Turn! Back to the village!''

Those with him faced about and reversed their charge. The distance between the village buildings and the shore was no distance at all; and almost immediately they ran head-on into men still coming out of the buildings, some of them still half awake and empty-handed, but some, at least, now armed with swords and shields and ready to fight. By the time Jim caught up, the mêlée was in full activity.

Jim cursed himself internally for not having thought to have brought at least a sword. It might not have fitted with his demon image; but he would have felt a lot better right now if he had something in his hand to keep enemies at a distance. He tried to make up for the lack of it by bellowing at the top of his voice and flailing his clawed arms in the air.

It was a few moments before he realized that he was not forcing anyone to stand back from him—for the very good reason that everyone was being very careful not to get close to him without being forced in any way. That included Sir Mortimor's men. But Brian was locked in tight combat in the midst of the fight, surrounded by half a dozen Moroccans.

He was a much better swordsman than any of those around him, and his armor was good enough to turn the edges of most of their blades; but there were entirely too many concentrating on him alone for Jim's peace of mind. Jim charged in his direction, therefore, making as much noise and trying to look as fearsome as possible. It worked. Brian's attackers caught sight of him coming, and ran. Jim came up to Brian, who was now leaning on his sword, its point shoved into the beach before him, and catching his breath.

"Damn it, James!" gasped Brian. "You frightened them all away!"

The use of Jim's name was safe enough. The hubbub around them would have covered up the sound of it, even if any of those nearby had time to listen; and none had.

"Don't be an idiot yourself, Brian," said Jim, likewise gasping for breath. His magic boots, which added a couple of feet to his size, had not made running easy and he also was out of breath. "There were too many of them!"

"I did not call for rescue—" snapped Brian, then checked himself. "But there, James, I honor your thought to aid a fellow knight possibly in distress."

"A fellow knight and an old friend!" said Jim.

"I would rather believe you would have given that response to any knight in my position," said Brian. "But there, let it be. I am sensible of your friendship, James. But look! It is all but over now. Those who were not slain, or too badly hurt to do so, have reached their ships and are putting out to sea, leaving their friends behind."

Jim turned to look. At first glance, it seemed all too easy, almost ridiculous after the undeniable alarm and concern up in the castle; but then he saw all the bodies lying around on the ground. The streets—if they could be called that—in the village, the pebbly shore down to the water's edge, was strewn with fallen men. Most of Sir Mortimor's warriors seemed busy in robbing the dead bodies of their enemies—also those of the near-dead.

"Brian," he said in a low voice, "I'll be glad to be out of here."

"And I also," answered Brian. "In God's name, I will be glad to be in Tripoli."

They were in Tripoli, four days later, but where in Tripoli was another question.

"Do you suppose the damn fellow really knows the way?" growled Brian.

"The shipmaster said he did," answered Jim.

Brian grunted. What Jim had just said was of course no answer at all. Jim sympathized, but he had nothing more to offer his friend in the way of reassurance. The trading ship that had brought them down from Cyprus to the port of Tripoli on what would be the coast of Lebanon—if the future of this medieval world followed the same pattern as the twentieth-century world from which Jim had come—had carried as master a villainous-looking fellow, who, however, had not overcharged them for the trip, according to what Brian's friends in Cyprus had assured them. Whether this meant he was honest in everything else, however, might be doubtful.

He was a lank-haired, shifty-eyed individual with a drooping gray-black mustache in a narrow olive-colored face; with the ample stomach of a glutton and the skinny arms and legs of a miser. He had hired the local man who was leading them to their destination, as well as the other two that were coming along behind and carrying their possessions. In their innocence, neither Brian nor Jim had any idea whether the price he had negotiated with these three was an overcharge or not; but they could not do without direction and porters, so they had no choice but to pay it.

But their guide had led them now through a completely bewildering maze of streets and alleyways so narrow in some places they literally had to turn sideways to get between buildings, the ground underfoot all but carpeted with human and animal wastes, particularly in the smaller streets. In addition, Jim—like Brian—was fully armored and weaponed, with a travel cloak over everything else, the hood of which concealed the knapsacklike bag in which Hob rode; and Brian was similarly armed, armored and clothed. All this in a climate that was showing a warmer spring than they were used to in England. They were hot and thirsty, and their tempers were beginning to wear thin.

It did seem as if the home of a local magician, to which their guide was supposedly leading them, could hardly be this much of a distance in a medieval town, which while crawling with population like an anthill, was also crammed tightly into as small a space as could be practical. On the other hand, thought Jim, the maze of streets could have deluded them with the notion they had walked farther than they thought.

"Yet another corner!" said Brian sharply. "That's enough! I'm going to confront the fellow. Here, you, come back here!"

The guide stopped, turned and met them halfway as they came up.

"Oh, master," he said, "thou shinest before my eyes like a flower beloved of Allah, and thy sweetness perfumes the air. In what way can I oblige thee?"

"Enough of that chatter," snapped Brian. "When do we get to the magician's house? How much farther is it? Answer me, fellow, and if your answer is not a good one, on your head be it!"

He put his hand on his sword hilt.

"Great lords and masters!" said the guide. "May I be blinded and cast down into the seventh hell, if we are not upon the place right now. It is but three doors down."

"You're sure?" snapped Brian.

"It is as I've said," said the guide. "In Allah's name, it is but three doors down."

"It had best be so," said Brian.

The man turned and ran ahead a short distance through the dim alleyway they were traversing, and stopped beside what seemed to be a solid wall.

"It is here, my lords and masters!" he called. "This is the place!"

"Let's go look," said Jim. He and Brian slogged forward, and there was indeed a slight indentation in the wooden wall beside which the guide had stopped; and in that indentation was a door that probably once had been painted green, but there was very little of that color left to it now.

"Lo, I have done what was promised. Pay me and those two who carry your wealth, and let us go," said the guide.

"Wait a minute," said Jim, as Brian reached up under his chain mail shirt for his purse. "Let's get them to answer that door and find out if we actually are at the right place, first. Then we'll pay you."

"Your wish is my command, O mighty one!" said the guide. Turning, he began to hammer on the door. He hammered for some little time, but there was no sound from within nor anything to signify he had been heard. He turned and looked hopelessly at Jim and Brian, shrugging his shoulders; but Brian was scowling now, and he quickly turned back to the door and began hammering on it again.

"Open!" he cried in a piercing, high-pitched voice. "Open, in the name of Allah, the beneficent, the all-hospitable. Two great men, beloved of Allah, the sultan and our Bey, here in Tripoli, are come to visit with abu al-Qusayr."

There still was no response, but Brian growled and the man kept up his pounding and his cries. Finally, there was the noise of bolts being drawn and bars being lifted, and the door opened to reveal a tall, stately-looking man in a rich, heavy robe of red. He was silver-haired and upright. He glared down at the guide.

"Dog of the wharf," he said. "Why do you clamor at this door? Do you not know what you risk by disturbing the mind of abu al-Qusayr?"

"Forgive me, O gracious one!" said the guide. "But with me are two great men, lords among the Franks and nasranies of the north, who are directed here by friends of abu al-Qusayr. Not for a king's ransom would I disturb so all-wise and powerful a man. But I think that these with me are expected by him."

The silver-haired man in the red robe directed his glance at Jim and Brian.

"Your names, sirs?" he asked, with a surprising change of speech to a courtly, even European manner.

"I am Sir Brian Neville-Smythe," said Brian. "With me is the Mage, Baron Sir James Eckert de Malencontri, whom your master is expecting."

"I must not claim the title of Mage, however," said Jim hurriedly, for the eyebrows of the silver-haired man had climbed up on his forehead on hearing that title. "I am a magician of relatively low rank; apprentice, however, to the Mage S. Carolinus, who has said that I would find friendship and direction from abu al-Qusayr, as a fellow member of the Magician's Kingdom."

The man in the doorway relaxed.

"You are expected, sir," he said—again with more of a European way of speaking than that of one of the locals. Jim wondered if his invisible translator was carrying him over what essentially was a switch from one language to another. Looking past Jim and Brian now, this man beckoned the two luggage-carriers forward and pointed just inside the doorway.

"Leave your burdens there," he said. "They will be taken care of."

"My pay! Our pay!" cried the guide. "O munificent masters, we have not yet been paid!"

Jim produced a silver coin and passed it to the guide.

"But it was to be a *gold* dinar," wailed the guide.

"That's not what the shipmaster told us," said Jim.

"It was to be gold! It was to be gold—" clamored the guide.

"Cease thy clamor," snapped the man in the red robe, "and get thee hence happily with what thou hast, lest devils and scorpions follow thee to thy grave!"

Ignoring the guide and the bearers, he turned once more to Jim and Brian.

"Enter, messires," he said. He stood aside to let them come through the doorway in the narrow space left between himself and their luggage. Then he closed the door behind them upon the sound of lamentations and protests from both the guides and the carriers. "Five drachmas would have been ample. You have been robbed, messires, but there is little help for it, I know, in a city like this, where you are not known and you do not know its ways. Come, Sir Brian, Sir James. Sir James, my master is indeed expecting you. Follow me."

He led them down the short, dim-lit and narrow corridor toward a farther door, from which several other men, obviously lesser servants, ran in, ducked past them and ran on to the outer door. Jim heard the sound of the bolts being driven home and the heavy bar being lifted back into place. They stepped through the inner door.

Suddenly, it was as if they had stepped back into a palace out of the Arabian Nights.

CHAPTER 16

T hey had entered a large room with a lofty, white dome-shaped ceiling and one wall that was not a wall but spaced pillars, showing either an open corridor or a balcony beyond them. Entrances, both high and wide, in the other two walls ahead, opened on further rooms beyond, giving glimpses of similar high ceilings and stone walls.

The stone itself was beautifully fitted, and jutted out to make a gallery on the wall to Jim's left, its floor some fifteen feet up. Shielding the gallery was a screen of worked stone, with intricately curved, small apertures piercing every part of it, so that it was in effect a screen of wrought stone to hide anyone who might be standing behind it and looking down. A few pieces of furniture, mainly hassocks, cushions and low tables, were lined up against the walls of the room, leaving the center of it completely open, increasing the appearance of its size—an appearance that was reinforced by the light-colored of the walls. Bright daylight seemed to be flooding in, not only through the pillars, but from other, hidden parts of the room, either by clever architecture or magic, so that the whole place seemed to float in mid-air.

"If you will follow me, messires," said the red-robed man; and led them off through one of the farther entrances which were rectangular to about six feet off the ground, and then swelled into an onion-shaped arch with a sharp upward point in the center.

They followed him, through rooms that were almost identical with the first they had seen. Carpets, with indecipherable figuring upon them, were everywhere. Occasionally they caught sight of men, dressed in loose green blouses and trousers, passing through the corner of a room—from doorway to doorway—in the same rooms they traversed.

Now that he stopped to think of it, Jim remembered that the servants that had run to rebar the door had also been dressed in green. The red-robed man paid no attention to these, however, so Jim and Brian also ignored them; and they went for some distance, always flooded by the remarkable daylight that seemed to penetrate into every room, even those that had walls on four sides and no visible form of lighting otherwise.

At last, they came to a small closed door, a rectangular door, not unlike the two by which they had entered from the street; but this door was of highly polished, dark, rich wood, with a handgrip in its outer side that seemed to be of shining silver.

Red-robe stopped before it, and Jim and Brian necessarily stopped with him. The silver-haired man spoke to the door.

"Master," he said, "Sir James Eckert, the Dragon Knight, is come. He is with me now, outside your door, with a companion, Sir Brian Neville-Smythe. What is your will, O my master?"

"They may come in," said a deep, quiet voice from beyond the door. "You may go, Majid."

"At once, my master," said Majid. He turned to Jim and Brian. "Abu al-Qusayr bids you enter."

He stood aside from the door, which opened softly and apparently of its own power. Looking through the entrance, Jim saw a smaller room than they had encountered so far, still high-ceilinged, but completely windowless, with all four of the walls windowless, but bright with the same ever-present daylight.

Against a far wall, a square-shouldered man sat cross-legged on a thick, white cushion, with a round table of black wood before him. On the table was a bowl apparently filled with clear water; and beside this stood some pieces of silver apparatus, very intricately fitted together and with jointed parts that were probably movable, but which now stood still.

The man, himself, behind the table, had a wispy white beard on a firm chin. He looked to be of something more than middle age, but his actual age was anyone's guess. He was a strong-looking man, sitting straight-backed, dressed in a long robe that covered his legs and feet completely in his present cross-legged position—a robe of the same color of red as that Carolinus habitually wore, a softer red than Majid's robe. His brow was lofty, his eyes dark and his face square and suntanned beneath a straight nose and a straight mouth.

He gave the impression of being utterly reliable, utterly to be trusted. The sort of person who is like a glimpse of land to someone helplessly adrift in a storm-torn sea.

Jim and Brian advanced into the room, and the door closed almost noiselessly behind them. Curiously, in spite of the warmth that seemed to emanate from the man himself, the air in here was cooler and strangely fresh. The man gestured toward other pillows against the wall, and three of these slipped out in front of his table, apparently on their own power.

"Sit down, Jim, and you too, Brian," he said. He smiled. "I see Majid didn't realize there were three of you."

"Three of us, sir?" said Brian, a little sharply as, more easily than Jim, he dropped into a cross-legged position on one of the pillows before the desk.

"You forget your little friend, whom Jim is carrying, Brian," said abu al-Qusayr. He turned to the already seated Jim. "Come out, little one. Don't be afraid."

Jim felt a stirring in the small hidden knapsack on his back, and Hob climbed out onto his shoulder. He stood erect, holding onto Jim's neck, his feet on Jim's shoulder and looking at the bearded magician.

"Come," said abu al-Qusayr, patting the table top in front of him. "Come and sit here, little friend."

To Jim's surprise, Hob leaped absolutely fearlessly forward onto the table top and sat down cross-legged on the spot indicated, staring interestedly up at abu al-Qusayr, who examined him in return.

"You are a Natural," said abu al-Qusayr. "What I believe is called a hobgoblin, back in the place you come from. Isn't that right?"

"Oh, yes," said Hob confidently. "Actually, I'm also Hob-One de Malencontri—but nobody but m'lord Jim and m'lady Angela can call me that. Maybe you can call me that. Do you suppose?"

"I suppose I could," said abu al-Qusayr. "But it's a long, rather formal name. I'd rather just call you Hob too, if you don't mind."

"I don't mind if *you* do it," said Hob confidentially.

"Good," said abu al-Qusayr. "How did you happen to come along with m'lord Jim and Sir Brian?"

"I came so I could hurry back and tell m'lady Angela if m'lord gets into any trouble at all," said Hob. "She'd like to know. She worries about him."

"I can understand that," said abu al-Qusayr. He looked at Jim.

"With all due respect," said Jim, "don't you suppose you could be asking me those questions?"

"I could, of course." Abu al-Qusayr stroked his small white beard. "But I was curious. I wanted a little conversation with your Hob. I'd never met his form of Natural before. Are you gentlemen quite comfortable? You may be a little overdressed for this climate."

"Why, damme," said Brian, almost wonderingly, "I was a little more than comfortably warm on the way here, but this house of yours is very airy, cool and pleasant. I'm quite at ease, now."

"And the pillows," said abu al-Qusayr. "Can you manage to sit on them comfortably? I know you people from northern Europe are not used to sitting in this position."

"We do it a fair amount, when out away from home or any other lodging," said Brian. "We'll sit like this around a fire of nights when we're far from any lodging. I find no discomfort in it."

Brian, to Jim's ears, was beginning to sound almost as trusting as Hob had, toward this magician. Abu al-Qusayr seemed out to charm them all. Jim waited, a little grimly, for the force of that persuasion to be tried on him.

"As for you, Jim," said abu al-Qusayr, with no attempt at all to put him at his ease, but speaking as if they had been old friends from the start, "trouble follows you like bees after a man smeared with honey. Have you been aware of a small brown dog around you, since you left the European shore?"

"You mean Kelb? The Djinni? He's already approached me about getting my protection," Jim said. "It seems his master was another, very powerful Djinni, who's angry with him for having escaped from a lake of fire into which the other Djinni had him thrown."

He heard his own voice coming out warmly and confidentially.

I'm already falling into the same sort of soft trap that this man got Hob and Brian into, he told himself. He stiffened his back and deliberately spoke coldly. "I told him I'd think about it. He's been hanging around me, but I haven't had any trouble with him."

"Well," said abu al-Qusayr, "he's perfectly right to be afraid. Sakhr al-Jinni is one of the most powerful of the Djinn. You, yourself, should be careful of him, also. I would counsel you to have little to do with this Kelb."

"I wasn't planning to," said Jim.

"Good," said abu al-Qusayr. "You're ranked as a C magickian, now, I believe?"

"Yes," said Jim, feeling a twinge of embarrassment, and becoming angry with himself almost immediately for feeling anything at all. Why, he asked himself, should it matter to him what rank this bunch of magicians chose to consider he should hold?

"I don't think a Djinni like Kelb should give a C-rank magickian any great problems," said abu al-Qusayr. "But you want to avoid anything that might lead you into getting mixed up with Sakhr al-Jinni. It's true he's only a Natural, but he's one of the very powerful Naturals, and one of the most vindictive."

"I was planning on avoiding him," said Jim.

"I thought you would," said abu al-Qusayr. "Still, no harm in mentioning it. But there's something else I unfortunately have to mention to you. Carolinus just passed word to me that he'd gotten notice of another complaint filed against you by a separate kingdom. The Grand Demon accuses you of impersonating a demon. Would you care to tell me your side of that matter?''

Jim told him.

"I see," said abu al-Qusayr, when he was done. "Excuse me a moment, then—"

He bent over the bowl of water or whatever it was on the table in front of him and stared into it. While Jim, Brian and Hob sat silently waiting— Jim with an uneasy feeling in his stomach—there was silence in the room. Finally abu al-Qusayr lifted his gaze from the bowl of water.

"Much more cheap and convenient, you know," he said to Jim, "doing your scrying in a clear bowl of water. You don't have to have a glass globe, as you northerners do. Everyone to his own taste, of course. Well, I would say that you'd have no trouble answering that accusation. I'll have to disqualify myself as one of your judges, of course—"

"One of my judges?" said Jim.

"Quite naturally," said abu al-Qusayr. "Naturally, I know this region, and I've had a few contacts with demons myself—just in passing, you understand. However, they would still have to call me as an expert witness because of my local knowledge; and what I can tell them should clear you completely. Not, actually, that you need my testimony. The facts are plain enough."

"You were looking at what happened a couple of days ago? At the castle of Sir Mortimor Breugel?" asked Jim.

"Yes," answered abu al-Qusayr. "As I hope you know, scrying is usually limited to events happening at the present or possibly in the near future; but under special circumstances, of which a capital accusation is one—"

"Capital!" echoed Jim. Capital crimes even in the first part of his twentieth century normally called for a death sentence. "What would happen to me if I was convicted of actually having violated the demon kingdom?"

"We'd have to turn you over to the demons, of course," said abu al-Qusayr. "Just as you would have had to have been turned over to the King and Queen of the Dead, if that earlier charge of willful trespass upon their kingdom had been proven against you. Of course, it wasn't. The guilt in that case actually lay with Malvinne, the French AAA magickian—and you saw what happened to him, I believe."

"I did," said Jim. He would never forget the sight—Malvinne being drawn up into dark clouds sculpted into the forms of the King and Queen of the Dead on their thrones; pulled up as if he had been a drowned rat at the end of a string.

"Well, as I say, it doesn't matter," said abu al-Qusayr. "As I just told you, even without my expert testimony, the facts are indisputable. You made it very clear, for the record, in speaking to Sir Mortimor, that you would not turn yourself into a demon. You only said you would produce one. You lied to him, of course, which is perfectly justifiable under circumstances where the magickian needs defense, but wishes to do no harm. You merely let him think you had produced a demon, which is not a violation of demon sovereignty in any way. The fact that Sir Mortimor, Sir Mortimor's men and those who were attacking his castle believed you to be a demon was their mistake, and their responsibility. You fulfilled the magickian's command to defend himself without harming anyone else. You did no harm."

"No harm," echoed Jim, in a low voice. In his mind's eye he saw the bodies of the Moroccans scattered all over the beach, being searched and even cut into by Sir Mortimor's men, to see if they had swallowed anything small but valuable to protect it from being stolen.

"Don't let it disturb you," said abu al-Qusayr, as if he had read Jim's mind. "If it hadn't been the Moroccans who were killed, it would have been Sir Mortimor's men, Sir Mortimor—and possibly you three as well. But come now, let's have something to eat and drink and talk about more interesting things."

Jim felt a sudden breath of air on the back of his neck; and a moment later a green-clad servant set down on the table top a tray of cakes and three tiny cups of what looked like very black coffee, one each in front of himself and Brian; and the third in front of abu al-Qusayr. He also put down a bowl of milk before Hob—who lapped it up like a cat. The bowl of clear water and the other apparatus on the table had vanished a second before the servant appeared.

Abu al-Qusayr immediately sipped from his coffee cup and nibbled at one of the cakes. Jim vaguely remembered from his reading that such was good manners in this part of the world. The host would eat and drink before his guests, to show that neither food nor drink were poisoned.

Jim lifted his own cup to his lips; and, sure enough, it was very strong coffee, very heavily sugared. He saw Brian tasting his; and a look of astonishment coming over his friend's face before he set the cup down. Brian, surrounded by transplanted Europeans, had obviously so far not been offered anything but wine and water until this moment. Still, Brian's manners were enough to keep him from making any comment on this hot, bittersweet brew.

"I am sorry I can't offer you wine," said abu al-Qusayr. "There is none in this house. The Koran, as you know, forbids it to true Muslims, of which I am one. As I understand it, Brian, you are in search of the father of your beloved, so arrangements may be made that she be given you in matrimony; and James, here, has out of friendship come with you on this trip—albeit a little behind you, catching up with you in Cyprus.''

"That is so," said Brian. He had only taken a couple more sips of coffee, but he had already eaten five of the little cakes. Jim noticed that they were magically replenishing themselves on the tray, as fast as those that were there were devoured. "My lady's father went off on a crusade, though few would do so, nowadays; but he hoped that good fortune would attend him, if he did. We had lost track of him until just lately. Then a knight returning from this part of the world gave her word that her father had been seen in Palmyra, which we understand is inland from this city of Tripoli.''

"It is indeed inland," said abu al-Qusayr, "on the other side of the mountains and then a distance. But it is still on the caravan routes and it is a city of merchants. Perhaps her father has become a merchant and that is the reason for his staying there. If he is doing well he may have chosen not to return home.''

"How do we get there?" asked Brian.

"I would say," answered abu al-Qusayr, "the only sensible way for you will be to join a caravan taking goods shipped from Tripoli to that city and others beyond. The route lies through the mountains, which are now dangerous because of a nest of Assassins that have flourished there in the Kasr al-Abiyadh, or the White Palace, in the last few years.''

"Assassins?" asked Jim, beating Brian to the question by seconds.

"Yes," said abu al-Qusayr, "at least they claim to be Hashasheen; and I would not risk doubting it. They are not, of course, of the original Assassins, which began with Hassan ibn al-Sabbah, who was the first 'Old Man of the Mountain.' He seized the castle of Alamut, in a valley near Kazvin, nearly three hundred years ago; and Alamut was their headquarters for many years, until the Mongols took them, one by one. Finally, Alamut itself fell to the Mongols; and the last of the Assassins' castles in Syria, Kahf, was conquered less than a hundred years ago. But still the brotherhood crops up from time to time. I do not know the name of the one who calls himself Grandmaster of this group in the mountains you will be passing through; but he was a Sufi, one of the Orthodox who worship Allah, but in their own strange ways. He felt called upon to become an Isma'ili and joined those Isma'ilis who are Hashasheen, or Assassins, as you would say. But the caravan itself will be armed and ready; and if you stay with the caravan, your chances should be good of getting to Palmyra.''

"That sounds not too difficult," said Brian. "Indeed a small bicker along the way would possibly be welcome, to break the tedium of the trip.''

"I'm glad to hear you so confident," said abu al-Qusayr. "I suggest, however, you keep an eye out. Not only for Assassins, but for other enemies, most of them Naturals. There are actual demons among those rocks, as well as ghouls and spirits of various kinds. You might even encounter a griffin or a cockatrice; although these are rare nowadays and are not likely to approach something as large as a caravan.''

Jim noticed Brian's face had paled. Hob leaped from the top of the table to Jim's shoulder and clutched him around the neck.

"Would they want me?" he cried at abu al-Qusayr. "Would any of them want a hobgoblin like me?"

"Never mind," said Jim, shortly. "I'll make sure that nothing from an Assassin to a cockatrice has anything to do with you."

Hob sighed with relief, and sat down on Jim's shoulder. Jim noticed that abu al-Qusayr was looking at him with a curious interest.

"Do you," said Hob, addressing abu al-Qusayr, then hesitating, "do you have a fireplace around here some place?"

"I'm sorry, little friend," said abu al-Qusayr. "There are no fireplaces here. However, there are fires in places like the kitchens. Sir Brian, I must speak privily with Sir James, here. Would you be good enough to allow yourself to be shown your quarters, now? On the way, then, you could be taken past the kitchen, and Hob could be shown what we have by way of fire and smoke in this building."

"I would be glad to do so," said Brian, rising smoothly and athletically from his pillow without even putting a hand to the ground. "We will be staying with you, then?"

"Just overnight, I believe," said abu al-Qusayr. "I have arranged for you to join the caravan to leave tomorrow."

Behind him, Jim felt another puff of air, and the voice of Majid spoke behind them.

"What is your will, master?" said the voice of the silver-haired man.

"Show Sir Brian to the room set aside for him and Sir James," said abu al-Qusayr. "On the way, go past the kitchen; so that our small friend, now on Jim's shoulder, can see the cooking fires there. Perhaps Hob would like to ride on Sir Brian's shoulder?"

Hob immediately leaped over to land on Brian's shoulder. Brian looked a little startled, but did not object as Hob took a firm grip around his neck. Jim turned his head to watch them go out through the door, which closed noiselessly behind them, then looked back at abu al-Qusayr.

"You don't even want Hob listening to what you have to say?" he asked abu al-Qusayr.

"In this case, I think it's just as well," said the older magician. "I'm glad you sounded so confident now about dealing with these other creatures that might threaten you in the caravan. Actually, the threat is small.

Most of them like to find their victims alone. On the other hand, if you see the Mongols at all, they may come in such force that the caravan will be helpless before them. In that case, I suggest you not resist them. Just explain why you're going to Palmyra. I've arranged for some wine, and a certain amount also of cooked wine—I believe in the north you call it brandy, as well as other names—to use as a bribe on the Mongols. You might promise them whatever you think it might take to give you safe passage. Also, it might be wise if you made the cooked wine appear as if by magick, whether you actually use magick or not—I understand you're limiting your use of it at the present, and I applaud that. But magicking the cooked wine into existence would keep them from thinking there's more of it hidden around the caravan, someplace; in which case they would tear everything apart. The Mongols are known to be fond of alcohol.''

"I've heard that," said Jim; and, indeed, he had, although he had not remembered it until just this moment. It was another tag of knowledge from the twentieth-century world he and Angie had left behind.

"What about my using magic?" he said. "How do you suppose the Mongols would react to that?"

"I think it would serve you very well," said abu al-Qusayr. "It may even gain you some respect among them. They will class you with their shamans, who indeed are magickians of a sort, although they are other things as well, including being religious figures among the Mongols.''

"Speaking of magic," said Jim, "I've been enjoying the control of temperature you have in this house of yours. That will be magic, of course?''

"It is my one indulgence," said abu al-Qusayr, with something very like a sigh, "as your Master, Carolinus, indulges himself with flowers and green turf through the year, around his small cottage. When you reach A level, my son, experience will have made you clever in knowing how you can achieve your ends without magick; and consequently you will have magickal energy to spend on an indulgence or two.''

He sighed again.

"I say an indulgence or two," he went on, "because the architecture of this home of mine reflects an ancient memory, an ancient, fond memory, of the time when ours was a great civilization here to the south of the Mediterranean Sea. We had builders and scholars and wise men of many kinds. But then Genghis Khan's Mongols came and the cities were conquered or destroyed; and with them went much of the ways of thought and wisdom. Now I live alone and quietly; and seldom do I have a chance for discourse with one who thinks and ponders what he thinks and looks at the world to try and understand what he sees in it.''

He paused, and then almost visibly shook himself out of what seemed to be a sort of half-dream.

"But I talk too much about myself," he said. "More to the point is that, speaking of wise men and scholars, there are still a few thinkers wandering the world. You'll encounter one in the caravan. He's a young man still—no more than thirty years of age I would say—his name is ibn-Tariq and you may find his conversation a boon to you on the long ride to Palmyra. Have you ever ridden a camel before?"

"No," said Jim.

"You will find it interesting," said abu al-Qusayr.

CHAPTER 17

"Interesting" was not the word Jim would have chosen for the experience of riding a camel.

The caravan with which he, along with Brian and Hob, had left was five days out of Tripoli on the route that would take it eventually through Palmyra, climbing the steep path into the mountains, and Jim had yet to get any real control over the beast he rode.

It had to be made to kneel in order for him to get on the saddle because of the enormous height of its legs; and anyone else in the caravan, except Brian who was having the same sort of trouble, could make it do so simply by tapping its neck with a thin stick. Jim could tap away lightly or strongly or any way he wanted; and the camel simply ignored him. What the trick was, he had yet to learn. Also, the camel was equipped with reins, with which he should be able to guide it like a horse. But it ignored Jim's attempt to do any such thing.

What it would do, entirely on its own, was plod along in line with the other camels as long as they kept moving. When the other camels stopped, it stopped. It smelled, it made noisy bubbling sounds, and it was as indifferent to Jim on its back as if he had been a piece of baggage.

The one welcome thing about it was its pace, after the familiar jolting of a trotting horse. The camel traveled by moving both legs on one side forward at the same time. The result was joltless, and gave an almost soothing, rocking motion to the saddle. It occurred to Jim that it would be almost easy to sleep on the move in such a saddle—even more easy than in the Tuareg saddle with its high cross before the rider on which he could sleep, resting his arms on the crossbar and putting his head down on them.

In fact, Jim had already seen one of his fellow travelers sleeping hunched in his ordinary camel saddle.

This was a small, black-haired, bullet-headed man, with a short, curved sword and a couple of knives stuck into his belt, who rode with his legs crossed on the camel's neck before him, and who, it turned out, was a Mongol.

His name was Baiju; and he was apparently one of a Mongol tribe or group that was in disagreement with the Mongols they might meet along the way. It was difficult to learn much from him; but there was a strangely dangerous air about him, and Jim noticed that the population of the caravan in general either avoided him or were careful about doing anything that might offend him.

But another traveler was indeed a blessing. He was ibn-Tariq, the wandering scholar and thinker that abu al-Qusayr had mentioned to Jim.

He was obviously a man of means. His clothes, his baggage, his voice and actions and even the way he sat his camel proclaimed the educated aristocrat. In any case, whether he actually was an aristocrat or not, he was most certainly educated.

Jim could not make his camel go to this man; but ibn-Tariq had no trouble bringing his alongside Jim, and telling him much about the country as they went through it, about caravans, trade, and the history of the land. He was a camel-portable encyclopedia.

Often, during their conversations, Brian would either manage to urge his camel up to join them, or else he would get the help of someone else to do it for him; for ibn-Tariq was interesting to listen to.

Baiju the Mongol, however, never came over to speak with Jim when ibn-Tariq was there; and came seldom enough when Jim was alone. It seemed to Jim that Baiju looked at him, and his inability to manage the beast he rode, with a certain amount of contempt. But it was a tolerant contempt, mixed with a remarkable amount of respect. Somehow, he had learned that Jim was a magician.

Jim wondered if ibn-Tariq also knew; but if so, he was having trouble thinking of a way to ask about this politely. Ibn-Tariq himself was a model of politeness.

"About the ghouls and demons and such in these mountains," Jim ventured finally during a conversation between them on the fifth day. "How likely are we to run into them?"

"I have no doubt they are all about us now, and will continue to be so for the length of our journey," said ibn-Tariq. Like Brian, he sat very straight-backed in his saddle so that he seemed taller than his actual height, which was actually slightly shorter than Jim's, but not by much. He had a high bridge to his nose, but otherwise his face was handsome in a lean sort of way, and remarkably relaxed. His brown eyes seemed to see beyond anything he looked at, as if he was aware of all the forces that moved it or caused it to be. "To say nothing of Djinn and the lesser devils, as well as Assassins, Mongols and wild tribesmen who would rob us if they could."

"Shouldn't we be taking more care to protect ourselves against them, then?" Jim asked.

"I think we have relatively little to fear," said ibn-Tariq. "The ghouls prefer a single man, lost in the wastes. To him they appear as beautiful women—only when they open their mouths, it will be seen that the insides of those mouths are green. As you undoubtedly know, they devour mainly the dead, but will not hesitate to devour the living who are helpless to keep them off. The demons prefer for their prey those who have transgressed against the laws of God as laid down in the Koran. You are a nasraney, of course; and as an infidel would not be of great interest to them. I understand there are demons in your part of the world who would be, however; and of course against those you would have the protection of your faith, such as it is. Here, of course, it would not protect you against one of our demons, who know that there is no God but Allah. But I am interested. In what way would you protect yourself against one of your northern infidel demons?"

It was a polite opening for Jim to hint that magic, though unlike that of a demon, was also his game.

"I'm not all that sure we have individual demons where I come from, any more," said Jim. "They actually belong more to pagan superstition than anything else. There's the Dark Powers, of course; and they make and use such creatures as ogres, harpies and Worms. But none of those could properly be called demons. They're merely creatures created to physically attack humankind. They cannot be turned away, as ordinarily can all the Powers of Darkness, by such things as crossing yourself or saying the Lord's Prayer."

"Ah, yes," said ibn Tariq. "The prayer of Jesus of Nazareth. He is one of our saints, too, you know. A Muslim can invoke the name of Allah and hope for his protection; but whether he receives it or not will depend upon Allah's will. Few men are so sure of that, that they would chance going unscathed among the creatures of darkness. On the other hand, as I say, it is often those who have transgressed in the eyes of Allah, whom these creatures deliberately seek out."

"And the Assassins or the Mongols?" asked Jim. "Any human enemies?"

"We are a large caravan," answered ibn-Tariq. "The Assassins like to outnumber those they attack. Like whatever tribes that would prey upon us and live in these mountains, they are probably not numerous enough to make an attempt against us. Against a force of Mongols, of course, we would be helpless. They would outnumber us and they are very fierce

fighters. On the other hand, a force of Mongols would not be interested in anything as small as a caravan. They would probably be happening across us in the process of going toward something more important that they intended to attack, like a city.''

He paused and looked at Jim, clearly inviting him to speak. Jim hesitated. It was very clear that ibn-Tariq wanted to ask if he had some magical powers that would allow him to defend himself, and possibly all of the caravan, against Mongols, if they should appear; but politeness would not allow him to ask the question in any direct or leading manner.

Unfortunately, a comparable wariness made Jim hesitate to bring it up himself. By this time he was almost certain that ibn-Tariq knew he was a magician; but that was not the same thing as the fact being openly acknowledged between them.

Jim's mind struggled for some subtle way of dealing with the situation. He was not capable of the intricate, polite ways of approaching the topic that ibn-Tariq possessed. On the other hand, ibn-Tariq was pointedly leaving it to him to be the one to establish the fact; and Jim, while not wanting to hide his magical status, on the other hand wanted to preserve as much as possible of his primary character as a bluff English knight. An English knight who might have many other failings, but had certainly had some schooling in courtesy—at least enough not to boast of his accomplishments.

It made for a definite awkwardness. Ibn-Tariq, as a traveling scholar, was eager to trade information for information. He would have liked to have learned from Jim as much about magic as Jim would tell him, the names of any particular magicians he had studied under, and so forth. He had been trying to prod Jim delicately into talking about this for four days now.

"I was fascinated," went on ibn-Tariq, when the pause had reached unnatural proportions, "to learn about the great nasraney magician of Córdoba, and how he saved the city from an attack once more than half a century ago."

It was another delicate feeler; clearly designed to give Jim the opportunity to talk of comparable powers and situations with regard to an appearance of the Mongols. Unfortunately, Jim had never heard of the great nasraney magician of Córdoba, a city in Spain which, during the eleventh and twelfth centuries, had been almost the center of the western world, as far as North Africa was concerned.

"Ah well," Jim said. "I suppose if the Mongols show up, we'll just have to be polite to them and hope everything goes well."

"*Inshallah*" ("It is the will of God"), said ibn-Tariq, defeated. "In any case, the sun is close to the mountain tops, now. Shortly we will be

stopping for the night. I will ride forward and find out what our chosen stopping place will be like.''

Ibn-Tariq rode on ahead, and Jim was left alone. He was not particularly disappointed in this because he wanted to think. He would have liked to have asked ibn-Tariq more about Palmyra, and the chance of finding Geronde's father there. But he hesitated to talk about that until this business of his being a magician had been abandoned between them. What he really wanted—and, in fact, he had been trying to get into words—was to ask ibn-Tariq to keep any information on both Jim and Brian to himself.

It could probably not be kept entirely quiet, but the problem was that the name ''magician'' in ordinary gossip and conversation easily slipped into being ''great magician''; and great magicians attracted great interest. Great interest would stand in the way of his and Brian's investigation of Palmyra and the whereabouts of the Lord of Malvern, by as many discreet routes as possible.

Jim's main difficulty lay in the fact that, even with the help of his invisible and undoubtedly magic translator, he simply did not have the clever control of his tongue that ibn-Tariq had. He had yet to think of a good way of meeting ibn-Tariq halfway about the subject; so that it could be acknowledged between them without ever being put into words.

He was in the midst of this particular study when he became aware that he was no longer riding alone. Another camel had moved in beside him, and it was the one with Baiju, the Mongol, on its back.

Baiju had been riding along with him for several minutes; but in his usual fashion, he seemed in no hurry to open conversation with Jim.

It was strange, thought Jim. According to all visible characteristics, Baiju should appear unimportant, if not ridiculous. He was not only a little man, but he seemed to ride hunched in the saddle, although Jim had finally decided that his posture was indeed not so much hunched, as completely relaxed.

In fact, he seemed more at home in his saddle than anyone else in the caravan. His face was dish-shaped, with slightly slanted eyes and high cheek bones and yellow skin. His very dark eyes were essentially expressionless. It was impossible to read anything from them as to how he was feeling, let alone what his intentions might be.

Still, he had been friendly enough, in his laconic way. He was the very opposite of ibn-Tariq, in that he did not so much reply to what was said to him, as simply utter flat statements. Jim knew he would not speak until Jim initiated the conversation.

''We will be stopping for the night, soon,'' said Jim. ''It seems to me it's already starting to get cool; but then, we're steadily moving higher into the mountains.''

He looked at Baiju, who, under a coat of mail, appeared to be wearing nothing but a thin shirt of dark blue color, made of what looked like some surprisingly modern, close-woven, thin material.

"You do not notice the cold of the mountain heights with only that shirt under your mail?" he asked.

"The shirt is silk," said Baiju.

Jim felt a little foolish. Of course the Mongols, with their connections to the Far East, would tend to have garments made of silk. In fact, now that he stopped to think about the robe he had seen abu al-Qusayr wear . . .

"Still," he said, "in the west, we're used to wearing a garment of padding under our chain mail. Don't you usually prefer wearing something like that? Or are ways of dressing simply different here?"

"It is silk because of the arrows," said Baiju. "When an arrow goes into the body, the silk is pushed in with it. It is then easy to remove the arrow by pulling gently on the silk."

Jim winced internally. He had never heard of such a way of dealing with arrows; but perhaps it made sense. Silk was an interesting cloth in many ways, and it might well have the characteristic of entangling the barbed ends of an arrow and the strength not to tear loose, but bring the arrowhead out when pulled, instead of just tearing loose when it was pulled upon. At the same time, having an arrow removed that way would not be the most comfortable of experiences—though, come to think of it, having the arrow cut out might be even worse.

"Are Mongol arrows always barbed?" he asked.

"Always," said Baiju.

"And do the arrows and suchlike vary from tribe to tribe?" Jim asked. "Maybe I should say from kingdom to kingdom—"

"They do not vary," said Baiju.

"In the west, our weapons vary," said Jim. "Generally, of course there's the short sword and the long; and various styles of them. But usually you can tell by the weapon and the way a man's dressed where he's from. How do you tell where another Mongol's from?"

"You look," said Baiju. Jim thought he would go on from those first two words, but evidently they were his complete answer.

"I suppose what I meant to ask," said Jim, "is what differences do you look for? What about him, his clothes or his weapons, or whatever, tell you who he is?"

"You look," said Baiju. "That is all. You look—and you know."

"I see," said Jim. "If we run into a force of Mongols, have you any idea which kingdom of Mongols they'll be?"

"They would be of the Golden Horde." Baiju leaned from his saddle and spat on the ground.

"Your people?" asked Jim.

"No," said Baiju. "I am of the Il-khanate," said Baiju. "We hold this land against the House of Juchi in the Golden Horde, to the north."

They rode in silence together for a little ways.

"Are the Golden Horde friends of the Assassins?" asked Jim, finally. "Are there any Mongols among the Assassins?"

"No," said Baiju. "The Assassins are not warriors. Mongols are warriors."

"Ibn-Tariq," said Jim, "said the chances were we wouldn't be disturbed by Assassins, anyway; because the caravan is too strong."

Baiju turned his head and looked directly into Jim's eyes. Then he looked away again. Jim was growing used to the little man's ways, and he recognized this as another gesture of contempt. Clearly Baiju did not think much of the caravan's fighting ability.

They had been climbing a rocky defile between two large stony cliffs that ended in what looked like razor-edged rocks. But now they came to the head of the defile and the walls dwindled on each side, letting them out into an open space, filled with boulders of all sizes, from that of a pebble to that of a small house.

It looked like an ancient water course; and indeed it had a stream running through it. The stream was from a spring jetting out of the near vertical wall of a cliff right before them. Jim could hear the cries of camel riders ahead of him, reining in their camels and beginning to make them kneel. The stopping place for the night had been reached.

As the sun disappeared behind the mountains, and the light dwindled, most of the camels were at least partially unloaded and tents or tentlike shelters were set up. Thanks to abu al-Qusayr, Jim and Brian had two baggage camels as well as the two beasts they were riding, and one of these carried a tent, which they had learned to set up for themselves.

They got it up, got a cooking fire started just outside its front flap, using dried camel dung for fuel—it having formed part of their load for this section of the trip over the mountains. Baiju had gone off by himself. As far as Jim could see, the little man had no tent and merely curled up next to his camel, or in any convenient shelter from the wind he could find.

Ibn-Tariq had evidently joined another group, barely visible between the boulders at some little distance off, but it looked like a gathering of half a dozen of the merchants of the caravan in a sort of communal meal.

"These infidel messes do not really feed a man," grumbled Brian, as they sat down to eat the stew, made up of foodstuffs that were also part of their camel loads, and courtesy of abu al-Qusayr.

"Meat is scarce in these parts, evidently," said Jim. "For one thing

they seemed to have nothing but goats—or perhaps sheep; although we haven't see many sheep so far."

"There were at least adequate sheep on Cyprus," said Brian. "A roast of mutton can fill a man's stomach. But a few strings of this goat meat can hardly make anything of a handful of vegetables."

In spite of what he was saying, Brian was managing to eat more heartily than Jim at this, their late meal of the day. They only had two, one on getting started in the morning and one after stopping at night.

"Perhaps we will see some wild goats, or other game that live in these mountains," said Jim. He started to take off the thick leather ankle-boots he had bought in Tripoli for this mountain crossing; then changed his mind. His feet would be warmer overnight if he left them on. "And be able to kill an animal or two to provide ourselves with meat."

"May St. Francis mercifully send it so," said Brian.

Hob had come out of his knapsack on Jim's back and was perched on Jim's shoulder. They were far enough away from other members of the caravan so that he would be invisible in the last of the twilight, and the faint illumination of the fire. In fact, anyone there seeing him would probably have taken him for a monkey—a hairless, rather strange-looking monkey, but a monkey, nonetheless. He was about the right size and shape.

In any case, he was good at being as near to invisible as possible. He reveled in these evening caravan stops; and went riding from one waft of smoke to another, over all the cooking fires of the caravan, to come back bursting with useless information; plus stories of demons and monsters he had overheard—in the talk of men who never thought of looking up into where the thinning smoke was lost against the darkening skies. Talk that he could hardly wait to tell Jim all about.

However, he was a considerate hobgoblin; and when he came back to their tent this night, to find both Jim and Brian asleep, he let them slumber peacefully. He went back out to lie on a waft of smoke from what was left above their own cooking fire; thoughtfully, when it burned low, stoking it up with more of the fuel that had been planned to last them until the end of their journey.

CHAPTER 18

Jim woke to the feeling he was being suffocated. His mind was stunned and baffled, but his survival reflexes were working at full capacity. He burst through the front flap of the tent and came to full awakeness rolling down a rocky slope just outside it, rolling over and over, tightly locked with a slighter, hooded figure, who had been trying to wind a cloth around his head and tightly over his mouth and nose.

With his mind working again, at least slightly, he shifted his grip to the shoulders of his attacker, thrust out a knee to incapacitate him at a moment when Jim was on top, and banged the other's head upon the stony ground. The figure went limp and he got to his feet, only to be knocked off them again by three other hooded figures, who held him down and wrapped another cloth tightly around him in the same way. He fought mightily; and something hit him on the side of the head so lightly he scarcely felt it.

But, curiously, that was the last he remembered for some little time.

He came fully to his senses finally, with a feeling that quite some time had passed. He was walking along a narrow ridge of rock somewhere in the mountains, with Brian ahead of him, his hands tied behind his back. Also walking ahead of both him and Brian were a number of robed, brown-skinned men, none of whom he recognized. But then, he had really known only two or three people in the caravan. Whoever they were, they were not hooded; but that was little help. They could, for all he knew, have been merchants from the caravan itself.

He was aware of others like them behind him; and he had a confused memory of being half-conscious at some time earlier. He also had the feeling he had been walking for a long time, as much as a day or two. The left side of his head ached. He instinctively tried to put his hands up to touch it and see if it was sore, and abruptly realized that, like Brian's, they were tied behind him at the wrists—uncomfortably tied, as a matter of fact.

He had a memory some time back of stopping while walking in order to be deathly sick for some little time. The men about him had been very annoyed by this; but someone who was evidently their leader had come back, riding on a horse, and ordered them sharply to leave him alone until he was fit to walk again.

He remembered the blow on the side of his head then, and the word "concussion" jumped into his mind. Those were some of the signals— the impact that was enough to make him lose consciousness, the present headache and the soreness of his head, which he was now feeling on the right side of his head, the opposite of the side with the headache. There was a medical term for that pair of symptoms he could not remember right now. But all these three things pointed to a possible concussion. If he had been concussed, he shouldn't be walking like this. He should be resting as much as possible.

A concussion could cause brain damage, he remembered, because the blow on one side of the head made the brain dash itself against the bony cage of the skull on the opposite side; and it was on that opposite side that the damage to the brain occurred. He was not quite sure about the rest of it; the brain was either bleeding on the side that had been hurt, or swelling against the immovable bone of the skull, causing the pressure there that made concussion dangerous. Someone with a bad concussion could suddenly drop dead a day or so after being hit, without even knowing he or she had been badly hurt.

Now that he had concentrated on how he was feeling, he was also aware of exhaustion, an unsureness of balance and a heaviness of his whole body; as if it had been worn out by trudging along through the mountains this way, with hands bound behind it.

It made no sense. These men had apparently sneaked into the caravan when everyone was asleep; but they had taken only Brian and him as prisoners and were now leading them off someplace. He could release both Brian and himself with magic. For that matter, he could also transport Brian and himself away from here with magic, probably. But that could be done later, if necessary. Right now, he wanted to find out why this had happened. It might just be moving them closer to Geronde's father, if they stuck it out until they knew more about it.

But he wished his head would stop aching so he could think more clearly. He also wished he could put his hands up and feel the sore side of his head and find exactly what kind of a bump or cut was there.

Well, there was one thing he could certainly do; and if there was ever a legitimate use of magic, this would be it. Magic could not cure disease, but it could heal wounds. The hit on the head he had taken was clearly a wound; his brain had been wounded. He had to fight the headache to do

it, but with a little effort he managed to visualize his brain as red and swollen on the side that wasn't aching; and then visualize both the redness and the swelling as going away.

It took a moment before he realized this had worked. The sudden stopping of his headache was the most noticeable thing of all. He realized that he had almost become used to that headache—now that it was gone.

That didn't matter, though. The main thing was, whatever danger might have been there from concussion should be gone. Indeed, his head was very clear now; and unfortunately, one result of this was that he was much more conscious of the way the thongs, or whatever it was that was binding his wrists together, had been tied so tightly that his hands were aching from the interruption in normal blood flow.

He was ready, unthinkingly, to simply visualize his bonds as being more loose, so the blood could get back into them. But a new thought occurred to him—one that he silently condemned himself for not having had sooner. This was a land of all sorts of magic and near-magic; much of it, in the case of the Naturals, unconscious and not deliberately controlled; but there could be some from other sources that was deliberate. It was just possible that if he used noticeable magic, he would draw to himself the attention of someone who wanted to catch him doing just that, demonstrating whatever powers he had.

Perhaps it might be better to see if he could not get the bindings loosened some other way.

While all this had been going through his mind, they had come out into an opening in the path, which had formerly been a ridge running along a mountain face. Now it was entering into another little stony valley, with another spring coming out of the mountains and a small pool underneath it, from which water over-spilled and trickled away down the mountainside.

Those of his captors ahead of him were already gathered around the pool of the spring and drinking. Jim himself was suddenly conscious of a raging thirst at the sight of the water. He lengthened his strides toward it, but came to a halt behind the bodies of the captors ahead of him who were still waiting their turn to drink.

"Stand back, nasraney!" snapped one of his escort who had come up from behind him. There was nothing compassionate about his voice, but Jim seized the opportunity to speak to him.

"Look," he said. "I don't know where I am, and there's no way I could get away from you now. Can't you take these ropes, or whatever they are, off my wrists? Or at least loosen them? They're so tight my hands have gone numb; and I won't be able to drink unless I can scoop up the water."

For answer, the man swung a backhanded blow at his face that was so completely unexpected Jim was nearly knocked off his feet.

Instantly there was a hubbub around him, and another figure pushed itself through the crowd—or rather the crowd parted to let this other man through. He came up to Jim and the man who had hit him.

"What happened?" he asked the man.

"He tried to escape," said the man.

"He lies!" croaked a voice.

It was Brian's voice, and Brian shouldered his way through the crowd that had now closed tightly around them to confront this new authority. "He only asked that our bonds be loosened. They should be. Mine also. We are unarmed and have nowhere to run."

"He did not try to escape?" asked the man he spoke to.

"He did not, damn your black souls all to hell!" said Brian. "I am an English knight; and my word is good."

Brian was a battered sight. Both eyes were black, his nose was a little crooked now and his face had been cut or torn open in a few places. Also, he had limped as he had appeared through the crowd.

"It is he who lies—" The man who had hit Jim was beginning again, when the man who had just arrived struck him the same sort of backhanded blow the other had hit Jim with; and the man went down.

"I shall judge who lies, here!" said the leader. "You lie. These infidels do not."

Jim was not so sure of that. If he did not have his magic to fall back on, he told himself, he would have no more compunction about lying than the man now on the ground.

"Take off the bindings on their wrists!" said the leader, turning away and heading back toward the spring. "And let them drink!" He added over his shoulder.

Fingers fumbled with Jim's wrists. The bonds fell away; and a moment later Jim felt as if his hands were being put through the cleverest of torture machines that any medieval mind could imagine. It was simply the blood returning to his fingers, but for a moment he almost regretted that his wrists had been untied.

However, Brian was giving no sign of how his hands must feel—and they could not feel much different from Jim's. Also, those captors standing close around them, it seemed to Jim, were plainly—almost eagerly—watching for any sign of weakness or admitted pain. Jim managed to keep his own face straight; and slowly, the pain began to ebb away. He passed through a stage where he could actually feel the blood pulsing in his hands. Then this, too, faded; and he was left with the soreness of his wrists as his main concern.

He lifted his arms before him and looked at his wrists. They were an unlovely sight. The cords, thongs or whatever they were had cut through the skin and the flesh was furrowed and coated with blood. He made use of the pool to wash them off after drinking—he and Brian were the last to be allowed at the water. Clean, the wrists showed themselves to be more bruised than cut. Magic could have healed them, too; but there was the danger of any more use of magic being observed—by someone. The less everybody knew about his capabilities that way, the better.

Brian also washed his battered face; and it looked better with the traces of blood removed. He and Jim were allowed to go on with their hands free. Jim's fingers had explored the bump on the right side of his head—or where the bump had been; for evidently upon taking care of the concussion he had also taken care of the damage from the blow that caused it.

He and Brian were even allowed to walk side by side, where the route they followed was wide enough. Most of their escort was walking also. Only the man who had come back and ordered that their bonds be taken off was on horseback, and he rode at a walk at the head of the troop.

Jim did not speak; and Brian did not speak. Their eyes had met in a glance that perfectly agreed on the situation. Their escort was close enough about them to hear anything they said; and undoubtedly this was not unintentional. For once, Jim found himself less than grateful for the fact that everybody on this world seemed, at least, to speak the same language.

If there had been the same welter of different languages here that there had been in Jim's twentieth-century world, he and Brian could have talked English and possibly not been understood by those who were guarding them. For that matter, they could even have spoken in the broad Somersetshire dialect of the part of England where they lived, perfectly understandable to an English ear but possibly not so to an unaccustomed middle-eastern ear.

In any case, there would certainly be sometime later on when they would have a chance to compare notes and discuss the situation.

Two hours after that they came to their destination; a castle, or rather a stone fortification. It was considerably larger than Sir Mortimor's on Cyprus, but placed in almost as strong a natural defensive position on the steep side of a mountain, facing downslope.

It had no moat, but a trench had been cut—very probably by human labor, since it was obviously not a natural part of the terrain—before the great door in the front of the structure. A wooden bridge led over it, a drawbridge with chains running back into the castle; and as they crossed the trench, Jim looked down.

A second later he wished he had not. The trench was deeper than the

height of a man; and its bottom had sharp spikes or spears set in it, pointing up, so anyone falling (or being thrown) into it would instantly be pierced by half a dozen metal points. In fact, there were dead bodies there—ranging from near skeletons to some not more than a few days or perhaps some weeks dead; and the stench was choking.

But they passed on and through the doors, which opened before them; and came into something that was a cross between a roofed-over, but very small, courtyard and an open-air stable. Here their leader dismounted and gave his horse to an attendant.

He gave an order; and a couple of the escort prodded Jim and Brian forward at knife-point, so that all five went off in a small group by themselves.

They passed through a farther entrance, along a passage and down a flight of steps into a shorter passage, lined with cells on either side of a narrow corridor. They had been created by iron bars sunk into the stone at top and bottom; and the cells were divided to make cubicles about ten feet square.

The cells were almost twentieth-century modern in appearance; and by medieval standards they were remarkably clean. What this meant, Jim had no idea; but somehow the very cleanliness of it stirred an ominous feeling in him. He and Brian were herded into one of them and were locked in by a bar placed in sockets from the outside, with a chain hook below, so that the bar could not be lifted unless the end of the chain were detached; and the other end of the chain was fastened to the stone floor, out of reach of anyone behind the bars.

All this time the leader of the expedition, as Jim judged him to be, had said nothing. But now he did.

"You will wait here," he said. "In time our Holy Grandmaster will have you brought before him. Do not hope to escape. There is no way out."

He and the two who had herded Jim before them down to the cells turned and left. Jim and Brian were at last alone, left in a silence so profound that it almost seemed to thunder in Jim's ears. They looked at each other in the yellowish, flickering light from a cresset at the far end of the cells, on the wall through which the stairs descended to enter this place.

Brian still looked badly battered. But he was ignoring the fact, and his blue eyes were bright with interest. Already he was carefully examining the bars and as much as he could see of the room around them, including the ceiling and floor. After a moment he looked back to Jim and spoke to him in a low murmur, speaking almost into his ear.

"I see no way by which they could overhear what we say to each other

here," he said. "But I will wager such exists. Still, if we keep our voices down, and speak only when close to each other, perhaps we can keep any from understanding what we speak of, even if the sound itself can not be completely unheard."

Jim nodded.

"Do you have any understanding of why they have brought us here?" asked Brian. "Or, James, do you have any plans about what we might do about it?"

Jim put his head close to Brian's and answered with equal softness in his friend's ear.

"I don't know a thing about why they carried us away—just us—from that caravan," he said. "The crazy thing is, it looks almost as if the raid was put on only to get the two of us. Of course, there's no way of knowing what else they might have taken from the caravan while they were there."

"I agree with you," answered Brian. "It is all passing strange. Where are we, do you suppose?"

"From the mention of a Grandmaster," said Jim, "I'd guess we're in the headquarters of the Assassins. Why, I don't know. Can you think of any particular reason why anyone in this land wouldn't want us to find Geronde's father, or why the Assassins wouldn't, either?"

Brian shook his head.

"Well, I'll tell you one thing, Brian," Jim said. "If necessary, I can use magic and get us out of this—that is, unless there's something in this castle, or in this country, to stop it from working. But I don't think there is. So I can almost promise you I'll get us away safely, no matter what happens. The reason I haven't used it before this is because I'm beginning to think that for some reason someone might be wanting to know just how much I can do with magic; so besides using as little magic as possible—I told you why I was doing that—I'm trying to use the least amount when I have to use it, and in its simplest form. That's why I haven't healed our wrists where they had us tied up. They'd notice that right away."

"Oh, those marks?" said Brian. "They are nothing, James. Nothing—that is, unless they interfere with you doing—whatever you wish."

"They don't," said Jim. "Anyway, we're undoubtedly best acting like any two ordinary people who've been snatched up and brought here; and all we can do is wait for an explanation. Actually I think one will—"

He was interrupted suddenly by an unexpected but welcome voice.

"M'lord!" cried the familiar tones of Hob; and they both looked over to see the little hobgoblin slipping between two of the bars. Just outside

the bars was a brown dog wagging its tail ingratiatingly. "Look who I brought, m'lord!"

"I tried to warn everyone in the caravan by barking," said the Djinni-dog. "There're no dogs in the caravan. But either they did not rouse, or they were fearful of looking to see what made a barking where no barking should be. But I did rouse your hobgoblin, here. I did my best to save you, master!"

"Did you?" said Jim, still suspicious, for Kelb was clearly trying to imitate the innocent, direct and almost childlike way of expressing himself that came naturally to Hob.

"Oh, that was one of the things I was going to tell you, that night, m'lord," said Hob quickly. "At every cooking fire I visited all the men were telling each other that they were going to sleep specially heavily. Then, after one of them talked about it, the others would all look at each other strangely, without saying anything more for a moment. But when I got back, you and m'lord Brian were both asleep—"

"What is this?" Brian was staring at Kelb. "A talking dog?"

"It's a Djinni that wants my protection," said Jim. "I haven't made my mind up yet—" he added, enunciating clearly and looking directly and very hard at Kelb. "But there's one interesting thing. He's not trying to keep his voice down at all, so everything he's said is being heard someplace in this castle. Hob, you should remember that yourself. Everything you say that loudly is possibly going to be heard and understood someplace. We're sure they've got ways of listening to us."

"But they aren't listening now, m'lord," said Hob. "They've all been having some kind of meeting."

"Meeting?"

"Yes, master," said Kelb swiftly. "They are being told of another raid such as the one on the caravan. Their Grandmaster is telling them."

"Hmm," said Jim.

He turned to Hob.

"But how did you two get here from the caravan, Hob?"

"Oh, I carried him here along with me on the smoke," said Hob anxiously. "Did I do wrong, too, m'lord? I didn't know what I could do to help; but I thought if I got here, maybe you'd have an idea you could tell me and then I could do it; and I would be helpful."

"They will not need you," said Kelb to him. He turned back to Jim and Brian. "Oh, masters, fear not. If for some reason you cannot yourself free yourselves from this place, I will free you and set you once more on your path for Palmyra and the one you seek there."

"What do you know about us seeking someone in Palmyra?" demanded Jim.

But at that moment there were voices to be heard at the top of the stairs that led down to this cell block. Hob scrambled along the bars to a dark corner where his gray body was all but lost in shadow; and Kelb literally vanished.

CHAPTER 19

The voices came closer. They descended the stairs and four of their captors came in, together with the one who had been in charge of those who had kidnapped Jim and Brian.

Without a word, they unlocked the cell door, motioned Jim and Brian out and pushed them ahead up the stairs. They went through several long corridors into a large, square room with a domed roof in which windows with glass in them had been built, so that daylight filled the room with afternoon light. At the far end of the room a man sat upon cushions, and continued to sit motionless as Jim and Brian were brought before him. Then he lifted one hand; and the leader, as well as the four with him, left.

Brian and Jim were left standing before the seated man.

He was a man of indeterminate age, but Jim guessed him in his late forties or even fifties. He was possibly slightly overweight, but that could be simply because of his position, seated cross-legged on the green cushions beneath him. He was wearing a dark green robe of almost the same shade as the cushion he sat on. He had a hat on his head that was rather like a beret that had been puffed out, and was white in color. His eyes were dark, his eyebrows graying and his face clean-shaven. It was a benign face, a calm face, an almost gentle, fatherly face, except for a rather round, aggressive chin and a firmly closed, straight mouth above it that lent a touch of sternness to his expression, at odds with the calm, unwrinkled appearance of the rest of his features.

"So," he said, "you find yourself brought before me."

"And who the hell are you?" snapped Brian.

The man moved his eyes slowly to focus on Brian.

When he spoke again the tone of his voice was exactly the same.

"Know," he said, "I am Hasan ad-Dimri, who left my father's home early to travel from town to town, with others like myself. After some years, people would give me gifts, and bowed before me to hear words of wisdom from my lips. But in the night, one night, a blessed angel came

and spoke in my ear, saying thus—'*Oh, thou who are by rights ruler of all the world, the time of the return of Isma'il is at hand. But the way must be prepared for him. Therefore go thou and take control of the Hashasheen of the White Palace, in the mountains; revive their lost glory, and set them to the work of cleaning out the foul weeds from among the faithful and unfaithful alike; so that when Isma'il does come, he shall come to an earth cleansed and kept as is a well-kept garden.*' "

His gaze came back to Jim.

"You are both nasranies," he said, "and claim to be in search of another nasraney. As such, you are a stench in the nostrils of true believers. But you, who call yourself James, are worse than the one with you or the one you seek, because you are also a nasraney magician. I am in the shadow and protection of Allah's hand, and your magics will not work against me. I fear you not. But there are, even among the faithful, those who may be weak or erring in their worship of Allah; and upon those, your foul spells may have some effect, turning them from the true faith and dooming them to everlasting death. Therefore, it is my duty to see that you do no such thing. My children, the Hashasheen that you call 'Assassins,' will guide and guard your friend on his way to his destination. But you, at least, must be put to death here, by men who are of true faith and will be untouched by any infidel magic you may bring against them—"

He stopped speaking abruptly, on a note that sounded as if he had more to say. His gaze went between and beyond Jim and Brian.

They turned to see what he was looking at; and there, standing just a little behind them, upright in his red robe, was abu al-Qusayr.

"*Salaam,*" said abu al-Qusayr to Hasan ad-Dimri.

"*Salaam aleikum.*"

Jim, his brain still reeling from the thought that he suddenly might be inches from an inescapable death, realized that for once his translator was not translating; but that thought was washed out by a powerful feeling of relief. Help had come without his needing to use magic.

It was true that the two words he had just heard were some of the very few he recognized in Arabic—ordinary words of greeting. But now abu al-Qusayr was continuing to speak in the perfectly understandable words of the language everyone spoke here.

"Allah has made it so," said abu al-Qusayr, "that those who are true to the faith may only be vulnerable to those who are also of the true faith—whatever that faith may be. Therefore I, who am a Muslim and whose faith is pure, have been sent as a representative from the Kingdom of Magickians to speak for this nasraney whose life you would end."

"I fear no magicians—" began Hasan ad-Dimri; but suddenly he was

speaking Arabic again, and abu al-Qusayr was answering him in the same language. Jim's mind, sharpened by the threat of Hasan, fumbled for the reason his translator was once more not translating. Their talk concerned him and Brian, because he heard the English names mentioned in the flood of Arabic. But for some reason, he was not to understand what they said to each other. Why should his unknown translator on this world suddenly become a censor? It never had before.

Then it came to him—ten to one, it was abu al-Qusayr who did not want him to know what was being said; and who had caused the change.

Suddenly, he felt Brian's elbow dig into his side.

"What are they talking about?" Brian whispered in his ear. "I do not comprehend these noises."

"I don't know, either," said Jim.

His mind was still whirling over Hasan's death threat. Of course, before letting himself be killed he would most certainly use his magic to transport himself and Brian safely home to England.

But Brian might not want to go. It could be that with Jim dead, the Assassins would even help Brian as Hasan had promised, to find Geronde's father, if he let them "guide and guard him" to his destination. On the other hand, Hasan could be playing with them both, and Brian could also be put to death as well—

"—Clearly, there is no more to discuss," said abu al-Qusayr, suddenly understandable again. He turned from Hasan to Jim and Brian. "I am sorry I could not be of help."

Jim was conscious of a shimmer all around them; and through the quiveriness of that part of the air that shimmered, he saw Hasan still sitting with the same expression on his face, and apparently looking through and past them, as if they were not there. Obviously, abu al-Qusayr had his magic at work again; and their present speech was private from the Grandmaster of the Assassins.

"You weren't able to help us at all?" Jim asked, staring at him.

"I'm afraid not," said abu al-Qusayr. "There is nothing more to say but goodbye. I will explain to Carolinus, of course, that I could do nothing."

"Wait a minute," said Jim. "What about us?"

Abu al-Qusayr shrugged.

"It is the will of Allah," he said.

"What is the will of Allah?" demanded Jim.

"That whatever will happen here between you and Hasan must happen," said abu al-Qusayr.

"You mean he's going ahead with the idea of killing me and doing

God knows what to Brian under the guise of sending him off with an escort?''

''I'm afraid so,'' said abu al-Qusayr. ''He believes himself completely invincible. He was a Sufi, as I told you, and Allah uses them in strange ways. Or it may be that Allah has deprived him of the power to understand who and what you are. What is certain is that there is an aura of power around this place. A low-ranked magickian like yourself, Jim, has probably not sensed it—but I do, very clearly. It may even be that he has acquired a Djinni for a friend, or one for a slave; and—knowing little of real magick—believes that nothing can stand against him.''

''Well, why was it just a matter of convincing him?'' asked Jim. ''You have real power.''

''I have, and you have, only *defensive* power, Jim—remember?'' said abu al-Qusayr. ''In effect, he left it up to me to force him to change his mind; and of course I cannot use force for that reason.''

He became strangely glum suddenly.

''It may just be, too,'' he said, ''that he has become too much an Isma'ili, with all their stubbornness.''

He cleared his throat and spat on the floor beyond the quiveriness. Hasan stared straight ahead, unperceiving.

''What are Isma'ilis?'' said Brian.

''Those who follow Isma'il instead of Musa, as the Seventh Imam,'' answered abu al-Qusayr. ''But now I must take my leave. What is written is written. Farewell.''

He disappeared. With him went the quiveriness of the air around them, and—happily—the results of his spitting on the Grandmaster's floor.

''Enough!'' said Hasan, as suddenly as someone waked out of a sound sleep. ''Take them away!''

Almost immediately, there were men back around Jim and Brian. Jim and Brian were hustled back to their cell.

''James,'' said Brian, when they were alone again. ''You must explain all this to me. I am an ordinary knight, who says his prayers daily, but leaves all such mysteries to those who are supposed to understand them. This Holy Land seems to be a place of a multitude of strange names and even stranger happenings. That man upstairs who called himself Hasten-something—''

''Hasan,'' corrected Jim automatically.

''Hasan, then,'' said Brian. ''Can he really think that I would go blithely off with an escort to wherever I wished with never a backward glance, if you were to be put to death? Has he no knowledge at all of what a knight is?''

''Actually,'' said Jim, ''he probably doesn't. But don't concern yourself

about it, Brian. I can easily use my own magic to escape from here; and take you along as well. We could be back in our own castles in a moment.''

"But I thought you were saving your magic." Brian frowned at him.

"Not in the case of emergencies like this," said Jim stoutly. "But I wasn't too sure that you would want to go back to England; and if you stay, I should stay with you."

"Well . . ." Brian looked uncomfortable. "Perhaps . . . the fact of the matter is, James . . . well, I took a vow."

"A vow?" asked Jim.

"In the height of my happiness over having decided to put the King's present to good use," said Brian, "I took Geronde with me, down to the small chapel Malvern Castle possesses—as you know—and there, before the altar and the cross, I vowed to never cease from searching for her father until either I found him, or came to certain knowledge he was dead. Could not your magic simply take us both to Palmyra, James, since you are willing to spend it, after all, to leave this place?"

"I'm afraid not, Brian," said Jim. "I can only take us to places I can visualize. We could go back to abu al-Qusayr's, or Sir Mortimor's; but I don't know any other route to Palmyra but the one we were just taking. We ought to be able to travel overland to Palmyra, too, down from the north; but I wouldn't know how to find my way. But, if we were anywhere on the Lebanon coast here, word would get back to the Assassins and they'd be on our trail again. If we'd been able to get to Palmyra using magic, I'd have been tempted to go that way in the first place, instead of with the caravan. But abu al-Qusayr understood, back in Tripoli, when he suggested the caravan. We have to travel like ordinary people; and somehow we have to get where we want and find out what we want to find out, like ordinary people.''

"But we are not ordinary," said Brian, "I am a knight; and you are not only a knight, but a magician."

"True," said Jim, "but neither of those things seem to be helping us right now."

"M'lord . . ." It was the voice of Hob, once again perched on a bar right above their heads, once more timidly entering the conversation.

"Hob!" said Jim. "I'd forgotten about you back here for just a moment. You don't know any way we could get away, riding your smoke, do you?"

"We'd have to have some smoke first," said Hob, "and I've lost the smoke waft on which I brought the dog-Djinni here. Anyway I can't carry two big people on the smoke with me. I could take one—but for smoke I need a fire. There must be fires someplace in this castle, but I don't know where, and I don't know how to get to them. Do you think if I went

and looked, that the people here would leave me alone—or would they chase me?"

"I think they'd chase you all right," said Jim. "In fact, they'd probably do their best to kill you. You stay where you are."

"But I've got to get you out of this, m'lord," said Hob. "You and m'lord Brian both. M'lady would never forgive me if I didn't."

"It's good of you to feel that way, Hob," said Jim, "but I don't know what you can do."

"Well, then, I thought we might talk to that Djinni once more," said Hob.

"Djinni?"

A whine sounded on his ears and drew his attention to the corridor between the cages. Outside the iron bars of their cell was the brown dog, again, wagging his tail.

"Kelb!" said Jim. "You're a fair-weather friend! If you wanted to be helpful, why haven't you been helpful before this?"

"I have been helpful, my master," said Kelb. "Know that when that which surrounds us was built, it was before there were any Assassins in it. It was built by a robber knight, a nasraney like yourselves, who preyed upon the caravan route. He had come here as other Franks from the north came, two hundred years ago, speaking of a Holy War against those who lived here. This is none other than the Kasr al-Abiyadh, which is otherwise now called the White Palace."

"White?" asked Brian.

"I don't know why it was so named," said Kelb. "But so it was; and so it is called in this day, even by the Hashasheen, themselves. In any case, I have searched for the secret way out and just now found it. And with your great magic, O my master, you can undoubtedly not only loose yourself and your nasraney companion from this cage whenever you want, but with my help find that secret way and escape."

An alarm bell went off in Jim's mind. Any fortified place that Jim had come to know of in these Middle Ages had such a secret way out. There was one out of Malencontri, for example—and knowledge of such ways out was usually the tightly guarded secret of the owners of the castle themselves. Sometimes the secret was lost when the castle changed hands by war; but very often it was rediscovered again, and once more kept secret by the finder and those valuable to him or her. But Jim had just come from nearly a week of polite prying by ibn-Tariq to find out about him as a magician. The thought had crossed his mind, while he had been dodging these questions of ibn-Tariq, that the other might have some ulterior motive for wanting to know how much magic Jim could wield.

He had not worried too much about it, however; but now he was sud-

denly wary. His wariness was reinforced by a glimpse of Hob out of the corner of his eye. The hobgoblin had left Jim's back and climbed the bars of Jim's cage first—almost like a monkey—and had gradually, but unobtrusively, gone over to the bars of the next cage and out on its door which was swung open. The result was that now he sat at the top of that door behind Kelb's vision and, sitting on top of that door, Hob was now shaking his head vigorously and making faces at Jim.

The hobgoblin's vigorous unspoken message crystallized Jim's suspicion.

"Very good, Kelb," he said. "That's a point in your favor. I will take it into consideration. Meanwhile, you may go. I must sit and think a while."

"Yes, O my master," said Kelb. And he disappeared.

As soon as he was gone, Jim beckoned Hob in until he was once more sitting on Jim's shoulder; and then Jim moved closer to Brian, who was looking puzzled.

There is a time for small magics, Jim thought to himself. He visualized Brian and Hob as being able to hear him when he thought at them; and he would be able to hear them when they thought back.

Now, Brian, Hob, he said, *I will talk to you without using my voice and you must simply think the words you want to tell me and I will hear them.*

Exactly like that, thought Jim. He looked at Brian again and saw that Brian was understanding. There was a tight smile on his face. *Now Hob, and Brian, you both know I'm trying to conserve my magic; so we're going to do this with as little use of magic as we can. To begin with, Hob, could you get some smoke from that cresset in the corner? Remember, just think, don't say the words.*

I don't know if I can think them without talking, said Hob—and looked at first astounded and then tremendously pleased. *I can do it! I can do it! The cresset hardly puts out a good waft, but I can gather enough I think— like I gathered the smoke for the boats. Yes, m'lord, I can climb up to that cresset. The bars go up within a few feet of it and then I can simply take a jump to the bracket that holds the basket where the fire is.*

You won't burn yourself? asked Jim.

Oh no, said Hob. *Fire and smoke are friends of mine.*

Fine, said Jim. *Hob, I want you to climb up the cresset, so that you can reach the smoke, and then ride some smoke through as much of the palace as you can, without people seeing you around the building, and find that secret way Kelb was talking about.*

Hah! said Hob proudly. *M'lord, I already know where it is. When the Djinni brought me here, the first chance I got to leave him alone, I rode the smoke around the building and it was no trouble at all to find out all*

*about it and particularly the underground tunnel that leads to the outside.
I'm sure that's what he was talking about—it's just like the one at Malencontri.*

Thanks, Hob, thought Jim. *But if I were you, I wouldn't mention the
tunnel at Malencontri in front of anyone but Sir Brian here.*

Oh. Yes, m'lord, said Hob. *Do you want me to take you on the smoke
and go out that way?*

He checked himself suddenly.

I forgot, he said sadly, *you're too big, m'lord, you and Sir Brian, to go
through the vents.*

The vents? said Brian.

The vents just above the cresset, to let the smoke out.

Yes, said Jim. *Do we have to go through areas of this place where there
are a lot of Assassins?*

Yes, m'lord, thought Hob. *The way passes through a part of the building
that contains a place they call Paradise, to which new Assassin people
are taken. They are all sort of drunk and funny there.*

I see, said Jim.

James? said Brian.

Jim looked at him.

*Do you think you can find a way there without magic? I vow it is beyond
my abilities.*

I guess I'll have to, said Jim. *I'll give it a try, anyway.*

He pondered for a little while, staring unseeingly at the bars and stone
walls in front of their cell.

"Kelb!" he said out loud.

Kelb appeared, wagging his tail.

"Tell me, Kelb," Jim said, "you can make yourself invisible any time
you want to, can't you?"

"Invisible, O my master?" echoed Kelb. "I do not understand."

"Are you capable of making yourself so people can't see you, even
though you're still there?"

"Oh, yes," said Kelb. "In fact, I do that a lot when I'm being chased.
I'll go around a corner and get out of their sight; and those who chase
me will come around the corner and see only a room or a corridor where
there is no dog to be found. They will wonder a moment; but then go
someplace else that I might have gone. Then I turn back into being seen
and go about my way—it's easier, you see, being seen. I can make myself
so they can't see me, but I have to keep working at it to stay so."

"And when you turn invisible, everything about you turns invisible
too?" asked Jim.

"Oh yes, master," said Kelb.

"Good," said Jim. "Then, I've got a job for you. You'll carry Brian and me out that secret escape tunnel you talked about. Now, I'll tell you what to do, Kelb. Just turn sideways and lean against the bars at the front of this cage of ours, would you?"

"If I do this, master," said Kelb, with a new, cunning note in his voice, "you will then take me under your protection against Sakhr al-Jinni? If so, I will be your most loyal follower."

"You can't be a loyaler follower than I am," said Hob quickly. He jumped on to Jim's shoulder and clung to Jim's neck.

"Yes, I can," said Kelb.

"No, you can't!" said Hob. "You absolutely can not!"

"Never mind that now," said Jim. "We won't worry about it. Hob, you are my old and faithful Hob of Malencontri. As for you, Kelb, you'll have to show yourself faithful over the same number of years that Hob has been faithful to me—"

"—Since m'lord and m'lady first moved into Malencontri," put in Hob hastily. "I know I didn't talk to you a lot at first . . . and so forth, m'lord. But a hobgoblin is always faithful to those in whose house he lives. And you and m'lady were people I loved from the first moment. I am the most loyal—the most loyal—"

"Yes, Hob," said Jim. "No need to get excited. Feel secure. And I'm glad you reminded me you were there. I was thinking only of Brian and myself for a moment. Lean up against the bars, Kelb; and, yes, I will take you on and promise you my protection—which I shall continue to do until you do something that causes me to cast you off. So you'd better be on your best behavior at all times."

"None shall be on better behavior than me," said Kelb.

"You can't possibly—" Hob began energetically; but Jim cut him off.

"Hob," he said, "never mind, now. I told you you were my old and trusted retainer, and as yet Kelb has got to win his place. Now, Kelb, we three are going to be small insects riding on your back; and you're to carry us to a secret passage out of this palace. Do you, or do you not, know how to find it?"

"I do," whined Kelb. "It's just beyond Paradise—"

"Good enough," said Jim. "Lean against the bars."

Kelb still hesitated.

"What does my master intend to do?" he asked, cautiously.

"Nothing important," said Jim. "I'll simply turn myself, Brian and Hob into fleas on you, hidden in your hair. You'll sneak through the corridors to the way out, and when you go invisible we'll be that way too."

"I know not if you will indeed become unseen when I do, master,"
said Kelb.

"If the dog can go invisible, why can't he make us invisible?" said
Brian. "That way we wouldn't have to be fleas."

"I can't, master," said Kelb.

"Why not?"

"He's a Natural, not a magician," Jim reminded Brian. "Let's not have
any more talk, now. Kelb—against the bars!"

"Ought to be able to," muttered Brian.

"Whatever," said Jim impatiently. "As fleas we'll be too small to be
noticed anyway. Now, Kelb!"

Kelb turned sideways and pressed himself against the bars.

Jim had never turned himself into an insect before. He had heard Carolinus threaten to turn humans, animals or Naturals into insects; and he
had actually seen Carolinus turn a thirty-foot sea devil into a very large
beetle. But Jim had never done it, or even turned himself into an animal
before. Still, visualization had lately been making everything seem possible, and he could think of no drawbacks to the idea. They would simply
ride Kelb all the way out of this Kasr al-Abiyadh, or White Palace. He
half closed his eyes and concentrated on visualizing Brian, himself and
Hob as fleas on Kelb's hide, and locked the picture firmly in his mind
and concentrated on it.

"Here we go," he said.

And so they went.

CHAPTER 20

As it turned out, luck was with them. Kelb encountered no one on his way up the stairs from the cell block, or after that for some distance.

It was just as well that things had fallen out that way, Jim thought later. Because his first reaction after transforming himself into a flea was to discover at least one of the unfortunate side effects of the transformation. He had forgotten entirely what the viewpoint of a flea would be, out of sight in the hair on a dog's back.

Basically, the view was of hair. Hairs like tree trunks, all around them and leaning over them. There was, of course, the skin of Kelb underneath him. He felt a momentary instinctive urge to try to get at some of the blood beneath that skin, but overruled it. However, meanwhile, as in a dense growth of something like bamboo, he was still completely fenced in by hair—hair not only enclosing him but reaching up to shut out any sight of what might be above its tips.

This would not do. What he needed was a viewpoint outside his flea body. He visualized the prospect as seen through Kelb's eyes.

However, what he found himself seeing, though recognizable, was—as in the vision of all dogs—in black and white; and so different that it took a moment for him to make out even the stone walls and stone roof overhead. This would not do.

What he wanted was human vision; but human vision that would be completely disembodied.

Well, there was no reason why that should not be achievable by a very small amount of magic. What came immediately to mind was a pair of invisible human eyes floating in the air just above Kelb's head. A concept that fitted into words easily enough, but was a little hard to picture in the mind. To begin with, how did you picture eyes if they were invisible?

He had wrestled with that for a moment until the obvious answer came to him.

Of course, the invisible eyes didn't have to be like a pair of human

eyeballs, only invisible. It could be as if his flea-eyes were magic glasses connected to an invisible television camera hookup, which could be swiveled around, up or down, to let him hear and see things in perfectly normal human fashion, in any direction from Kelb's head.

He had visualized such a camera arrangement, then made it invisible, then turned it on; and suddenly he had achieved a good view of the corridor down which Kelb was trotting. It was a corridor perfectly bare of any kind of decoration, no carpet on the stone floor—that accounted for the sound he now heard of Kelb's claws clicking as he moved. The only thing that broke the corridor walls on either side were occasional entrances, either to rooms or other corridors; but Kelb was proceeding with apparent confidence, giving every indication of knowing where he was going.

"Where are we?" Jim started to ask the Djinni-dog. But even before the words were formed, he realized he had nothing to form them with. Not only was he so tiny that his voice would probably not be heard by Kelb; but he had no vocal apparatus as a flea.

It was true, he remembered, that the watch-beetle that Carolinus had summoned up on Jim's first acquaintance with the magician had spoken in a high tinny voice, but that might simply have been made possible by Carolinus's magic. Jim also remembered that Rrrnlf the giant sea devil, reduced to beetle size, had apparently had no voice at all. Though Carolinus had appeared to hear him saying things then, and talked with him in a conversation of which only Carolinus's side was audible.

What he wanted now, Jim decided, was to be able to speak inside Kelb's mind.

He tried to visualize what a Djinni's mind might look like. A sort of place of shadows? He had discovered sometime since that his visualizations did not have to be correct to work. It was the concept behind the visualization that made the structure on which his creative ability could act.

He concentrated on his place of shadows; and in his own mind he spoke to the dog.

Where are we?

Kelb came to an abrupt stop.

"Master?" he said, in a voice that quavered with what—if it was not fear—was a very good imitation of it.

That's all right. It's me, thought Jim. *Where are we?*

"I am concerned, master," said Kelb. "We're now in the quarters of the ordinary Assassins; and I would have thought we'd run into some of them before now. I do not understand this, unless a number of them are now out on some raid or other."

Jim realized that Kelb was speaking his words out loud.

You don't have to actually say what you tell me, Jim said. *Just think it. I'll hear it. Think the words.*

Indeed, you are a great magician, said Kelb, thinking the words. *Do you hear me now?*

I hear you loud and clear, said Jim. *You were just saying a number of the Assassins might have been sent off on a raid—against the caravan again?*

Oh, no, said Kelb. *But there has been talk for some time of the fact that the Golden Horde Mongols were planning a foray down here into what is actually Il-Khanate Mongol territory; and during the last two hundred years Mongols have taken many Assassin castles. Hasan ad-Dimri could have sent out many of his men in a strong group to see if any such Mongol force is coming this way; so he can take measures for defense. That's the only thing I can think of—*

He broke off suddenly, as two men barely in their twenties stepped out of one of the entrances ahead and turned to stare directly at him.

Kelb went invisible, and began to try to sneak up along the wall at his left, which was farthest from where they were standing. He moved with surprising softness, his nails no longer clicking on the floor. Jim suddenly thought of Brian and Hob. He turned his mental camera view back on himself and his fellow fleas, and discovered they were being carried along in mid-air, quite visible themselves—but only as specks.

It suddenly occurred to him that the amount of magical energy required to make three fleas invisible would be hardly any amount at all. Accordingly, he did so. He spoke mentally to Brian and Hob—meanwhile making sure that when they tried to speak back it would be a mind-to-mind contact—though where a mind could hide in the body of a flea, he had no idea. He did not know much about a flea's anatomy; but he was fairly sure that like most insects it did not have a brain.

Brian? he asked. *Hob?*

M'lord— Hob began on a note of alarm; but Brian interrupted him.

James? he said. *Where are you? I don't know whether I was seeing you or just feeling you close here; but I can't do that now.*

I'm right here, said Jim. *I made us all invisible and inaudible, so that those two Assassins up ahead won't hear or see us. Kelb's already made himself invisible.*

I noticed, thought Brian, a little sourly. *James, this is not my favorite way of traveling.*

It's the best I can do at the moment, Brian, said Jim.

Oh, I'm not blaming you, James, said Brian. *It's just that fleas are foul creatures. I don't like being one—craving your pardon, James,* he added hurriedly, *since you yourself are also a flea at the moment.*

No offense taken whatsoever, Brian, said Jim. *I quite understand how being a flea could bother a knight. I'm not too bothered myself, possibly because of being a magician, and being more used to this than you.*

Of course, said Brian, *naturally. Pray forgive my bad manners.*

They aren't bad manners, Brian— Jim broke off. They were now almost level with the two men, who were talking to each other in low voices. To Jim's surprise their faces were a pasty white.

"I saw a dog," one was saying. "I'm sure of it."

"I saw no dog," said the other Assassin. He was a little bit taller and possibly a year or so older than his companion—at least somewhat more mature-looking. He closed his eyes. "I saw nothing, I heard nothing."

"But I was sure—" began the Assassin who had been first to speak, uncertainly.

"Allah curse thee for the donkey wits thou wast born with!" snapped the other. "O, fool! Were there ever any dogs in the White Palace?"

"No . . ." said the other.

"Could a dog get in here without passing the guards at the gate?"

"No, of course not—"

"If a dog was to be allowed in, would we not have heard about it— unless such as you or I was not supposed to know it was here?"

The jaw of the smaller Assassin dropped.

"So," went on the taller Assassin, "I say it again. There is no dog, no voice! Do you see a dog now? Do you hear a voice now?"

"No."

"Then there was none; and I, at least, was never here."

The smaller Assassin's face had now whitened further, possibly to the shade of a well-laundered ghost.

"Neither was I," he said, and ducked back into the entrance out of which they had come, colliding with the taller Assassin, who was already on his way out of sight.

What now? asked Brian, as they passed the entrance into which the two men had vanished, and got a glimpse of a short hallway with a green door at the end, tightly closed.

I'm not sure, thought Jim. *Kelb?*

Yes, my master? said Kelb, becoming suddenly visible again.

How close are we to this secret way out now? Jim asked.

We have only to pass through Paradise, said Kelb. *It is the place to which they bring the new recruits. There will be some there, undoubtedly, but it will not matter if they see us, or hear us, because we will simply be something else in what they believe is Paradise; and they may not even see us as we are.*

Paradise? said Jim thoughtfully. *Why do you call an indoctrination center for recruits 'Paradise'?*

Forgive me, master, said Kelb, *my understanding does not extend to knowing what 'indoctrination' means. But it is the place where they take those newly committed to being Hashasheens, after filling them with hashish first, and then telling them they are going to paradise; and to them, under the drug, it is as if they went.*

We'll go through it invisible anyway, said Jim.

Master, it is not necessary—

You will stay invisible, said Jim.

Yes, master.

Shortly after that they turned down one of the other entrances into a corridor that led for some little distance, but ended in a wide high door painted a yellow-gold color that filled the full height and width of the corridor. Kelb's voice came out of nothingness.

"Forgive me, master," he said timidly, "but I can pass through this door without opening it. Is it so with you, master?"

"Thanks for telling me," said Jim. He hastily visualized himself and the two other fleas passing through the door as if it was no more than a projected illusion; quickly adding the magic stipulation that he, Brian and Hob should do this while still in connection with the skin of Kelb.

They passed through.

Within was a very large room indeed.

Its domed ceiling and much of its upper walls were painted a bright sunlit blue. Beneath this was what seemed to be a rather crude mock-up imitation of an oasis—the kind of imitation that inexperienced amateur theater stage carpenters might have produced. The trees that surrounded them were all fake palm trees, reaching up to an umbrella of false leaves at the top. From somewhere relatively cool air was blowing through the place, there was a pool of water in the center of the room, and in the middle of the pool a fountain spurted some three feet in the air and splashed back into the water.

Around the edges of this pool, sitting with their backs propped up against imitation palm tree trunks, were a number of young men, most of them seemingly lost in thought, or with their eyes shut—whether asleep or not he did not know. There were also a number of women around, most of them middle-aged and rather businesslike in expression, who seemed mostly concerned with gathering in groups, talking and eating. Nearly all the male figures lying around had trays of food near them, but very few were paying any attention to them. They looked dazed.

The women, however, were busy with their conversation and food. Occasionally one of them would break off to go over to one of the recumbent

figures and stroke some fingers under his chin, possibly murmur to him or pay various sorts of little attentions, then carefully evade the slow grasp which might respond to these attentions—but by no means always did—and then return to the group; or go on to give the same sort of momentary touching and talking to another of the recumbent figures. The women were dressed in what seemed to be layers of filmy, semitransparent silk garments that covered them from neck to wrists and ankles, and were of various hues.

The clothes, in fact, were lovely. The women, Jim decided, on the whole were not; nor did they seem to be making any effort to be so.

What are those round things they are eating? Brian demanded, staring at the gathered group of women.

Sheep's eyes, answered Kelb.

Jim gagged, mentally, but nonetheless uncomfortably.

Say you so? said Brian, in an interested voice. *I wonder what they taste like. What about those long ropelike things that they chew on?*

Sheep's entrails, said Kelb, *stuffed of course with rice and sugar and cinnamon and other good things.*

Hah! Like a Scot's haggis, eh? said Brian. *There were certainly Scotsmen with the first crusade. They must have gotten in among these infidels—*

He broke off.

They are not particularly dainty about how they reach into the communal pot of food, however, he went on. *It is true they wipe their hands, but only so often; and I have seen more than one hand go in to the wrist. Also they feed each other, and those beneath the trees.*

This last was true, Jim noticed. One of the things done by these women, who must be playing the part of the Houris, the women with which the Blessed were solaced in Paradise, would be to occasionally make a small ball of food from some of the foods on the tray beside a recumbent figure and put it into his mouth. But not always. Very often she just gave the dazed man a pat, or a stroke—and went on to the next one.

They skirted the pool and went on through the fake palm trees, with the figures against them becoming fewer and fewer until they saw a wall ahead of them. Low down, the wall was unpainted; and as far as Jim could see, there was no door in it. But Kelb carried them right to the wall, regardless.

Arriving at the point where the sand of the floor met the wall, he sniffed doglike along the line where wall met sand until he reached a spot where he began to dig industriously with his front paws. Sand spurted backward until he finally exposed what appeared to be part of a tiled floor, blue and white squares of glazed tiles alternating in a checkerboard pattern.

He pressed one of the blue tiles with a paw, and in front of him the apparently seamless wall slipped downward, revealing a rectangular opening.

"We now enter, my master," said Kelb, aloud.

He went in. In the dimness of the narrow, walled passage, he hesitated.

"Are you still with me, master?" he asked.

Jim remembered the fact that the Djinni could probably no more feel them than see them.

"We're here, Kelb," he said, also allowing his words this time to come out as spoken sound.

"I am much relieved, my master," said Kelb. He went back to the opening in the wall, and using his paws pulled sand back over the tile that he had exposed earlier. Then he returned to approximately where he had stood before, and slowly but silently, the stone of the entrance slid up to fill the aperture through which they had entered.

As it did, an utter blackness descended on them. Kelb's voice came out of it.

"Master, there is no more need for you and those with you to ride as fleas upon me. If you will return to your ordinary bodies, you will find to your right, on the wall, a rack of torches, and at the end of the rack, a flint and steel wherewith to light them. There is a powder on the thick end of the torch that will make them light easily if you get a spark to them."

Jim made the necessary magic adjustment. Still in darkness, but now feeling the slight weight of Hob at the back of his neck, and also feeling rather than seeing Brian's presence beside him, he reached out. He rammed his fingers rather painfully against a hard wall surface. Then he ran his hand over it, up and down, moving along as if he was using a brush to paint it. Finally he touched what felt like a curved wooden stand.

In the stand, he felt a row of upright bundles of something that felt more like tightly rolled paper than anything else.

He lifted one from its hole, groped again, and found, dangling on a cord, the flint and steel that Kelb had mentioned. Holding the torch in his left armpit, he struck the flint and steel together with both hands until a spark jumped in the right direction to touch the upper, thicker end of the torch. A flame burst into view, spreading and brightening until it illuminated the end of a long tunnel in the rock.

It also revealed Brian, still looking somewhat battered, but cheerful, and Kelb in his dog form looking expectantly up at him.

"Hob, are you all right?" asked Jim.

"Yes, m'lord," came the small voice just above his left shoulder; and he remembered suddenly that, like Brian, he had been sleeping in his travel clothes for warmth, when the Assassins had captured them. But he had not felt Hob climbing back into the knapsack.

"Should I come out?" Hob asked.

"There's not much to see," said Jim. "We're just in a dark tunnel. Perhaps you'd better just stay where you are."

"Yes, m'lord."

They went forward, Kelb trotting confidently a little ahead, but still within the circle of torch-light. The tunnel was longer than Jim had expected, considering that it clearly had been hewn out of solid rock. In the end, he judged they must have walked close to a quarter of a mile before Kelb stopped and waited for them to join him. They were facing a similar wall that seemed to bar off the tunnel at this point.

"I have pressed what needs to be pressed to cause this end of the tunnel to open," said Kelb in an apologetic voice, "but, my masters, it is evidently stuck. Would you mind very much jumping up and down on the floor? I think that will jar it loose and it will go up."

Not surprising, thought Jim. Mechanical contrivances here in the fourteenth century could hardly be expected to work better than those in the twentieth century.

"In that case," he said, "we'd better jump together, you and I, Brian. I'll say one, two, three and then we jump—that way we should come down together."

"Hah!" said Brian. "Infidel magic! Of course it doesn't work right!"

Jim was not exactly sure what he meant; but there was no point in going into the matter now. He counted off and they jumped. They came down hard on the stone floor; but evidently that was just what was needed, for slowly the stone slab before them began to move upward—but jerkily, as if it needed oiling.

"It is not used much, you see, my masters," said Kelb, "and anyone who is brought here, except the Grandmaster, must of course die after he has seen this tunnel. Therefore it is necessary that he be slain and his body be taken out to be left at some little distance on the mountainside, that he shall not be connected with the entrance, here, once it is closed again. But for us, we need but step outside now."

He had timed his words excellently. As he finished, the stone stopped jerking upward, and there was room to duck under it out into the star-lit night of the mountainside. There were a few bushes around them, and the rocks all but closed them in. Kelb did something behind them, and they heard the door scraping downward and finally ceasing to make any noise.

"It is closed now," Kelb said in a satisfied voice.

"That's good," said a voice out of the darkness. "And the place of its opening is now known. That will be useful. Abu al-Qusayr spoke truth to me, though I am not of his faith. So, now I find you all again, Franks."

It was the voice of Baiju, the Mongol from the caravan.

CHAPTER 21

Jim looked in the direction of the voice, but he could still see nothing but what seemed like three or perhaps four patches of pale white, which might be or might not be there in actuality, but which seemed to waver and change outline slightly.

"Night-devils!" cried Kelb. "Master, protect me!"

"You?" said Jim. "A Djinni? And you're afraid of night-devils?"

Jim could feel the dog's body pressing against the back of his legs.

"Afraid?" said Kelb quaveringly. "Who, me? I am the most—the most powerful of Djinni. But some of these night-devils can be very cruel, master."

"Send the Djinni away," said the voice of Baiju. "I will talk to you alone."

"Go," said Jim to Kelb.

"But, master—"

"And don't just make yourself disappear," added Jim. "I'll know if you do; and then you'll wish it was night-devils got you instead of me!"

It was a completely empty threat, of course. Aside from the fact that Jim knew nothing of what night-devils were, or could do, he knew very well he could never bring himself to treat even a Djinni with deliberate cruelty. Nonetheless, the pressure of Kelb against the back of his legs suddenly ceased.

"I don't understand this," said Jim, speaking in the direction of Baiju's voice. "How do you happen to be here? And why?"

"Some time back, in Tripoli," said Baiju, "but after he had seen you and the Brian-Sir with you, I happened to visit abu al-Qusayr to find out when those of the Golden Horde that are coming this way would come; and how they might be stopped. He looked into water and told me only two things. One, stopping ibn-Tariq was the key to stopping them; and, two, you were the only one who could stop ibn-Tariq. I should try to find

you at this time at this place in the night, and help you to get to Palmyra before the caravan.''

"And so you came, and showed up here, just on the basis of that?'' asked Jim. Baiju had not struck him as a particularly trusting or credulous individual.

"That was all he said he could tell me,'' said Baiju. "You are a magician yourself. I paid the price he asked for in gold—gold, not silver—and he gave me his answer. You would know better than I if a magician would cheat me after setting a price and getting it.''

Baiju had a point, thought Jim. Magicdom's rules were very emphatic about that. Abu al-Qusayr could not play anything but fair with someone who had struck a bargain with him—once the bargain was accepted. If this was generally known, even among the Mongols, then it was just possible that Baiju would, indeed, have trusted the elderly magician. It also meant that even abu al-Qusayr had not known why stopping ibn-Tariq could stop the other Mongols.

"Let me see you,'' Jim said to Baiju.

"Yes,'' said Brian's voice at his shoulder, "and any who are with you, Mongol!''

Baiju gave a brief snort of laughter.

"Then make a light, magician,'' he said. "I will make none. You are not that far from Kasr al-Abiyadh that any light will not be seen by one of those on watch from its higher towers.''

"If that is so,'' said Brian, "mayhap it is better to forgo the light. What think you, James?''

"I think you're right,'' said Jim, "and particularly if you think so, Brian.''

"It is ordinary sense,'' said Baiju, with a contemptuous edge to his voice. "Come, then. I have white camels from Basra, for each of us. Not only are they faster, and do they go farther, than the heavy beasts of the caravan, but we will push harder. We will push very hard. In five days I will bring you into Palmyra.''

Jim felt a return of the pressure at the back of his legs; and Kelb's voice spoke.

"O, mighty master, forgive your willful and unruly slave for coming back without permission. But what of me?''

"He is a Djinni,'' said Baiju. "Let him find his own way to Palmyra.''

"Master—'' began Kelb again.

"No,'' interrupted Jim decisively. "You are a Djinni, as Baiju says. We'll meet you there. Go then—however you can go. I will call for you again, possibly when I get into Palmyra.''

"Master—''

"Go!"

The pressure against his legs ceased.

"He's gone," said Jim. "Now what?"

"Come toward my voice," said Baiju.

Jim felt Brian's hand on his shoulder and stepped cautiously forward, over what was obviously fairly rough terrain. He stumbled once on what was either a large pebble or a small boulder, and almost lost his balance but regained it again. A moment later he smelled Baiju's breath. It smelled of alcohol. The little Mongol had evidently been drinking. But he sounded sober enough.

At the same time Jim began to make out the white wavering shapes in the darkness, which turned out to be the camels Baiju had mentioned. Baiju helped both of them to mount; and a moment later, with the Mongol on his camel leading, they were making their way up the steep slope amid the rocks.

Jim could not remember how long a time the caravan had been supposed to take in making the journey to Palmyra; but it was now six or seven days since it had left Tripoli. Still, five days more from here to the city seemed like making very good speed indeed. He was encouraged.

Later, he wished he hadn't been.

It was true they were near the top of the mountains; and it was only a few hours from the time they had met Baiju before they rode through the dark pass at the peak, with the absolute blackness of rock walls on both sides and a narrow slit of night sky sprinkled with stars far above them. It was also true that the following day after a few hours sleep just before dawn they reached the bottom of the far side of the mountains looking toward the desert valley area, in the midst of which Palmyra was placed; and as they went in the days that followed, the air grew warmer, and somewhat less dry—although it was far from being what might be considered balmy.

All in all, Jim ended up with the conclusion that he would just as soon not make another forced march with Baiju. The little Mongol drove them from before daybreak until after dark; and if they had let him have his own way they would have had no more than three hours of off-camel sleep a night. The camels themselves stood up to it admirably. Brian said nothing; but his face began to look a little more gray with each day passed, and he was definitely showing exhaustion by the time they got to Palmyra.

So it was not a pleasure trip. Their camels might indeed, as Baiju said, be jewels among their kind, and bred for racing; and it was undeniable that their gait, if anything, was smoother than that of the camels Jim and Brian had ridden in the caravan.

But Jim and Brian, both of them, were worn out by the time they all finally reached Palmyra.

At last, slumped in their saddles and swaying with fatigue, they entered the city in late afternoon. It was a good-sized place of tents and more or less lightly constructed wooden buildings, which had risen on the foundations laid out for an early Greek or Roman city.

At that time, clearly, the city had been constructed on a regular pattern; and the main street running east and west in the center of the city had ruins still standing of a double portico called the Great Colonnade. It was close to this Great Colonnade that Baiju at last brought them to a caravansary where they could lodge.

Jim and Brian were shown to a room. It was not until then that Jim realized neither of them had their usual baggage. Their heavy armor and weapons, their extra clothing and—worst of all—his personal, deverminized mattress were missing.

To hell with it, he thought exhaustedly, and chose a clean patch of floor. He visualized a magic line around it that would send all vermin and suchlike running from it in fear, and lay down, pulling his cloak over him. He had just enough consciousness left to magically make the splintered wooden floor underneath him as soft as a bed—and he fell ocean-deep in slumber.

They were wakened by Baiju. The Mongol showed no signs of weariness from the trip, just as he had shown no signs of weariness during it. They woke to find him standing over them.

"Will you sleep forever?" he demanded.

"Not any more, in any case, with your braying!" said Brian. "James, I must have breakfast—and a sword. We must both get swords. But food now! Where do you get some food in this hell-bound place?"

"Rise and come with me," said Baiju. Without waiting for them he turned and started out of the room.

"Wait a minute," said Jim. Unlike Brian, who woke up with a nasty temper until fed, but came fully awake at once, Jim needed a little time to reach full alertness. "If you walk out that door without us, you'd better count on not having anything to do with me from now on. I need a little time."

Baiju spun about on his heel.

"I brought you here," he said dangerously, "and now you will not repay me as you should?"

"I didn't make any bargain with you," said Jim. "Abu al-Qusayr told you I might be useful to you; and the only reason you helped us get here was because of that. If you've got any disagreements, go talk to him."

He switched his attention away from Baiju completely.

"Hob?" he said.

"Yes, m'lord," said a small voice from behind him. Out of the corner of his eye he saw Baiju go pale and rigid, and his eyes opened very wide.

"That's all right," said Jim, answering both Hob and Baiju's superstitious alarm at once. "I just wanted to make sure you were there and all right. It must have been pretty boring for you this trip. I know you don't sleep."

"That doesn't matter," said Hob. "Any hobgoblin is used to going a long time with nothing happening. We just sit and think about happy things that happened to us in the past, without sleeping."

"I will wait for you downstairs in the room where everyone eats and talks," Baiju said, less pale now, but walking hastily out.

Jim had all but forgotten him already. He was coming all the way awake; and it struck him that he felt hot, sticky and uncomfortable. He would have given almost anything for a shower, twentieth-century style, but of course that was impossible.

A bath was an alternative; but the bathhouses that might be available were more trouble than they were worth. Jim only wanted to get clean. He did not want to be offered female or male company, food, drink, drugs or anything else. Particularly he did not want people pretending to help him bathe, and then asking a price for it. It was not so much the price that bothered him as the annoyance of having to get rid of such gadflies.

He could magic himself and his clothes clean—but he had been nibbling away at his magic reserves, in spite of his good intentions to use them as little as possible.

"I'm ready," he said to Brian. "How about you?"

"You should wear your mail shirt," said Brian reproachfully.

Jim looked at the pile of metal links on the floor by his mattress with sourness. That was right. He had taken that off before collapsing in sleep. Now, wearing his shirt and undershirt alone, he was quite comfortable in the passably warm atmosphere here, and it would undoubtedly get warmer during the day. To wear the mail shirt, with its sewn on, interior quilted padding, would be to make himself uncomfortably hot. Still, Brian was right. They were in a strange city, among strangers; and the rule of the fourteenth century, whether you were in England, the Middle East or any place else, seemed to be "Go protected, and be ready for anything."

Regretfully he put on the mail shirt. He was almost immediately prickly with heat; but hopefully, his body would adjust to it during the day. Brian was on his feet, standing in the clothes he had been wearing all through the trip and moving from foot to foot impatiently.

"I am ready," Brian announced. "If you are too, let us go."

"No offense, Brian," said Jim. "But you stink."

"And so do you, James," said Brian, "though no worse than before. But it is better to stink and live than not stink and be dead. The chance will come for us to get our weapons and some other clothes or clean the ones we have. Meanwhile I need food; and I cannot believe but what you do as well."

He led the way out the door and Jim took a few long strides to catch up with him.

When they got to the coffeehouse, restaurant, or whatever it was that was part of their lodging place, it was enclosed by a circular wall of ancient marble in which were niches. Each niche had a low table and pillows on which to sit cross-legged around it. They looked about for Baiju, but he was not there.

"Well," said Jim, after they had sat down and ordered whatever was available for breakfast—Jim included a large container of cool sherbet with his. Having done this and watched their server leave, he looked around, saw no one was sitting close enough to overhear easily, and spoke to Brian in a low voice.

"Had you any plan for how we might go about finding Geronde's father here?" he asked Brian.

Brian finished gulping down what was in his mouth and answered.

"To be honest with you, James," he said, "I had planned to do as I have done all the way here so far, to search out an English knight, or at least a French or other knight of good repute, and ask his help and guidance. But this place seems singularly free of any but the local infidels. Yet we might ask."

He looked around the eating place they were in, caught the eye of the man who had served them and waved him over. While waiting, he dipped into the single dish that had been put down between Jim and himself, picked up another mouthful of it with the tips of his fingers as he would have done in England, and stuck it in his mouth. The server arrived at their table, as Brian was hastily trying to get this chewed and swallowed. Brian got it down just in time.

"Fellow," he said to the server, "by the way, what kind of meat is it in this you have brought us?"

"It is a tender young she-camel, masters," said the server. "One who broke a leg in the stables of Murad of the Heavy Purse, and which we were fortunately able to buy for slaughter. Is it not flavorful and good to eat?"

"Well, it is, at least, not goat," said Brian. "Tell me, do you know of any English knights here in this city?"

"English knights?" said the server, looking puzzled.

"Yes, yes," said Brian. "You know—English knights! Knights from England."

"Master," said the server, wonderingly. "Of Frankish knights I have heard; but I do not understand what you mean by these that are called English."

"I was speaking of England," said Brian, speaking the word slowly, and pronouncing the word slowly and more loudly. *"England."*

"My friend is speaking of a lord from his own country," said Jim. "And that country is England—an island not far from the land of those you call the Franks."

"Is it so indeed?" said the server. "There are no Franks in Palmyra either, may Allah be thanked."

"Are you sure?" asked Jim. "Couldn't there be one around in this city who you haven't heard of?"

The server shook his head.

"If there was such a man, masters," he said, "surely I would know it, since those who pass through here in caravans, and others speak of many things, and never fail to mention those who are strangers to our land."

The server went off; but his place was almost immediately taken by Baiju, who sat down next to Jim on a cushion in the niche where they were seated, and drew his legs up in cross-legged position. He reached out and helped himself from their bowl of food.

It was only after he had taken a mouthful and eaten it that he looked at Jim and Brian.

"Now what do you plan?" he said to them.

"The fact is," Jim said, "we're looking for someone who might be here in Palmyra. He—"

"But swords, first. We must buy ourselves weapons, Mongol. As for telling him about Sir Geoffrey, you need not bother, James," said Brian. "I have already told Baiju about our search."

"When did you do that?" asked Jim.

"Oh, one of the times in the caravan, when you were talking with that wordy fellow ibn-Tariq—or should I call him a gentleman?" said Brian.

He looked at Baiju, who was industriously eating.

"Was he a gentleman?"

Baiju shrugged and took another handful of food.

"In any case I told Baiju what Sir Geoffrey would look like," said Brian, "in case he should see him. You have not seen him, I take it?"

He was still looking at Baiju, who shook his head and went on eating.

"We are at something of an impasse," Brian told him. "Leave the food alone for a moment, if you please, Mongol, and give us your attention.

There is reason to believe that he is in this town; but we have no idea of how to go about searching for him.''

"Look!" said Baiju, pausing only briefly as far as feeding himself went, and staring at Jim and Brian. "Look—and ask to see if anyone else has seen him."

"We just did," said Jim. "We asked the server here who brought us this food. He said that if there was someone like that in Palmyra, he would know it because those who pass through here on caravans and by other means usually stop and eat here; and the word gets out of any strangers in the land."

Baiju gave a momentary short sound that was somewhere between a cough and a laugh.

He looked around the room, and focused on the server who was busy with some people in another niche a quarter of the circle around.

"Come!" shouted Baiju.

In the other niches, the men in flowing robes eating there stopped, looked at him, looked at each other and spoke to each other in low tones which were unintelligible to Jim and Brian sitting in the booth, but which were pretty clearly—judging by the hand gestures and the facial expressions—either shocked or contemptuous statements about Baiju's manners. The server deliberately kept on doing what he was doing for a few moments, as if he had not heard, then turned and almost ran across the room to Baiju, all smiles.

"My master called?" he asked.

"Tell me," said Baiju abruptly, "are there any Frankish slaves in Palmyra?"

"Assuredly, there are, master," said the server. "But how many, or to whom they belong, I could not tell you. Who keeps track of slaves?"

"You told me there were no Franks in Palmyra," said Jim.

"So I did, master," said the server. "But slaves—"

He shrugged his shoulders and spread his hands.

"We are looking for a Frankish slave, then, taller than you by a hand placed sideways," snapped Brian, "with graying hair that has gone halfway back on the head, and a small mustache which is perhaps pure white. It could be that he is beardless and that the hair is white. But he is not old and feeble, but still upright and strong, with blue eyes and a scar across a corner of his chin and jaw. He will have other scars as well, but this is the most notable one. Have you seen such a slave?"

"I have not, O master," said the server. "I could ask those who pay attention to such things if they know of any such? Perhaps in a day or so I would hear."

"He will reward thee," said the Mongol. "It will not be a great reward.

But it will be a certain one if you have found the slave I speak. Do you understand?''

"Indeed, understanding comes clear to me, O generous and beneficent master," said the server, salaaming. "Is there any other thing I can do for you?"

"Yes," said Baiju, "bring us more of what was in this bowl."

"Yes, master," said the server. He took the empty bowl and hurried off.

Baiju leaned back against the padded wall of the niche. He sighed contentedly, looked at Jim and Brian and belched.

Brian had grown accustomed to this eastern way of expressing satisfaction with the meal. Jim had learned to control his face at this, but he still winced inside; even though he knew that here it was a way of saying, "That tasted good!"

Baiju grinned at them, a fierce and sardonic but undeniably humorous grin.

"Ibn-Tariq is here," he said. "I caught sight of him earlier in the day, before you were down."

CHAPTER 22

B oth Jim and Brian stared at him.

"The caravan is in?" said Jim.

"No," said Baiju. "Yet he is here."

"How could he be?" said Jim, remembering how they had pushed their camels for long hours during the day, snatched a little food and sleep and gone on again day after day, to the limit of their endurance.

"I do not know," said Baiju. The server brought a new bowl of food and Baiju dug into it.

"I do not know," he said again, after eating a couple of mouthfuls. "It is barely possible—his camels were good, possibly as good as ours—and if he started not two days after you had been taken, as we did, but at once. If he started as the sun came up, or before, with one camel, alone but taking enough food and water. If he did that and knew the way well, it is just possible a house-dweller could be here by this time. In any case, here he is. I saw him buying a headdress in the souk. He did not see me."

"Did he look like a man who'd pushed himself to the limit, when you saw him?" Jim asked.

"Do I?" said Baiju sardonically. "If he could make such a trip, he could be able to travel even as I do. Do not judge the world by yourself."

"Let us go to this same merchant he visited in the souk," said Brian, "and examine his wares. Mayhap in conversation we can discover from him something he may have learned about ibn-Tariq; such as where he is lodging here in Palmyra, and even perhaps the reason for his hurrying to this place. Furthermore, it was in the souk here that Sir Geoffrey, my lady's father, was seen by the knight who brought news to her of catching sight of him. So, we ourselves might be lucky enough to catch sight of him. It may be he is no slave but a merchant, or someone concerned with one of the merchants of the souk, but hiding the fact he is an Englishman. He will be changed, perhaps—it has been over six years now—but he cannot have changed so much that I will not recognize him."

"Well enough," said Baiju. "I will eat some more here, and then we will go."

"Fine," said Jim. "In that case, I'm going to step upstairs and get that small friend you know of, Brian. I want to bring him along with us."

Baiju had stopped chewing on his latest mouthful and was staring at Jim. Jim ignored him.

"Is that wise, James?" said Brian.

"It is, if he has to act in an emergency." He looked hard at Brian to remind him of the fact that Hob was with them to carry word home on the smoke at high speed, to tell both Geronde and Angie if anything happened to them. Brian frowned, then slightly nodded.

"As you will," he said. He looked back at the second bowl, which still contained a fair amount of food. "I might have a bite or two more myself, while I'm waiting."

Jim went upstairs. He had already decided that about the only way to manage things would be to wear the cloak that had the secret pouch for Hob on his shoulders and at the back of his neck—the same cloak he had worn with the caravan, and had in fact been sleeping in when he was captured. If he was going to be hot anyway, he might as well have Hob with him. Then if anything happened to them, the hobgoblin would be along to know of it.

It was fortunate, he told himself now, that Hob had not been in the cloak at the time he and the Assassin had rolled over and over down the stony hillside. Hob would have been squashed. But then Hob must have been in his favorite spot, lying on top of the smoke of the fire in front of their tent.

The cloak, he decided now, looking at it up in their room, and he was once more tempted to use his magic to control the temperature inside the cloak, so that he would be comfortable.

But no, better he just toughed it out. Carolinus had never given any advice yet that had not turned out to be important. He reminded himself hopefully that the cloak would hide the chain mail he was wearing, not only from public view but from the direct rays of the sun, which might otherwise heat up the metal links to make matters even more uncomfortable.

"Hob," he said, before picking up the cloak where he had left it, "you're back in your pouch there?"

"Yes, m'lord," Hob's voice came back.

"All right," said Jim. "I'm going to put the cloak on and we'll be going out to go through the souk—that's a sort of market they have down here. Do you still have that special tinder? And do you remember the magic word I gave you to say to make it light up and create smoke, so

that you ride the smoke right out of the pouch and be out of people's reach before they even know you're there?''

"Yes m'lord," said Hob. "And I remember the magic word to light the tinder very well. It's—''

"Don't say it!" said Jim hastily, and a little more loudly than he had intended. He lowered his voice. "That's only to be used if you need to hurry home to the Lady Angela with word Brian and I are in serious trouble. The minute you say the word, that tinder is going to kindle; and you'll be in a pouchful of smoke.''

"I'd like that," said Hob.

"Yes," said Jim, "but you realize that once you've used it you won't have any other way of making smoke in a hurry if trouble crops up.''

"Oh," said Hob. "Very sorry, m'lord.''

"That's all right. Just remember the word is for emergencies only," said Jim. "I'll try to call out your name when the time comes you should go. But if for some reason whatever happens to us doesn't give me a chance to, then it'll be up to you to decide when to make your smoke and start back for England as fast as you can.''

"I'll watch everything very carefully," said Hob. "Is it all right, then, if I peek out of the pouch, or ride on your shoulder? Somebody said something to you about my being taken for a monkey, I think they said, if they saw me here.''

"I suppose it'll be all right," said Jim. "But if you can see by peeking, I'd like that better. After all, I'd just as soon not have anyone know that there's anyone riding with me.''

"Yes, m'lord," said Hob.

Jim put on the cloak and went down. The second bowl was empty; and both Brian and Baiju seemed in a good humor. Jim paid for their meal—there was evidently nothing such as putting your meals on your hotel bill in this place—and they sallied forth.

The souk, Palmyra's open-air market, occupied what must have been the location of the chief Sanctuary of Palmyra at one time; now, in this fourteenth century, the remains of the Roman architecture were generally buried by an accumulation of dirt and filth. In the time of Jim's original world, he remembered reading once, a French expedition of archaeologists had uncovered four porticoes and a ritual basin plus a large altar for sacrifices as well as other pieces of architecture in this area.

Certainly, at the present moment there was nothing architecturally remarkable about it. Most of the shops were half-tent and half-shack, and the lanes between them wandered like trails in the wilderness, barely broad enough for three people to walk abreast.

The one thing the shops all had in common was an opening fronting

on the lane that passed them, in which samples of their wares were displayed. Baiju led the way, first to a weapons shop, where they did not seem to have swords but offered long and heavy knives almost as large. For want of anything else, both Brian and Jim bought one, plus scabbards, and sashes to go around their waist and hold the scabbards.

Next Baiju took them to a shop that had both headwear and other items of clothing ready-made, plus bolts of cloth.

"What is this?" Baiju demanded of the shopkeeper, a blocky, not unkindly-looking man with a graying mustache and a striped headdress.

"It is the finest silk from beyond the Great Wall in the far, Far East," said the shopkeeper.

Baiju dropped the silk as if he had discovered it was suddenly unclean.

"It is Egyptian silk," he said flatly. "I had a friend who bought a headdress from you this morning, and spoke of silk this color. I would have been interested if it had indeed been silk from beyond the Great Wall, or even the silk of Hind."

"Allah pity me!" said the shopkeeper, wringing his hands. "And I bought it believing it to be the true Eastern silk. How will I ever recoup the great amount I paid for it?"

"By finding some other idiot who cannot tell Egyptian silk from the Eastern cloth," said the Mongol. "How else? But I see my coming has been wasted, as another friend of mine from whom I would buy knows silk—though not as I do. He believed you had better stuff than this."

"I have indeed some better silks—silk that would ravish your soul if you knew the true materials," said the shopkeeper. "It is in the back of my shop. But do you truly wish to buy? I would not expose it to the light before one who was not serious about buying."

"How can a man know if he wishes to buy until he has seen what is for sale?" said the Mongol.

"This silk is very carefully wrapped and protected and deep under other piled goods of great value. It would be some labor to get to it. A shopkeeper cannot go to such trouble for any not serious."

"Ho, as for buying," said Baiju, waving a hand at Jim, "the buyer is here with me. I have come with him merely because I know silk. But he is interested in many things, and silk was only one of them. If it is too much labor for you to find this fine silk of yours, undoubtedly we can find some elsewhere in the souk; and meanwhile he can be gaining information and possibly buying other things which he wishes."

"Indeed?" said the shopkeeper. "What might these other things be?"

"They are too numerous to mention. But perhaps you might point the way for us to the slave market. He has a fancy to buy a Frankish slave.

Being a Frank himself, and being able to indulge his wishes, he prefers to have Frankish slaves only around him.''

"Alas," said the merchant. "There is no slave market today. There will be one in a few days, perhaps. But Frankish slaves are not normally found in Palmyra.''

"Yet my other friend, the one who bought the headdress from you," said Baiju, "spoke of seeing a Frankish slave here in the souk. He saw him for only a moment before he was lost in the crowd, but recognized him immediately for what he was.''

"I know of no Frankish slaves about the souk, or in Palmyra at all," said the shopkeeper. "It may be that those with much wealth might have one or two. But the price would probably be very high. Is he indeed willing to pay such a price?''

"He cannot know that until he sees the slave," said Baiju.

"Such a slave is merely a curiosity, of course," said the shopkeeper, "but I do not think one would ever come cheaply. The price would be much more even than that for my finest silk.''

"Price is not the problem if the slave is what he wants," said Baiju. "The problem is that he is staying but a few days only in Palmyra; and then he will be traveling on. It is a pity you do not know of any Frankish slave. He would be grateful to one who could direct him to finding one, particularly one that was for sale.''

"What is not for sale?" said the shopkeeper. "But, if the owner has little intention of selling, of course, the price may be—possibly I could be of help in getting him a better price. I am, of course, a merchant in cloths only, and slaves are of no interest to me. Still, I hear things, and I know the ways of those who buy and sell here. It is just possible that before he leaves I might hear of such a slave. If so, perhaps I could get word to him. It would be an effort, of course, on my part and I would welcome his gratitude for my finding such a slave for him.''

"I am sure that he would not forget gratefulness in such a case," said Baiju. "If you should hear something, and if it should lead to what he wants, and if the purchase was practical, certainly the matter of his gratitude will be something he and you can discuss between yourselves when the time comes.''

"Certainly—" the shopkeeper was beginning, when the attentions of all of them were suddenly attracted to a hubbub that had broken out at some distance down the lane between shops. It was enough of a distance, and there were too many people crowded around, for them to see exactly what was happening, but voices were being raised, and even sticks were being waved.

Without warning, a figure broke through the crowd of people and ran

toward them down the lane. All those in his way hastily got out of it, and the mob he had momentarily left behind tore after him, all but catching up with him and striking out at him with sticks. Only a few of the blows got home, but they kept him running; and in a moment he was up to the shop where Jim and the others stood, level with them and gone on, and there was a jostling, shouting and screaming crowd filling the lane in pursuit of him.

But in that instant, Jim had a momentary glimpse of a tall, brawny man with black eyebrows and black mustache and the sleeve of his nearer arm torn completely off, showing some unsightly disfiguration, which could have been a scar, running almost from wrist to elbow, or a wide, grayish-white rash. His face, glimpsed for a moment, was white and staring, his mouth half open as if he was screaming; but if he was, he could not be heard over the noise of the crowd on his heels.

"Allah protect us," said the shopkeeper, "it is Albohassan Karasanij, the Persian—the leather-seller. It has been suspected for some weeks past now that he might bear the curse of leprosy secretly among us. He has sworn that he was only subject to boils; but someone must at last have torn off part of his garment to make sure."

He cast a glance up the lane in the opposite direction, then shrugged his shoulders and brought his gaze back to meet those of Brian, Baiju and Jim.

"Those with the shops on either side of him will have gained all his goods by this time," he said with a touch of regretfulness in his voice. "It is the will of Allah. Now, what else would please you?"

"I think that's all," said Jim. He wanted to get away from here.

"I will send word if there is any word to send," said the shopkeeper. "Depend upon it. Where may you be found, O my masters?"

"At the caravansary of Yusuf," said Baiju.

"Good, I will send word there then. I am Metaab, the silk merchant. All men know me."

Jim, Brian and Baiju moved off. It was a relief to Jim to be away from the shop with its association with what had just happened and what he had just seen.

"Where to, now?" Baiju said.

Jim found he did not want to go back to the caravansary.

"Actually," he said, "as long as I'm here, I'd like to see Palmyra while there's time to do it."

"You want to see a city?" said Baiju, staring at him. "You are seeing it now."

He waved his hand at the shops in front of him.

"No," said Jim, "I mean the whole city."

"Come to think of it," said Brian, "I would like that too. Particularly let us look around the oasis from which the women are carrying water on their heads. I am curious as to how they do it. Besides, it is always wise to look around any new place you are in."

"Perhaps," said Baiju, "but a city! They are all the same."

There would be no point, Jim knew, in mentioning to either Brian or Baiju the remnants of architecture that betrayed the hand of Rome, and civilizations before that, here in this place. The caravan route must be as old as time itself. But whatever they did it would be better than going back to the caravansary, staring at the wall and seeing the reputed leper, running.

He still kept seeing—as if in a sudden still shot made by a camera—the staring eyes, the half-open mouth of the fleeing, hapless leather merchant. Strangely, the sight had moved neither the shopkeeper nor Baiju at all. Nor, for that matter, had it evoked any emotional reaction from Brian. In fact, he was now talking to Baiju about the European way of handling such situations.

"—Our lepers are given a bell and must wear a garment that covers them completely head to feet," he was saying. "The leper rings the bell as he moves, that all clean people may safely move out of his path."

"Simpler just to kill him," said Baiju. "With arrows, from a distance."

They had reached the end of the souk—or at least one of its edges. At any rate, they were coming out from among the shops.

"If you must wander about this dung heap, I had best go with you," Baiju went on sourly. "Your customs are clearly not their customs; and you are just as likely to end up dead instead of back at the caravansary, through not understanding what you should do or should not do. Come with me, then."

He led them about the town and passed the oasis. In spite of what Brian had said, it was on the women, rather than on the water-filled pots on their head, that Brian's eye lingered.

"If it's the women you want," Baiju said after watching him for a little time, "I can find you places where you can see much more of them than you can here."

"That would be instructive, would it not, James?" said Brian, looking across at Jim, for Baiju, being shorter than either of them, was walking between them, which was the most convenient position for conversation among all three of them.

Jim did not feel any particular urge to follow Baiju's suggestion; but since his only interest was in keeping from the caravansary, he agreed.

In the end Baiju took them to a place where coffee was served, but also where they were given the opportunity to buy, since they were obviously

not Muslims, a thin astringent white wine at which even Brian made a face, though he drank it.

There, one by one, women came out and danced. They were still clothed, however, though in layers of gauzy cloths that, while evidently calculated to tantalize, actually were little less revealing than the complete coverings of the women getting water from the oasis.

All in all they killed about four hours and by this time Jim had managed to come to terms with the memory of the leper—although he had a notion that the memory would continue to haunt him for the rest of his life. It had not been just the fear of the crowd that had put that look on the man's face. It was the horror of what he, himself, now believed—or was at last acknowledging to himself—what afflicted him.

Even if he himself had truly believed he did not have leprosy, he was now facing a future in which he would have to live closely with actual lepers; and being a man of his place and time in history, he undoubtedly profoundly believed that it would be only a short time before he would catch the disease from them.

Jim, Brian and Baiju were finally back at the caravansary. There they were met by one of the regular workers, or employees—whatever they were—in the place as they came in.

"One waits for you," he said, as they came in. "His name is ibn-Tariq; and he waits in the eating place of this caravansary."

Jim would much rather have headed toward his room; but Baiju and Brian had immediately started off toward the caravansary eating place, and Jim went along with them. They found ibn-Tariq there, seated cross-legged on the cushions in one of the small niches, with what looked like some sort of pancake, grilling rather smokily on a brazier set up by his table.

"Ah, my friends," he called, seeing them. "Come. Sit with me!"

They continued across the room, and as the smoke from the brazier met them halfway Jim stifled a cough that he thought might be considered impolite.

"Are you all right, m'lord?" said a small, concerned voice in his ear; for the cough had only been partly silenced.

"Fine, Hob," murmured Jim. "It's just that smoke."

"It's not the best smoke," said Hob. "But there's no such thing as bad smoke."

Not, thought Jim, *to a hobgoblin, maybe;* but they were now at ibn-Tariq's niche, and greetings were being exchanged. There was no chance to utter the thought aloud.

"—A storekeeper in the souk, who was to specially make me a head-dress, delivered it to me not an hour ago," ibn-Tariq was saying. "He

enclosed a message that you three were here, had visited his shop and mentioned me. He also said you were seeking a Frankish slave. It happens that I have acquaintances here in Palmyra, having been here before, and it may well be that I can help you find him you seek.''

CHAPTER 23

Jim gulped at the small cup of incredibly sweet, incredibly strong coffee that had just been put before him by a server, scalding his tongue but ignoring that in his need to get some stimulant in him to sharpen his wits. They were now seated with ibn-Tariq at his table in a niche.

Seeing the man was shock enough. His seeking them out like this, on top of their knowing that he must have pushed himself as hard or harder than they had pushed themselves to be here at this time, had rung every warning bell in Jim at ibn-Tariq's first sentence.

There were several things wrong with his offer. In the first place, it was far too suddenly made, according to the rules of normal conversation in this part of the world, where the practice was to talk for anywhere from fifteen minutes to an hour about unimportant things before getting to the point. Also, it was remarkably direct for somebody like ibn-Tariq, personally, who had shown an almost machiavellian indirectness in his conversation.

But the man was looking at him now, smiling, with the open countenance of someone who was no more than delighted by being able to bring good news to someone he liked. It was true, Jim and ibn-Tariq had found a good deal of common ground in their talks, riding together in the first few days of the caravan; but they had certainly not become friends, in any real sense of that word.

"Ah," Brian was saying cheerfully, "the silk merchant."

"Yes, it is Metaab, the silk merchant you spoke to," said ibn-Tariq. "There are several other silk merchants in the souk. But I have always found Metaab the most honest."

"He promised to help us, too," said Jim. It was the first thing he could think of to say.

"That would be like Metaab," agreed ibn-Tariq. "However, his conversations are with those in the souk, in the street and in other low places. Those I know live on rather a more important level; and some are in

positions to ask questions for me. I got the impression that this Frankish slave was more than casually important to you," said ibn-Tariq. In the easy, casual way in which such matters were regarded in these parts, he went on to ask, "An old lover of yours, perhaps?"

Jim, who had taken another, somewhat larger mouthful of the hot coffee, had trouble swallowing it politely.

"No," he managed. "Merely a neighbor to whom I owe a duty."

"Ah," said ibn-Tariq, "it is too seldom that duty is highly regarded in this world. I have gone about the lands, talking and asking, and seldom do I find pure examples of any of the virtues enumerated in the Koran—"

He was interrupted by a sudden outburst of noise at the entrance to the eating place; and they all looked around to see five men wearing helmets, curved swords in scabbards and carrying long weapons that were halfway between a spear and a halberd. For a moment Jim simply assumed they were going to one of the niches on either side of them; but—no, they were coming directly toward himself and the rest.

They came right up to the niche and stopped before it. They did not look friendly. They were all dressed more or less the same in brownish-white robes. Four of them wore boiled leather jackets, and their helmets were also of leather. The fifth one, who was in advance of the others and seemed in command, had a steel helmet and a chain mail shirt.

He had a narrow, long face with cold brown eyes that looked hard at them.

"You three are under arrest, by order of the Dey!" he said, arriving. "I see you are wearing knives. You will give them up. Now—hilt first."

"Hah!" said Brian, and his hand was on the handle of his knife, but not in such a position as to pull it out and offer it hilt first; and immediately four of the long weapons were leveled at him from no more than half a foot away.

"Brian!" said Jim warningly. But ibn-Tariq was already speaking.

"Calm yourself, my friends," he said. "I'm sure there is a mistake here. Officer, may I speak to you apart for a moment? I am ibn-Tariq, and my name is not unknown in this city."

"Forgive our disturbance of your meal, O ibn-Tariq," said the officer graciously, with a circular outward wave of his hand. "I assure you there is no mistake; but of course, if you would wish for a word—?"

Ibn-Tariq got up and the two of them walked a little away. The four men stayed with their spears still leveled, although now at least one pointed each at Jim, Brian and Baiju.

There was a matter of some minutes of rather tense waiting. Brian looked fiercely at the four spears. He had taken his hand from his sword

and dropped it to his side. In appearance this seemed a move to make himself look more harmless, but Jim knew better and the knowledge made him uncomfortable.

Knights were not supposed to need what Jim's twentieth century was to call "hold-out" knives; but Brian had explained to Jim a long time ago, near the beginning of their friendship, no one who could afford a second knife ever went without one hidden about him.

In Brian's case, he had at least one Jim knew of. Up the sleeve of the arm behind the hand that Brian had just taken from his sword hilt, his friend carried a short, but heavy knife, hiltless, but with a leaded center to give it special weight, and a wide double-edged blade with out-curving edges that would ensure a cutting blow.

A snap of Brian's wrist could slide the hilt of it into his hand, and it would come out, tearing its way easily through his sleeve, ready for a backhand strike at whatever he wished. The blade was heavy enough to shear through at least one of the wooden staves behind the metal spear points that were aimed at him.

"I think we can give ibn-Tariq a chance," said Jim out loud to Brian.

Brian looked at him without disagreement. Baiju was also looking at him, but with something more like contempt.

It was after only a few moments, by the standards of eastern conversation, that ibn-Tariq and the officer came back.

"I'm afraid you'll have to go with this officer," ibn-Tariq said to them. "But I'm still convinced that a mistake has been made. I will see about having it corrected right away. This officer is under the command of the military governor here in Palmyra, whom I know. I would strongly suggest that you go quietly, without complaint; and leave all to me."

Baiju gave one of his snorts that could have been laughter or not as the case might be.

Jim hastily pulled out his sword and offered it hilt first to the officer, who disdainfully stepped aside and motioned for one of the spear-carriers to take it. The man did, still keeping his spear leveled on Jim. Seeing Jim had done this, Brian reluctantly gave up his sword but made no move to hand over any of the other weapons he might be carrying. It was quite possible, thought Jim, that he had more blades about him than the one up his sleeve.

Baiju stood up, letting the spear point in front of him come right against his chest, piercing his skin beneath his clothes. He lifted his own short, curved sword from its sheath with his left hand and, reaching forward, rammed the hilt into the stomach of a spear-carrier opposite him, who hastily snatched at it and took it.

"Now," said the officer, "we go."

They were led out into the street, attracting a crowd as they went, and marched for some distance followed by the same crowd. They went by various turns through alleyways until they reached one so narrow that the officer seemed to lose his temper with the onlookers, and told off two of his soldiers to block it behind them against any who might follow.

That left him and the other two soldiers now behind Jim and Brian and Baiju, herding them forward. They continued on, following the directions of the officer to turn here, or turn there, until they came to a door in a stone wall, with another soldier standing beside it.

The officer had moved in front of them by this time, since they were out of the narrow confines of the alley. He was highly visible; and at his approach the soldier standing beside the door hastily opened it. Without a word the officer marched Jim and his companions in and through a small dirty room where three other soldiers, all heavily armed with swords and wide, curve-bladed knives long enough almost to be swords, lounged on dirty cushions. They were herded farther through a very narrow door—so narrow that only one could pass at a time—down a dark flight of stairs, down, down and finally into a passageway that had earth underfoot and stone walls all around.

They went a little farther by the flickering light of a torch on one stony wall, until the passageway widened out to become a room divided by metal bars into cages. There were a couple of barely human, barely alive individuals in the first two cages they passed, dressed in rags. Then Jim and Brian were pushed into another, empty cage together and its door slammed on them. Baiju was left outside.

"Not you, Mongol," said the officer. "We've got someplace else to take you."

He and the three guards from the room above, who had evidently followed him down, surrounded the little Mongol and they moved off together, leaving Jim and Brian staring at each other in the empty cage.

A single cresset provided poor lighting to the whole room in which the cages stood. However, it happened to be fixed to the wall just behind the empty cage to Jim's left, almost within arm's reach; and this allowed them to see each other, and their immediate surroundings fairly well.

"What will they do with that small man, do you suppose?" Brian asked Jim.

Jim shook his head.

"I don't understand any of this," said Jim.

"I should not ask, perhaps," said Brian, "but is there some way in which you could use your magic—"

He left the end of the sentence hanging.

"Of course," said Jim, "but things aren't that desperate yet. There's

always magic if everything else fails. But we ought to be braced for the fact that there're some situations magic won't deal with.''

He looked around him.

"I wish I knew more about this place where they put us," he said. "Does it look like a city jail to you?"

"Not exactly," said Brian doubtfully. "City jails tend to be earth dungeons, like the one you got me and Giles out of, under the French King's lodging place in Brest, the last time we were in France. These are not only dry but clean."

"Clean?" echoed Jim, looking around himself in disbelief.

"Oh, yes," Brian went on almost cheerfully, "the sort of place you would have to lock up someone of rank. I do believe that's a chamber pot in the corner there."

Jim decided not to be drawn into any further discussion of the luxury of their quarters.

"I think you're right," he said to Brian. "I'd like to know what the rest of this building looks like. But I don't want to use my magic to do it. I'm beginning to get a strong suspicion that there may be other magic going on around here—maybe keeping an eye on us."

He stared thoughtfully at the guttering light of the cresset, and the soot-blackened ceiling just above its flame.

"On the other hand, now, there's some smoke right there. And there has to be some way for that smoke to get out of here—some kind of ventilation opening. Maybe Hob could ride the smoke out such an opening, possibly using the smoke of other torches, or cooking fires, or whatever, and then come back and so tell us about the place."

He half turned his head.

"Hob?" he said. "Do you think you could do that?"

There was no answer from behind him.

"Hob?" he repeated; and when there was still no answer, he put up his hand to feel the pouch behind him where Hob should be. It was limp and perfectly empty.

"He is gone?" said Brian, staring at Jim's face and his groping hand.

"Yes." Jim let his hand drop. "I know he was there with us when we went in to talk to ibn-Tariq, because the smoke from that cooking device almost made me cough; and he spoke to me."

"He surely wouldn't have left us without permission or orders?" said Brian. "What? Leave his Lord without permission? What sort of hobgoblin is he?"

"I think they're all like him," said Jim thoughtfully. A cold fear had crept into him. "You don't suppose he thought this was a sort of emer-

gency where he was supposed to go home to England and tell Angie and Geronde about it?''

"Back to England? Tell Angela and Geronde?" Brian stared at him. "What's this?"

"Part of what I arranged with Hob before he and I left England. I told you about this at Sir Mortimor's castle—remember? There might be a situation where I wouldn't be able to order him to go and carry back to Angie and Geronde a message of what had happened to us. In that case he was to use his own judgment when to leave. He must have thought our being arrested was that kind of situation, and ridden the smoke of the brazier off as we left. We might not have seen him go because he was trying not to be seen by anyone else there. Besides, as we left, we were looking toward the entrance, and everyone else was watching us go. Also, there was no one else in the niches next to us. I'll bet that's just what he did!''

"But if he did," said Brian, "and if it could be done . . ."

"Oh, it can be done, all right—or rather, a hobgoblin can do it," said Jim. "And I got the impression that the farther it was, the faster he could travel. He seemed to think he could get from wherever we might be to back home in a few hours, no more."

They looked at each other.

"And he'll be telling the Lady Angela that we've been taken by soldiers and locked up, our weapons taken away?" Brian demanded.

Jim nodded glumly.

"But it will only serve to disturb her—and Geronde, when she is also told!" said Brian.

"That's what I'm thinking. I mean," said Jim, "that's what I'm worrying about. Angie'll have been told we're in a dangerous spot; and there she'll be back in England, a couple of thousand miles away and not able to do anything about it."

"They'll want to come to our aid, of course," said Brian. "I can assure you Geronde will."

"So will Angie, of course," said Jim. "Luckily, they won't be able to. How could they possibly get here?"

"How will we possibly get there?" said Angie, striding up and down the solar of Malencontri. Geronde was perched on the edge of the bed, and Hob was sitting on a waft of smoke that had politely extended itself into the room from the fire that burned in the fireplace, though it was a fresh spring day outside. The walls of the castle would still be cold for another month or more yet.

"I could probably scrape together the money to travel," said Geronde. "But after that it would still take us months."

"That's the thing," said Angie, still pacing. "As far as that goes, I can lay my hands on enough money right here in the castle, along with a gem or two we could turn into money in any city of any size if we needed more along the way. But you're right, it'd take us months; and who knows what would have happened to them by the time we got there? We not only need to get there, we need to get there quickly."

She stopped pacing suddenly and whirled about to stare at Hob.

"M'lady?" said Hob, his eyes growing large.

"Hob—Hob-One de Malencontri—" said Angie, "Jim told me how you took him for a ride on the smoke. You can take Geronde and me to them, just the way you took Jim."

"Oh, m'lady!" said Hob. "We're only really supposed to take children. It was just because you're m'lord and m'lady that it was probably all right to take either one of you. But I really can't take anyone else, like m'lady Geronde. And anyway the smoke won't carry two big grown-up humans along with me. One is as much extra weight as it can carry. I might take two little children—if they were really little."

"Bah!" said Geronde.

"No, he can't help it," Angie told Geronde. "He'll do whatever he can, I know. Won't you, Hob?"

"Oh yes, m'lady."

"All right!" said Angie energetically. "If we can't do it one way, we'll do it another. I've got an idea how we could manage it."

"What idea is this, Angela?" asked Geronde.

"I'll tell you up on the roof of the tower, when there's no one around to hear," said Angie. "Come on, Geronde. You too, Hob."

She led the way out of the solar and up the short flight of stone steps to the top of the tower, which was actually the roof of the solar. The sentry on duty there gaped at them—not so much at Angie and Geronde as at Hob, sitting on the waft of smoke. But then, he was a seasoned member of this household of a magician; so it was beneath him to show any real alarm or emotion.

"You can go downstairs, Harold," said Angie. "I'll call you when I need you; or if you haven't heard a call in an hour, then come back up by yourself. If we're gone, pay no attention."

"Pay no attention, m'lady?" The seasoned member of the household was beginning to weaken in his self-control.

"You heard me," said Angie. "Down the stairs with you, now!"

Harold obeyed. When he was gone, Angie turned to Geronde with a smile.

"Well?" demanded Geronde.

"Geronde," said Angie, "remember not too long ago when Jim and I in dragon form landed on your tower, and you came up and tried to shoo us off thinking we were dragons that were looking for Malencontri and landed on your tower by mistake?"

"I remember, Angela," said Geronde.

"Well," said Angie triumphantly, "we'll turn ourselves into dragons and fly there!"

CHAPTER 24

Geronde stared at Angie. If it had been anyone but her, it would not have been too much to say that she gaped open-mouthed. But Geronde was too much like Brian, too fierce a person to look slack-jawed and foolish.

"You can do magic also, Angela?" she asked.

"I've never tried," said Angie, with her own brand of fierceness. "But the day we landed on your tower-top, Jim had turned me into a dragon. If I've been a dragon once, I ought to be able to be a dragon again. And if I can make myself into a dragon, I ought to be able to make you into a dragon."

"But how will you do it?" asked Geronde.

"How exactly, I don't know," said Angie. "That's beside the point. I've watched Jim often enough. If you live with a man as long as I have, Geronde, you get so you know him very well—very well indeed. Stand back and I'll try it."

Geronde backed off a few steps.

Angie stood where she was. She took a deep breath. Her hands were at her sides, and she clenched her fists and closed her eyes. She stood tensed.

Moments ticked by.

Geronde parted her lips to say something, and then changed her mind. She waited.

Angie exhaled exhaustedly and opened her eyes. She stood a moment limply, breathing deeply with her whole body relaxed.

"I tell you," she said to Geronde, "there's a way to do it! Jim sort of believes in his magic in his own mind; and he believes enough so that it happens—something like that. If I believe I can do it, then I can. If he can do it, I can do it."

"Of course you can, Angela," said Geronde.

Angie took another deep breath, closed her eyes and clenched her fists, and again Geronde waited.

"I am a dragon, I am a dragon, I am a dragon . . ." muttered Angie between her teeth. Another little period of time passed while Geronde waited. Then Angie gasped, opened her eyes again and relaxed.

"I tell you I can do it!" she said angrily to Geronde.

"Of course you can, Angela," said Geronde.

"The irritating thing is"—Angie began to pace up and down on the tower-top—"that I really know how he does it. I'm close enough to him to feel him doing it. Now, if I can just get that feeling. Bear with me, Geronde. I'm going to try again."

She tried—with no success.

"Angela," said Geronde gently, "don't you think, perhaps—"

But Angie's eyes were closed again and she was not listening.

Also, suddenly she was a dragon.

Geronde took several involuntary, extra steps backward.

"Angela . . ." she said. "Angela, are you in there?"

The dragon turned its head on a gracefully curving neck and looked at her. It was a very big dragon, in spite of its overall gracefulness.

"It's me, Geronde," said the dragon. "See? I told you I could do it. Now all I have to do is turn you into one, too."

"Oh, yes!" said Geronde enthusiastically. She added in a tone of curiosity rather than fear, "Does it hurt much?"

"Not at all," said Angie. "Now, just stand still and I'll concentrate on believing you're a dragon. I don't know just what I did, but I'm sure I can do it again; only for you it may take a little longer to manage. We mustn't be impatient."

The dragon closed its eyes, bunched its clawed feet into fists and took a deep breath.

"Geronde is a dragon, Geronde is a dragon, Geronde is a dragon, Geronde is a dragon . . ." it intoned.

The dragon that was Angie tried very hard for quite a while; but nothing happened to Geronde. Geronde stood patiently waiting. Hob was gazing at them with awe and delight from his waft of smoke, though both women had long since forgotten he was there.

After several pauses Angie drew an unusual series of deep breaths and looked at Geronde.

"You know," she said, "it might help if you too, close your eyes and say to yourself, 'I am a dragon, I am a dragon . . .' while I'm trying to make you one."

"Of course, Angela," said Geronde. "Should I also—"

There was a bang and a puff of smoke; and Carolinus was standing in

front of them, looking nine feet tall. His beard bristled with rage.

"THAT WON'T WORK!" he said. Both the dragon and Geronde opened their eyes and exhaled. They stared at him.

"Angie," he said, "this is the end—well, almost the end! One of you is bad enough. That husband of yours, leaping around the world, burning up magickal energy right and left as if it could be had for nothing, doing everything wrong and coming up with the right answer by some sort of miracle every time, using some of that other-worldly whatever he brought in his head with him when he came. Two would be too much. I'm an old man. Angela Eckert, this will not do!"

"I've got to find Jim!" said the dragon.

"Well, you're not going to do it that way!" snapped Carolinus—and suddenly the dragon was gone and Angela was there again.

"How dare you!" cried Angie.

"I only took back what you had no right to have in the first place!" said Carolinus. "Angela Eckert, you are not going as a dragon, to search for Jim, let alone turning someone else into a dragon and taking her with you. In fact, you're not turning yourself into a dragon at all. If Jim chooses to turn you into a dragon, I can't stop him. That's within his prerogative. But you can't turn yourself into a dragon. You can't turn yourself into anything. There. It's done. You weren't only breaking every rule in the *Encyclopedie Necromantick*, you were doing it, as unlicensed as a sorcerer, without the supervision of a senior magickian and no sort of permission from anywhere. The whole balance of Powers trembled there for a minute, I'll have you know!"

"Let it tremble," said Angie. She seemed to grow a few feet herself and glared back at Carolinus. "I'm going to get Jim out of whatever he's in, and you can't stop me. If your stopping me from turning into a dragon turns out to make things so that I won't be able to save him in time, you'd better look out, Carolinus. I mean that!"

"God bless my soul!" said Carolinus, for Angie had been utterly convincing in what she had said.

"Just remember that," she said, now, in the same voice.

"Angie," said Carolinus, "this is nonsense. Don't you know that you can't possibly manage to harm a Master Magickian like myself?"

"I'll find a way!" said Angie ominously.

"Bless my soul," said Carolinus for a second time, in a wondering tone. "I had no idea, Angie, that you—"

"Well, you know now," said Angie.

"My dear," said Carolinus patiently, "believe me. I feel for you, I feel for Jim. I would help if I could. I can't. If you can save him on your own, without magick, I will be there cheering when you do it. But what you

were trying just now can not be, will not be, and has been utterly closed to you. I'm sorry, Angie. That's the last word.''

With that, he disappeared.

Slowly the rage leaked out of Angie. She looked at Geronde; and Geronde looked back at her in silence.

"Don't worry, Angela," said Geronde, after a moment. "We'll save James and Brian. We will. We'll find some way.''

"What way?" said Angie emptily.

Hob cleared his throat. It was such a small noise that if there had not been a perfect silence on the top of the tower as Angie and Geronde gazed at each other, the two women would not have heard it. They looked at him.

"Er-hem," said Hob, clearing his throat again; and shrinking a little as the direct gaze of two pairs of eyes drilled upon him. "I had an idea . . .''

Angie relaxed.

"That's all right, Hob," she said, wearily but gently. "But tell us a little later, would you? We've got things on our minds right now.''

"No, no!" said Hob excitedly. "But this is a way you could get to where m'lord and m'lord Brian is, in a hurry, after all, using the smoke—maybe.''

They stared at him.

"But you said—'' began Geronde.

"Oh, I know what I said," said Hob simply. "I said I couldn't carry two of you on the smoke at the same time. But I've thought of a way around it, if I can just get some help. I mean, if I can get an agreement.''

"Agreement?" asked Angie. "What sort of agreement?''

"Oh, not from you, m'lady, or m'lady Geronde," said Hob. "But Lady Geronde, your Malvern Castle has its own hobgoblin, of course. I don't know him well. I've met him a couple of times when we were both out on the smoke at the same time and our paths crossed. But if I could carry Lady Angela, then your hobgoblin could carry you—if he would.''

"If he would?" echoed Geronde. Her face hardened. "You mean he can and he'd refuse?''

"Oh, please, m'lady," said Hob. "Please don't think of trying to make him do it. He's not like me, you know. He's very timid and not used to going far from home. Quite different from me. Let me talk to him. I'll go talk to him right now; and why don't the two of you come over to Malvern Castle on horses, or however you want to do it? With luck I'll meet you there with him at the top of Malvern's highest tower—just like this one— and maybe we can simply all take off from there.''

"Hob," said Angie, "do you seriously think you can talk him into it?''

"I wouldn't want to promise anything, m'lady," said Hob, "but I'll do

my best; and I really have high hopes. As I say, he's timid, but maybe I can rouse the fierceness that lies way down deep in all us hobgoblins.''

"I certainly hope so," said Geronde, with an ominous note in her voice.

"I'll try my best, m'lady," said Hob anxiously. "I really will, believe me!"

"We believe you, Hob," said Angie. "You just have to understand. The Lady Geronde wants to get Sir Brian safely back, as much as you and I want to get your Lord back safely."

"I know," said Hob. "I think it'll be all right. I'll meet you there."

His waft of smoke accelerated away into the sky toward the east, picking up speed as it went. In a few seconds it was out of sight.

"Will they never feed us? Will we stay here until Judgment Day?" said Brian. "Do you suppose?"

He had been pacing back and forth in their cage. Jim had found something that might be considered a bed, also in the cage, except that it was small enough for a child. He had sat on it, gingerly at first, but it had borne his weight. He was sitting there now.

"I know what you're thinking, Brian," he said. "I promise I'll use my magic if I have to. But I want to put it off until I know it's really necessary. I wouldn't be so close with it if it wasn't for something that really impressed me, Brian."

"Hah," said Brian doubtfully.

"But I was," said Jim. "When Carolinus told me about using as little as possible of it, there was something about the way he did it. He was more serious than I think I've ever seen him. I've seen him wave his arms and be emphatic; but this was different. He was trying to get something across to me; and the trouble with all this magic business is that, as he always insisted, he can't just tell me things. I've got to find them out for myself; and he can only point me in the direction where they're to be found. I think I'm beginning to see why I have to find them for myself. It's because, if someone else tells you, you never really believe it the way you need to until you run into it as a necessity in a real-life situation—"

"Hush!" said Brian, interrupting him, low-voiced. "Someone's coming. The less they learn from us the better, whoever they are."

They both fell silent; and into the room of cages came the same officer they had seen before, this time with four guards much more neatly and finely dressed. Also, their clothing was of blue and white and they all wore helmets and mail shirts made of steel.

"Come!" said the officer, unlocking the door. The tone of his voice was now perfectly neutral. There was nothing to indicate whether he was being pleasant, or speaking with the same voice of authority he had used

before. "These men will take you to a place where you are expected."

Jim and Brian walked out of the cage, the four men formed up around them, and they reascended the stairs, with the officer somewhere behind them. This time they followed the corridor to an opening that led them into a wider, cleaner corridor which ran for some distance and changed into one with carpets on the floor, and walls that were faced with marble.

Eventually they came to a wide entrance on the right-hand side, and the officer indicated with a wave of his hand that Jim and Brian should pass through it. The guards themselves stood back. From the moment Brian and Jim had first seen them, they had not said a word.

Brian and Jim went in, passing through a short but opulent corridor and into an equally opulent room, only differing from the corridors they had recently been passing through by the fact that cloths hung like curtains from some sections of its walls, suggesting that there might be further semihidden entrances behind them.

Baiju and ibn-Tariq sat there on cushions, with a tray of food between them, almost touching the knees of their crossed legs, and coffee cups on small, highly polished black wood stands beside each man.

"Food," said Brian ravenously, under his breath.

"Ah, my friends!" cried ibn-Tariq, seeing them. "We have been waiting for you. Come in, refresh yourselves and I will explain why you were put to such distress."

He clapped his hands. In the wall just behind him two areas of the stonework slipped backward, then off to one side, and four men came out dressed in robes of the same rich, deep blue and gleaming white as the guards that had brought Jim and Brian here. Even before the two of them reached Baiju and ibn-Tariq, cushions had been set down for them; and next to these, little black wooden stands were set, and coffee was being poured into the coffee cups on top of the stands.

"You're all right?" Jim asked Baiju.

"I was never otherwise," said Baiju.

"Luckily," said ibn-Tariq, "I was able to straighten out things before our friend here was taken to a somewhat less—"

He paused, watching Brian, who was popping small pastrylike foods into his mouth like a child eating bits of candy. He clapped his hands; and when the four men who had come out of the wall stopped and looked at him, he jabbed a fingertip twice toward the tray. They went off into the wall.

"—Less pleasant quarters than yours," ibn-Tariq went on. "Actually, it was never intended that any of you should end up just as you two did. But, what can be done—"

He broke off, for the four serving men had come back, bearing four

trays. These were arranged around so that while one was within reach of each person there, three of them were more or less clustered around Brian.

"—I ask you?" continued ibn-Tariq. "In any matter of government, complexities occur, and mistakes will happen."

Jim had devoted himself to the coffee, to begin with; and that black liquid dynamite was, as usual, brightening him up inside.

"Is this the place of the military commander of the city?" he asked.

"No," said ibn-Tariq, "it is not. It is the house of Murad of the Heavy Purse, with whom I am acquainted."

"Then I take it," said Jim, helping himself to one of the small items of food on his tray and watching his cup being refilled with coffee by a man who had apparently appeared out of nowhere, "that Murad of the Heavy Purse is the military commander of the city?"

"No," said ibn-Tariq, "he is not. But he is a man of many possessions, and of importance in the city; and the military commander let him use some of the soldiers. Unfortunately, as I say, the instruction given to those low fellows was garbled when it reached them; and they took you for offenders of some form or another."

That first foodlet he had eaten had awakened Jim's hunger. He felt as ready as Brian was showing himself to be to wade into the food; and was trying to do this discreetly while talking at the same time. It was not easy, but he persisted.

"All right, then," he said, around mouthfuls, "can you tell me why we were brought here?"

Ibn-Tariq spread his hands.

"I must express my own personal deep regrets that it happened," he said. "Murad of the Heavy Purse wished only to do me a favor, by bringing our friend Baiju here; so we two could speak without arousing undue interest in the streets. It is not unusual to see such a one as a Mongol being arrested by soldiers of a city. But, as it happened, before the soldiers were sent out—and this may have contributed to the confusion of their orders—I discovered that one of the matters Baiju and I need to discuss fully turns out to involve you two to a certain extent, although to what extent I am not quite sure."

He looked inquiringly at Baiju, pausing as if to give the other an opportunity to speak. Baiju looked back at him, poker-faced, and said nothing.

"As all men know, the Mongols conquered the castles of the Assassins in Persia, whereas we of Egypt—for that is my native land—conquered all those here. However, in recent times, these Assassins have revived in the shape of Grandmaster Hasan ad-Dimri and his White Palace, to which I believe you two were taken after you were captured and stolen from the

caravan. Recently the sultanate of Egypt was approached by people speaking for Hasan ad-Dimri, and offering friendship to our Bahri Mameluke caliphate—may something be done for you, my friend?''

His last words were addressed to Brian.

"Wine—or water!" said Brian thickly. "I choke on cinnamon!''

"Of course," said ibn-Tariq. He clapped his hands, and within seconds Brian was diluting the cinnamon-loaded foodlet he had tried to swallow with the help of a tall vessel like a vase full of water.

"—As I was saying," ibn-Tariq continued to Jim, "Hasan ad-Dimri has been making approaches to our Egyptian caliphate. It was not long before it was found there was a reason for this offer of friendship. Hasan had gotten word of the Golden Horde's push southward toward Persia, with possibly its ultimate aim being Egypt; but it had been announced that they came to take out Hasan and his foul nest of Assassins. As a friend of a friend among the Mamelukes, I undertook to speak with one or possibly more of the Mongols who might be coming and inquire if this matter could not be settled otherwise. We of Egypt would prefer to destroy Hasan ad-Dimri ourselves; and intend to. Therefore there is no need for the Mongols to come this way. Indeed, the arguments in favor of this are overwhelming; we are closer, in a better position to do so, and our Mameluke soldiers are better suited to the task than nomad horse-riding ones—I say that without any intention of offense to friend Baiju."

He paused and smiled at Baiju, who looked back at him with the same unchanged expression.

"But then word came to me, just before we were going to have Baiju conducted to where he and I could talk, that he had recently acquired some information through you two that would give the Mongols perfect confidence they could take the White Palace with great ease. I have no idea what this information is; but it caused me to ask the soldiers to inquire whether you would join Baiju and myself in our conversation. As you know, that order to take you from the caravansary was badly misunderstood."

"Hah!" said Brian quite distinctly. He had finally succeeded in satisfying his hunger and was just now availing himself of a basin of water and a towel being held for him by one of the servitors. In the process, he checked suddenly; and Jim realized that he had caught the eye of Baiju, and it was looking at him with a particularly deadly intent. Jim had a sudden strong guess that the little Mongol was regretting that he had not killed Jim and Brian before they could be trapped into such a situation as they were now, where undoubtedly torture could—and undoubtedly would, if necessary—be tried to extract the secret of their escape from the White Palace. The Mongol must have allowed them to live this long be-

cause he intended to use their experience of the secret way out of the White Palace. Now he was regretting he had done so.

Jim turned back to ibn-Tariq, only to see that ibn-Tariq was occupied at the moment, by a servant who was whispering something into one of his ears. As he looked, the servant stopped whispering and went back into the wall of the room; and ibn-Tariq turned to him with another of his ready smiles.

"I have just had word," he said. "Murad of the Heavy Purse is now able to meet with you. Will you do me the honor of coming with me, then?"

There was a noise—not a large noise, but a shuffling of feet and a slight clinking of metal, and Jim, looking around with Brian and Baiju, saw at least a dozen of the soldiers dressed in the colors of the house, armed with spears this time, as well as their swords, coming in through the entrance through which Jim and Brian themselves had entered just a moment before.

"Perhaps we could go now," said ibn-Tariq mildly.

CHAPTER 25

They were conducted politely enough, but also effectively, with half the armed men behind, half in front and themselves in between; as a group effectively filling even the wide corridor through which they were ultimately taken.

They did not turn down any side passage. This last corridor led directly to the spacious entrance of a very large room, empty of furniture or anything else except at the far end, where, beneath a canopy under the domed ceiling high overhead, a very wide, big man sat on cushions with trays, cups and beakers around him.

He was, thought Jim, as they got closer in the great room, not merely big but almost unbelievably huge. Not only that, but his face was almost buried under an amazingly full, fluffy, white beard that seemed to start right under his eyebrows and bury his features—chin, neck and all—in a beard that would almost make a mattress for a bed. The only thing really visible was the red interior of his mouth, as he picked up some morsel and it disappeared into that aperture.

He wore a turban on his head and a massive, overflowing gown of silk in purple and red that made him seem even bigger. It must, thought Jim, take at least four of his servants to help him even get to his feet.

It was just at this juncture that he was a little startled to hear Brian's voice, low-pitched and hoarse in his ear.

"Is that this fellow with the heavy purse?" muttered Brian. "There's something false about all this, James. As if I'd seen him somewhere before."

"Where?" Jim would have asked, but they were already too close to the massive owner of this establishment for any further low-voiced conversation.

"Welcome!" said the enormous man in a heavy voice. "Pray be seated."

Servants rushed forward with cushions, trays, stands. To Jim and Brian

they gave tankards; and to Brian's obvious delight, they filled them with a red liquid that was all too clearly a wine.

"O, Murad of the Heavy Purse," said ibn-Tariq, "these are those I have spoken to you of: Baiju the Mongol, Sir James and Sir Brian—the noble Franks."

"They are welcome, very welcome!" said Murad. "Am I right, my guests, that you, being unknowing of Allah, believe yourselves free to drink alcohol?"

Jim suddenly noticed that Baiju also had a flagon. Not only that, but he was already drinking out of it in a way that would have it emptied in a few more seconds. Ibn-Tariq had not said anything; so Jim supposed it was up to him or Brian to answer.

"You are right, Murad of the Heavy Purse," he said. "We thank you for this wine, it being a familiar drink to us."

"I wish my guests to be pleased and furnished with whatever brings them pleasure," said Murad. "I appreciate my food and drink—and I wish all others to appreciate theirs too. As Allah has commanded, I feed all those who are truly hungry who come to my door; and to the best of my guests I offer their choice of my food."

"All know that, O Murad of the Heavy Purse," said ibn-Tariq, while Jim was still hunting for a polite form in which to make an answer.

"It is well," said Murad. "O Franks, I understand you are looking for a Frankish slave; and my great friend ibn-Tariq is aiding you in this search. I myself will do what I can to help. What sort of man would he be?"

"When I last saw him, some years ago," said Brian, "he was an erect man somewhat taller than I, but not as tall as Sir James, here; with black hair just beginning to go gray, a small mustache, a high, arched nose and a jaw that came to a point in front. A scarred and somewhat small jaw, for the rest of his features, which were big-boned and strong."

"A search shall be made," said Murad. "I have connections and affairs with many people; and the search shall be an extensive one. We will hope that it finds what you need."

"Are not the ways of Allah marvelous, Murad, my friend?" said ibn-Tariq. "That the emirs of the caliphate of all Egypt should need information which possibly these Franks can supply; and they should be led directly to you, who are in a best position to answer the Franks' own need to find this long-lost other Frank?"

"It is so," said Murad. And a small brown dog came out from somewhere behind him and sat down, beside the cushion on which he rested, looking directly at Jim. "The wonders of Allah are beyond all men's comprehension."

"But perhaps some of the wonder may be guessed at," said ibn-Tariq.

"Egypt is by rights the source and headwater of a mighty empire and so destined to be. The caliphate with its many emirs does not always move as swiftly as it might. Perhaps the time has come for another like Sala-ad-Din was—may Allah keep him forever in His arms—a Kurd as thou art a Kurd, O Murad. Some master of wisdom and possessor of infinite courage, who will lead us into this new empire."

"Blessed indeed, be the name of Sala-ad-Din," answered Murad. "It would indeed be well to think that someone like him might arise again, and even that he might be a Kurd. But we must not look beyond the present moment."

While this flowery speech was going on between the two men, Jim was looking at the brown dog and the brown dog was looking back at him. It was a ridiculous situation.

He could not say to the dog, "What are you doing here?" in spite of the fact that he was sure that the dog he was looking at was none other than Kelb, still in his canine shape.

Likewise, he could not say, "Kelb, I told you not to show up again unless you were called by me." And in fact something suggested that if the two of them were alone together, even then it might not be wise. There was an air of insufferable arrogance about the dog's yellow eyes, which were meeting his unblinkingly at the moment.

There had to be, of course, an outside chance that the dog was not Kelb. Small brown dogs were small brown dogs, particularly when they had obviously been pushed around by circumstance; and were scruffy and unkempt, with short hair.

But if it was Kelb, then what possible connection could he have with Murad? Jim looked into that question and saw possible different answers stretched out apparently without limit.

He gave up on it, for the moment. There was no point in exercising his imagination on it now. He returned his attention to Murad and ibn-Tariq. The compliments were still flowing back and forth between them.

"If Sala-ad-Din were to be once more among us," Murad was saying, "he could do no better than appoint you as his Vizier, ibn-Tariq—" Murad was saying. But Jim missed the last of that particular verbal flourish, because Brian had just caught his elbow between thumb and middle finger and was digging those two fingers into his flesh to attract his attention.

Brian had an iron grip, and it would have been hard to ignore this example of it in any case; but Jim only glanced sideways out of his eyes, enough to see that Brian, although he had hitched himself a little closer to Jim, was also pretending to look straight forward and listen to the dialogue between ibn-Tariq and Murad. However, he was also now close enough so that he could murmur out of the corner of his mouth to Jim.

"James!" he said. "That server, just going back into the wall. Look quickly."

Without turning his head, Jim slanted his gaze swiftly over in time to catch a glimpse of a relatively tall but bent man with gray hair, thin almost to the point of emaciation, going into the wall. Before he could see more, the wall closed behind him.

"Sir Geoffrey! Geronde's father!" muttered Brian. "James, I'm sure it was him!"

Jim thought swiftly.

"We'll have to wait, Brian," he murmured back. "Wait until he comes out again."

"But he hasn't come out before this!" said Brian urgently. "He may not come again!"

This was all too possible, Jim realized. Murad seemed to have as many servants as a queen bee had workers feeding and caring for her. His mind raced.

"Give me a chance to break into the conversation," he said to Brian, and resolutely returned his attention to ibn-Tariq and Murad.

Their talk had wandered off to matters dealing with Sunnis and Shi'ites—which, as Jim vaguely remembered from the days of his twentieth-century education, were the two major sects of Islam. In fact, if he remembered rightly, the Sunni were the orthodox, and perhaps by far the largest sect; but the Shi'ites were numerous enough to be formidable. At the moment, Sunnis were being spoken of with approval and Shi'ites not so. Jim got the strong impression that both Murad and ibn-Tariq belonged in the Sunni camp.

"—A change is coming, O Murad," ibn-Tariq was saying, "I tell thee. We must be ready; and there is no time like that which is now."

He paused and Jim jumped in quickly, before Murad could speak again.

"If you will forgive me, O Murad of the Heavy Purse and ibn-Tariq," he said, "a remarkable thing has just happened. My friend Sir Brian and I have just seen a man that greatly resembles the one we seek. He was dressed as one of your servants, O Murad of the Heavy Purse, and has but a few moments ago left us through that entrance there."

He pointed to the wall that had now closed up again to Murad's right.

"A servant of mine? Are you sure, Frank?"

"I cannot be sure," said Jim. "Neither can Sir Brian. Would it be possible to have the man back so that we can look at him?"

"Indeed, this is a time of wonders," murmured ibn-Tariq, stroking his neat mustache.

"What manner of man was he?" demanded Murad.

"He was elderly—more elderly than any of the others who have served

us since we have been here," said Brian. "He is gray-haired, somewhat stooped and thinner than I remember him; but he is very like Sir Geoffrey, the man we seek, if he is not indeed Sir Geoffrey himself."

"In my own household!" said Murad. He clapped his hands three times.

The door through which Jim and Brian had seen the man they were interested in disappear opened again; but this time what came out was a tall old man with a wispy white beard and a tall staff, with some sort of gold ornamental top on it. He salaamed, bowing very low to Murad.

"Is there something in which Murad of the Heavy Purse needs to be served?" said the old man.

"Yes," said Murad. "There has been, within a short time here, a servant who came into the room, more elderly than any of the other servants, stooped and gray-haired, which two of my guests think they recognize and would like to see again. Find that man and send him back out here again."

"The command of Murad of the Heavy Purse will be obeyed," said the bearded man. He backed into the aperture in the wall, which closed upon his exit.

"Did you know him very well?" asked ibn-Tariq, turning to look at both Jim and Brian.

"I knew him very well," said Brian, "though it was some years back and I was younger then."

"Well, we will soon see," said Murad.

In fact, it was only a few moments before the aperture opened again and the man Jim had just caught a glimpse of came back into the room, followed by the bearded man with the staff, who herded him around to face Murad. Even though his face was half averted, Jim could see a sort of worn hopelessness in it. He did not raise his gaze to meet Murad's eyes.

"How art thou called?" demanded Murad.

"I am called 'the Nasraney,' " said the man in a rusty, worn-out voice.

"Thou art a slave, then," said Murad. "So much the better. Look toward those who sit before me, so that they may see your face clearly," said Murad.

Wearily, the man turned, but his eyes were still on the floor.

"Lift up thy head!" said the bearded man sharply.

The man lifted his head.

Brian stared almost fiercely at him, although Jim, ibn-Tariq and Baiju were also looking.

"I had never thought to see a man so changed," said Brian at last, in something very close to a deep growl, "but I think it is him. Sir Geoffrey?"

The man lifted his head a little more, staring at Brian.

"Answer him," commanded Murad.

"I—" The man seemed to stumble in his speech. "I was once . . . Sir Geoffrey de Chaney."

Brian leaped to his feet, took three steps forward and threw his arms around the man.

"Sir Geoffrey!" he said, kissing him on both cheeks. "Do you not recognize me? Brian—Brian Neville-Smythe? Recall how I often used to be at Malvern, almost, in fact, growing up with your daughter Geronde?"

"Geronde . . ."

The man seemed stunned. He had not returned Brian's embrace. Jim was feeling a strange uneasiness. There was nothing wrong with what was happening—in fact, it was probably the most fortunate thing in the world; but it came very, very close to being a whopping coincidence—that they should meet ibn-Tariq, who knew Murad of the Heavy Purse, who just happened to have as one of his household slaves the one man they were seeking for in all of the Near East.

"Sir Geoffrey, speak to me!" Brian was saying.

"Perhaps," said Jim, "this is all a little too much for a man who has not seen one of his own kind for some years. Perhaps if Brian and I could have some time alone with him . . ."

"Whatever wits he had are gone," said Baiju harshly.

"More likely it is simply the suddenness of meeting someone he used to know from a long time back," said ibn-Tariq. He turned to Murad. "Perhaps this suggestion of Sir James is not unwise. O Murad, of thy mercifulness and great generosity, wouldst thou allow this slave to be alone with your two infidel guests, here?"

"Let it be so," said Murad, with a dismissive wave of his hand. He looked at the man with the beard and the staff and made a motion with his finger. The man with the staff stepped forward to Brian.

"Follow me," he said. The slave turned automatically, Brian went with him, and Jim jumped hastily to his own feet and joined them.

They were led back to the entrance of the large room, and there a portion of the wall opened up again, and they were ushered through into a narrow corridor, but one still richly furnished, that led them a short distance to a small room furnished the same way. Here the bearded man stopped and took a step back from them.

"You will stay here until Murad of the Heavy Purse summons you," he announced, turned on his heel and walked out.

As the sound of his feet died away on the stone surface of the corridor they had just come along, the slave gradually raised his eyes to Brian.

"Is it really you, little Brian?" he said, in a broken voice. "Brian, you
are you, aren't you? You are real?"

"Yes, Sir Geoffrey," said Brian. "Come—"

He took the older man by the arm and led him to one of the walls of
the room where some pillows were piled up.

"Sit down, Sir Geoffrey," he said. He almost had to push the man into
a seated position on a cushion, where the older man automatically crossed
his legs in eastern fashion. Jim and Brian sat down with him.

"Brian," said the man, in a wondering voice, "do you recall going
looking for hobgoblins in one of our chimneys, and getting stuck? Geronde came screaming to me, sure that something terrible had happened to
you. I had to climb into the chimney myself to get you out."

"I remember it well," said Brian, chuckling. "And well I remember
the beating you gave me for doing such a foolish thing."

"It was but a child's adventure," said Sir Geoffrey. "I was too impatient in those days . . ."

He put up his one hand and lightly stroked one side of Brian's face.

"And now you are a man and a knight, with scars!"

"And do you remember," said Brian eagerly, "the Christmas that no
one was expecting you home and you came just the day before. It was
when I was fourteen years old; and Geronde and I thought we would be
alone all through the twelve days of Christmas—and then you showed
up?"

Sir Geoffrey nodded.

"And then the Easter that . . ." Brian went off into a flood of reminis-
cences. Jim stood aside, forgotten. Sir Geoffrey was nodding to everything
Brian suggested, but Jim could not be sure whether he really remembered
all that Brian mentioned, or was just agreeing to keep the flow coming.
His face looked happy.

There was nothing for Jim to do while the two renewed their acquaintance. It was probably just as well, thought Jim. Finding Sir Geoffrey was
not the end of all their problems. In a sense it was just the beginning of
them.

Murad had spoken of Geoffrey as a slave. That meant that he was
property that Murad owned. Would Murad let him go? Probably. But,
what kind of enormous price might he not ask, now that he must have
gathered that getting Sir Geoffrey back and taking him home to England
must mean a great deal to Sir Brian, and supposedly to Jim as well?

Jim moved restlessly about the room, his mind searching for a point
from which to attack the several problems that had presented themselves
to him all at the same time. Brian still had most of the capful of gold
coins he had received as the winner of the tournament. The coins were

now sewn into the padded vest he wore underneath his chain mail shirt; and since, as commonly done, the vest had been sewn directly to the chain mail, the weight of the gold coins, hopefully, would be masked by the weight of the steel shirt.

By English standards, it was a princely sum. But what would it look like to someone like Murad, who evidently was the equivalent of a billionaire—judging by this place, these servants and the submissive attitude ibn-Tariq had been showing to him? Even assuming the gold pieces, perhaps with Jim's money added, were enough to buy the freedom of Sir Geoffrey, the three of them would still be far from European friends, or any other help in this city.

How, to begin with, would they pay the expenses of their trip home? How, indeed, would they even be able to get out of Palmyra and back to Tripoli, where Brian could possibly find some English or connections that would lend them enough to get home on? From what he had seen of this land, credit was not something that came easily to strangers—come to think it, credit never came easily to strangers anywhere, he reminded himself.

Then there was the matter of ibn-Tariq and Baiju. The fact that they both had been on the caravan was now somewhat explained by the fact that there seemed to be some kind of political business between them with this matter of the Mongols of the Golden Horde coming down from the north into Lebanon and the attitude toward this of either the Mamelukes, or the Egyptian caliphate—or perhaps the last two were one, and ibn-Tariq represented them both.

It could be that both ibn-Tariq and Baiju might have prices of their own to demand for the freedom of Sir Geoffrey. Baiju had not simply supplied them with camels and brought them from the Assassins' fortress to this city with such speed because he was a generous soul.

Nor, in spite of his repetition of the word "friends," was ibn-Tariq simply a fountain of generosity. Moreover, ibn-Tariq was entirely too well connected, and in exactly the right place at the right time too often, for Jim's present peace of mind. Could it be possible that ibn-Tariq had somehow already known they were searching for Sir Geoffrey?

But if so, how? And, if so, had he planned to lead them to Geronde's father, so that he could set some price on his assistance in getting Sir Geoffrey into their hands?

It was not beyond the bounds of possibility that ibn-Tariq, who seemed the most polished of politicians and possibly one of the most clever individuals that Jim had met here in the fourteenth century, had gotten word from Cyprus of an English knight searching for Geoffrey. But why should that interest the Egyptian?

But if he had such an interest, having learned this much, ibn-Tariq could then have joined the caravan and tried to pump Jim for further information. Failing in this, he might then have somehow arranged with Hasan ad-Dimri to have Brian and Jim kidnapped and brought into the White Palace.

But could he have foreseen their escape from there?

Baiju, according to what the Mongol had said, had learned from abu al-Qusayr where to wait for Jim and Brian and on what day and at what time. That suggested something very strongly. Which was that abu al-Qusayr had known ahead of time they would be taken to the White Palace, but then escape by the tunnel. If he had somehow known this—he was a senior legal magician, after all—though he pointedly mentioned scrying would not show the future—he might have told Baiju to provide some help for Jim. That was the sort of thing Carolinus might do . . .

Jim's head began to spin. I'll stop thinking about it, he told himself, and come back to it later.

In his wanderings around the room, Jim had half-unconsciously drifted into examining the walls that surrounded them. With the exception of the entrance, the walls showed no openings. There were not even windows to be seen, and the only light came from several torches burning around the room, although these shed a remarkable amount of light for their size and the activity of their flames. Jim found himself running his hands along the walls as he passed, absently feeling for any difference.

He had seen both the wall in the first room where he had met Baiju and ibn-Tariq in this house, and the wall behind Murad of the Heavy Purse, open and reveal a space through which a servant could enter the room. It was not beyond possibility that this room had something like that. And if it did . . .

His mind was only absently considering this possibility when he felt under his fingers a slight vertical edge, the almost invisible upper side of a joint between two of the carefully fitted stones of the wall. He stopped and ran his fingers up and down it—finding it continuous, stone to stone, from floor level to just above his head.

Now that he knew what he was looking for, he could see that the joint also ran crosswise from its highest point, over to another line that descended again to the floor. The outline of a possible secret door was made less obvious by the fact that this wall, like all the others he had seen in the rooms where he and Brian had talked with ibn-Tariq and Murad, was faced with square slabs of polished marble; and the lines where they joined, both vertically and horizontally, helped hide the joint his fingers had discovered.

But finding the doorway was one thing. To open it could be a more difficult matter. He tried pressing and pushing at the slab which faced the

door, and running his hand up and down just inside the joint on either side.

He was not sure exactly when he touched the place that opened it, but suddenly the stone facing before him moved back some six inches and then without a sound slipped sideways. Unthinkingly he stepped into darkness, and then hastily on out to the daylight two steps farther on.

He had expected to find only some sort of secret passage, hidden in the thickness of the wall between this room and whatever was next to it. Instead, he now came out into another room, this one with one side plainly open to fresh air, or whatever else was beyond being hidden by several layers of filmy curtain.

Excited, he went across and tried to part the curtain just enough so he could see through it. By gathering almost a full armful of sheer cloth, he managed it finally; and what he saw beyond was a sort of interior courtyard with a fountain in the center, and trees growing around it.

The trees were not very tall, but were heavily laden with what seemed to be oranges and lemons, some half-ripe, and some clearly ready for picking. Over-topping these trees and beyond them, Jim could see what apparently was an exterior wall, protecting this garden spot—and he thought as he peered through the tree trunks that he could see a green door at ground level in the wall that might lead to freedom.

His happiness over this discovery suddenly tripped and dropped into a cold sensation more like despair.

Even if they did escape, how could they take a valuable slave from Murad of the Heavy Purse and hope to hide with him? Particularly in this city where Murad evidently had so much power, and undoubtedly many people to search and locate them. In fact, they could almost surely not leave even this part of Palmyra without being seen; and once they were seen, Murad would hear of it.

He was struggling to pull himself back up from this sudden fall of spirits, when suddenly two wafts of smoke came through the curtains between him and the garden as if the curtains were not there; and also coming through the cloth as if they were not there, riding on the smoke, were Hob and Angie on one, Geronde on the other, riding with another hobgoblin.

The smoke deposited Angie and Geronde on their feet on the floor directly in front of Jim. The two hobgoblins stayed, perched where they were.

"Jim!" cried Angie, wrapping her arms around him.

He kissed her gratefully and heartily; then, remembering, came up for air long enough to say over her shoulder, "Geronde, we found your father. He's in the next room."

"You found him?" Geronde stared, and Angie suddenly let go of Jim
and stepped back.

"You did, Jim?" said Angie. "That's marvelous. Let's go to him right
now!"

"There're some complications—" Jim was beginning, but even as he
said this, he saw Brian and Sir Geoffrey enter the room through the still-
open wall door, looking inquiringly in the direction of the voices. Brian
raced to Geronde.

"Look, Geronde!" Brian was saying, a moment later, as he came up
for air. "We have Sir—"

But Geronde had stiffened, and a cold look had come over her face as
she stared at the elderly man. She broke in now, icily, before Brian could
finish talking.

"That's not my father!" she said.

CHAPTER 26

"Geronde!" said Brian. "He is much changed and aged, I know, but he remembered the time I got stuck in the chimney looking for hobgoblins at Malvern Castle—he mentioned it first to me, before I ever mentioned anything about the castle yet he—"

"What of it?" said Geronde fiercely, glaring at the man. "He may remember what he likes! But he is not my father—favor me with your understanding, Brian! I should know my own father, should I not? And this man is not Sir Geoffrey de Chaney!"

Brian looked helplessly at Jim and Angie, who were standing, stunned, looking from Geronde to the man.

"Sweeting—" the man said, advancing with his arms outstretched. Geronde recoiled.

"My father never called me 'sweeting' in his life!" she snapped. "Stand back!" From somewhere about her clothing she had suddenly produced a small but undeniably useful dagger. The man halted as if he was on a tether suddenly jerked taut.

"Brian, what made you pick up this impostor?" said Geronde, fiercely turning on Brian, the dagger still in her hand.

"Geronde—" Brian ran out of words and looked helplessly at Jim, Angie and the man who had just been labeled an impostor.

"If this man is an impostor, Geronde," said Jim, "the situation is more complex than you can imagine. We're all going to have to do some quick thinking. Put that knife away, will you please, Geronde? Whatever the situation is, I don't think much of the blame attaches to this man if he's not Sir Geoffrey."

Geronde reluctantly slid the dagger back out of sight through a slit in the cloth behind the belt that gathered her full gown at the waist. Jim turned back to the man.

"Well?" he asked. "Are you Sir Geoffrey, or aren't you?"

"I am Sir Geoffrey!" said the man, and Geronde snorted. "This child

of mine is merely . . ." His voice dropped off and failed. He looked at
the floor at his feet. "What is the use?" he said in a dead voice. "I have
been expecting death every day for the last twelve years. It will come
now, one way or another. It makes no difference."

"Who taught you things that only Sir Geoffrey could know?" demanded Jim.

"It was Murad of the Heavy Purse, himself," the man said. He raised
his head suddenly and his face had become stern. "I was a knight once.
Sir Renel de Oust. I was a knight and a man once. But twelve years of
being a slave have made me nothing, nothing at all."

"For heaven's sake, Geronde!" said Angela to Geronde, who was still
sneering at Sir Renel. "Have some pity for the man. This must have been
his first and only chance to escape—"

She turned to Jim.

"How did this whatever-he-was-of-the-Purse know to tell this one about
it?" she asked. "Perhaps he has the real Sir Geoffrey hidden somewhere
around here."

"That I can answer for you," said Sir Renel, still in the same dead
voice. "I have been here the last three years as a slave. I can tell you, on
the faith of the man I was once, he has no other here who, like me, was
once a gentleman and a knight."

Jim's mind, which had been poking halfheartedly—in fact, more or less
hopelessly—at their problems since the moment of their arrest in the caravansary eating place, suddenly snapped into high gear and began to work
with welcome clarity. It was something that had taken place in him during
a number of crises, both large and small, in his life. The closest thing he
could compare it to was the way a sudden awareness of oncoming danger
brought mind and body together in an instant alert.

He remembered it happening to him one time during a critical term-end
physics exam as an undergraduate. He had sat through nearly half the time
allotted for taking the exam, being defeated one at a time by each question
in the test. He had felt exactly as if he was facing a solid barrier in which
there never had been and never would be an opening. Then suddenly had
come this moment of wakening; and the wall dissolved. Suddenly, all that
he knew, all that he had absorbed over some months of the class, was
back with him and, going back to the beginning he found the test questions
to be child's play—obvious. The same thing happened now.

"Hob," he said.

"Yes, m'lord," answered Hob.

Jim looked at him. The two hobgoblins on their miraculously hovering
wafts of smoke hanging in place in midair in the room were almost identical. About the only difference was the fact that Hob had a cheerful

look and sat proudly upright on his smoke, whereas the hobgoblin from Malvern was not only thinner, but sat hunched up in a small gray ball, as if hoping no one would notice him.

"Would you introduce us to your friend?" Jim asked.

"This is Hob from Malvern Castle, m'lord."

Hob from Malvern Castle hunched himself even smaller.

"I see," said Jim. "Could you, and possibly Hob Malvern with you, then, go out into that garden? There's a fountain there. See if you can't find something to bring some of the water in to me. You know how big a soup plate is?"

"Oh, of course, m'lord. You want some of the water brought you in a soup plate. I don't think there are any soup plates in the garden, though," said Hob.

"Not in a soup plate," said Jim, "in something the size of a soup plate."

"Oh, then that's easy," said Hob.

He wheeled around on his smoke, Hob of Malvern following him, and they both vanished through the curtains in the direction of the garden.

"What do you want water for, Jim?" asked Angie. "Or are you and Brian thirsty?"

"No, we're fine—" Jim began. But before he could even finish the sentence, Hob and his counterpart from Malvern were back in the room; and Hob had brought him the water he had asked for, cradled in the bowl-shape of—some smoke.

Jim stared at it for a second, then recovered.

"Put it on the floor, Hob," he said. There was no place else for it. Hob put it down on the carpet under their feet, and Jim got down on his hands and knees to stare into it.

"It's for scrying," he said to the room at large. "Back in England we use crystal balls, or mirrors. Here they do it with water. Brian and I watched a magician in Tripoli scrying that way. If he can do it, I can do it."

Scrying was a use of magic, and he was still trying to conserve his. But there was no other way to what he wanted to discover.

He concentrated on the water, willing himself to visualize the room he and Brian had just left a short while ago; and where Baiju, ibn-Tariq and Murad of the Heavy Purse, with Kelb beside him, should still be.

The image of the room formed in the shimmering surface of the water. But the room was empty. None of those people was there. Neither was Kelb.

"I don't see anything," said Angie, peering interestedly over his shoulder.

"You wouldn't," said Jim absently. "You have to have magic."

"Oh, of course!" said Angie. "How could I be so stupid? And of course I can't possibly have any magic!"

She strode off and peered through the curtains, as if her gaze would penetrate their thickness to show her the garden beyond.

"What?" asked Jim, still absent in his mind. He had a vague notion that Angie had just said something important, but he could not remember just what it was. He returned to his scrying, trying to summon up a picture of ibn-Tariq and Baiju, wherever they might be.

The picture formed. The two were in a room not much different from this one, except that it had a little more in the way of furniture. Ibn-Tariq was talking, Baiju was listening; and sitting watching both of them was Kelb.

"Good," muttered Jim to himself; and he immediately began to search in the water for an image of Murad, and his present surroundings, whatever they might be.

He had suddenly remembered that Kelb—and he was fairly sure the brown dog was Kelb—had kept his gaze solely on him and Brian. The memory backed up his sudden suspicion just now that the whole business with Murad, and Sir Renel playing the part of Sir Geoffrey, had been a show of some sort for his and Brian's benefit. Sir Renel had clearly been fed to them as surely as a card trickster "feeds" a particular card to someone who thinks he is picking a card from a deck at random.

In any case, now the necessary thing to discover was where Murad himself was. Jim concentrated on the bowl of water. Gradually shapes began to form.

Slowly, they solidified. He saw Murad, lying on his back in a bed that would have been nothing but a huge mattress on the floor of a room, if it had not been so opulent and thick that it raised the possessor of the Heavy Purse a good two feet off the floor.

"Hob—and Hob Malvern—" Jim said. "Come here and look in the water. I want to show you something." Whatever Angie had said a few moments ago finally registered somewhere in the back of his mind, along with a clear feeling that she was displeased over something. "Oh, Angie, if you'd like to see what things look like in the water, do you want to come and look now? I'm making one of the pictures visible to anyone."

"No, thank you," said Angie from the curtains, without turning. She was still furiously angry—at Carolinus, at Jim, at Brian . . . she was even more than a little annoyed at Geronde. Geronde knew why she was angry. The least Geronde could have done, as a friend, was to come and show a little sympathy.

Then it occurred to Angie that if Geronde had done that, just now, her

own response would have been to snap at Geronde; and Geronde, never shy in such matters, would of course, immediately have snapped back . . . the whole thing was ridiculous. Angie suddenly found herself smiling, the anger gone abruptly.

Jim just doesn't understand, she told herself, *of course. He never will.*

She turned and went back to Jim and leaned over his shoulder with her head close to the heads of the two hobgoblins.

"What is it?" she said. "Oh, who's the big man with the beard?"

"Someone called Murad of the Heavy Purse," said Jim. "He owns this place we're in. Hob, could you and Hob Malvern go to that opening in the wall behind me there? That's where I came in here. I didn't really look as I went through, but I think there's enough thickness to the wall, so that there's a chance of a passageway. These walls have passages like that all the way through them. Could you and Hob Malvern search through them on your smoke and try to find the way to the room that has the man you see in the water here?"

Both hobgoblins stared at the image of Murad.

"I don't see why not," said Hob. "It's just like looking through chimneys, only straight through instead of up and down."

"Can you find him quickly, do you think?" asked Jim. "He's alone right now and I'd like to get to him while he is alone, as quickly as possible. If you can, find a route to him for me that won't have me running into other servants who just happen also to be in the same passageway."

"You don't have to have them search," said the voice of Sir Renel. "I know where he is. It is one of his private rooms. He's just resting—as he often does—for about an hour at a time. I can lead you there; and if we run into other servants, I think I can keep them from being curious."

Jim looked up.

"Brian," he said, "what do you think? If we can be alone with Murad for a little while, we can learn a lot more from him about this situation than we know now. What do you think about trying to get to him and find out something?"

"I would say it is a most excellent idea," said Brian. "But I will go first, even though de Oust points the way." There was a flip of his hand, and the knife from up his sleeve was in his fist. He looked at the two women.

Geronde produced the useful little knife again, so swiftly that it was like a conjuring trick. Angie was slower, and had a smaller knife, but she too had been carrying one concealed in what she was wearing. Jim reached down under his eastern-style robes to some very western, and twentieth-century-style, socks that Angie had made for him; and came up with a knife very much like the *skean dhu* favored in Scotland. It was short, with

a blade broad next to the hilt but tapering quickly to a needle point; and it fitted comfortably into his hand.

"We are hardly properly armed as a group," said Brian dryly. "Nonetheless, provided you, Angela, and you, James, are not squeamish and hesitate about using what you have, I think we may do fairly well against unarmed servants in a dark passage, if necessary."

"It won't be," said Jim. "At least, I don't think so. Sir Renel, show us the way."

"Heaven bless you, Sir James, for speaking to me as knight to knight," said Sir Renel. "For that alone I will go bare-handed into whatever may befall us, that I may do one worthwhile thing before I die. But you must let me lead, Sir Brian, for that will be quickest. I know the way and you do not. If you still have doubts of me, you have your knife at my back."

"I would not be truthful if I said I did not doubt," said Brian. "Should my mind become less doubtful at any time along the way or in the near future, perhaps I can give you something to fight with."

"That would be the way to die! God send the chance comes to me! Now, follow, all of you."

He led them back to the opening between the two rooms, and as they stepped into it, Jim realized that the wall had been thicker than he thought, but it was apparently solid on both sides of the opening. However, Sir Renel turned to the solid portion at his right, touched it lightly, and it swung back to show a dark passageway. They could go no more than two abreast, and possibly it would be best to go single file.

"Hob. Malvern Hob?" Jim called over his shoulder. "Are you with us? You hobs can see pretty well in the dark, can't you?"

"Yes, m'lord," answered Hob's voice from behind Jim. "Very well."

"Brian," Jim said, "I suggest we let Hob and Hob Malvern go ahead of us on the smoke, staying about fifteen feet in front, to give us warning if someone is coming toward us. They can travel silently on the smoke; and aren't likely to be seen in the darkness here. Even if we hit a passage with torches, they'll be hard to see."

"Let it be so, then," said Brian.

Jim felt a breath of air past his ear that signaled the passing of the two hobgoblins on their wafts of smoke. They moved into the dark, chain fashion, each touching the one ahead to find their way. Moving so, they forged ahead, moving more rapidly than Jim would have expected, since Sir Renel strode through the darkness with the confidence of someone long accustomed to it.

After a distance, light grew ahead of them; and they emerged into a wider passage that had torches at intervals along it. They passed down this as well, without encountering anyone; but then Sir Renel led them off

to go into a maze of other turns and passages, all lit, and all as empty as the ones they had met so far—until, entering a new one, Hob came flying back to Jim.

"A man!" he whispered in Jim's ear.

"Brian—" Jim began; but before he could finish what he was going to say, in a voice just loud enough to reach Brian's ear, the man was upon them and had almost bumped into Sir Renel.

"Nasraney!" he said. "What do you do with all these—"

"Do not ask!" said Sir Renel in a strong, hard voice. "And do not remember!"

Startled, the other servant stared at him for a moment, then hastily sidled past them all with his eyes turned away from them, to the wall.

"We must hurry." Sir Renel's voice came back from the front of their column. "He may be silent a little while; because normally I am a servant of servants and do not speak up to anyone. He will think that I must be under orders, to talk so boldly. But sooner or later he will tell someone, and the news will get back to all in the palace—to Murad himself."

Sir Renel did indeed pick up the pace. Jim found himself walking fast behind Brian. Luckily, there was light—enough at least to keep him from bumping into Brian from behind, and those behind from bumping into him. In the gleam as they passed under the occasional torch he was able to catch a glimpse of Sir Renel out in front. Now, suddenly under one torch, Renel held up a hand and stopped. Again, his voice came back.

"We turn to the right here," he said. "There will be more light; but there will also be people close to the walls on either side. So make no noise. We are very close to the room in which you saw Murad."

He made the turn. They followed him; and a moment later he made a final turn, stopping before what seemed to be solid wall. But it opened to his touch, and he led them into the room where Murad lay asleep on the overstuffed bed.

Once they were all in the room, the aperture in the wall through which they had entered closed automatically behind them. Sir Renel turned and looked at Brian, who himself turned and looked at Jim, who was examining their surroundings.

Now that they were in the room he saw that an open archway in the wall beyond the bed led to another room, in which he glimpsed curtains, and the lemony-orange smell of the garden came to him.

"We'll have to wake him up," said Jim, looking back at Murad.

He walked to the edge of the bed, reached out and took hold of the nearest wide shoulder. To his surprise, his fingers sank into it, as if there was nothing there. He moved his grip up closer toward the neck, and felt something solid under the clothing that was more like a shoulder. It was

only then, getting a look at it behind the beard, that he noticed the neck was relatively thin, compared to the rest of the big body. He took a strong grip on the solid portion of the shoulder and shook the figure.

Murad's eyes flew open.

"What—who . . ." He sat up in bed with surprising nimbleness for someone of his size and his gaze took them all in, but fastened on the face and figure of Geronde.

"Geronde!" he cried. It was as if none of the rest of them were there and she was the only person to be seen. His eyes moved enough to take in Sir Renel. "How could you bring her to me?" he cried.

"Because I remembered what I once was," answered Sir Renel.

"Damn you!" said the false Murad, the real Sir Geoffrey, or whoever he was. "I might still have had a chance if you'd played the man!"

He literally bounced off the bed and stood up, towering over Sir Renel.

"Say what you want. Do what you will," said Sir Renel, meeting his eyes unflinchingly. "Yes, all that I once was had left me years since. But I recovered it, leading them here to you. Do what you will."

He turned away indifferently. The real Sir Geoffrey glared after him for a moment and then turned his eyes toward Geronde.

"Daughter—" he said awkwardly.

Geronde drew back. Her face had grown cold and forbidding again.

"If I am daughter of yours—and one thing is certain, you have my father's voice and manner—it is only by a fault of nature!" she said grimly. "You, who would blame this gentleman for leading us to you, have you looked at yourself? A vile, gross figure. So, you found the riches you sought at last, turned Musselman, and no doubt live happily here with a hareem and all the other infidel vices!"

"But Geronde, listen to me—" began Sir Geoffrey.

"I do not need your words, sir!" said Geronde, withdrawing as he took a step toward her. "I need only your vile body back in England, dressed like an English gentleman, and at least pretending to be so and a Christian, long enough to give me permission to marry Sir Brian Neville-Smythe, here beside me now. Do that and you can return to your Musselman ways, and the women of your hareem for all I care!"

CHAPTER 27

"**B**ut you don't understand!" repeated Murad-Geoffrey. "Wait!"

His fingers dived into what were apparently openings in his robes and worked there. As they watched, he seemed to fall apart down the front. Then his hands withdrew from the sleeves of his robe, the two halves of his body on either side of the opening parted, and a slim, gray-haired, clean-shaven man, very like Sir Renel indeed, stepped out of all that had been Murad—even the fluffy, white beard—leaving it standing there upright on the floor of the room, as if the robes were made of something stiff and solid, rather than cloth.

"It is true that all Palmyra believes me a Muslim," said Sir Geoffrey earnestly to Geronde, "but the hareem—you don't understand. There is so much here that I can't explain to you. But I am your father, Geronde. I've always been your father. I have always loved you—"

"Hah!" said Geronde.

"But—" began Sir Geoffrey.

"You never loved me!" said Geronde, suddenly and wildly. "You didn't even know I was there, until I was old enough to take on the duties of chatelaine at Malvern—at the age of eleven. Eleven years, Sir Knight, my father! You left me to do a job that would have been heavy for a grown woman with experience. But I did it; and you came home when you wished and went when you wished, hardly ever noticing that the castle was in order and strongly protected, that the lands were productive, that our tenants were loyal. I had done all that. You never even noticed!"

"I was hoping to do something for you," said Sir Geoffrey. "I had hoped all my life to do something for you and your mother—only she died too soon. But you were still young and strong and I had hopes; and I kept trying. We needed money—"

"*You* needed money!" said Geronde. "You needed money to try a hundred things that would cost. Money to get you to where you wanted to go, money to engage you in some endeavor that would bring back a

fortune. Well, you have won that fortune—long since, evidently. But did you come home to me with any of it? No! So how can you stand there and say that any of it was for me?"

"You do not understand!" said Sir Geoffrey desperately. He looked at Jim and Brian. Jim felt a stir of sympathy in him for the man, although he found it hard to believe the good intention he professed. At the same time he noticed that Brian's face was as cold as Geronde's; and Angie's face was almost as condemning. "I'm not really a Muslim. I still am a Christian."

"Then prove it!" snapped Geronde. "Find a priest in this God-forsaken city! Confess to him; and tell him truthfully you are my father and give permission for our marriage; and stand there while he marries us. Then we will happily leave you forever to your sins."

"There is no priest in Palmyra," said Sir Geoffrey.

"Then we will wait until one comes through with a caravan, on his way to some mission or other Holy duty, somewhere else!" said Geronde. "Then you will confess, give us permission to marry, and we will be rid of you! You can go back to being whatever you are here."

"Even if a priest came through," said Sir Geoffrey, "I could not do that, either. I cannot tell you why. Just believe me. I could not do it any more than I could go home with you—and Geronde, believe me, I yearn to see Malvern again."

Geronde laughed jaggedly.

"Oh, aye. But you can not do anything that will see to the purpose for which we came!" she said. "I am sorry, my father, but I do not accept that you are unable to do what we need!"

She pointed to her right cheek.

"You see this scar?" she demanded. "I got that scar because you were not there to protect me. Because you were not there to lead the defense of the castle. Malvern was as good as taken, and I was in the hands of a man who said he would disfigure me slowly, day by day, until I agreed to marry him. After which, with the help of those he had bribed at the King's court, he would have had you declared dead in the Holy Land, myself awarded him as wife, and he would own Malvern. I did not give in to him. I saved Malvern—against your homecoming—sometime, maybe. I did that for you, Father. But you will do nothing I need!"

Sir Geoffrey closed his eyes. The lines of his face had gone deep, so that all at once he looked twenty years older.

"I can not," he said. "And I can not tell you why I can not. Think of me what you will. But what I do is far better for you than giving in to what you want. You must believe that."

"I will never believe it," said Geronde; and she turned her back on him.

Angie went to her and was about to put her arm around Geronde's shoulders when Geronde spoke to her.

"Do not touch me now, Angela," said Geronde, without turning her head. "I would do you a hurt. But stay with me."

They stood side by side in silence, their backs to the others.

Sir Geoffrey took a deep breath, backed up, and started to step back inside the framework of whatever held up his Murad disguise in position on the floor by his bed.

"Just a minute, Sir Geoffrey," said Jim. "Do you know me?"

"No," said Sir Geoffrey, in a disinterested voice.

"I am Sir James Eckert, a neighbor of yours, now in Malencontri."

Sir Geoffrey stopped in his attempt to fumble his way back into his disguise, and turned to look at Jim.

"Malencontri?" he said.

"Yes," said Jim. "I took it from that same ill-knight who marked your daughter's face. I'm a close friend of Sir Brian and Geronde, both; as is Lady Angela, my wife, who is standing with Geronde now. I suggest you wait a moment before considering there is no possibility of your escaping whatever you feel has you entrapped here. I am known in England as the Dragon Knight, because I can also take on the form of a dragon. In fact, I'm a magician, an apprentice of S. Carolinus, who you ought to know as well as I do."

"A magician?" Sir Geoffrey stared at him.

"Right," said Jim. "I don't use magic lightly; but I'm in a position, by knowing it, to sometimes see more than those who aren't magicians. Perhaps, if you told us more about what holds you here I might see something I could do—something you'd never imagine was possible yourself—to free you, after all."

Sir Geoffrey stared at him a moment longer, then slowly shook his head, with a sad smile.

"Not even a magician can help me in this," he said.

"You show small courage for a knight," said Brian grimly.

"It is not a matter of courage, Brian," said Sir Geoffrey to him. "There are some things against which it is hopeless to attempt to fight. You cannot fight the tempest, nor the cold in winter that may kill you before morning if you are lost in the woods. No man, no knight, no magician can change such things."

"No," said Jim, "but an open human mind possibly can."

For the first time he was beginning to get a little warm-tempered himself.

"An open mind, for example," he went on, "could show you a way to build a shelter to survive overnight in those woods. It might also show you a place to hide from, or ride out the tempest—if you were on the sea when it blew. You've only got one mind, Sir Geoffrey, and it sees no way out. But that does not mean that another mind, like mine, or Sir Brian's, or Geronde's, or my wife's—or all of them put together—might not find a way you have never thought of. Think. What will it cost you to tell us what holds you?"

"Too much," said Sir Geoffrey. "The one price I can not pay."

He looked once more appealingly in Geronde's direction; and Jim, following his gaze, saw that both Geronde and Angie were moving toward the entrance into the other room. A moment later they had passed through it and were gone.

Sir Geoffrey turned back to face those left, and took a couple of steps toward them. There was a sudden new light in his eyes. He lowered his voice and spoke.

"Renel, go you into the other room also. This is for the ears of Sir Brian and Sir James alone."

"I am a man again, not a slave," said Sir Renel. "I am at no one's orders, not even yours. I no longer hope for freedom, but only to die as a man should. I will stay."

"Then you will run the same risk these two will run," said Sir Geoffrey. "I would rather speak for their ears alone. If I ask you to go—not as what you know me to be, but as a fellow knight, an old companion—would you do me the favor of going?"

"It is true," said Sir Renel, turning to Brian and Jim. "Once he and I were companions in a foolish adventure to raise a last crusade and wade knee-deep in infidel gold and gems. In those days we looked much alike, so that people took us for twin brothers, although we had fallen together merely by chance and were no real kin. But we went different ways; and the next time he saw me, I was in the slave market here in Palmyra. He had become Murad of the white beard and Heavy Purse. How he did that I do not know; but he rescued me from a worse slavery by buying me himself and bringing me back here."

He stopped and looked at Sir Geoffrey.

"For that I still thank you," he said. "Though I think you had other reasons for it, even then."

Sir Renel turned back to Jim and Brian.

"He secretly favored me when none of the other servants were around, and finally proposed that I should go back to England as him, and take over lordship of Malvern and the name of Sir Geoffrey de Chaney. He would help me escape. Indeed, we had this planned; and then for some

reason he could not tell me it became difficult and had to be put off. While the months went by and I still hoped, there suddenly came you people upon us. Now you know everything that I know. How he became Murad I do not know. What magic he uses to look like Murad, I now know. As you see, not even the beard is his own. We could change places right now; and if he went back between the walls, the other servants would take him for me. With all that between us, why should I leave?''

"I don't think you should," said Jim. He looked at Sir Geoffrey. "What do you say, Sir Geoffrey?''

Sir Geoffrey raised his hands in a helpless gesture.

"Perhaps it will make no difference," he said. "Stay, then, Renel."

"I will stay; and insomuch as I can still fight I will fight for you and what you need as things may turn out. I pledge you that.''

"And I pledge you equal succor," said Sir Geoffrey. "Renel, you are a friend I do not deserve.''

"Neither of us deserves much," said Renel with a tight smile. "Enough of that. Let us listen to what you have to say.''

"Very well, then," said Sir Geoffrey, lowering his voice even more, so that Jim and Brian and Renel all had to move close to him to hear. Out of the corner of his eye Jim saw the two hobgoblins on their smoke also edging closer. He looked at them.

"No," said Jim.

"Beg pardon, m'lord," said Hob as both wafts of smoke backed up hastily. "Should we leave the room?''

"No," said Jim. "Just stay far enough away so that you don't hear and we have privacy.''

The two little Naturals backed off even farther, nearly the width of the room. Jim turned back to Sir Geoffrey and the others.

"I am under a curse," said Sir Geoffrey, quietly and simply. "The curse will fall upon me if I cease to do the bidding of him who is my master—and that is Hasan ad-Dimri, Grandmaster of the Assassins. It happens—I do not know how, it is undoubtedly magic—that as I move around through the passages in the walls of this house of mine, I can find myself coming out, not here in Palmyra, but in the White Palace up in the mountains where Hasan rules. I will know then that he has called me for some reason. I know my way around there, also, as I know my way around my own house here. I will go where I know I would find him; and when I find him he will tell me what he wants, and I will obey.''

"Why?" asked Brian bluntly. "If he has no weapon but the curse, he can only use it once and—''

"Not so. It was a curse on him," said Sir Geoffrey, "that I agreed to take from him, in exchange for all this—''

He waved his hand in a wide, level sweep about him.

"How—?" began Brian.

"Let me go on," he said. "Also, when he wishes, Hasan comes here. The servants see him but do not know who he is. He takes what he wants and does what he wants here. The hareem is his, not mine. I have not been near a woman, slave or free, ever since I came to dwell here. It is part of the curse Hasan gave over to me. Also, I can go to rooms where there is tremendous wealth, silver coins heaped high and gold as well, and other precious things. But I can no more touch them than I can touch a woman. They are Hasan's."

"How did you come to be under such evil influence?" asked Brian.

"That which makes me look like Murad," answered Geoffrey, "was something I had once learned to construct from a man in Italy who made masks, devil costumes and other such things for religious festivals. He was very clever. But I learned quickly; and when I left him, I knew enough to be able to make myself appear as various different people. It happened that I fell upon evil times—it was after we had parted, following the battle in the mountains, Renel—"

He had turned to his friend for a moment; but then he turned back to concentrate on Jim and Brian.

"After that, I went back to England for a while, then was other places—no need to tell all that—then came this last trip here; when it happened I found that in spite of my armor and weapons I was in danger. I had to sleep sometime; and it was only a matter of days before I would wake to find my throat being cut and all I had taken—and that would be the end of me."

He paused, glanced around him and lowered his voice even a little more.

"It was necessary for me to pass as a Muslim. Not only that, but as one whom other Muslims would not only accept but see benefit in dealing with, rather than killing. I still had some silver and gems with me from a recent battle and our sacking of—a place. I went into the first place that could sell me what I needed, and took this off into the desert. There, where I was alone and safe, I made up a Kurd disguise I had perfected. It turned me into one with the appearance of the Murad you have seen; and I used what wealth I had left in the manner of one who is a rich but parsimonious Kurd merchant. I was traveling down toward Tripoli, where I hoped to find at least one friend left; so that I could lay aside my disguise and borrow the extra money I needed to start me homeward to England. But before I got there, the group with which I was traveling was waylaid by Hasan's Assassins; and I was taken with the others to his White Palace."

He stopped speaking.

"Then what?" asked Jim.

"Then Hasan offered me all this that you see around you, the wealth I told you of, the hareem, the power, the position—provided I would accept his curse," said Sir Geoffrey. "I was in his power. He could do anything with me he liked; and I thought it most likely he would have me killed if I did not agree. Also, at that time I foolishly thought I could find some way of getting free of the curse. I was wrong."

"And what is this curse?" demanded Brian. "What happens when it strikes you?"

"That," said Sir Geoffrey, "is the one thing I will not tell you. I will only tell you this. It is a curse that no sensible man would wish to dare— let alone pass it on; for it was that if I managed to escape him after accepting it, the curse would follow me to the ends of the earth to still fall on me, and then it would also fall on my descendants unto the seventh generation."

"Hmm," said Jim. "Where would a human get the power to lay on a curse like that—and come to think of it, what about Kelb?" asked Jim.

"Kelb?"

"A Djinni," said Jim. "Don't try to tell me you don't know about him. He came out and sat by you when we were all gathered talking in that large room a little while ago."

"The brown dog is a Djinni?" Sir Geoffrey stared at him. "I knew only it was a dog; and that it had been set to watch over me at certain times. I suspected it was Hasan's messenger, or spy, or what you will. But I did not think of it as being a Djinni."

"That's interesting, too," said Jim.

"May I ask why?" asked Sir Geoffrey.

"Because a Djinni is a Natural," said Jim. "And a Natural doesn't have the power to curse, either."

Sir Geoffrey stared at him.

"Tell me something," went on Jim. "Do you know the place is in this house of yours that takes you instantly to the White Palace? And can you take me there?"

Geoffrey hesitated.

"In fact, I do," he said at last. "It is one of two places, first one, then the other, taking turns to put me in the stronghold of Hasan. Do you mean you would wish to go to the White Palace?"

"Yes," said Jim.

His words dropped into a pool of silence. All the rest of them were staring at him.

"James," said Brian. "Is this wise? We are not even armed. If somehow we could get swords—"

"I don't think this is going to be a matter of swords, or weapons of any sort," said Jim, "and I was only talking of me and Sir Geoffrey going."

"What, put your head into the lion's den without me at your side, James?" Brian said emphatically. "Never!"

"Well," said Jim doubtfully, "then, if you come, Brian—and it's a foolishly risky thing for you to do—you'll have to simply trust what I do in this instance. I won't be able to explain things to you as I go along, and give you reasons."

"Of course, I need no reasons," said Brian. He added wistfully, "But, I would I had a sword."

"We can pick up a sword for each of you on the way I will show you," said Sir Geoffrey.

"Fine," said Jim. "Give me just a minute."

He left them, walked over to the entrance and stepped through it into the other room.

"Angela," he said, "Brian, Sir Geoffrey and I are just going to leave you for a little while. We want to look into something down in the passages."

"Oh, no, you don't," said Angie. "If you're going someplace, I'm going with you."

"So am I," said Geronde.

"That's going to make us too much of a crowd," Jim said. His original idea of going with Sir Geoffrey alone had suddenly developed into something more like an expedition. "Besides, if you come, we'll have to make it our main duty to take care of you; and I don't want to take you where we're going, anyway."

"The two hobs can carry us away from any danger," said Angie. "It's settled, Jim!"

She pointed a little to the side and past Jim. He turned and saw the inquisitive faces of a couple of hobgoblins on their smoke right behind him, having evidently followed him into the present room. Jim gave up.

"Hobgoblins," he said, "we're going to the Assassins' fortress."

"You understand?" Angie asked them.

"No," said Hob of Malvern. It was the first actual word Jim had heard from him.

"I'll tell you as we go," said Hob—Jim and Angie's Hob. "You'll like it. It's exciting."

The Malvern Hob gulped and nodded.

Jim gave up. It was something he was used to doing, and he no longer wasted extra energy fighting with the inevitable.

"Come along, then," he said, heading back into the next room.

Sir Renel was waiting for him there.

"Surely, Sir James," he said, "you were not thinking of leaving me, alone, behind?"

Jim sighed internally.

"I guess not," he said.

"Damned caravan," muttered Brian.

"Equally surely," said Geronde, "you had never been thinking of leaving me behind here, had you, Brian?"

"No. Of course not," scowled Brian. "Damned caravan . . ." he muttered again under his breath, but in such a low voice that Jim, who was closest to him, was probably the only one to hear it.

Some fifteen minutes later, besworded—including the women—they were going down one more of a number of almost lightless, narrow passageways, between the walls they had traversed; and the voice of Geoffrey, in the lead, came back to say they were not far from their goal.

"I wish I had my boar-spear," Geronde said wistfully in the gloom. Geronde's boar-spear was her favorite weapon, light enough for easy use and very effective.

"No boar-spears here," said her father.

There was silence after that until they came to one of the things Jim was beginning to get used to encountering in these between-the-wall passages, simply a blank wall that ended a corridor.

"You can open it, of course?" he said to Geoffrey.

Geoffrey nodded, pressed at various points on the wall, and it slid downward out of sight. Ahead of them was complete darkness.

"Follow me," said Geoffrey, plunging into it and disappearing almost immediately. Jim and Brian did so, followed by the rest of their group.

It was a little like stepping into a pool of ink—even to the point where the air that touched them in this darkness felt almost liquid, heavy and clammy against them.

"Don't worry," came Sir Geoffrey's voice, "just walk forward."

They did so, blindly; and suddenly they were in a room that was less than half the size of Murad's bedroom, but completely unfurnished—bare stone floor, ceiling and walls, with the only illumination being the late afternoon light coming from a single arrow slit in one of the walls.

Jim turned to see if everybody else had got through all right. They were there. Angie, Geronde and the two hobs on their smoke. Brian was with him and just behind them were Sir Renel and up in front was Sir Geoffrey.

The place had no door. No place of entrance or exit. It was solid wall all the way around except for the arrow slit.

"How do we get out of here?" asked Brian.

Jim had been turning to Sir Geoffrey to ask him the same question; but

now he saw the knight beckoning him from one of the walls. He walked over and saw that there was a chink between two of the squared rocks that made the wall, hidden from casual view by the fact that one rock protruded enough to hide the slit except from a certain angle.

"Look through that," said Sir Geoffrey.

Jim looked.

He saw, from what seemed to be about fifteen feet above its floor, the large square room with a domed roof he remembered from his visit to Hasan in the White Palace—a domed roof with windows now filled with the fading pink sky of new twilight. Inside the room torches had been lit; and these burned most brightly at the far end to Jim's right, where Hasan ad-Dimri was in conversation with ibn-Tariq. Baiju, with both wrists and both ankles bound together, sat on the floor almost at Hasan's feet; and, sitting just beyond him, looking like a third partner in the conversation with Hasan and ibn-Tariq, was a small brown dog.

When abu al-Qusayr, the Tripoli magician, had come to speak with Hasan on behalf of Jim and Brian, he had told Jim after failing to help that there was someone or something aiding Hasan—that a power was at work here; though Jim, as a low-ranking magician, possibly could not sense it. Jim had not been sure about such a power then; but he could feel it now, in the room below.

It was like a cold pressure, emanating outward from a point in the room that was like the depression in the center of a whirlpool of water. He could feel it pushing like a large, open hand against him; but also, oddly, it seemed to him, he could almost smell it—a strange, bitter smell. Also, as these things impressed themselves on him, he became aware that the ordinarily fully lighted room below now seemed to have acquired, to his sight at least, all sorts of strange, hard-to-see shadows; lurking not only in corners but in mid-air, moving to and fro, some darker than others—but all becoming invisible when he tried to look directly at any one of them.

Whatever all this meant, there was certainly no question about where the center of the whirlpool of the power he felt was. It was centered not upon Hasan, but upon ibn-Tariq.

Down below, the brown dog turned its head to look up in the direction from which Jim was looking down on him. Jim felt a distinct shock, as if he and the canine were face to face.

"We are observed." The dog's voice floated upward clearly to Jim's ear.

CHAPTER 28

"Welcome, O visitors," said ibn-Tariq softly.

Abruptly they were, all of them, down in the room Jim had been looking into, standing before the four who were there, but at a little distance from them.

Jim was acutely, immediately conscious of matters of measure—shape and shadow. Without any need to calculate, he knew that he, standing in front of the rest, was exactly three lengths of his own body from ibn-Tariq, who was the closest of the three. He was aware that ibn-Tariq, the dog and Hasan ad-Dimri marked the points of a triangle, enclosing Baiju at its center, that had exactly three equal sides; and that a globe enclosing all four of them would have a diameter that was exactly twice Jim's own height.

It was as if the nonexistent globe could be the heavy, if invisible, head of some massive hammer, the handle of which reached half the length of the distance from them to him. He found himself imagining, as he might have imagined a sudden strike out of darkness, the hammer rising on the base of the handle, pivoting up to fall down again upon him and those with him, crushing them all. A hammer controlled by any one, or possibly all three, of those who sat at the points of the triangle.

This was power of a magnitude he had not encountered before. Power only to be found otherwise in a senior magician—perhaps not as great as that he had faced in his original battle at the Loathly Tower to free Angie—but then Carolinus had been there to deal with it. Here, he was the only one who used magic. The vortex of this power was still with ibn-Tariq; but it could be that the other two, Hasan and the dog Kelb, had not yet shown their hand. He had an uneasy feeling that there might be more here than had yet appeared.

But, he realized, it could not be Hasan. Hasan could not be a magician if he was heading up a group like the Assassins. The activities of the Assassins were flatly against the rules of Magicdom. Also, if Hasan had

been anyone else with magical powers, abu al-Qusayr would not merely have reasoned with him, then backed off. That left only the two who could be direct opponents of his in this moment. Ibn-Tariq alone was at the vortex. But he also could not be a magician and act as he was acting now—aggressively. That left only one thing he could be.

"You're a sorcerer," Jim said to ibn-Tariq.

Ibn-Tariq smiled.

"And stronger than any you ever expected to encounter," he said. "Is that not so? You thought Julio Eccoti, the counselor to King Jean of France who made the alliance with the sea serpents you defeated—you thought he must have the utmost strength of we who study and use the *Whole Book of Spells*. But the truth is Julio learned only a little; and then ran out into the world to become rich with it. I stayed, and never ceased to study with the masters of my art. Already, my strength overcomes yours."

Jim abruptly became aware of something he should have noticed earlier. In the dome above them, the windows showed a sky in which late afternoon was moving toward twilight. It was not natural that evening could have come so soon—but then time was now an area beyond the actual. The dimming sky now made almost visible the shadows he had first felt, rather than seen from the room above, and which now had gathered and thickened in the hall. Also, they were moving in on him and his small group.

They, too, he realized now, were creatures of angles and distances. Each had its own particular size and pattern; and the total of those patterns was closing in on Jim and those with him, slowly, but always more and more tightly.

There was no time left to waste. Now a full understanding came to him of why Carolinus had warned him to hoard his magical energy against some great possible need.

Theoretically, his drawing power there was "unlimited." In practice, there had to be a limitation. Otherwise, he could break the bank—call for all the free magical energy there was, and leave no reserve supply for any other of the world's magicians. But now he needed everything he could get, for he could feel that what he faced was stronger than he was. Gratefulness washed through him that he had not wasted any more of what had been available to him.

He reached for that available amount, now—and found himself climbing a steep, stony mountainside, toward a peak, gray against a bloody-colored sunset. Far and high the top of the mountain stood dark against the light; and he knew without needing to be told that the staff he had come to get was only to be found at that top.

His will almost failed him. It was too far to go in the small period he

dared be absent from the domed room in the White Palace. But suddenly, there was Carolinus, standing on a great boulder above him along the path upward he must go, and looking down at him.

"There will be time," said Carolinus, "but save your strength to reach the very top; or you may fail with what you face."

He stood for a moment more, looking at him.

Then Carolinus was gone. A little wind whispered and whistled among the boulders and smaller rocks to either side of the narrow path on the rocky mountainside Jim saw before him. There was nothing growing anywhere. All was rock.

The small wind whistled and sighed among the stones. It stroked his face and chilled his body inside his clothes as he drew the air deep into his lungs. Deep, for the air was thin as well as cold. Leaning forward to balance himself against the steep slope, he started up the path that wound between the bigger rocks.

Now there was sound in addition to the talking of the wind. He had not realized how complete otherwise the silence had been. But now he heard the grating of pebbles and the rasp of immovable stone below his boot soles; and he felt a moment of gratitude for that night back in the caravan encampment when the Assassins had kidnaped him, when he had left his boots on as he went to sleep, to keep his feet warm in the air that grew mountain-cold at night there, too. The foot-sound, and the sound of his breathing, seemed loud in the otherwise perfect soundlessness around him. No far-off rocks fell, no solitary hawk called, high overhead.

He climbed. If it was not a path he followed, he told himself, it was another old, dry streambed that had once snaked down this mountainside; and it was well it was there, because as he looked to right and left he saw nothing but a wilderness of stones, large and small, through which he would otherwise have had to climb and squeeze his way. But the path was becoming even steeper now, and the going was not easy. The cold began to reach deeper into him. He pushed it back with the inner heat of his determination to get to the top.

He walked so for some time, leaning farther forward as the way grew steeper. The muscles of his thighs began to ache lightly as he went on upward, and the path or watercourse narrowed, winding up and up until he could have reached out and touched the taller stones on either side at once, as he went.

The wilderness of boulder-tumbled mountainside came to an end, abruptly, as a forest stops almost neatly at the edge of a meadow.

The pathway narrowed and ended. He turned sideways to pass through the last large rocks, and came out in an open space, at the edge of a sheet

of ice—gray, smooth ice with no sign of snow on it, stretching like a river itself up the mountainside.

There was a darkness at the far end of it. More rocks, he assumed; but he was breathing so hard now and his eyes were misting, perhaps because of the dryness of the air, so that he could not make out exactly what the dark shape was. In any case he would have to climb the ice, and it was as smooth and clean as a fresh-shaved skating rink. It was like the out-reaching limb of a glacier, except for its glasslike clarity; like a river of ice; and, thinking of it as a river, for the first time, he looked over at the far side of it.

The brief stop while he looked had allowed him to catch his breath, and his vision had cleared and sharpened. On the other side, he saw what looked like spaces between the rocks there that went up also toward his goal and might give him an ice-free place to climb. But he would have to cross the river to get to it.

His hand had reached for the hold-out knife that Brian had taught him to carry, and which he had produced when they had all begun to follow Sir Renel between the walls of Murad's palace. Leaning out over the edge of the ice, he began to chip hand- and footholds in it.

Slowly, building his way as he went, he crossed the ice—and he had been correct. On the far side it had not flowed completely in among the rocks and there were spaces of flat, dry stone that required only an inter-mediate hand- or foothold chipped in the ice to get him from one to the next stony space. With the help of his knife, he worked his way up the far side of the ice river until the line of rocks began to run out and the river itself narrowed.

He had forgotten to look ahead in his absorption with making his way. Instead, the knife in his hand had reminded him of Brian, of Geronde and most of all of Angie—and then even of the hobgoblins, Sir Geoffrey and Sir Renel. There was a living warmth in thinking of them that counteracted the cold that seemed to be stiffening all his movements now; and with this in mind he had been feeling as if he was almost to the staff. So it was a shock when he came to the end of the ice floe, and the end of the rocks alongside it where he had been moving, almost running into it before he stopped and saw what was there.

It was a long slope of scree—pebbles and broken stones—that must have come down as a landslide over the ice river. It offered a dry route toward the top; and for the first time he could see how close the top was. It loomed only a hundred feet above him.

He went faster now, seeing himself so close. It was moments, only, before he got to the scree and started up. He took his first two steps with confidence, but his feet slipped and he fell, for the surface under his feet

might as well have been made by an avalanche of glass marbles. It rolled and slid, one pebble and fragment over another, as his weight came upon it. He could go upward only by climbing with both hands and feet.

But the scree did not stretch far. He struggled up it, not looking ahead, until he was stopped by a wall of rock.

He lay, the loose stones hard against him, his lungs pumping, pumping the thin air in and out to get enough oxygen to slow his racing heart. This was the darkness he had not been able to make out from farther down. It was a cliff, like a wall built to keep him back at the last.

Gradually the pounding of his heart slowed, breath and calmness came back together upon him. He looked up at the cliff. The red of the sunset was gone from the sky overhead now. The twilight was moving in, and darkening. But still, sharply outlined against what was left of the illuminated western sky, was the top of the mountain not far away. The cliff did not rise straight upward. It leaned back, but at a near-vertical angle. There were handholds and bosses of rock sticking out. It could be climbed.

He breathed for a moment more, and then began to try to make his way up it.

He had believed he could do it when he started; but by the time he was halfway up, that confidence was dying in him. The muscles of his arms were trembling and weak; and his body seemed to weigh many times what it should.

He hung where he was, doubting that he could go on, sure that he would fall if he tried to go back.

Then a hatred of his body took him. His body was only an animal, after all, he told himself. It had to do what his mind told it. Slowly he began to climb again, not thinking any more about a time when he would stop climbing but ready to climb forever. And, after some time beyond measure, his right hand, reaching up, went over the top edge. He had reached the end of the climb.

With what seemed the last of his strength he pulled himself out on to a little space of flat rock, tilted upward, but by comparison with the cliff almost level. He lay there, once more working to get oxygen back into his body. It was a strange thing—that the stopping should seem to be so much harder than the going on; and for the first time he began to notice the cost of his struggles.

His feet hurt and his hands hurt. His knees hurt. He looked at his knees and they were naked, the clothing over them worn away. His boots were hardly more than collars around his ankles and the top of his feet. Like his hands, his feet were icy from their contact with cold ice and the cold rock; but now he felt pain in them as well, and looking more closely at

his hands, he saw the cuts and tears in them. He did not try to see the soles of his feet.

But he was very close to the top now. He looked to see above him the spire of rock that it was; and for the first time his courage died within him. Between him and it was a last, short stretch that was a jungle of large and small boulders. There was no path. There were only the tops of rocks, some rounded, some jagged, but all with spaces between them, into which he could slip as into the jaws of a trap. Now, so close, but barred like this, tears came to his eyes.

He made himself think again of Angie and the others; but now it was as if they were at a distance, and he did not rouse at the thought of them. Something inside him was sure that if he tried to cross those rocks he would fall between two of them and be caught forever—or slip and fall on some sharp spine or spire of frost-broken boulder, and spear himself on it.

He was aware of Carolinus once more beside him. He rolled a little on to his left side to look up at the red robe, the white beard, the old face and the faded blue eyes, looking down at him.

"Why?" he asked.

What he had meant to say was *Why does it have to be so hard?*

"Because," Carolinus answered, as if Jim had spoken the words aloud, "the staff is made by your effort in reaching it. If you give up right now, you will still reach out and gain a staff. But it might not hold the strength you need. You could have stopped anywhere before now and gained whatever that much had earned you. But the stoutness of the staff is measured against your will, the strength of your spirit, which will be tested against the strength of what you'll need to use it against."

It seemed to Jim suddenly that he had known this from the beginning, only he had never put the knowledge into words. Known it, not merely from the beginning of his climb, but from the beginning of the moment that he and Angie had found themselves back here in this fourteenth-century world where they did not belong—where they were foreign matter introduced into something that had no room for them, like grit into the crankcase of a running engine.

From the beginning he and Angie had known they had to make a place for themselves in this different world; and it had been their choice to stay—they could have left. It was too late to change that choice now. Even without thinking, he found his body move, beginning to climb the first of the rocks in the jungle between him and the top of the mountain.

That last cold and impossible distance he did not really see or feel as he made it, nor after was he able to remember. But after a time he could not measure—going beyond all things in him, beyond his strength, beyond

his courage, beyond his desire, beyond his love for those still back in the reception room of Hasan now with the shadows moving in on them—he came to the end of the rocks; and half fell into an open space; and the staff was there, standing straight and upright against the last of the red glow in the western sky, which disappeared even as he looked.

He reached out and took hold of it—and he was back in the domed room with the others.

He had returned almost to the moment he had left; people were still all in their same positions. "—my strength overcomes yours." Ibn-Tariq's words still echoed in his ears.

But during the small moment between, the shadows had moved closer. He lifted the staff and they drew back . . . not far, but they drew back. He glanced for a moment down at himself. His clothes were untorn, his shoes complete again, his hands unlacerated. Angie was looking at him penetratingly, but outside of that, none of the others showed any sign of being conscious he had been away.

"Your rod is no threat," said ibn-Tariq.

Jim risked a glance at his staff. It was neither as tall as nor as thick as Carolinus's had been in those first days when they had come and with Carolinus's help they had made the assault on the Loathly Tower to rescue Angie. Then Carolinus's rod had held back the Dark Powers while he, Brian and Dafydd ap Hywel fought its creatures and won.

This that he grasped would not hold as much power as Carolinus's had; but it was straight and weathered. It fitted like a talisman in his right hand. Its lower end now rested on the floor of the room; and the floor, through various underpinnings, reached down finally to touch the earth itself, drawing strength upward from the planet into the staff and him.

"I say," came the voice of ibn-Tariq again, "the staff is no threat. We are Muslim. Your Christian magic cannot attack us, as you yourself know. Lay it down. You will suffer less from us."

"Not all of you are Muslim," said Jim. For the first time he noticed that Baiju, seated with knees drawn up to his chest, had his wrists bound tight to his ankles.

"Baiju," he said, "if it is what you wish—come stand with us."

As he spoke, he visualized it. A small lightning flickered from the top of his staff, burning through the cords that bound Baiju—and the little Mongol appeared behind Jim, standing on his feet. Baiju gave a grunt, but that was all.

"So much for magic," said Jim. "I went a long way and a hard way for what I hold; and you're right—I'm not allowed to attack with it. But I'm not here to attack, but to defend those who need defense. Even you—

I will defend you, too, if you'll come to me. But you'll have to leave your own unlicensed sorcery behind.''

Ibn-Tariq's gaze sharpened like that of a cornered hawk.

"Am I only an apprentice in my art," he said, "to think I might need the aid of one like you?"

Jim did not answer.

His mind was fully open and understanding, sharp and clear now that he had the staff in his hand.

"To begin with," he said, "you could have wanted only to stop Brian and me from finding Sir Geoffrey and taking him back to England. Then you found out about us by chance, probably from abu al-Qusayr—carefully hiding the sorcerous element in you when you dealt with him—that our success would mean the end of all you planned—"

Ibn-Tariq's eyes glittered.

"I hide from no magician!" he said.

"If that was true, you'd be a fool," said Jim, "and you're not that. So, you found out about me, and that I was one of the junior grades of magician, who ought to be easy to handle. But when you couldn't get me to talk about magic, so you could get some idea of my powers, as we traveled in the caravan, you arranged to have Brian and me captured by the Assassins; and tried to trick me into showing what magic I had by forcing me to escape with it, didn't you?"

Ibn-Tariq only smiled.

"But then when we escaped, using no important magic, but learning of the secret way in and out—knowing which could allow the Golden Horde Mongols to get in and conquer the White Palace easily—we became a real danger. But why should we, or even Baiju, who met us as we left the secret way, tell those of the Golden Horde about this?"

"He is of the Horde," said Hasan, behind ibn-Tariq.

"*Ya barid!*" snapped ibn-Tariq, turning on him. "Fool!"

Both Hasan and the dog cowered away from him. Ibn-Tariq turned back to face Jim; but Jim had already looked back to meet the eyes of Baiju.

"Is that true?" Jim asked. Baiju met his gaze unyieldingly.

"No," he said. "I am of the Il'Khanate, those of the first horde who hold Persia, as I told you in the caravan. I thought you, with your magic, would understand."

"I didn't then," said Jim, "but I do now. By letting them think you were of the Horde, you hoped to learn what the Mamelukes of Egypt planned for the Horde."

Baiju did not nod or speak—but he smiled tightly.

"So," said Jim, "you never were their spy. But your learning the exit

point of the secret way out of here was still a threat to ibn-Tariq, who
wanted the White Palace to survive.''

He turned back to face ibn-Tariq, who spread his hands before him,
calm once more.

"I?" he said. "I have something of a friendship for Hasan ad-Dimri,
but why should I be concerned with the White Palace or the attack on it
by any Mongols? And what could one sorcerer do, in any case, against
an army?"

"One sorcerer alone might not be able to do much," said Jim. "But a
sorcerer connected with an army of Mamelukes coming to oppose Mongols is something else again."

"I have no connections with Mamelukes," said ibn-Tariq. "Though I
have friends among them, of course."

"I think you have," said Jim. "You're what, where I originally come
from, is called a 'politician.' I wondered, when I first saw you here just
now, why you talked to Murad in front of us about a new leader being
needed to make Egypt into an empire. A leader like Saladin, who was a
Kurd—as was Murad. Why say this to Murad, when you and he knew he
wasn't really Murad, but Sir Geoffrey? Of course, it was all for my benefit.
For our benefit, Sir Brian's and mine, to reinforce the image of Murad,
so we'd not even suspect he could be Sir Geoffrey. It was your idea,
wasn't it? To arrange for us to catch a glimpse of Sir Renel?''

"And when did you come to these wild imaginings?" asked ibn-Tariq.

"As I say—when I first looked down on you here through a crack in
the wall of that room above us that connects with the palace of Murad,"
said Jim. "If you knew Murad was Sir Geoffrey, why talk to him like
that when the only ones listening were Brian, myself and Baiju?"

"So," said ibn-Tariq, "then you think I see myself as a second Sala-
ad-Din, taking the fire and sword of Egypt over half the world, like Al-
exander; and then weeping because there are no more worlds to conquer?"

"No, I don't," said Jim bluntly. "I think you're interested in something
much more manageable and practical. Reviving the nests of Assassins and
increasing their power, by combining it with sorcery. Your plan must be
to recruit younger, less trained sorcerers to work with the other Assassin
nests you'd create; and you would be the master of those apprentices, the
shadow Grandmaster of the sorcerers behind the power of all the Grand-
masters of the Assassins."

"You dream," said ibn-Tariq.

"I don't think so," said Jim. "You dreamed—of an empire. But you'd
only just started to build it with the White Palace here. You built your
power over this particular nest of Assassins by offering Hasan power and
wealth when he was a Sufi. If he would become leader here, you'd help

him to gain power. It was something easy for you to do for him, using sorcery to impress the Assassins already here.''

"You guess, only.''

"I'm sure enough,'' said Jim. "Hasan was a good man in his own way and you turned him to evil. The White Palace has survived and grown since then; but the beginning of your private empire isn't ready yet to stand up to a Mongol attack. That's why neither Baiju, Brian nor I could be let survive; and Hasan still had to be held by the curse.''

"You weave lies into a cloth of falsity,'' said ibn-Tariq coldly. "Hasan ad-Dimri is under no curse, as you know. It is your Sir Geoffrey who bears the curse.''

"Yes,'' said Jim. "But there were things about curses that, being a sorcerer, you didn't know; or else you wouldn't have had anything to do with them. Curses are like some vile disease. They eat away at the person they've touched. You saw the signs in Hasan too late to cure what had already been done to him. You'd undermined his faith by tempting him away to lead Assassins. That started the decay in him; and it was gradually eating away all his strengths. Strengthless, he'd be no good to you. So, you arranged to have his curse transferred to Sir Geoffrey; and all the wealth and luxury you promised him became only a step from the White Palace, moved sorcerously into the home of Murad of the Heavy Purse in Palmyra.''

"Sir Geoffrey is a Christian,'' said ibn-Tariq. "How could I, a Muslim sorcerer, take a curse from someone else and place it on him?''

"You,'' said Jim, "couldn't. A sorcerer can't, any more than he can lay curses on persons in the first place—any more than a Muslim sorcerer can work magic against a Christian, a Christian against a Muslim, or either against a Holy person of their own faith. And it couldn't be done by Kelb. Or is Kelb really Kelb?''

"No!'' A voice boomed out that echoed off the walls and rang down again from the cup of the domed ceiling—and where Kelb had been there was a puff of smoke and then nothing, only the voice—

"I am Sakhr al-Jinni! Kelb was always the least of my slaves and still is. I put on his shape to watch you on Cyprus. Solomon, David's son, locked me in a bottle and threw me into the sea. But now I am free. It is no weak demon or sorcerer you face here, but Sakhr al-Jinni, Djinni of Djinn!''

The smoke thinned; and standing on the platform was the hideously ugly turbaned figure with the mismatched eyes and misplaced mouth that Jim and Hob had seen on Cyprus when Jim had asked to see Kelb in his Djinni form.

"Thou hast always been overproud and boastful!'' said ibn-Tariq to

him with sudden startling savagery, "and it seems thy time in the bottle taught thee nothing! Of all here, thou art the weakest, not the strongest. Now, a dog thou chose to be—be therefore that dog and not otherwise for ninety-nine lifetimes!"

Suddenly, where the Djinni-figure had been, was a small, ugly brown dog that yelped and vanished.

"Enough talking, James," said Sir Brian. "We have our swords. Let us move on this hell-begotten infidel and his—his Djinni! A Muslim or a Natural can feel the edge of a Christian sword, or else the Crusades never were!"

"And likewise turnabout!" said Geronde sharply. "Hush, Brian!"

"What you suggest, too, is a lie," said Jim, still speaking to ibn-Tariq. "No Djinni—not even Sakhr al-Jinni—can lay a curse on anyone, Muslim or Christian. Below the one you Muslims call Shaitain, only the beings of a few kingdoms can. And the only ones of those available to a sorcerer are those who inhabit the Kingdom of Devils and Demons."

"So you think," said ibn-Tariq.

"So I know," answered Jim. "Only the Devils and Demons are creatures of pure hate, set in this world to test the children of humans. But Devils and Demons are penned in their own kingdom. They are released into human affairs only to plague humankind, or upset the balance between History and Chance—which is what reviving the Assassins and blending them with sorcery would do. But Djinn can't call them up. Sorcerers can!"

He looked over at the puff of smoke, to where it was now shredding into nothingness, then back at ibn-Tariq.

"We magicians, too, could raise Devils and Demons," he went on, "but our rules forbid us. Sorcerers have no rules. You, ibn-Tariq, called up a Demon to lay that curse on Hasan. Now he is free and you cannot lay him again. Now you must tell me, in the name of all the Kingdoms, what Demon was it that you called?"

Ibn-Tariq's face changed. It did not pale, so much as go fixed—like a stilled picture in three dimensions of his features.

Awareness like a jolt of cold electricity all through him made Jim look up. The talking had gone on too long. It had distracted just enough of his attention from the shadows; and they had gained on him. Now understanding failed him. The shadows were not controlled by ibn-Tariq, but by the Demon.

They were close now, hardly an arm's length away from one or other of the humans clustered behind him. In the aftermath of the shock of seeing this, a rage that someone like ibn-Tariq could free a being with these powers rose and burned his mind clear.

He struck out at the shadows, with all the power in the staff, so that its

top burned with small lightnings, scorching them back and back—not as far as they had been before; but enough so that he could again take some small part of his attention from them, for just the moment necessary to delve into his memory of all that was written in the *Encyclopedie Necromantick*, inside him and magically a part of him.

Somewhere was the permission he needed. Still holding the shadows at bay, he found in his memory the section marked *Devyls & Deamons* and read swiftly from the huge type of the prohibition against any magicians having to do with them, down and down to the smaller and smaller type, until he found what he was searching for.

Yes, there was an exception. One special situation in which it was permitted.

He snapped back to full attention on the shadows. They had crept forward once more; but again he drove them back, until they were a safe distance from him and those with him.

Only then, with breathing space, he raised his voice.

"Demon who has been summoned and is loose in this period between History and Chance, by the power and right of the Kingdom to which I belong, I call on you to name and show yourself. *Now!*"

The air around them was partly sucked away for a moment. As if some giant, almost as large as the earth itself, had inhaled. Next, a great whisper, but a whisper only, spoke soundlessly in Jim's head—and he knew it would be speaking also in the heads of everyone else there as well.

"I am here," it said. "I, Ahriman, Demon of Demons."

Around them, the walls, the domed roof overhead, melted toward invisibility; becoming as insubstantial as mist.

Jim, all those with him, ibn-Tariq, Hasan ad-Dimri and the space where Sakhr al-Jinni had revealed himself, were left standing together on nothingness, far above the earth.

It was as if they were now so high in the atmosphere that they could see beyond all ordinary horizons. Their gaze went out and out until the sky around them and the landscape below merged in the far distance to a sort of dark mist. Below them was a landscape that was a pattern, a crazy quilt of not only space, but time.

In one area, far below and beyond ordinary vision, in bright sunlight a battle was being fought. It was 'Ayn Jalut, two centuries past, and the Egyptian Mameluke leader was winning over a force of Mongols—Baybars, who was first to deal a defeat to the Mongols and went on to drive out the Christian forces from Lebanon. Closer, and more directly below them, at this moment a sandstorm was destroying crops and burying the homes of villagers. Things now, and things in the past, were all taking place at the same time, somewhere in that vast landscape.

"Answer me," said Jim aloud. "Ahriman, is ibn-Tariq now your master?"

The Whisperer who was Ahriman laughed voicelessly in all their heads.

"Who calls a Demon and is its master?" it whispered. "When a Demon is summoned, the Demon becomes master. I rule all; and ibn-Tariq is my creature. Look at him."

Jim looked across the airy space that now existed between him and ibn-Tariq, and the man was still unchanged—as if he had become a wax figure of himself—the look on his face still the same.

"Now look down at what else I have done."

Jim looked; and perhaps a week's march away to the north, he saw a force of Mongols coming toward the mountains in which the White Palace was hidden.

"Look now south and east."

Jim looked, and the Mamelukes were there less than three days' march from the mountains holding the White Palace—much closer than the Mongols.

"The Mongols believe they have only to reduce one more nest of Assassins, as they have reduced so many before," said the Whisperer in their heads, "but this time they will find a fortress armed, prepared and ready to resist them; and with an army of Mamelukes much larger than theirs, already in position, encircling them, but out of sight until they have come in, before the White Palace. The Mongols will die to a man; for Baiju will not have been able to tell them what he knows. And you will have told them nothing. In the end there will be nothing but a whole world, aflame with war between Mamelukes and Mongols."

There was whispering laughter.

"And Murad of the Heavy Purse will take up his work again. Hasan ad-Dimri will sit as ruler of all, but puppet of ibn-Tariq, who is puppet of mine. You and these with you will be gone."

"No," said Jim. "We will not."

As Ahriman talked, a part of Jim's mind was reviewing what they all would have to do.

He turned to those behind him.

"Now, if you'll help," he said, looking at them, "with luck, we can win. The world can win, and Ahriman can be dealt with."

CHAPTER 29

H e watched their faces as they all looked back at him. There was something like joy in Brian's face, there was trust in Angie's, and in the hobgoblins'; and an echo of Brian's fierce joy of battle in the face of Geronde. Some of that eagerness to be at grips with the enemy was there also in Sir Geoffrey and Sir Renel—and Baiju grinned.

"If he wins, we die," said Jim. "But if we hold together, we can drive him back to his own place, where his power here will be ended. But you're going to have to ask something more of yourselves than you've ever asked before. Each one of you, once you join hands, must hold until it is over. You must never let go, for the sake of something in you that you would die for—something more important than life itself to you."

He waited a second to see if they all understood, then went on.

"If we, holding to what we would die for and together, all have that, we form a human chain Ahriman can never break through. All together, we can drive him back to his own place."

"There are not enough of you," said the Whisperer. Jim ignored him.

"Who can join hands under that condition?" he asked.

Angie smiled and put her hand into Jim's one free hand. With her free hand, she took one of Brian's.

Geronde had already slipped one hand into the other hand of Brian. Hob—Jim and Angie's own Hob of Malencontri—reached out and proudly put his small hand into Geronde's free one. Hob of Malvern reached out and took Hob's other hand.

"I want to be brave, like you," he said to Hob of Malencontri.

"You will," Hob told him.

Sir Geoffrey had earlier reached for Geronde's free hand, but she had pulled it away from him. Now, ignoring him, she looked past him at Sir Renel.

"Sir Renel?" she said in a clear, hard voice. "Have you something to die for?"

"Yes," said Sir Renel. "My honor, which I lost and found again."

He stepped forward and took the free hand of Hob of Malvern, then turned and offered his other to Sir Geoffrey, who took it; and they both smiled, gripping each other like old friends meeting after a long time. The human chain was complete, from Jim to Sir Geoffrey.

"Good," said Jim. "Now, make a semicircle with me—"

He broke off suddenly. Ibn-Tariq had stepped forward and taken the only free hand remaining—that of Sir Geoffrey.

"I would be free," he said, looking across at Jim.

"We can use your strength," Jim said—and at that, Hasan ad-Dimri came and took ibn-Tariq's other hand.

"I would be as I was in the years before this," he said.

"All hold together then," said Jim. "For if any lets go, the chain loses its strength. Now—make a semicircle and we'll herd him back."

"You will fail," said the Whisperer.

Jim ignored the words.

"Ahriman," he called. "By the staff I hold, and the rules that bind you in your own kingdom, I call on you to make yourself visible to us!"

A hiss answered; a continuing, wordless, malevolent hiss in their heads that was dizzying in its effect. But ahead of them—and it was impossible to tell whether it was at the horizon or close to them—had appeared something like a black sun.

Like the sun, it was impossible to look at directly. It glared, and seemed to shimmer and move, if the eyes tried to hold it in focus; as if it was one black disk swiftly overlaying and melting into another one a little out of place from where the original was. Now, from it, came something like a powerful but pressureless icy wind that numbed their wills, rather than their bodies.

It was not a wind that could push them backward, or even take them off their feet. But it was like a great hand laid against each of them. It tried to drive them back, without any real feeling of touch; but only with the tremendous, reiterated threat not to approach the black and burning sun-shape.

"Hold to each other. Keep going!" said Jim.

He took the first steps forward; and the rest moved with him. They felt the pressure hard against them, not only on their faces, bodies and limbs, but within them—to the very marrow of their bones.

But they went forward; and each step of theirs was like a five-league stride across the space-and-time surface far below them. Even with their first few steps, the black sun grew larger and closer. The pressure against them increased. It reached into them and tried to suck the life from them. Their steps slowed.

"Keep moving!" said Jim. "Never stop!"

The strain was on their linked hands, numbing their wills to hold together. It became harder and harder to do so. But now the knowledge was clear in each of them, unspoken but in all their minds—there was no way but forward. To stop, to go back now, meant that the blackness ahead would follow and destroy them.

Jim, at his end of the chain, a little in advance of all the rest and with the staff held before him, risked a glance at the faces of the others. So far, they were holding.

Brian was single-mindedly engaged in the struggle, as always. His hand held Geronde's and Angie's hands firmly but with the gentleness of strength and confidence. Angie's face was calm, and Geronde's was alight with fierceness. The two Hobs had fixed, steady expressions on their small, dark faces that gave no clue to how they were feeling.

Beyond these two, Sir Renel and Sir Geoffrey showed something of Sir Brian's joy in the battle, but with it something more—almost a hunger for the ultimate meeting. As if they had just been freed from chains they were so used to that they had hardly realized they had been carrying them about. The face of ibn-Tariq, beyond the two of them, was knifelike and expressionless, but with no sign of yielding.

Only at the end, the whole face and body of Hasan ad-Dimri gave an impression of crumbling inside. His body seemed to have grown smaller, as if he was falling in on himself; and his face was pale and fixed, like a man in whom doubt was like a rising tide, lapping on the pilings of his courage until it threatened to overflow and drown him.

Of them all, Hasan seemed to be the only one showing signs of weakening so far. Jim looked back, marveling at the two hobgoblins. Of all of them, he would have expected the most frailty in those two small wisps of life, used to running and hiding from all things. But this was a battle of wills, not of muscle and bone.

Angie, Brian and Geronde, he knew, would go to the end. Sir Geoffrey and Sir Renel might do the same. Possibly, too, ibn-Tariq had an equal courage in him. It would not have been easy to make himself a sorcerer of the power he controlled.

True, he would be pricked on now by the spurs of the thought of his own mistake in raising Ahriman—his ignorance of the fact that the Demon would be free and independent once he had obeyed his raiser's original command—a piece of simple knowledge he would have had if his studies had been in magic, rather than sorcery.

In its own way that knowledge would now cast shadows of doubt on all he would have studied for most of his life.

But also, there was a strength in him. Hasan, only, looked like he might

fail. Yet, he must have also had a strength of his own, when he was a Sufi, before he let himself be seduced by ibn-Tariq's offers of power and wealth.

They were few enough together to try to drive back a being as powerful as Ahriman. Fighting on their side was only their individual faiths; and the knowledge that the here and now was their place, not Ahriman's. Time was the crucial thing. The longer it took, the greater the chance that the weaker ones in the chain must break. Time was all.

"Faster!"

The word had come to Jim's lips without his intending it. But the others heard—and they tried. Their leagues-long steps above the landscape far below could not be hastened, but they were making longer ones. Ahead, Ahriman had seemed to grow tremendously, as they got closer to him. Now he blocked out a quarter of the sky ahead; and seemed not merely to face them, but to tower and loom over them.

But something like a collective fury had taken them, like the frenzy of battle. Consciousness, all logical thought, was set aside. Their awareness was only of Ahriman ahead, of the hands they gripped at either side, and the consciousness of being part of a team, a single-minded fighting unit; and their own intent to do what was before them. They had lost all thought of themselves as individuals, caught up in the unity of their effort.

They were very close to Ahriman now. Whether they had not been that far from him to begin with, or whether the enormous distances they seemed to be covering in their steps above the landscape below were actual, the fact remained that there was little farther to go. But now, at the end of the line, Hasan ad-Dimri stumbled and almost fell.

But did not—for ibn-Tariq had held tightly to his hand and for a moment literally held him up.

"It is the will of God," ibn-Tariq said, looking straight into his eyes.

Hasan straightened upright, bearing his own weight again.

"Yes!" he said, and a light had come into his face. "God wills it!" And he went on strongly.

"He's going back, m'lord!" cried Hob of Malencontri suddenly, in a high, thin, triumphant voice.

Jim stared. It was true. The sky had become like dark blue velvet, with night above; and in that darkness the lights of stars were to be seen. By ones and twos these points of light were emerging into view from behind Ahriman as he backed away from Jim and the others. Hob had been the first to see it; but it was there and it was so.

"Yes!" Jim called out to the rest. "Listen! Those in the middle hold back. We at the ends go forward, to deepen the pocket; so we can enclose him completely when he backs all the way to the borders of the Kingdom

where he belongs. Give him no chance to escape to either side. He must have no choice but to go backward into the Kingdom where he belongs!''

Jim himself lengthened his stride; and Hasan struggled forward at the other end, with ibn-Tariq close beside him now, and all but physically helping him forward. The two Hobs, Geronde and Brian sagged backward. In a deep cup formation they moved on Ahriman. Finally they were so close to him that he seemed no more than two steps away—and his black brilliance was blinding.

Now they saw that he had no real shape. He had seemed a sphere from a distance; but now he appeared as many shapes, constantly melting into each other.

But he was alive, and he was still strong and vicious. They could feel his rage hammering at them; and Geronde, herself, stumbled—but for just a second. She caught herself back up without any help from Brian or anyone else, and pushed forward enough to make a small bulge in the pocket of the semicircle.

Ahriman's rage was now something they were close enough to hear, as well. It came through to them like a high-pitched keening in their ears; and a feeling that was not—but greatly resembled—the searing sensation of the heat from the open door of a furnace, with a fire raging inside it. Ahriman had slowed in his backing now.

"He's close to the edge," said Jim, for the awareness of that frontier came to him through his staff in a way he could not have explained, but of which he was certain. "Hold fast, move forward," he went on. "I'm going to let go of you, Angie, and move to the center of the semicircle. I'll try to push him over with the staff."

He let go, and Angie gave his hand a small squeeze as she released it—a small squeeze and a quick smile. He grinned back briefly and moved, with effort because it seemed as if the air had become almost solid, until he stood in the center of the cup their bodies made. Then he held the staff out in front of himself.

"Back, Ahriman!" he said. "By the power in this staff—by all the laws of all the Kingdoms—back, back, back to your proper place!"

The keening, or whatever it was that was so close to keening, rose and rose until it was like a shrill scream of terrible pain. Then, all at once, it ceased.

There was silence. They looked at each other.

"You can all let go," said Jim wearily. "We've put him back; and there he'll stay, unless he's called up by someone else. May it never happen!"

They were too exhausted to voice agreement. Hands fell apart, and they flexed aching, bloodless fingers. They looked at each other, amazed to find

themselves only the humans they had always been, mere mortals and victorious.

"I'm free!" said Sir Geoffrey suddenly, in a wondering voice. "It's gone—the curse is gone. I can feel it's not with me any more."

"All that the demon did," said Jim, "for ibn-Tariq, and on his own, will now be wiped out of History. Look below us."

They looked.

Off in time and distance, Baybars had almost won his battle against the Mongols. But nearly everything else below them had otherwise changed. The village that was being buried and destroyed by the sandstorm was untouched. There was no storm and no sand. The streets were free and the villagers moved back and forth along them.

"Look north," said Jim.

They turned their eyes that way; and there was no force of Mongols coming south toward the mountains and the White Palace.

"The attack from the Golden Horde was something instigated by the Demon, after he found himself no longer under the orders of ibn-Tariq, and out of his own desire to see humans killing and destroying each other," Jim said.

He looked at the sorcerer; but ibn-Tariq only smiled with his lips tight closed.

"The Mamelukes will not be there either—look. All these things, like the curse, have gone back into what now never will be. Ahriman has failed. If he had been able to accomplish any of what he wished, a death, a change in History, then those things would have been permanent. But because we stopped him before they could be accomplished, all he tried for is lost and gone."

Jim looked across at ibn-Tariq.

"From here," he said to the sorcerer, "I think my people and I—and you, with Hasan ad-Dimri—go different ways."

"We do," said ibn-Tariq.

Almost with his words, he and Hasan were no longer with them.

Jim turned to face the rest. Weary faces brightened.

"Now," he said, "I think I can risk spending some magic to take us all back to England without any more delay. Whose destination is it to be? Will you come to Malencontri, or Castle Smythe—"

"Oh pray, m'lord!" piped Hob of Malvern. "Malvern? Pray?"

He had been looking as he spoke, not at Jim, but at Sir Geoffrey.

"Yes," said Geronde harshly. "Best it be Malvern. I must stay there until I am properly wed."

She looked across at her father.

"But I will occupy a different part of the castle," she said. "You can have your own old quarters."

"Geronde—" began Sir Geoffrey. But then his voice died in his throat, and the hand he had raised toward her dropped to his side again.

Hastily, Jim visualized them all in the great hall at Malvern, on the dais that held the high table—and they were there.

CHAPTER 30

"Ah!" said Brian, his eyes lighting up at sight of the table. "A servant here for my lady! Ho!"

No one responded immediately; then a young man who was actually rather low in the serving-room hierarchy cautiously sidled into the room. He stared at all of them.

"Food and wine for my father's guests!" snapped Geronde automatically. "Quickly, man!"

But the servant stood where he was, staring blankly at Sir Geoffrey.

"Yes, yes!" said Geronde impatiently. "That is your Lord, come home again. Now, fetch what I told you. Now!"

The servant turned and ran into the serving room and out of sight.

They stood looking around themselves and at each other awkwardly. The Great Hall at Malvern was almost as big as the Great Hall at Malencontri. But after the buildings they had all recently spent some time in, at this moment it appeared dark and bare, with primitive-looking furniture.

The table on the dais, the high table, had its top unfolded and laid out upon its trestles. But the two low tables stretching away at right angles from it on the regular floor level were trestles only, with their table tops folded and leaned against the wall. Only a few slitlike windows let the late afternoon light of a raw spring day into the room. The two Hobs, bereft of their smoke wafts, and therefore standing on the floor, looked like thin little dark-skinned rabbits. They gazed wistfully at the cold and empty mouth of the single wide fireplace in the Great Hall; for of course, with the castle's Lady gone, there was no fire in it. The air of the hall was chill.

"Oh!" said Geronde suddenly, like someone waking up from a deep sleep into automatic courtesy. "Pray be seated, m'lady, sirs!"

They all mounted the dais and sat down in the padded chairs at the top table, which looked like—and, in many instances were—literally barrels, partly cut out to make a chair with a back and a seat inside. The middle

chair at the table was politely left open for the host, but Sir Geoffrey quickly took a seat near one end; and, with a second's hesitation, Geronde sat down in the middle chair.

They had barely seated themselves before not one but four servants were back, spreading a tablecloth, putting mazers in front of each person and pewter plates, with a large spoon on the side. Two other servants were starting to lay logs for a fire in the fireplace.

Brian and Jim had automatically reached for the knives at their belt, but Sir Geoffrey and Sir Renel, after automatic hand movements toward nonexistent belts, sat looking embarrassed.

"Eating knives for your lord and Sir Renel," snapped Geronde.

One of the servants ran off toward the serving room.

"Stay!" said Brian to the servant who had just filled his mazer. He drained it and held it out for a refill, which was immediately given him.

"Sir Brian!" said Geronde sternly.

"Damn it to hell, Geronde!" said Brian. "I'm thirsty. After what we've just been through, you'd deny me a fast first cup? You have my promise to sip nobly and politely from now on."

"Sirs," said Geronde to Sir Geoffrey and Sir Renel, "do not stand on manners, I beg you. Drink!"

The two men rather hesitantly picked up filled mazers—which neither of them had touched in years and which they handled with unusual caution—and conveyed them almost reverently to their lips. Geronde herself set an example by drinking from her own mazer.

Angie, Jim was glad to see, was already drinking from hers. Encouraged by this, he drank almost as deeply of his first cup as Brian had done. With the taste of the wine, the last of a feeling of being out of place left him. He drank almost as deeply from his mazer as Brian had done—and almost choked. None of them had thought to water their wine, though there were water pitchers on the table. His mazer was already being refilled, even though it had not been emptied.

Angie smiled at him. He smiled at Angie.

"Oh!" said Angie, setting her mazer down. "The Hobs!"

She turned. They all turned and looked. Hob of Malencontri and Hob of Malvern still stood side by side, small and forgotten on the floor.

"There will be a good fire already going in the serving room, little ones," said Geronde gently. "Take your guest there, Hob Malvern!"

The faces of both Hobs lit up.

Hob of Malvern took Jim and Angie's Hob by the hand.

"Come with me!" he said, and together they ran off into the serving room.

"See that none disturbs the small creatures!" said Angie severely to the closest server. "They are to have whatever they want."

"Yes, m'lady!" he said, and followed the Hobs into the serving room. Those at the high table took to the food, when it arrived, gratefully; for in fact, no one there had eaten recently. But better than the food was the release of tension that came with the eating and drinking. Gradually, even Sir Geoffrey and Sir Renel relaxed enough to take part in the nearly forgotten pattern of the social conversation they had been used to back in their homeland.

They talked only to each other, however. At the other end of the table, Brian's normal ebullience revived with the food and drink; and he led the conversation there into something very much like normal chatter between himself and Jim, Angie and Geronde. But there was still a certain constraint even in Brian's talk, Jim observed.

Geronde's hardness toward her father had not softened, and there was a consciousness of this among the others that added an uneasy note to the gathering, even though everyone pretended that it was not there; and the manners of the day caused Geronde to speak to her father—when she did speak—with the same respect she would have shown if he had never left home. As if he had always remained Lord of the castle and in the castle.

Sir Geoffrey replied in the same manner. But it was clear to everyone that he would happily have traded all this courtesy for one word from Geronde that would indicate that the antagonism in her had diminished a little, and that she might sometime forgive him for all those things of which she had found him guilty.

There was nothing worse, Jim thought, than a *polite* dinner party; where everybody was avoiding what was foremost on the minds of all there. He found himself feeling almost as wistful about the ill feeling between daughter and father as the Hobs had shown standing forgotten on the floor, before Geronde had sent them to the serving room fireplace.

This would have been a very happy, celebratory occasion, he found himself thinking, if the daughter-father feeling had not been present. But it was—like a ghost with them at the table. It pushed them all into formal manners that were not in key with what should have been a celebratory occasion. A little anger stirred in Jim that neither Angie nor Brian—nor yet even Geronde herself—had ever chosen to tell him of these deeps of resentment in her toward her father.

Perhaps they had not known, either; but it was hard to believe that people as close to her as Brian and Angie had not.

Jim could see that the unhappiness was pressing on them, too; and gradually, after everyone had taken the edge off his or her very real hunger, and begun to reach the point where food and drink did not have such a great deal of interest, talk began to slow at both ends of the table.

"But you must be tired!" said Geronde to Jim and Angie. "Will you stay overnight here"—she cast a glance down the table—"with my father's permission, of course?"

"Oh. Certainly, certainly, stay, I pray you, m'lord, m'lady," said Sir Geoffrey hastily. "I have scarcely had time to meet either one of you, and to thank you. I know it would pleasure me; and I am sure it would pleasure Geronde."

Angie cast a meaningful glance at Jim. Under the manners of the period, it was his job to announce whether they would stay or go; and Angie was clearly signaling that she believed they would do no good by hanging around here. Jim's guess was that she sensed that Geronde, herself, in spite of her invitation, would just as soon have all her visitors out of the way, so she could stop being hostess and be herself with her father—except, of course, when servants were present.

"You tempt us, Geronde," Jim said. "But you know, with Angie as well as myself gone from Malencontri, we need to get back there. There's something about your own roof, you know, that calls you back. Also, as you know, while our servants are pretty well trained now, they can't compare to yours; and they've been on their own with both of us gone. Something'll have gone wrong. I've no idea what—but something will have. It always does when neither Angie nor I are there. You understand?"

"I do indeed know the way of servants," said Geronde. "Therefore, though I would love to have you, I will not press you to stay."

She turned and looked down the table to Sir Renel.

"Sir," she said. "You are welcome to stay here as our guest until you have reason to go someplace else, of course—"

"I'm afraid, Geronde," interrupted Angie quickly, "that Jim and I are guilty of having hoped to invite Sir Renel to stay with us. Particularly, it would pleasure us to take him back with us now; and then after he is settled down a little bit, perhaps he can come back for a visit with you and Sir Geoffrey. Besides, you'll feel a duty to entertain him; but I know how busy you'll be getting ready for your wedding."

Whatever insensitivity Sir Renel originally had to the attitudes and emotions of those around him, it had been burned away by his years as a slave.

"Indeed, m'lady," he said to Geronde, falling back with remarkable ease and a certain amount of obvious relish into the formality of earlier years, "blithe I would be to stay with you and Sir Geoffrey. But also I was hoping to visit with Sir James and his lady wife. I am most interested in one whom Sir Geoffrey tells me has renown as a Dragon Knight. Also, as Lady Angela has mentioned, I would not be a burden to you with your present cares and needs."

"Alas," said Geronde, "it cannot be denied there will be certain pressures upon me"—she darted a glance down at Sir Geoffrey—"but I will indeed have much to do; and would enjoy seeing you with more freedom of time on my hands, and more of a chance to enjoy your company. I must sound like an ill hostess to you, but perhaps Lady Angela is right and it would be best that you return with her and Lord James to Malencontri."

After a few more stilted verbal exchanges that fooled no one and were not intended to—Jim had heard their exact counterparts a number of times as he had been leaving social gatherings back in his own twentieth-century world—it was established that Sir Renel would not consider Geronde an ill hostess; and Geronde would not consider Sir Renel an ungrateful guest who was scorning Malvern's hospitality, because of a preference for the company of Jim and Angie. Sir Renel would leave with Angie and Jim. But now Jim himself was beginning to feel more and more uncomfortable.

He could not shake the feeling that there was something wrong with all this, the three of them going off (four, counting their own Hob, of course, though indeed the little hobgoblin might be at Malencontri right now, having returned there on a waft of smoke from Malvern). There was something badly wrong about leaving Sir Geoffrey here alone, abject and despairing, and Geronde as hard toward her parent as only Geronde could be.

It was not right. They were all on their feet now, ready to go their separate ways.

"Hold on!" said Jim.

He had spoken without thinking, but his anger was now out in the open. It was aimed primarily at Geronde, but also at Sir Geoffrey and all the rest of them, including himself.

He was stared back at awkwardly. He had broken the glass curtain of sociability with which they were covering up an uncomfortable situation; and the two responses to that in their historical period were to challenge him on it, or pretend to ignore what he had just said. Ignoring it had become a little difficult. On the other hand, Brian was his closest friend, Geronde would be in a sense acknowledging the situation by saying anything, Sir Geoffrey owed him his freedom from something very like slavery and Sir Renel had literally been rescued from that state.

Jim was aware of all this, and of Angie moving closer to him and looking back at the rest of them with him, and he had no solution to the impasse he had created. But it did not matter. He was now in the full tide of his own emotion, and he charged ahead without bothering to sort out his words ahead of time.

"This is all wrong!" he said. "Sir Geoffrey, tell your daughter why,

though you had the palace that she saw you in and the wealth to go with
it, you couldn't come back to her, much less bring back what you had
with you. Tell her!''

Sir Geoffrey stared at him with a white face, saying nothing.

"Tell her, man!" said Jim. "Tell her, or I will!"

Jerkily, moving like a jointed doll, Sir Geoffrey turned to face Geronde.

"I could not," he said to her. "I was under a curse."

"Could not?" said Geronde with emphasis on the first word. Her lip
did not exactly curl contempt, but it looked as if it might.

"I dared not," said Sir Geoffrey then, bluntly.

"Dared not, Sir Father?"

"Tell her the whole story," said Jim. "The curse had originally been
laid on Hasan ad-Dimri, he transferred it to you and you accepted it from
him. Tell her why."

"Hasan offered me the palace and all that went with it that you saw in
Palmyra, Geronde," said Sir Geoffrey. "That was to be my price for
accepting the curse and lifting it off him on to myself. It offered, I thought,
all I had been searching for. But he laughed when I accepted."

"Why did he laugh?" said Jim relentlessly.

Sir Geoffrey was still looking only at Geronde.

"He laughed, and I did not mind it, then," said Sir Geoffrey. "He
laughed because he told me that now I had accepted, if I should ever try
to escape from him, the curse would follow me wherever I went. Not only
that, but it would be extended."

Sir Geoffrey ran down again.

"Tell it all to her," said Jim, more gently now.

Sir Geoffrey looked at the ground, away from Geronde's eyes.

"He said part of the curse was that if I did escape, its effect would go
with me. It would not only fall on me, but on my descendants unto the
seventh generation. That was why he laughed. *Think of your sons, and
your son's sons,*' he said, '*all of them suffering it, down to the seventh
generation!*' ''

Sir Geoffrey took a deep breath, and without raising his eyes went on.

"I had gathered as much already from what he had said, although he
had not made it plain in words until then," he said. "But I was sure I
would find some way to get out from under the curse, you see; and manage
to take much of what I now had back to England. Indeed, I doubted a
curse that would hold a Muslim would have any effect on a Christian. I
was wrong; but when I found out how wrong, I could not come back. I
could never escape the curse—but I could not bring it back to you."

He raised his eyes to Geronde.

"So," she said cuttingly to him, "as you say, in the end you *dared* not."

"Tell her what the curse was," said Jim. "Geronde, you saw Ahriman. He was real enough. What would have followed Sir Geoffrey home would have been real enough too."

"I am not afraid of curses!" said Geronde, raising her head proudly. "Even if my father is."

"Tell her what the curse is," said Jim. "She may think differently after she hears."

Sir Geoffrey looked at him, the knight's face drawn and old.

"Surely, I need not—" He stopped.

"Name it," said Jim. "Don't you see that you're going to have to name it, for Geronde to understand?"

Sir Geoffrey took a deep breath and straightened, stiffening. He looked back at Geronde.

"I could not bring it back to you, my daughter," he said in a harsh voice. "The curse was leprosy."

"Leprosy!"

Brian's and Sir Renel's voices spoke together. As for Geronde, she said nothing; but the blood left her face.

In England, as Brian had told Baiju, lepers were not driven into a desert by men with clubs and sticks; but certainly, here too, they would be as surely put out, not only of the society of those they knew, but of their home and family—to wander, begging and ringing a bell to warn everyone out of their path. The horror of the disease as it was known in England during the Middle Ages was no less than it was in the Near East.

"That was why he would not come back, Geronde," said Jim softly.

Geronde's eyes moved. She stared at Jim for a second. She made a small choking sound, looked once more at her father for another second. Then she leaped up, whirled and ran, down from the dais and out through the doorway leading toward the stairs to the tower, where her own solar room was—leaving silence behind her.

After a long moment Angie spoke, her voice clear in the hall.

"Sir Geoffrey," she said, "I think what's been between your daughter and yourself will begin to heal, now. But it will take time, and you will have to prove yourself a different man."

The table was silent for a long moment.

"God send it so," said Sir Geoffrey.

CHAPTER 31

They were wing to wing, soaring on the broad river of air, home to Malencontri.

"Are you sure Sir Renel really wanted to stay at Malvern after all?"

Jim nodded, then realized the ridiculousness of this in his dragon body.

"Yes," he said. "He's a stranger here, and the situation'd gone through a large change since we had talked about taking him home with us. After all, Sir Geoffrey's the only one he actually knows, and they were close friends once, evidently. He'll be better off with a friend around, particularly if things are going to be starting to mend at Malvern."

"We hope. No, I shouldn't say that," said Angie, as they began to circle upward on another thermal. "Things will mend. I'm sure they will."

"So am I," said Jim, and meant it.

He was happy; and he knew that Angie was too. Happy to be going back to Malencontri. Happy that they would be alone there—alone, that would be, except for young Robert and the castle staff—and both were welcome elements in homecoming. In a way it was almost as if he and Angie had shared in the reconciliation of Geronde and her father.

He winced a little internally, thinking of the shock to Geronde—to learn that her father had been ready to accept leprosy for himself, rather than inflict it on her. Particularly after the way she had been thinking of him for years.

In any case, she understood him better, now. He and Angie had never had to suffer that way; and right now, for both of them, the world was good. Warm in their dragon bodies, riding the air currents together, it seemed to Jim that the sun had a special brightness.

Above, the sky was almost cloudless. Below them, a little of the rawness of winter still survived in the leaves that were still curled up tight in buds—too tight to show green on the dark limbs of the trees; and even farther down on the ground black patches of wet earth still showed through the drab carpet of soggy leaves revealed by the melted snow of a winter

now vanquished. But the whole world, nevertheless, seemed to be demanding summer just as soon as it could get there; and birds called loudly. The smell of early spring was in the rushing air around them. Jim snuffed it through his dragon nostrils with pleasure.

He was happy Sir Renel had decided finally that he would remain at Malvern, even if it had only been after everybody thoroughly assured him he would offend nobody by staying; and Geronde would echo that assurance if she was with them.

So, with no reason for Jim and Angie to go home on horseback, as they would have if they had taken Sir Renel with them, it was a natural decision to bedragon themselves and fly. The others had waved them off from Malvern's tower.

"I'm going to be really glad to be home," Jim said to Angie.

"Me too," she said. "I hope everything's been all right with Robert."

"I'm sure it has," said Jim, and a moment later, they were landing on the tower roof. The man-at-arms on lookout gave what sounded more like a whoop than the usual ritual shout, on seeing them; but by the time they had changed back into their human bodies, clothes and all, his face was unusually rigid.

"Well, we're back, Harold," said Jim to him.

"Yes, m'lord," said the guard, without giving up a bit of the stiffness of his expression.

"Super-formal!" said Jim under his breath to Angie, grinning once his back was safely turned to the guard and they were going down the flight of stairs into the solar. There was no one on duty at the outside door; and inside there was a fire in the fireplace that was a very low fire indeed— just enough to "air the cloth," as the servants put it, coming from a profound belief that clothes hung in a room without a fireplace would overnight become damp and mildewed.

Actually, there was some reason for it, since many castles were afflicted with dampness most of the year around. Jim stood, gazing about himself with pleasure. What a homelike sort of space it was, he told himself.

"I'll go see Robert," Angie said, vanishing out the door toward the separate room created for Robert out of the solar floor.

She was back in a minute.

"He just fell asleep, the lamb," Angie said.

Woken out of his pleasurable contemplation of their private quarters, Jim automatically went to add some of the logs standing beside the fireplace to the flames. Angie stopped him just in time.

"Oh, yes," said Jim, suddenly reminded that people would be along to take care of this in a moment—in fact, the man-at-arms overhead could

be heard shouting something from the top of the tower down to the courtyard below right now.

Undoubtedly, the message was being passed that the Lord and Lady of
the castle were back. The servants would be very upset if Jim had needed
to pick up a log with his own hands to lay it on a fire. Indeed, there was
only time for Jim to take off the mail shirt he had practically lived in
these last weeks and settle himself in one of the comfortable chairs he
had caused to be made for the solar, while Angie also got rid of her
traveling cloak and sat down, before there was a scratching at the door.

It was opened without waiting for the order to come in; several servants
entered, one of whom rebuilt the fire, another who went around straight-
ening and dusting things, and a third who was already carrying a tray with
wine and cakes into the room.

"Put it on the table, Beth," said Jim. He was still too full from the
meal at Malvern to want anything more; and he suspected that Angie was
in exactly the same condition. But to simply send the food and drink back
could hurt servant feelings.

"Yes, m'lord," said Beth, a serving woman in her late twenties, her
lips now thinned a little bit. She spoke without looking directly at him.

The others finished their tasks and they all went out, backing through
the door, saying with the same odd stiffness the sentry had shown, "With
your permission, m'lord!" and "Crave pardon, m'lord and lady, for the
disturbance!"

After the door was shut behind them Jim looked at Angie.

"Did you notice anything?" he asked Angie. "It seems to me they're
all acting unusually strange. I thought they were just being extra correct.
But it's something more than that."

"It is," said Angie. "I don't know why."

"If this is their way of welcoming us back," said Jim, "I wish they'd
get over it. You don't suppose they were upset by both of us being gone?"

"I don't know why they should be—" Angie was interrupted by another scratching at the door.

"What is it?" called Jim.

"Crave pardon, m'lord." The voice of a male servant came back,
loudly. "John Steward is here to speak with you, m'lord. If your Lordship
permits."

"Send him in!" said Jim. He looked at Angie. "Whatever's going on
here, we ought to get a handle on it from John."

The door opened and John Steward came in. They had inherited him,
as they had the blacksmith and nearly all the other servants, when they
had taken ownership of Malencontri. He was a tall, rectangular-framed,
stern-looking man in his forties.

He had been steward here during the times of the last three owners of the castle; and he was proud of having most of his teeth, though two of these were missing in front. He smiled seldom, either to hide the gap, or simply because he believed his air of unquestionable authority required it. His black hair, still untouched with gray, was combed straight back; and even indoors he always wore a hat that was shaped like a loaf of bread, and a cast-off robe from the castle's former lord that had once been a dark blue in color. He was heavily boned and broad shouldered enough to make a good man-at-arms, rather than a steward; but of course, from his present position he looked down on all men-at-arms below the rank of squire.

"I hope I am not intruding, m'lord, m'lady," he said, once he was in and the door was closed behind him. He stood a good eight feet from them, upright as a post, and frowning down on them like a schoolteacher at a couple of pupils.

"Not at all, John," said Jim genially. "We're glad to be home and to see you all. How have things been? Happily, your Lady was not gone long, so I suppose there isn't much to tell."

John Steward looked at him for a long moment, his expression unchanged.

"Yes, m'lord," he said flatly. "If your Lordship so desires it."

"Desire?" said Jim. "What's my desire got to do with it?"

"I am entirely at your service, m'lord," said John Steward, still in the same voice. Belatedly, it occurred to Jim that the magic with which he, Angie and the rest had been involved might have caused some kind of backwash affecting the castle staff.

"Has something been changed, for all of you, here at the castle?" he asked.

"I would not say so, m'lord," pronounced John.

The suspicion in Jim of something being badly wrong, which had been faintly woken by the manner of the tower sentry's greeting, suddenly blossomed. Jim's happiness at being home was rapidly evaporating. He knew John well enough by this time to read in the other's voice that the answer he had just heard had hinted at things unsaid.

"No nonsense, now, John!" said Jim. "If it's been different for you people, I want to know about it. How long did it seem to you that m'lady Angela was gone, for example?"

"Since you asked, m'lord," said John Steward, "it has been ten days."

"Ten days!" Jim stared at the steward, then got himself under control. "Is that so? Well, that's something I hadn't expected. But it may have been because of what we were doing. Anyway, the people of the castle shouldn't be surprised if we're gone for any length of time. We'll always

come back. Now, if we were gone ten days, perhaps you've got things to tell us. What happened while we were gone?''

John looked at him for a moment, like a physician considering whether a patient was strong enough to be told bad news.

"Well, m'lord," he said deliberately, "Mistress Gwynneth Plyseth, who as your Lordship knows has charge of the serving room, spilled a great jug of your lordship's finest French red wine.''

This was not exactly earth-shaking news. The wine John was talking about was something normally reserved for their most special guests, and brought out only on special occasions even then. The loss of a great jugful was at least a gallon and a half, which was certainly regrettable, but not the sort of thing to send either Jim or Angie into fits, and John knew it. There was something behind all this.

"What else?" he asked.

"She was clearly at fault, m'lord," went on John, inexorably, "but she had some reason. Mage Carolinus had just appeared beside her.''

"Carolinus?" asked Jim, sitting up in his chair. "Carolinus was here while we were gone?''

"Yes, m'lord," said John heavily.

"Why was he here?"

"He came, m'lord," said John, "because the blacksmith's foot had been stepped on.''

"Foot?" said Jim.

"Stepped on?" said Angie.

"Yes, m'lord and lady," replied John.

"A horse, I suppose," said Jim. "Still, I'm a little surprised that Carolinus would come here just for that.''

"It was not a horse, m'lord," said John. "The devil did it.''

"The devil?" said Angie and Jim together.

"The devil from the sea, m'lord," said John. "You had scarce been gone three weeks when he came seeking you. You know of whom I speak, m'lord. He's been here before. He is a giant devil.''

"You mean Rrrnlf!" said Jim.

"Yes, m'lord," said John. "He wished to speak to you; but I spoke to him myself and told him you were not here. And when he would speak with the Lady Angela, I must needs tell him that she was not here either. So he settled down in the courtyard to wait for your return, like he did before when the serpents attacked—you remember, m'lord. A terrible time the stablemen had getting horses in and out, for he fell asleep in such a position that there was only a little space to get past his arm into the stables with the horses; and the horses grew very skittish when led close to him.''

"I'll bet," said Jim. "Well, I'm back. I can see him now."

"Now, m'lord, he has left," said John. "Crave pardon if I exceeded my duty. But in desperation I had sent one of the men-at-arms to the cottage of the Mage Carolinus, to ask if something could be done. The Mage returned, bringing the man-at-arms with him—both carried back by magical ways—so that they suddenly appeared in the courtyard. The devil was still asleep, but Carolinus told me and all else to go inside the castle. He would speak privily with the devil. He did so and then disappeared. The devil was still here, so I went to see what had occurred; and the devil said that he had looked for you in Cyprus and not found you and then come here and not found you; but he would return to speak to you at a later time."

"Oh," said Jim, sinking back into his chair. "That's all right, then. And it explains Carolinus being here. Carolinus didn't say anything to you about me or anything else, did he?"

"He did not, m'lord."

"Oh, by the way, John—" Jim began, and then changed his mind. "No, on second thought that's all right. Thank you. You may go now."

"Yes, m'lord."

John Steward bowed himself out. He was the one person in the castle who could bow properly; although Theoluf, the man-at-arms who had become Jim's squire, had gotten better at it since his promotion. Jim suspected him of practicing privately.

"I was going to ask him directly about the way people are acting," Jim said, looking at Angie. "But it wouldn't have been any use. He'd never tell us right out, whatever it is. We'll just have to wait and see what develops."

He stared into the flames of the fireplace.

"Not that it matters . . ." he said to the flames in a low voice.

"You've been through a lot," said Angie, getting up to go to the fireplace and kissing him as she passed his chair. She took the poker and jabbed at the logs. Sparks flew upward and the flames reached higher. She put the poker back and came down and sat in her chair. Jim was still staring into the flames.

"Tell me," Angie said, after a moment, in a conversational voice, "where did you go just before you got your staff?"

"Go?" Jim started as if he had been woken out of sleep. "Staff?"

"You told me once that Carolinus said he had to go a long way for his staff when he helped you at the Loathly Tower to rescue me," went on Angie in the same gentle voice. "You must have gone a long way too."

"What made you think I went at all?" asked Jim. "Did I disappear?"

"No," said Angie. "But I could feel you were gone. The *you* wasn't

there. It was more than a moment for you, wasn't it? What did you have
to do to get the staff?''

"Climb a mountain," said Jim. "It was . . ."

He looked at her, wanting very much to tell her, but unable.

"I don't think I can tell you about it right now," he said finally. "Let
me have a little time. Get away from it so that I can think about it differently; then I'll tell you all about it."

"But I'm right, aren't I?" said Angie. "You had to go a long way too,
like Carolinus, didn't you?"

Jim nodded.

They sat in silence for a little while and the fire crackled as another
small burst of sparks went up.

"It's all part of a whole," said Jim, looking at the fire again. "It's like
this business now with the servants acting so funny. You know as well as
I do they wouldn't do that with any Lord or Lady of the castle who was
born and raised here in the fourteenth century. We may dress like they
dress in this time, we may use their manners and talk the way they talk;
but we're different and these people who have to live with us feel it."

He looked over at Angie again, grimly now.

"We just wanted to stay in this time because we liked it," he said to
Angie. "Remember? We didn't want to change anything. But that's what
I've been doing. I never planned to be a magician, either. But I'm a
magician whether I like it or not; and I'm doing things to their magic. I'm
twisting it in twentieth-century ways, using it with twentieth-century
twists, just like we're infecting these people in the castle here with us with
our twentieth-century attitudes."

He paused but Angie said nothing. There was, he thought, nothing much
she actually could say to what he'd just said.

"We can't help it and they can't help it—but it's happening," he went
on. "I'm like something put in the oil of an engine that was running
smoothly, but now with me there, it runs differently. I think I can tell you
what's bothering everyone in the castle right now. They resent our leaving
them."

"Oh, I don't think so," said Angie.

"That—or something just as bad," said Jim. "They've got all sorts of
advantages having us here—they can boast about having a magician for
a Lord; and we're the most easygoing superiors that any fourteenth-
century castle help ever had. They can twist us around their finger, and
they do that all the time. Now they're letting us know that we shouldn't
have done anything like going away without checking with them first and
getting their permission."

"Jim—" said Angie.

"No," said Jim strongly, "I'm right about this. The way we make them feel—things like the hypocaust that warms this room from underneath its floor, all the things that I thought I was so clever about changing around the castle—all these have to have been going against the grain for them. And they're right. They should have their world the way they made it, without me messing it up. I think secretly they've come to hate us. They won't even admit it to themselves, probably, but that's how they feel; and now it's beginning to show. Wait and see if that isn't what we find out behind this new attitude of theirs."

He stopped speaking, and Angie sat looking at him for a long moment.

"You really must have had a hard time getting that staff," she said at last, gently. "But I think—"

There was a scratching at the door.

"Now, damn it—what?" said Jim, looking up.

"Come in!" called Angie.

John Steward entered once more, carefully and quietly closing the door behind him.

"M'lord," he said formally, "Mistress Plyseth is here from the serving room and wishes to crave pardon and mercy from you for her spilling of the wine."

"Your Lord will see her," said Angie before Jim could answer.

"Very good, m'lady," said John, going out and closing the door behind him. There was a little pause and then the door opened again and John ushered in Gwynneth Plyseth, with a tear-streaked face and wringing her hands. She made directly for Jim and started to fall on her knees before him.

"Stand up!" said Jim harshly.

Gwynneth Plyseth caught her balance with an effort and remained upright.

"M'lord," she said in one fast, garbled string of words, "the - fault - was - all - my - own - and - I - acknowledge - it - freely. Whatever - your - Lordship - feels - should - be - done - to - me - is - only - right. Yet - for - all - these - years - I - have - served - you - may - I - crave - your - mercy - and - your - pardon?"

It was a set speech, but Jim was in no mood to pick on that fact.

"It's all right, Mistress Plyseth," he said, still harshly. "That's all. We'll say no more about it. You can go now."

"Wait a minute!" Angie's voice cut in. Only a month or so earlier, in addition to Robert's room being partitioned off from the solar, the remaining, still large, circular area had been divided into two lesser rooms—there was plenty of space in it to do so, since the original space had occupied one complete floor of the tower—and now there was a living

room and separate bedroom, with an extra fireplace in the bedroom. Angie
pointed at the door of the bedroom, now. "Go in there and wait for me,
Gwynneth. I'll be in in a moment. John, you can go now."

"Yes, m'lady."

John took his stiff-backed way out.

Angie got up from her chair again.

"I'll find out for you why the servants are acting this way," she said
to Jim. "Gwynneth and I get along very well together. We think alike.
I'll have an answer for you. Just stay put."

She went into the bedroom, closing the door behind her. Jim sat where
he was. After a while, mechanically, he got up, poured himself some wine,
sat down again and sipped at it. The division between the rooms had been
made with stone blocks like those that made up the rest of the castle.
These, in fact, had been stolen from lower levels to make the partition
wall. They were effectively soundproof; but through the door, which was
just an ordinary door of wood, Jim could hear Angie's and Gwynneth's
voices, without being able to make out what was being said.

Not that it mattered, he told himself. He had never been cut out to be
a fourteenth-century knight and magician. He should have realized that
from the start.

Anyway, his mind was not really on what he was hearing from the
other room, which could make no difference in what he now understood.
He sat staring at the fire and thinking black thoughts.

After a little while, the sound of someone weeping roused him from
these, however. It was almost certainly Gwynneth. Angie did not weep
easily, like that, on the rare occasions when she wept at all.

"The whole thing's a charade," he muttered to himself, sipping at the
wine and staring at the fire. "I'm just playing the part of Lord of the
castle. I don't belong here and everybody knows it. The hell of it is, it's
become home—and I don't want to be anywhere else."

He felt bleak inside. Whether he even had enough magic available now,
to take Angie and himself back to the twentieth century, he did not know.
He doubted it, after what he must have spent to get the staff. But right
now, his mind refused to come up with any other possibility but magic
transfer back to the twentieth century, where at least the most damage he
could do to anyone else was what he could do as his ordinary, nonmagical
self in his native time.

The door opened suddenly and Angie came out, followed by Gwynneth.
Gwynneth's face was still wet, but happy.

"It's *so* good to have you and m'lady back!" she said to him, bobbed
a curtsy, hurried to the outer door and let herself out. Jim stared at Angie,
who had not sat down again but was standing over him.

"What happened in there?" he asked.

"I found out what's going on," said Angie. "She couldn't keep up the act with me—just as I thought. Jim, our people here didn't resent our being gone. It never occurred to them they had any right to resent it. Jim—they *love* us! But they thought it'd be presumptuous of them to show it. They were very happy to have us back safe—when people leave you in this time, remember, you're lucky to see them safe and sound again."

"But," said Jim, "the way they were acting—"

"They were trying to act as if our coming back as good as ever was nothing important—when they really wanted to celebrate. Jim—we should make an excuse to let them celebrate!"

Jim stared at her. He was having trouble adjusting to everything she said. He started at the first unbelievable statement.

"Love us?" he said. "What for?"

"What does it matter what for?" said Angie. "They love us because they love us. And we like them—we love them, too. We love it here. Here loves us. You must've been carrying this worry around with you for months now, haven't you?"

"As a matter of fact . . ." said Jim, his voice trailing off into silence for a moment. "Maybe it began when I first started to feel that Brian and Dafydd and Giles and all our other friends were giving me way too much credit . . . I don't know. And then, gradually they were all seeming to be so glad to have us around because they had a false idea of what I—I don't know. It's been upsetting, sometimes. Angie, you know what I am. All I am—all I've ever been—is myself."

Angie came to him, sat down in his lap, put her arms around him and kissed him.

"Jim Eckert," she said, solemnly, looking into his eyes, "that's all you ever have to be!"

There was a scratching at the door.

"Oh, no!" said Jim. Angie sprang to her feet.

"Come in!" she snapped.

Once more, John Steward came through the door. It was hardly perceptible, but now Jim saw that there was a change in him. He was back to being his old self, rather than the stern and distant master of lesser servants he had been, talking to Jim and Angie earlier.

"I do beg pardon, m'lord and lady," he said, apologetically, "but the Devil is back. He's in the courtyard right now and wants to talk with you. And he's got an ugly little man with him."

Jim looked at Angie. Angie looked at Jim.

"Tell him I'll be down in just a while," said Jim.

"Yes, m'lord." John went out.

Jim and Angie exchanged glances again. Slowly, Jim relaxed. He sighed, and shook his head. Angie smiled widely at him; and gradually he felt himself beginning to smile back, in spite of himself. Then they were both laughing.

"Maybe you better go take care of your Devil before he decides to take another nap," she said, wiping her eyes.

He sighed deeply but happily, and got to his feet.

"Ah, well . . ." he said; and headed out the door.